*Dear Lue
I hope
reading —.
cousin (x2) Barb Howard*

First Class to America

Joyce Senatro

FIRST CLASS TO AMERICA

Joyce Senatro

ISBN: 978-1-940224-92-3

Copyright 2015

All rights reserved. No part of this book may be reproduced or transmitted in any form or by any means, electronic or mechanical, including photocopying, recording or by any information storage and retrieval system, without permission in writing from the author or publisher. This book was printed in the United States of America.

Cover layout by White Rabbit graphix.com

Dedicated to my daughters:

Edie
Faun
Patty

Strong women who make me proud

Part I

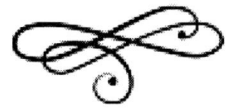

ITALY and NEW YORK
1883 - 1901

1

Gaeta, Italy, 1883

    Seven year old Teresina Santora sprinted out of bed before dawn, eager to put on the beautiful white dress and veil her mother made for this special day. Mamma brushed her only child's long, wavy brown hair and curled it to perfection before they made their way to church.

    A short time later, Teresina and the other members of the Annunziata Holy Communion Class processed toward the front of the church, eyes downcast and lips moving in the prayer of unworthiness they had been taught. *Lord, I am not worthy that Thou wouldst come under my roof, but only say the word and my soul will be healed.* If Jesus really loved her, young Teresina couldn't understand why she must continue to be so unworthy. Sister Maria Giuseppe said she was not to understand the mysteries of faith, she was just to accept them.

    Deep in thought about such mysteries, Teresina missed a step and hurried to catch up with her partner when she heard a snicker. Glancing at the nearby pew, she saw Leo Legattia grinning at her. He saw her look his way and winked. She almost tripped, but he didn't laugh. Teresina told herself that one day she would walk down this aisle, as a bride, with that handsome Leo.

***

    "I see you watching the Legattia boy in church on Sundays and smiling at him," Mamma said one day when Teresina was twelve. "You are too young to be fussing over boys. Sixteen is soon enough, and then you should not be looking at just one. You want to make sure you pick out the right one."

"You always tell me that, Mamma, and I know I am too young. But it doesn't matter how many I look at, I know Leo will be the right one for me. I'm just afraid one of those older girls will get him first." Teresina sighed. "I'm five years younger than him. He probably thinks I'm a baby."

"And does he pay a lot of attention to those other girls?"

Teresina looked to the ceiling, thinking for a minute. "You know, Mamma, he doesn't really. He often walks away from them and carries my books home. I can tell they don't like it, but he knows I don't have a brother and I think he watches out for me." She sighed again. "He treats me like a little sister—like a child."

"Well, that is very nice." Mamma carried plates from the table to the crude sink and began pumping water. "And you remember, you are a child. Now help me with these dishes."

Wait until I'm sixteen. I'll let Leo see that I'm no child.

Teresina became Teresa, growing into a comely girl in her mid-teens who gave the promise of becoming a stunning young woman.

And then one morning a twenty-year-old Leo showed up at Domenico Santora's workshop. Teresa saw him through the window and couldn't resist walking outside to listen around the corner.

"Buongiorno, Signore Santora." Leo nodded to the older man. "I want to tell you that my father and I may be away for a while. We understand that the fishing is very good off the southern coast, near Positano. We plan to fish there for two or three years and build a little savings before we come home."

"Well, then, I wish you good luck, young man, though I'm not sure why you tell me this. Is there something I can do for you or your father? He is a fine man. I am happy to help if I can."

"Oh, no, sir. It's not that. It's your daughter, Teresa. I know that she is only fifteen now, but when I return I would like your permission to court her, *Signore*."

Teresa's loud gasp caused both men to look outside. Papa scowled, while Leo grinned.

"I'm sorry, Papa. I didn't mean to eavesdrop. I came out to—to—and I heard…" Her hands covered her burning face.

"Uh, huh." Papa nodded, still scowling. "And what do you think I should say to Mr. Legattia?"

"Yes, Papa. Please tell him yes." She could not look at Leo.

Domenico cleared his throat. "You understand that you both may feel very different in two or three years. But you are welcome to come by when you return to Gaeta, young man. We'll see how you feel then." Domenico offered his hand, which Leo pumped vigorously before he turned to Teresa.

"I will see you in a couple of years, *Signorina*. Take care of yourself." He bowed, turned and sprinted toward the coast.

"You take care of yourself," Teresa called.

***

She kept busy with her studies, sewing and dressmaking, helping Mamma in the garden and kitchen, and playing her *pianoforte*. A dying friend of Mamma gave it to them when Teresina was nine.

"I have no one else, Maria," the woman told Mamma. "Maybe Teresina will learn to play."

Teresa thought the instrument was the loveliest thing she ever saw. One of her school teachers taught her the musical notes on paper, and she practiced every day for hours, learning them on the piano until she could pick out simple songs. When Mamma had extra change to give her, Teresa would go to town with Papa to buy a piece of music at the general store. Now she vowed to teach her children—hers and Leo's—how to play. There would always be music in their home.

Girlfriends urged Teresa to be mindful of the attention she got from numerous young men. Instead, she counted the months. As two years neared, she walked to the coast—more than half an hour each way—two or three times a day to watch the fishing vessels come in. By the spring of 1894, she was convinced something had happened to Leo, or that he and his father had decided to stay in southern Italy and she would never see him again. With a heavy heart, she ceased her daily walks to the harbor.

Mamma baked a delicious chocolate cake for Teresa's eighteenth birthday in July, and made her a lovely new dress. "Cheer up, my precious. There are many young men here who would love to court you."

"I know, Mamma." Teresa said. But there is only one Leo, her heart cried.

That September, she was weeding in the garden one beautiful fall day, her hands full of dirt, telling herself that she must move on with life.

"Ciao Bella." "Hello Beautiful." She stopped breathing. It had to be her imagination. Then she looked up and there he stood. She didn't even think about the dirt, or that this was the first time in almost three years they saw each other. She ran into his open arms. With the back of his hand, Leo wiped away her happy tears, kissed her on each eye, and then brushed his lips against hers. He stepped away, holding her at arm's length, while he looked her over.

"I have dreamed about you every night since I left, Teresa. I knew you would be waiting." He hugged her again. "I have enough money for us to start a life. I want to ask your father if we can marry. Will you say yes, *mio amore*?"

"Yes, oh yes."

***

They would have married at once, but the church required a waiting period, and Leo wanted to have enough money to buy their own home. They set their wedding date for the first week in August.

"We don't want to live with our families, Teresa. I want you all to myself, and the extra time will give me a chance to earn more toward the home we want. We'll be able to start our family."

Teresa smiled. "Two girls and two boys, Leo. A boy first. We'll name him after you." They sat on top of a hill overlooking the coast where Teresa came to watch the ships when Leo was at sea.

"No. The first one will be Dante, after my grandfather. He taught me how to fish when I was a young boy. I'll teach my son."

"All right. Dante, then. The children will go to midnight Mass with us at Christmas, and we'll take them to see the processions and holiday lights." Teresa put her arms around Leo and held him tightly. "And I'll miss you so every time you're out to sea. Please don't ever go away for such a long time again."

"My trips will be short," Leo promised. "I'll be too anxious to get back to you."

Then it was late July, and Mamma had Teresa's dress finished. Everything was ready. The couple sat in the porch swing Papa had made.

"I don't like you going away now, Leo. Can't you skip this trip?"

"It'll just be a couple of days. The fishing should be good, and it will give us enough extra money for me to take you on that honeymoon to Rome we've talked about."

The next morning, Teresa was up early to see him off. They held each other until Leo's shipmates threatened to come back on shore and drag him to the ship.

"Ciao, bella." He kissed her again before starting toward the fishing boat, and then turned back to wave. "Remember, my beautiful bride, even when I'm at sea, I'll be with you."

An unexpected storm came up the following night, and two days later Teresa learned there was no sign of Leo's ship or any survivors. A few weeks later she realized she was pregnant.

***

In the midst of her smothering grief, Teresa thanked God she would at least have Leo's child. But how would she tell Mamma and Papa.

"There's only one thing to do," a distraught Domenico said after he absorbed the news. "You have to go away, Teresa. There are homes in Naples. They'll find a good family for your baby."

"No," Teresa screamed. "Mamma, talk to him. Papa, please, I can't give my baby away."

Domenico stood and walked outside, while Maria wiped her own tears and held her sobbing daughter.

Teresa saw the lantern light shining from Papa's shop long before dawn the next morning, and guessed that he had a sleepless night like she did. She walked softly to not wake Mamma, and groped her way to the shop door.

"Papa, I can't give up Leo's baby. I can't."

Domenico stopped sawing and looked into the tear-stained face of his daughter. He sighed and turned away to blow his nose before looking back at Teresa.

"Think of the disgrace to our family if you stay here, not married. And think of the shame the child would have to live with."

"I'll go away. I'll live somewhere else. I can't give up this child, Papa."

"And what would you do? Beg on the streets? What kind of a life could you give your baby? You have to do what's best for the child, Teresa."

They heard a creak. Both had forgotten about Nico Barile, who stood in the open doorway, listening. Ten years older than Teresa, he had come to Gaeta shortly before Leo's death and worked for Domenico as a carpenter's helper. Teresa pushed past him, stumbling out of the shop with her head down and her eyes flooded with tears. She sank to the ground, gasping sobs of desperation. Then she heard Nico talking to Papa.

"I couldn't help overhearing what you said to your daughter just now, Domenico. I have no family, you know. I would be willing to marry Teresa and be a father to her child."

No, Teresa thought. She couldn't marry a man she didn't even know, and wouldn't love. Papa knows that. She pushed herself up and ran into the house.

***

"He's a good worker, Teresa, and he is willing to be the papa to another man's child. What else can you do if you want to keep this baby? It's a perfect solution." They sat at the kitchen table that evening.

Mamma agreed. "I do not want you to go away, Teresina, but it would be too hard for you to stay here with a baby and no husband. Nico is a handsome man. I know you don't love him, but love can grow."

Teresa stumbled through the fog of the next couple weeks while Mamma sewed for days to make her a wedding dress and a fine suit for Nico. Maria then baked for several more days to have a suitable reception for friends and relatives.

Praying that Leo would forgive her, Teresa's trembling voice vowed she would "love, honor, and obey" the man—almost a stranger—standing beside her at the altar of Annunziata Catholic Church, "until death do us part." The priest pronounced them man and wife two weeks after Nico's offer of marriage.

The next day, Mamma pulled her aside. "I know you married Nico to keep Leo's baby. It is the right thing to do, Teresa, but you must remember that marriage is forever. Whatever happens, Nico is the head of your family now. There is something else I want you to remember." She held Teresa by the shoulders and looked into her eyes.

"A woman needs money of her own that her husband doesn't know about. Find a way to put aside enough to take care of yourself and your children. It is a woman's only chance for independence, and sometimes her only protection. Never give up your dream of living first class."

***

They still lived with her parents six months later, when baby Dante was born. Teresa knew Nico expected to take over her father's business one day. Her heart told her that was his reason for offering marriage. However, barely enough work existed to support even one family anymore. Crime had increased and businesses struggled or closed, especially in southern Italy.

Nico grumbled, "We'll never get ahead here. I hear there's plenty of work in America."

Her son was less than six months old when she became pregnant with a second child. Hard as life was, Teresa was sure they could find a way to make a living somewhere in Italy. She couldn't think of her children growing up in another country.

"I understand it's better in the north," she said. "Why don't you try up around Venice, Nico? I'm sure you'll find work there, then Dante and I can join you after this baby is born."

Nico continued to insist America would offer opportunities they'd never find in Italy. Teresa's uncle in New York agreed to sponsor them. With Papa's help, Nico finally saved the $95 fare and arranged transportation for their trip to the United States.

On a warm May day in 1898, Nico carried one year old Alberto and Teresa held tightly to Dante's hand, afraid of getting separated from her two year old son as they squeezed into the steerage section of the large ship. She thought she would never again see her parents, or the land where she had found and lost the love of her life.

Three struggling years later, they received the news in New York that her mother was dying and Papa needed her.

2

Thousands of immigrants streamed into New York harbor that January morning in 1901, while Teresa Barile couldn't wait to get out. Though much as she wanted to see Italy again, this trip would be bittersweet. If only she could take her boys—

Teresa heaved until she thought her insides would spill out. She bent over the rusty bucket that served as chamber pot, fresh water carrier, wash basin, or whatever the need was. It sat on a wooden plank—a make-shift counter in their tiny, cramped cold water flat. The claustrophobic room served as kitchen/dining and living room, next to an airless, windowless, even smaller bedroom. The little she had for breakfast already floated in the pail. Her patched cloth tote bags, packed and ready to go, waited on the floor.

"Look at you," Nico chided in their native Italian. "You're sick thinking about getting on that ship. You'll never make it. What a waste of money. I told you this trip was a stupid idea."

Teresa lifted her head and wiped her mouth with the corner of a dirty, ragged towel that lay on the counter. "It's only nerves, Nico. I'll be fine. I pray Mamma will live 'til I get there. You know Papa couldn't afford the money he sent. He wouldn't ask me to come if he didn't need help."

Nico said no to many things, but not to the father-in-law who helped finance their passages to America. Uncle Sal's wife, Clara, had reluctantly agreed to care for the children during Teresa's absence.

"I wish I could take the boys," Teresa said. "I don't like the way Clara treats them."

"We talked about that. Do you understand *no?* You and your fine education," Nico sneered. "I might only had three years in school, but I can say *no* in English or Italian."

"I just want Mamma to see her grandsons once more before she dies." Her voice cracked. She would miss Dante's fifth birthday the next week, and Alberto's fourth the end of April.

"They're not going back to Italy." Nico's face reddened. "Everyone gets sick on those ships." He grabbed her bags. "At least everyone like us who gets shoved into the bottom, with the damn thing rocking back and forth all day and night. It's bad enough that you go."

Teresa grabbed her stomach. It was true. She hated the thought of the trip, but she had to go. It would be the last chance to see the mother who made Teresa believe she could do anything she put her mind to, no matter how hard life became. Teresa never forgot Mamma's words. She only had a few coins, garnished from rare sewing jobs that Nico didn't know about—coins she kept hidden in a handkerchief in the middle of her undergarments where he would never look. Someday there would be enough to make life better for her children.

She so wanted to have her sons along, but Nico would know that keeping the boys here was his only guarantee of her return. He roughly nudged her toward the door. "If you got to do this, get going. Just don't forget to be back in six months or you can't take the exam for citizen—"

"I know, Nico, I know."

Nico headed for the stairwell, leaving her to shut the door. Teresa followed her husband down the four flights of stairs, listening to him grumble all the way, but glad he insisted on walking with her to the trolley stop. Even three blocks, alone through Little Italy, made her nervous.

If Nico knew about her pregnancy, he would never let her go. But he didn't know…yet.

***

After almost four weeks of throwing up in the closed belly of the steamship, and a harsh two and a half day horse-cart drive from Naples to Gaeta, Teresa knew she was a pitiful sight by the time she reached her childhood home. It took less than an hour for her dying mother to get out of bed and become the caretaker.

"You are better than medicine for your mamma," Domenico said.

"Being home in Italy, with you and Mamma, is better than medicine for me." She smiled, then her expression became serious. "But what's wrong with her, Papa? What does the doctor say?"

"The doctor doesn't know," Papa said sadly, "but he's sure there is no medicine to cure her. He thought your visit is the best thing for her."

Maria did rally with her daughter there, and Teresa treasured their special moments together. Her mother's approaching death gave both of them the urgency to say things they didn't want to leave unsaid. When Papa was not around, Mamma talked about the two miscarriages she had before Teresa was born.

"Your father never knew how much I mourned for them, but I made a memorial for each one. If you go to the small hill behind the church's cemetery, you will see two little markers under the big shade tree. I said prayers there every week, 'til I couldn't walk anymore. Your papa and I will be buried nearby."

Tears blurred Teresa's eyes. "I'll visit for you while I'm here, Mamma, and say the rosary for them."

Her mother's faint smile showed resignation and peace. "I thought I would never have a child. Then God gave me you. You are my miracle."

First Class to America

Teresa leaned into Mamma's outreached arms as they sat on the couch. She remembered when Mamma had made the bright flowered slipcovers that were now worn and faded.

Then they talked about Leo. Pain stabbed Teresa's chest as hard as it did the day she got news about his ship. Here in Italy, she could still feel his presence—tall, strikingly handsome, always smiling Leo.

She pictured him running up the beach from his fishing trips, anxious to gather her in his arms. *"Chiao bella."* The melodic voice rang in her head, making her hands even now reach back to smooth her hair. A smile touched her lips for a brief moment, before she remembered that he was gone forever.

"I know how you loved him," Mamma said. "I know how it hurt your heart to marry Nico when you loved Leonardo. But your father thought it was the only way. I wish it could have been different."

"Oh, Mamma, so did I. When Leo was lost at sea, I wanted my life to end, too. But I had to live for our child. He's the only part of Leo I have left."

"Does Nico treat him like a son?"

"Well, he may favor Alberto a little more sometimes, but I try to make up for it with Dante, and Nico is fine with him most of the time. And Mamma, if I hadn't married Nico, I would not have Alberto. He is so precious. I wanted you to see them again."

Mamma's eyes watered. She looked tired, so Teresa helped her back to bed.

"I've missed you so much, Teresina. I wanted to have you and my grandchildren near me, but life doesn't always work out the way we plan. This one, though," she patted Teresa's bulging stomach, "I pray God will let me see my new grandbaby."

"It's already June, Mamma. Only another month, and you will see this baby. This one is going to be born in Italy, like Dante and Alberto."

Maria smiled as her eyes closed briefly and then opened again. "Tell me about America, Teresina."

Teresa looked into her mother's eyes for a minute before she answered. "It's just like Uncle Sal said, Mamma. It's a land of opportunity."

※※※

It took weeks for letters to reach America, too long to let Nico know when Teresa would return to New York. She sent two letters, both to Uncle Sal since Nico couldn't read. The first told of her safe arrival, finding Mamma still living, and the realization of her pregnancy. The second told of their daughter's birth in July.

> *She's so beautiful. I named her Lauretta Maria, after my grandmother and mother, but we call her Laura. The doctor said Mamma does not have long to live. I have to stay here and help Papa care for her until she passes. I know that may keep me away longer than six months, but the doctor said he will write a letter, and I am sure the immigration authorities will make an exception. I will come as soon as I can.*

While she waited to give birth, Teresa used the time to clean and brighten the deteriorating house that had always been lovely and homey to her. Papa helped her paint some of the peeling walls. She pulled out Mamma's ancient sewing machine and made new slipcovers and curtains with material Mamma bought before she became so sick. Then Teresa went into the garden, pulled weeds and planted new flowers from bulbs and seeds neighbors gave her.

"You lift my spirit, my darling," Mamma said, watching the flowering plants and smiling more often than she had in a long time. True joy shone through her eyes, however, when she held her newborn granddaughter.

"She is beautiful, Teresina, the very image of you," Mamma said, blinking away happy tears. "God can take me anytime now, and I will die a happy person."

God gave Maria two more months to enjoy the baby that even Papa said was "the prettiest, most perfect baby I ever saw."

She and Papa cried afterwards, trying to adjust to the too quiet house, sorting through her mother's belongings and picking out items they could sell to pay for a modest funeral.

Neighbors took advantage of having Teresa there, using the dressmaking skills Mamma had taught her. Income from several sewing jobs helped with expenses for the funeral and toward Teresa and her baby's trip home. She had promised Nico her father would pay for the return voyage. She did not tell him Mamma's illness took all the money Papa had saved.

"I wanted to take care of you, Teresina, not have you take care of me," Papa said. They sat in the small kitchen, which Teresa had been cleaning, trying to make it shine like she remembered.

"Papa, you took care of me all my life. We could not have gone to America without your help. I'm worried about you here by yourself."

Her father had always been an outgoing, positive man. Whenever Mamma insisted the world was falling into doom and gloom, he remained cheerful and optimistic. It broke her heart to watch him now.

He smiled through sad eyes, and leaned over to kiss her cheek. "You are not to worry about me. I have good friends to help take care of me. I am the one to worry about you. My brother wrote to me about your life in America. I should not have sent you and Nico. I thought he would do better. But he is your husband. I can't change that now."

"You didn't tell Mamma, did you?"

"No—no. She always thought your life was, well, the way you wanted her to think."

"Thank you." Teresa walked to her father and put her arms around him. "Don't you worry about us. Nico works hard, and something better will come along. We are going to be all right, Papa." She prayed they would be.

***

Her time in Italy, longer than expected, meant that her pending citizenship could be in jeopardy. They would have to make a special appeal to the Bureau of Immigration.

It was early November when she boarded the *Karamania* in Naples. "Nico will be furious," Teresa told herself. She would have to deal with that when she got back. Now, as she turned to say goodbye to her beloved Italy, her tears fell on baby Laura's blanket. She prayed that one day she and her children would come back, and vowed they would travel first class.

3

Teresa pulled the collar of her worn, woolen coat more snugly around her neck, and tightened the shawl sling that held Lauri close to her body. The November cold was relentless in the steerage section. She tried to picture the warm rooms and fireplaces that first and second class passengers enjoyed. Third class had no private sleeping rooms, or libraries, or dining rooms, or other luxuries found on the main decks.

When the disgruntled men and boys weren't arguing or fighting, though, brief patches of relief from their daily miseries came from passengers like the tall, handsome Frenchman Maurice. Teresa watched him walking her way, with his arms out.

"I take bebe." If Laura was fussy, a dance with Maurice always quieted her.

A smile crinkled Teresa's eyes as she watched the Frenchman hold Laura in the air, waltzing around and leading groups in song while his laughing, matronly wife pumped an accordion.

Most of the immigrants intended to stay in New York and look for work, but others would scatter. Maurice planned to settle in Pittsburg, Pennsylvania. It might as well be another country.

A few mornings later, as the ship neared New York harbor, Teresa finished packing and lashing together the straw basket and cloth tote bag she had found in Mamma's attic. Cheers from above meant they were passing the Statue of Liberty.

"America, the land of opportunity!" she muttered. She wanted to tell the others that the only opportunity for immigrants in America was the opportunity for ship owners, employees and landlords to take advantage of them. She joined the other steerage passengers, packed into the hallway waiting to disembark—waiting for the upper class to go first, of course. One day...

"Not much longer now, bambina," Teresa whispered to the whimpering baby in her arms.

"Teresa, Teresa."

She heard the panic in Gina's voice from somewhere behind her. Gina and her ten month old baby, Luca, had slept in the upper part of the bunk Teresa and Laura had occupied. They were part of over two hundred parents, or single mothers traveling with children, packed into the foul smelling room. Lumpy, moldy-smelling thin mattresses offered little chance for comfort. The cacophony of the ship's creaking noises, scratches of rats skittering across the floor, and discontented grumbling of fellow passengers made a full night's sleep impossible.

Now Teresa felt a tug at her sleeve and looked over at Gina, who finally pushed her way through the crowd.

"I am so nervous," Gina said in Italian. "How am I going to answer the inspector's questions if I can't understand them?"

Teresa spoke English better than her husband and most of their neighbors. After seeing how victimized Italians were, as they clung to their homeland's language and traditions more than other nationalities, she was determined to learn and use English at every opportunity. She had helped Gina learn a few basic American phrases.

"Answer the questions we talked about, and don't let them know you feel sick." She worried about the pale young woman. "You'll do fine. Make sure your tag is tight."

She pointed to Gina's coat and the required document each immigrant had pinned to their outer garment. It showed the manifest number of the ship, with the page and line number of the registry book that held the passenger's name.

Teresa checked again to make sure hers and Laura's were secure. Her birth date, July 16, 1876, and full name, Teresa Maria Barile, were written correctly, unlike that of many of the immigrants who couldn't read or write.

Tightening her hold on Laura, she whispered a promise to the baby that they would soon be on their way home. She hated that her baby girl had to be taken to such a place, but she couldn't wait to put her arms around her sons.

Teresa reached down to move the bags along. Besides her clothes and the baby clothing that Mamma's Italian friends had given her, she managed to tuck in some special, personal items of her mother's, including the cameo pin. Outlined with tiny pearls, it came from her maternal grandmother. Teresa had only seen a picture of her, but Mamma often said, "You look more like my mother than I do, Teresa. And you have her beauty and softness in your ways."

She didn't feel either soft or beautiful as she pushed back a strand of hair from her face and brushed fingers over cheeks that felt like leather. When she got home, she would find a way to crush the olives she brought from Italy to make a soothing skin lotion.

Most of the immigrant women, including Gina, wore babushkas to keep their heads and ears warm. Teresa had on a pretty, royal blue soft hat that fit uncomfortably over the crown of her head, with attached ribbons covering her ears. She wore a beige woolen dress that she had sewn in Italy, from material she found in Mamma's closet. There had been enough extra to make a shirt for each of her boys and Nico.

Laura squirmed in her arms. "At least, little one," Teresa whispered, "you and your brothers were born on Italian soil. No one can ever take that from you. One day you will go back to visit, and one day you will wear fine dresses, my darling."

Thinking about seeing her sons in a few hours excited Teresa as much as a child anticipating Christmas morning. Dante was more than five and a half now, and Alberto, four and a half. Would they remember her?

***

Teresa and Gina were herded onto the third barge that anchored at Ellis Island two hours later. Amid the crowd of weary, nervous immigrants, they squirmed their way to a wide staircase that led to the main processing hall. Inspectors pulled aside those too weak, or impaired, to climb the stairs easily. Trying not to show the effort it took to get her tote bags and baby to the top, Teresa lost sight of her friend.

When she reached the upper level, she turned around and spied the girl sitting on the stairs, cradling Luca and crying. People stomped around her and tripped over her. Teresa could not get through the crowd. "Get up, Gina," she called.

Gina struggled to stand. Thankfully, a young man came by and helped, carrying her bags until she made it to the top floor.

Chaos greeted them on the upper level, where hundreds of immigrants sorted through mounds of luggage and trunks. Facility workers stored baggage in the back of the room and shoved family groups and singles into long lines separated by iron railings. Teresa and Gina were moved to the same line.

"Don't forget, my sister's name is Lilly," Gina said. "She and her husband will be waiting for me. If I don't make it through, try to find her and tell her I am here."

"Lord willing, we'll both get out tonight. But I promise I will look for Lilly. You showed me her picture. I'll remember."

Everyone gripped their identification papers. Tired, scared and hungry children whined and hung on to their mothers' skirts. Laura cried for a feeding. With no seat available, Teresa lifted the infant from the makeshift sling, fumbling to get layers of clothes unbuttoned enough to expose her breast to the baby's hungry mouth for a few minutes. The shawl kept Teresa modestly covered, though she hated the lack of privacy.

The line inched slowly toward the Inspectors, and Teresa's heart pounded. She and Laura were healthy, but the least suspicion of anything wrong would have her shuffled off for further examination by a doctor. She felt nauseous. She had been too nervous to eat that morning, and couldn't have stomached the food anyhow. A Hail Mary passed her lips in prayer that she wouldn't faint or throw up.

At last, she stood in front of an Inspector. Like the others, he had on a formal dark uniform and hat. A name tag sewn onto his jacket, eye level to Teresa, read *Inspector Victor Gauginn*. More than a head taller, and probably as old as her father, he had none of the soft expression that her father wore, nor the kindness heard in Papa's voice. The thin inspector's facial features included a sharp nose and eyes that held no smile. He spoke to her in a flat voice, without lowering his head. She had to stretch her neck and raise her face to meet his gaze.

First, he had her hold up Laura while he felt the baby's arms and legs, and then checked her scalp and eyes. Laura wailed, and Teresa bit her lip to keep from screaming at his insensitivity. She took a deep breath when the man finally expressed satisfaction at the baby's condition.

Next came Teresa's turn. She cringed as the man's hands felt the bones in her shoulders and arms, and then pressed down her back and along her sides. His fingers unnecessarily cupped the edges of her breasts. He had her stand on one leg at a time, and then used sticks to make parts in her hair and check her scalp. Then came the part

Teresa most dreaded. The inspector took a buttonhook out of his coat pocket and used it to lift her eyelids, looking for signs of the eye disease, trachoma. Widespread in southeastern Europe at the time, it had become the most common reason for failing the examination. Strained from standing still so long and holding on to her crying baby, Teresa feared her head would move and the buttonhook would be thrust into her eye.

At last, the inspector indicated she could move on to the money exchange line. Until she took a step away, Teresa didn't realize how badly she was shaking. She moved out of the way and held Laura close to soothe her before wrapping her snugly in the sling again. Glancing back, she saw Gina in the middle of her inspection. Teresa motioned toward the moneychangers to let Gina know she was going on. Then she saw her friend slump to the ground.

Baby Luca screeched. Teresa froze. If they didn't make it out by five-thirty, she would be locked in for the night. She couldn't be any help to Gina and she couldn't afford to lose her place in the money line. She watched as an aide rushed over to take the wailing baby. Another assistant pulled Gina up and walked her toward the detainee room.

Gina looked around frantically until she spied Teresa. "Find my sister," she mouthed.

Teresa nodded as Gina and Luca disappeared behind the door. Shaken, she moved toward the teller cages. She had to make it out in time.

Nico had warned her about the moneychangers. "They'll take your money and give you back half or less in American dollars." The clerk had short-changed him when they came through in 1898.

Teresa promised him she would not let it happen again. Her hand clutched the paper that listed every Italian coin and its worth in American money. She knew she had enough. A woman alone needed at least ten dollars in order to be released from the facility.

Her turn finally came. With paper in hand, she prepared to argue when the curt teller told her, "Those aren't current rates, missus. Our rates change every day and your list is outdated."

She didn't believe him, but what could she do. Panic made her speechless. Then she heard another voice.

"I'm afraid my friend has been too busy today to see the latest exchange rates. They've gone up again." The kind looking teller at the next window, with a deep, eloquent voice, nodded to Teresa and then turned to his colleague.

"Ed, I guess you didn't get the message. You owe the lady a couple more dollars." His soft tone had a no-nonsense firmness.

"Here," Ed snarled. He thrust the rest of the money toward her under the cage bars. The second teller watched the exchange before returning to his own customer.

Maybe immigrants actually would be treated better in the future. There had been a rumor on the ship that the new American President Roosevelt was determined to improve treatment of immigrants. "We'll see, little one, if life gets better for us with this new President." She moved toward the luggage line.

Teresa stated her husband's name, address, and employment before getting permission to pass through. It was twenty past five. Ten minutes left. She frantically rummaged through the baggage, so nervous she almost tripped, and finally found her bags. Laura cried again from hunger, but tending her would have to wait.

Darkness already enveloped the cold winter evening. A guard locked the door just after she squeezed through, leaving less fortunate passengers moaning on the other side. Teresa crossed a foot bridge that led to the mainland. The wind, whipping across the water, funneled through the small open space between her neck and coat collar. She shivered and pulled Laura's sling closer, looking for a place to sit.

She hadn't eaten all day. If she didn't sit for a few minutes, she would faint from hunger. She tried not to think of the dangerous street, praying that God would keep them from harm. She would have to spend five cents on the trolley and get as close to their tenement as possible.

The bridge led to a small park, where dozens of family members waited. A young couple sat on one of the benches. The man stood up and motioned for Teresa to sit.

"Oh, *grazie, grazie,* thank you very much." It would take at least two more hours to get home. Teresa slumped onto the seat, and then watched a lamplighter reach up to light a nearby street lamp.

"Excuse me, do you speak English?" It was the woman sitting next to her.

"*Un poco,* a little." Teresa realized she needed to get used to speaking the local language again.

"My name is Lilly Bianchi. I wonder if you might have –"

"You are Gina's sister." Teresa hadn't paid attention when she sat down. Now, even in the dim light, she could see the image of the woman in her friend's picture. Lilly looked like an older version of Gina, with an attractive round face framed by dark brown curls.

"You know my sister?" Lilly's face lit up.

"We had the same bed on the ship. She was up," Teresa pointed over her head, "and I was down." Her finger pointed down. "She showed me your picture and said look for you."

"Thank goodness," Lilly exclaimed. "Is she all right? Why isn't she here?"

Teresa explained what happened. "They will keep her tonight, but if she is better tomorrow, she can come out. I am sure she will be better."

"If she's not coming tonight, Lilly, we'll come back in the morning." The tall, slim man who had given her his seat said, "I'm Lilly's husband, Paul. Is there anything we can do for Gina tonight?"

"No. Come back tomorrow morning. Tell the authorities you are here and can take care of your sister."

Lilly thanked her and stood up. They started to walk away, and then stopped. Teresa saw them talking. They came back.

"Is someone meeting you?" Paul asked.

"No, my husband did not know when I would come."

"Where are you going?" Lilly asked.

When she told them, Paul said, "You can't go to that area by yourself at night. It's too dangerous."

"I am very careful. I have to go home."

Lilly looked at her husband. "Paul, we can't let her go."

"You will stay with us tonight, and get a streetcar home in the morning." His tone was decisive.

"We have Gina's bed for you and the cradle for your baby to sleep in," Lilly said.

Exhaustion and hunger gave way to argument. Much as she wanted to see her sons, Teresa worried about her safety on the streets at night, especially with Laura. "Thank you. God sent you."

4

She sat up with a start, and then took a few seconds to orient herself to the small neat room. Hearing her baby stir, Teresa breathed deeply and stretched as she looked around.

Bright quilts covered the bed and cradle. Matching curtains decorated a large window that framed bright light and the view of a prosperous looking neighborhood. She patted the soft bed made of real bedding material, not matted smelly straw that crawled with bedbugs. Oh, to live like this.

The delicious aroma of coffee, fresh bread and bacon drifted into the room, scents that brought happy memories of childhood mornings in Mamma's kitchen. But Teresa had to get Laura up and fed so they could start for home.

When they came into the kitchen, Lilly reached for Laura. "You will not leave here without having a good breakfast. You eat while I hold this precious baby."

Paul nodded as he passed a plate of bacon and eggs to Teresa.

She argued with little conviction, not knowing when she might eat this good again. She couldn't remember the last time she ate bacon. It tasted wonderful.

"It is so pretty, your home." Teresa's eyes scanned the spacious apartment.

"Thank you. We like it." Lilly shifted Lauri to her shoulder. "We were in a very small flat for almost three years until we could afford this."

"Gina will stay with you?"

"Yes. Did she tell you about her husband's death in the mine accident?"

Teresa nodded. "So sad."

"And she was just pregnant. It was terrible for her," Lilly said.

Teresa nodded again, understanding too well. She finished the delectable breakfast, thanking them repeatedly, and then tucked Laura into the shawl sling. Paul insisted on carrying her bags to the trolley stop. He had just picked them up when they heard a knock at the door. Lilly opened it and shrieked with delight.

"Jakob, we didn't know you were here. How good to see you." She threw her arms around a good-looking man who tossed his Derby on the table as he hugged her.

Paul dropped the bags, reached out and pumped the other man's hand briskly while they exchanged greetings. His friend's gaze drifted to Teresa.

"Forgive me. Jakob, this is Teresa Barile, and this," he pointed to Laura, "is her beautiful daughter. They were on the ship with Lilly's sister, and we invited them to stay over with us since it was so late. Teresa, this is a dear friend of ours, Jakob Hahn."

He looked familiar to Teresa. Where would she have seen him? Not likely anywhere in her world, not anyone as refined looking as this handsome man. It must be that he reminded her of someone—someone with light brown, smiling eyes.

He and Paul were both about a head taller than Teresa. Both men had well-trimmed mustaches. Jakob wore his dark blonde wavy hair a little longer than Paul's short cut.

Jakob took Teresa's hand and bowed. "It is indeed a pleasure, Mrs. Barile. Would we have met before? Did you say you came in on a ship yesterday?"

That voice. Where had she heard it? "Yes, the *Karamania*."

"That must be it. You may have come through my line." He looked at Paul and Lilly. "That's why I'm in New York. President Roosevelt wanted me to spend a few days at the Ellis Island Receiving Center and make sure our immigrants are being treated with respect. I was working at the money exchange windows yesterday."

Of course, the man who made the teller, Ed, give her the right exchange. "I remember you," Teresa said excitedly. She described what had happened.

"I do remember," Jakob Hahn said. "It was very keen of you to have the exchange rates written."

In a rare rush of pride, Teresa felt a blush color her face.

"So what will happen to others, with tellers like Ed, when you're not there?" Paul asked.

"I'm recommending he be replaced. The President is determined to have honest people work with our newcomers."

"How long can you stay, Jakob?" Lilly asked. "Paul and I were just leaving to walk Teresa to the trolley. Then we have to go back to Ellis Island for my sister."

"No, no," Teresa said. "You stay with your friend. I will get the trolley. You already do too much for me. Thank you."

"Just a minute, Mrs. Barile. I'll not have plans changed on my account. I have a carriage outside and I will take all of you wherever you need to go," Jakob said. "I do have to get back to Hartford, but it doesn't have to be today. Why isn't your sister here, Lilly?"

They had Teresa tell him what happened to Gina.

"Come with me and we'll make sure she gets through all right," he insisted.

As Teresa reached for her bags, Paul stopped her. He looked at Jakob. "Teresa lives in Little Italy. Do you think we could drive her home first? I know it's not on the way, but we don't like her going through that area by herself."

"Of course we can. I have room, and we will still get to the Island in time."

Teresa sighed with relief as she thanked them again.

***

Little Italy bustled with its usual crowds, noise, and a combination of pleasant and offensive street odors. There were merchants selling their wares, children playing stickball in the streets, and men and women talking in groups. The men, mostly unemployed, smoked cigars and drank liquor they couldn't afford, and gambled away money they didn't have. If they won once, like Nico they had no memory of the many times they lost. The women complained and gossiped. Even on such cold days, visiting on the front stoops of apartment houses offered better alternatives than being closed up in the intolerably cramped, depressing tenements. Teresa joined them occasionally, when she felt the walls closing in on her.

A horse and carriage like Jakob Hahn's—a rare sight on their street—caused more than a little curiosity. The cab, closed in the back where Lilly and Teresa rode, had two padded bench seats. The men sat in the partially open front section, with Jakob handling the reins of a fine looking chestnut mare.

Anxious to see her sons, Teresa paid little mind to the gawkers. She hoped this was not the time of day Mrs. Marketti would be tossing her garbage—or worse, emptying her chamber pot—out of her third floor window onto the street. The woman never looked to see who was below.

Nodding to neighbors as Jakob helped her out, she assumed the women stared at her because of the way she arrived.

Paul picked up her bags. "I am carrying these to your door." His tone that left no room for objecting.

As they climbed chipped, creaking stairs and passed filthy hallways, permeated with odors of urine, rotting vegetables and dry decaying foods, Teresa felt increasingly embarrassed by her surroundings. "It is not like your pretty apartment," she said when they reached the fourth floor.

"It's much like the first apartment Lilly and I lived in when we came to America," Paul said. "That's how most of us start out in this country. I'm sure things will soon get better for you."

"I hope you are right." She stopped in front of her door and turned to face Paul. "You and Lilly are so kind to me. How do I say thank you?"

"Your being home safe is our thanks."

Teresa did not invite him in. He set the bags down, said goodbye and started to leave, but looked back when she gasped.

Teresa was turning the doorknob when a stout, middle aged woman yanked it open.

"Who are you?" Teresa said in alarm.

"I thought I heard someone at my door." The woman's Italian tone was harsh.

"Your door? This is my apartment," Teresa said.

"You are mixed up, missus. We lived here over two months."

Panic churned in Teresa's stomach. She glanced around. Surely she had the right place, but as she looked past the woman into the small space, she didn't see anything that was familiar. She looked up at the faded number on the door: 4-12. It was the right flat.

"This is where I live with my husband and our children. What are you doing here?"

"Maybe you lived here before, but not anymore."

Teresa's chest hurt. She couldn't breathe. She couldn't talk. She grabbed the doorframe to hold herself up.

Paul took her arm, looking at the woman in the doorway. "*Signora*, can you tell us where the family is who lived here before you?"

Teresa took a deep breath and translated, her voice shaking.

"I can't tell you nothing. We needed a flat, and the super said a family just moved out, so we move in. I don't know nothing more. I'm sorry." She glanced at the stricken Teresa, her voice softening. "I don't know where they went. I hear ladies say the wife is gone—I guess that's you—and the papa moved away with the children."

Paul seemed to understand enough. "*Grazie, Signora*. Come on, Teresa, we'll find them." He picked up her bags and took her arm. "You said the boys were staying with your uncle. I'm sure they'll be there. We'll take you. I think your husband must have found a better place for you to live. You'll see. It'll be fine."

Teresa let herself be led, unable to think clearly. She heard Paul's calm words, and told herself he must be right. Nico had found a safer place for them to live. The boys would be with Clara at this time of day. She should have remembered that. She would see them in a few minutes. Her heart still slammed against her chest, but she was able to breathe again.

Downstairs, a group of children and teens surrounded the horse and Jakob, while he instructed them on how to handle and care for horses.

"What's wrong?" He looked at Teresa.

Paul told him what happened.

Saying goodbye to the boys and girls, Jakob asked Teresa for directions to her uncle's tenement as Paul helped her into the cab.

"Fine. It will be on our way to the island," Jakob said.

In her concern, Teresa had forgotten about Gina. "I am so sorry. You have to go on."

"Not until we get you to your family," Lilly said. "As Jakob said, it's on the way."

***

Teresa insisted the others continue to the harbor after Paul carried her bags to the front door. She waved goodbye and bounded up to her uncle's second floor apartment.

"Well, look who decided to come back from Italy." Plump Clara, eye to eye with Teresa, stood in the doorway. Salt and pepper hair, pulled into a bun on the top of her head, framed her round olive skinned face. Teresa often wondered why the woman rarely smiled, since Uncle Sal—her father's brother—had a happy, pleasant nature.

"Clara, the boys are here, aren't they? I am so anxious to see them." Looking behind the woman, apprehension grabbed Teresa's stomach when she heard no sounds. "Where are they?" Her voice quivered.

"You didn't get the letter?"

"What letter?"

"The one Sal sent to your father a couple weeks ago?"

"Oh, Clara, it takes about two months for letters to get to Gaeta. Tell me what it said. Where are my boys?" She felt faint.

"Don't worry, nothing happened to them," Clara said matter-of-factly. "They're in Philadelphia."

Teresa almost collapsed with relief. Her boys were all right—but Philadelphia? Where? Why? "I have to sit down." Her legs were shaking.

Clara pulled out a chair by the kitchen table for Teresa. Laura began crying. "So this is the baby girl you didn't tell Nico about when you left?"

Teresa ignored the sarcasm. "This is Lauretta Maria, and I have to feed her." While the baby nursed, Teresa looked up at Clara, questions pounding in her head. "Please tell me where my children are and why Nico took them so far away? Are they all right? Who's taking care of them?"

"Far as I know they are just fine. Don't worry about that." Clara pulled out another chair and sat down, watching the nursing baby. "She's a pretty thing. Looks like you when you were a baby."

Teresa couldn't remember Clara being in their home in Gaeta more than two or three times, but she did remember that Clara once said she wished she had a daughter. She and Sal had two grown sons who worked in Uncle Sal's grocery store.

"She's a good baby," Teresa said. "But Clara, please tell me about Nico and the boys. Why did they go to Philadelphia and when are they coming back?"

"Far as I know, they're not coming back, but Sal knows more than I do. All I know is one day Nico tells us that a man he met by the railroad yard told him about a German couple in Philadelphia who ran a boarding house. I think the man used to board there. Anyhow, I guess they were moving and needed someone to run the place. The man said Philadelphia was the New York of Pennsylvania and told Nico this job could be a goldmine."

She knew the word "goldmine" would lure her husband. "But Nico doesn't know anything about running a boarding house. And who is taking care of Dante and Alberto?" She pictured them wandering the streets.

"He expected you back much sooner, you know. I guess he thought the two of you could do it. He was gone on the train two days later. Just packed up the boys and left." Clara threw her hands in the air.

"But how could he have afforded to do that?"

"I don't know. But he said he was going to pack up your clothes so he'd be ready to go when he got the money. The next day he came by and had tickets already bought. He told us to give you the address and tell you to come to Philadelphia as soon as you got here. He said you would have enough money from your father."

Nico told them he was going to pack up her clothes. Teresa knew where he got the money. He had found her savings.

***

She spent an anxious, sleepless night at Uncle Sal's. He added little to what Clara already told her. She had no appetite for breakfast the next morning, but the rumbling in her stomach—by the time she reached the train station—made her wish she had eaten something.

When the already crowded train arrived, Teresa walked through three cars until she found a seat. She squeezed in beside a heavy set man who breathed loudly through his mouth. He fell asleep quickly, but nearby passengers covered their ears to ward off the impact of his snoring. Nonetheless, his sleeping through most of the trip gave Teresa some privacy to feed Laura. She closed her weary eyes for what seemed like seconds. They snapped open when she heard the conductor calling, "Next stop, Philadelphia."

Part II

PHILADELPHIA
Teresa and Nico
1901 - 1903

5

"All out for Philadelphia, Reading Terminal," the conductor shouted.

Teresa tightened her grip on Laura, who still slumbered on her chest. Snow flurries fell as the train braked in front of a huge brick station, several stories high. She struggled to gather her bags and hold onto the baby as her rotund seatmate waited impatiently to get out.

She thanked the doorman for helping with her baggage. "Please tell me where we are."

"This is downtown Philadelphia, Miss. You're on Market Street. Watch your step." He helped her step onto the platform.

Laura awoke and howled with hunger. Teresa walked into the station, holding onto her baby with one arm and lugging her bags with the other. She faced an immense room with rows of ticket windows along the wall ahead and long pew-like benches, back to back, in the middle section. She picked one of the benches, secluded from the stream of passengers, where she could feed Laura and think about what to do next.

Hunger pangs attacked Teresa, and her bladder screamed for relief. She looked around and spotted a door with a "Water Closet" sign. "Thank you, God," she whispered. The room also had a pump for water. Teresa fished a cloth from her bag, pumped water onto it and wiped her face and neck.

Refreshed, she made her way to the ticket cages, holding the paper Uncle Sal had given her with the boarding house address written on it. A pleasant clerk advised her to catch the South Philadelphia trolley.

"It won't get you all the way, but you should be within a few blocks of here." The young man tapped the address on her paper and smiled. The brief smile boosted Teresa's spirit. She thought this must be a friendlier place than New York. Her sagging shoulders lifted.

"*Grazie, grazie.* Thank you." Teresa forgot her hunger for a while as she walked onto Market Street to search for a trolley. Instant cold wind, funneling between the rows of tall buildings, slapped at her. She raised her coat collar and pulled the shawl tighter around Laura. With weary bones and aching feet, Teresa felt a growing concern about what she would do if she didn't find Nico. She looked up at the tall buildings as she walked. It didn't seem that anyplace could be as big and congested as New York, but Philadelphia must be a close second.

In spite of the weather, people filled the sidewalks, dodging Teresa without looking at her. Fashionably dressed women passed by, or climbed into carriages, with large bags of shopping goods. Men in nicely tailored suits—overcoat collars up around their necks—walked by with hands in their pockets. Deep in conversations, their breaths clouded the air in front of them.

The streets bustled with hansom cabs, horse drawn merchant wagons and street cars. Teresa felt bone-tired and weak from hunger. "It was so dumb of me not to eat this morning." She looked at Laura, sleeping snugly in her sling. "But we'll be there soon, little one. We have to be."

The bags pulled at Teresa's arms and the baby grew increasingly heavy. Looking for a trolley that said South Philadelphia, she almost slipped off the curb into the path of a carriage. The world spun as she jumped back and crumpled onto the sidewalk.

***

Teresa's eyes opened to blurred faces peering down at her and a hand cradling the back of her head. She blinked, aching all over. As her vision cleared, she saw a woman kneeling beside her.

"Can you hear me?" The woman's voice and touch were gentle.

"Where is my baby?" Teresa struggled to get up.

"She's right here, a little jolted, but nothing bruised or broken that I can see." A nice-looking, middle-aged mustached man was rocking Laura in his arms.

"How do you feel?" the woman asked.

"I am all right." She sat up, and then slowly got to her feet with the woman's help. It felt good to have someone to lean on. By then, most of the curious on-lookers had dispersed.

Teresa peered up at one of the handsomest women she had ever seen—not beautiful, but strikingly attractive. Thin and two or three inches taller than Teresa, she looked about forty. The woman wore a lush, dark green coat that was surely made of warm, soft wool. It hugged her slim waist, and the color matched a hat that Teresa could only dream about. She wanted to reach out and touch the soft black velvet on its large rim. Teresa had seen fancier hats in New York, but none more elegant.

"Are you sure you're all right?" the lady asked again.

Teresa nodded, but as she took a step her legs gave way. The woman held onto her.

"You aren't strong enough to walk. My carriage is right here. You almost stepped in front of us...gave me and Donal an awful scare." She took a deep breath. "My doctor is just a few blocks from here. I want him to check you and the baby. If you are both all right, we'll drive you home. My name is Letta Wunders. This—" her nod indicated the man holding Laura, "is my driver, Donal."

"I ... I can't pay for a doctor, but thank you." Teresa reached out to take Laura. "We will take the trolley. Thank you."

"Mrs.—what is your name?" Letta Wunders still clutched Teresa's arm.

"Teresa Barile." She reached again for Laura. Donal held the baby out, but pulled her back when Teresa wobbled.

"Please get into my carriage," the woman insisted. "Look at you shivering. You can't walk any further, and I don't expect you to pay for the doctor. I'll pay if there is a charge, and there probably won't be. Dr. Janys has been our family doctor and a personal friend for years. It's not far."

Teresa argued briefly before giving in. With her bags and Laura to carry, she would never make it on her own. Gratefully, she climbed into the enclosed, four passenger carriage. Sitting on the soft maroon cushion, her hand swept over cloth that felt like velvet.

She wished Mamma could see this fine carriage, so far removed from the wooden carts they rode in Italy. Nico would be impressed. Teresa could hear him wondering how much a carriage driver was paid, and thinking it would not be a bad job. He would feel important being this close to wealthy people, even though he spoke of them with nothing but contempt.

As Donal guided the horse back onto the street, Teresa watched the huge buildings and crowded streets turn into quieter neighborhoods with large, luxurious stone and brick homes. It seemed only a few minutes before the carriage stopped in front of a pretty three-story gray stone house that filled a corner lot on 19th Street. Rows of tall evergreen trees, on two sides of the property, offered a bright comparison to the huge, leafless trees in front that were sure to provide welcome shade in spring and summer. Donal took Laura again. The baby cooed and smiled at this stranger.

A few minutes later, they waited for the doctor.

"You must have a house full of children," Teresa said.

"Ah, I wish we did," Donal sighed. "My wife and I both wanted a family. We were never blessed with little ones, but Mrs. Wunders' children have always been like our own."

"You have worked for Mrs. Wunders a long time?" Teresa looked at them both.

"Donal knew my husband and his family before I did," Letta Wunders said. "He and his wife are godparents for—" she hesitated and glanced briefly at Donal—"for both the children. Donal taught Abbie to handle the horses when she was still a toddler. She took to them more than her older brother did. Lance liked to ride, but he wasn't much of a groomer."

"That Abbie girl perched right up on me shoulders when we went out to feed the horses." Donal's smile reflected happy memories. "I miss havin' the little tykes around, 'cept they aren't little anymore." He looked up as the doctor walked out to meet them.

Teresa thought Dr. Janys, a little shorter and probably a few years older than Donal, looked like the American Santa Claus. His eyes twinkled with friendliness, and a head of thick white hair matched his full beard. He introduced himself, and then took Laura in his arms with the ease of one who had handled children for years.

In the exam room, the doctor checked Laura first, then Teresa. "Your baby is fine, Mrs. Barile. You, though, are much too thin. When did you eat last?"

Teresa told him about her train trip from New York and the subsequent events that brought her to his office. A few minutes later, he led her from the office to the living part of his home, into a kitchen unlike any she had been in before. Beautiful maple wood cabinets lined the walls, and the counters would allow room enough to fix food and pastry for several families.

Letta and Donal followed, chatting comfortably with the man they obviously knew well, while the doctor sat Teresa at a round table covered with a bright yellow cloth. Three big windows allowed in enough light to brighten the room even on this gray, snowy day.

Beatrice Janys, the perfect Mrs. Santa match to her husband, placed a plate in front of Teresa that held a thick turkey sandwich on homemade bread oozing with butter. There were pickles on the side and a large bowl of steamy vegetable soup sat next to it.

"I am sure I can't eat so much," Teresa said.

"You just eat what you can, honey," Mrs. Janys said. "Whatever is left will go with you." She raised her hand when Teresa began to object. "No use protesting. It's doctor's orders."

Teresa reached for the sandwich, trying not to show her hunger. A half hour later, she left with a jar of vegetable soup, a quart of apple sauce—"the children will love it," Mrs. Janys insisted—a loaf of bread, and enough turkey for several more sandwiches.

***

After leaving the cobbled streets of the main city, they meandered on dirt roads another two to three miles into the outskirts of Philadelphia. City buildings—brick, cement block and brownstones—gave way to majestic country homes, all three and four stories high, on acres of land. The high pitched roofs reminded Teresa of the castles in Italy. Their lawns looked like sculptured parks.

Then more crowded neighborhood communities emerged, reminiscent of the New York tenement areas. Her chest tightened.

"This is south Philadelphia," Mrs. Wunders said. "We should be getting close."

Dusk was closing in when the carriage turned onto South 9th Street. "Uncle Sal's directions say look for a sign in the front window that says *Yost Boarding House*," Teresa said. Donal spied it first and pulled his horse to the curb.

By then, Letta had learned the story of Teresa's trip to Italy and back, though Teresa did not expand on the hardships of the trip. She did share her apprehension about the move to Philadelphia.

"It's a lovely city, dear," the woman told her. "It was the capitol of our country for a short while, you know, and is filled with so much history. Its growth over the past few years is a mixture of good and bad. Crime has risen, unfortunately, but so have job opportunities. Many new industries have their headquarters here now. Overall, I don't think you could have found a better place to put down roots for your family."

Donal helped both women out of the carriage in front of a three-story brick building that was squeezed between similar structures. Narrow passageways, sandwiched on either side, were barely wide enough to walk through. Four wooden steps led to a front stoop. A small window below the stoop apparently belonged to the cellar. Wide brick chimneys, one on each side, indicated at least two fireplaces. From the outside, Teresa noted that the building looked dingy, but not filthy like so many in New York.

Mrs. Wunders handed Laura back to her mother and slipped a note into Teresa's hand. "This has my name and address on it. I hope you will visit me when you get settled. And please, Teresa, promise that you will let me know if there is anything I can do for you." She kissed Laura's cheek before climbing back into the carriage.

Donal deposited the baggage and food on the stoop and took Teresa's arm to help her up the steps. He tipped his hat and wished, "…the best of everything life can give you, Mrs. Barile." He kissed Laura's forehead before replacing his hat and returning to the carriage.

"We're waiting until you make sure this is the right address," Letta Wunders called to her.

Stomach in knots, Teresa walked up the steps of her new home with the daughter her husband had yet to see. She took a deep breath and knocked on a peeling wooden door that appeared to have once been white. As it opened, she looked past the middle-aged, buxomly woman in the entry. Behind her in the hallway stood older versions of the young sons she remembered leaving in New York ten months earlier.

Her heart beat wildly as she gave a quick wave toward the carriage, sure she would never again see these kind people. She knew this part of the city was not simply "on the way home" for Letta Wunders. Then she burst past the startled woman in the doorway and reached for her boys.

6

Teresa had no time to be concerned with another transition in her life. Nico's move, whatever his intentions, got them out of the slums. Now she prayed they could stay out.

She had much to learn. At night, sandwiches for the men's lunches were made and the table set for the next morning's breakfast. Her reluctant body rolled out of bed by 4:00 a.m. She sliced and toasted bread, percolated coffee, fried bacon, eggs and potatoes, and put homemade jam and canned fruit on the table for the seven men who started their workdays with breakfast at 5:30 a.m. A second breakfast had to be ready for the five hungry night shifters who straggled in between 7:30 and 8:00 a.m. All to be done again in the evening. There was weekly laundry and ironing for twelve boarders and her family, and housecleaning that included the upstairs six bedrooms. She stayed tired and never had enough time to spend with the children.

Gertan Yost, the owner of the building, brightened her days, though. She showed Teresa the cellar stock of canned fruits and vegetables stored for the winter. "In the summer, grow what you are able in the small backyard garden. Canning fruits and vegetables will help you save. The rest you will have to purchase."

A few days after her arrival, Teresa looked at her new friend. "Gertan, I will never be able to manage all of this myself, and I do not know how Nico can do it without Carl."

"You are not to worry," Gertan said in her German accent. "Carl has the house fixed good and word gets round about a decent place to board. You and Nico will do fine."

The Yosts claimed family and business pulled them back to Germany, but they didn't want to sell. "Someday, we want to come back."

They would rent the boarding house, with a bank official collecting payments each month and returning a portion to Nico and Teresa. All expenses were to be approved by the official.

***

"I should be collecting the money myself, not having to deal with this Woodhill man at the bank, but Germans don't trust anyone." Nico shook a finger in Teresa's face. "You have to make sure we keep the house full."

They were across the hall from the kitchen, in their ten-by-twelve-foot bedroom that served as sleeping quarters for the whole family. "You almost ruined this, staying so long in Italy. If it was up to you, you'd still be on holiday there, not even thinking about your own family."

"Nico," she gasped, "how can you say that, with my mother dead. Holiday! You know I didn't want to leave the boys."

"But you didn't care about leaving me, did you, or losing the chance for your citizenship," he snarled. "And the baby—do you expect me to believe you didn't know you were pregnant when you left?"

She shook her head and turned toward their bed. "I wasn't sure, Nico, and I am too tired to talk about it now. Anyhow, this is where we are, and we have to do the best we can now—oh!"

The breath whooshed from Teresa as the punch against her back slammed her onto the bed.

"Don't ever turn away when I talk to you."

She lifted her head and rolled over. Nico stood above her, arm raised in a threatening stance, his face purple with rage. Her mouth went dry, but she did not want to show the fear she felt.

"Nico," she whispered hoarsely. "You'll wake the children." She had to calm him. "I have to get up early and I am so tired. Please, can we talk tomorrow? I promise I will try to do better."

"You'll do everything you are told. How do you think I looked to the Yosts these past weeks, telling them my wife was coming to help, and you never came," he said through clenched teeth.

That was it. She had caused him embarrassment. "I'm sorry. I promise I will learn how to do everything quickly."

She did learn. She wrote down all Gertan had told her about the men and their schedules, information about the best places to shop, delivery times for ice and milk, and other helpful tidbits.

The washing machine with a wringer was on the front porch, and it fascinated Teresa. Gertan showed her where to pour in gas that fired the engine, and how to light it for the machine to work.

"Stand back so the flame doesn't shoot out at you," she said.

"Oh, Gertan, it is wonderful." Teresa gaped with disbelief at the amazing machine that could wash clothes. She worried about having to do the men's laundry before seeing this unbelievable contraption. It would still be a big job, but not to have to wash all those clothes by hand—what an invention!

She learned to use the old wood-burning stove in the kitchen. In spite of its age, it cooked fine. Within a few days, she knew everything that had to be done, though she dreaded facing it all without Gertan. Teresa told her so as they worked in the kitchen.

"You have been here barely a week, Teresa," Gertan said, putting a damp cloth over the bread dough. "Look how much you've learned. The work is not what concerns me, my dear."

Teresa turned from the sink, where she washed breakfast dishes in water she pumped out and then heated on the wood-burning range. "What is it, Gertan?"

"You need friends—women friends. You are not taking care of yourself. You should be the one going to the market. And you could go to church and meet neighbors there."

Teresa walked to the kitchen table, pulled out a chair and sat, leaning an elbow on the table. Her other arm reached over to rock the cradle—kept in the kitchen during daytimes—where the baby, now called Lauri, slept. Her adoring brothers found the name easier, and it stuck. Their laughter drifted in from the next room where they played.

"I tried to go to Mass in New York, but it was not safe there. I do miss church, but how would I have time? The men have to eat, even Sundays."

"I'll tell you how," Gertan said. "You put out sweet rolls with some fruit and cheese. Have coffee ready, and the men can serve themselves. They like to do that at times."

Picturing herself at church services filled Teresa with a surge of energy. "That sounds wonderful, Gertan, but Nico wouldn't like me leaving the house that long."

"You let me and Carl talk to Nico. He will be pushing you out the door."

***

After the children fell asleep that evening, Teresa sat on the edge of the bed brushing her hair while she watched shadow figures playing on the walls from the flickering lantern flame. Gas lamps lit the kitchen, dining room and parlor, but oil lanterns were still used in the bedrooms.

Nico walked over and looked down at her. "The Yosts say if we want to keep the house full, you have to get out to the market and church. That's where you meet people to send boarders here. Gertan is going to church with you and the children this week. It's about a mile, not a bad walk. And Carl is going to take me to a Knights of Columbus meeting Wednesday night. It's a new men's organization in the Catholic church."

Teresa listened without moving, not allowing her expression to change. "If that's what you want me to do, Nico, I'm sure I can learn to manage it."

He looked her in the eyes, authority in his voice. "That's what you will do."

***

Gertan held the boys' hands while Teresa carried Lauri in her sling that Sunday. Even trudging through snow didn't dim Teresa's excitement about being out of the house. She breathed in the frosty air with relish, thinking out loud of the beautiful mountains that surrounded Gaeta. Gertan listened to her tell how her village radiated with festivity this time of year.

"Fifers and bagpipers parade down the mountainsides to start the season. There are big celebrations and fairs all over Italy during Advent. The town air is full of steamy breaths from all the people who come out to visit different churches, to see which ones have the most exquisite crèches. It's such a wonderful time, Gertan." Teresa stopped walking. She closed her eyes and put a hand over her chest for a moment.

When she moved again, excitement still filled her voice. "The Yule Log burns from before Midnight Mass on Christmas Eve until New Year's. In Italy, you know, Catholics believe the Virgin Mary comes into their homes at midnight to warm her infant by the fire while the family is at Mass. And everyone eats a lot of fish.

Mamma always made at least three fish dishes for Christmas dinner, and baked bread with fruit in it, and had lots of nut dishes." She heaved a big sigh.

"You should keep some of those traditions."

Teresa took a deep breath. "Christmas foods cost so much now. I will fix something special, though. Maybe Nico will let me get one fish, and some figs and nuts that I can bake in a sweet bread." After all, it was Christmas.

"Did you have an Advent wreath in Italy?" Gertan asked.

"Oh, yes. Mamma gathered evergreen and, ah, what do you call..." She made a tent with her fingers.

"You must mean pinecones," Gertan said as Teresa nodded.

"Yes, we made the wreath and Mamma lit a candle and we said prayers every Sunday until Christmas."

"There are still some pines around the church. I'll help you gather a few and we'll make a wreath."

Teresa stopped in mid-step and turned to look at the woman. "You make me feel so much better, Gertan. I can't afford candles, but we will make a wreath. Thank you." She reached over and gave her new friend a hug. Women didn't travel alone at night, but maybe Nico would come to Midnight Mass with her. She sighed, remembering her dreams of going in Italy, with Leo and their children.

At unexpected times she felt Leo's presence. It surprised—almost frightened her at first, but then she remembered his promise to always be with her. It became comforting to know he watched over her and Dante. She breathed in familiar whiffs of sea fragrance from his body and sensed him brush against her arm. Sometimes she felt the ever so slight brush of his lips against hers.

Their son looked more like his father as he grew into boyhood. Teresa kept her only picture of Leo—her most precious possession—tucked carefully behind the lining of her handbag. She so wanted to show it to Dante someday, but how could she explain?

"Do you have anything for the children's Christmas?" Gertan asked, interrupting her thoughts. They walked carefully, helping the boys step over slushy puddles of snow and mud stirred up by passing horses and buggies.

"I brought pretty colored papers back from Italy. Dante and Alberto can help make paper circles to decorate. I am hoping someday we will have a tree—not this year, I know. Papa gave me a little bag of marbles for each boy. I will save them for Christmas, for in the shoes."

She shifted Lauri, who slept peacefully in her sling. "In Italy, children put shoes by the fireplace Christmas Eve and La Befana puts a toy and goodies in them. When I was a little girl, I couldn't wait to check my shoes on Christmas morning."

"I suppose La Befana is the Italian Santa Clause," Gertan said.

"She is like a lady Santa Clause. If the child is bad all year, he gets only coal in his shoe. I don't know any child who only got coal. That would be awful."

The walk to and from church didn't seem far at all. Gertan had been right—it helped lift her spirits. Teresa already looked forward to the next Sunday, except it would be the last week that Gertan would be with her.

***

Six days before Christmas, the Yosts said good-bye to the boarders, hugged Teresa, shook hands with Nico, and stooped down to give the boys a crushing squeeze. Dante and Alberto cried. Teresa saw how attached they had gotten to "Aunt Gert" and "Uncle Carl" and how often they sought out Carl instead of Nico.

"You *kinder* come over to Germany and see us someday when you get bigger," Carl said. "You will have a good time there. And bring your mamma and papa along."

A friend from church brought his carriage to take them to the train station. Teresa didn't want to let go when she hugged Gertan good-bye. She waved until they were out of sight. Panic rose in her chest when she turned back to the house, until she remembered what Gertan had told her the day before.

"You didn't even notice that I've done nothing the last couple days except be there and talk to you. You have done everything, and you did it just fine, like I knew you would. You don't need me anymore."

But she did need Gertan—not for the work, but for her friendship. The loss left Teresa with a big, empty spot inside her chest.

Shivering, she climbed the porch steps and pushed the boys inside as the wind whipped fresh snow against the building. She turned to close the door and saw a carriage stop in front of the house. The Yosts must have forgotten something. Then she recognized the driver. It was Donal.

7

A puzzled Teresa waited for Letta Wunders to appear. She watched Donal step to the ground, but instead of opening the carriage door, he pulled something from a compartment under his seat.

Closing the door to keep the boys inside, she walked toward the carriage, arms wrapped around her body against the cold wind and snow. "Hello, Donal. Such a surprise to see you. Is Mrs. Wunders here?" She shouted to be heard through the increasing wind. Then she saw him pull out a small, beautiful evergreen tree.

Donal nodded his head to Teresa. "Mrs. Barile, nice to see you again, ma'am," he said pleasantly, as though it was a balmy day. "Mrs. Wunders could not make the trip today, but she thought you might have a place to put this tree. She had four cut for her house, but could only use three."

He stood there with the tree, in the middle of what was becoming a heavy snowfall. A cold shiver darted through Teresa's body as snow blew against the back of her neck.

"Goodness Donal, come inside." She turned and hurried up the porch steps, holding the door open. Donal propped the tree by the stoop while he brushed snow off his coat, slapped his hat against the railing and stomped his feet. Then he picked up the tree and shook the powdery flakes off before bringing it into the front hallway.

"Ma'am, I hope this isn't an intrusion. I'll just leave the tree and …" stopping in mid-sentence, he raised an index finger. "I forgot the box. I'll be right back." He hurried out the door and down the porch steps, plopping the cap onto his head.

Teresa had assured Nico she would never again see the people who had given her a ride after she fainted. She expected him to be angry, but instead he had admonished her for not getting information on how to contact them.

"They may be the kind of people we need to know here. You have to think about that now, Teresa."

She hadn't told him about the doctor's visit or Letta's invitation to visit, thinking he would consider it accepting charity. She was concerned about what Donal might say now.

He came back carrying a large box as Dante and Alberto ran up behind Teresa. They stood gazing at the tree and the snowy man at their front door, then inched closer to their mother, each grabbing a handful of her skirt.

Donal looked the boys over, smiling at them. "You lads are as handsome as your mother said."

Dante, a thin but sturdy five year old, tall for his age, had curly dark hair and dark brown eyes that watched Donal cautiously. Alberto, considerably smaller and rounder, had straighter hair with blonde streaks. Not moving from his mother, his light brown eyes peered at the man.

Donal set the box down and squatted to Dante's height. "My name is Donal, and I think yours would be Dante. How do you like that? Our names both start with a D. And is this your brother Alberto?"

Dante nodded and let go of his mother's dress. Teresa was surprised that Donal would remember the names from their brief conversation.

"Mamma, what's that?" Dante pointed toward the box.

"You'll have to ask Mr. Donal."

"What's that, Mister Don'l?"

"Why don't you just call me Don, and I'll call you Dan? We'll be like twins. Do you want to help me open this?" He looked at Teresa. "My apologies for all the trackin' into your house, ma'am. I almost forgot the decorations for the tree. Mrs. Wunders would have me back here right away, storm or not."

A Christmas tree and decorations. Teresa gasped in disbelief. "I…I …" she stammered.

Donal stood quickly. "It's my fault, Mrs. Barile. It's the weather that got me distracted. Mrs. Wunders told me to be sure and ask if you wanted it first and what did I do…just plopped it in here. She'll be upset with me for sure. I'll take it back right away, ma'am. I didn't mean …"

"What's going on?" Nico interrupted, walking out from a back room.

"Nico, this is Donal—I am sorry, I don't know your last name."

"It's Malone, ma'am, but please just call me Donal. It's a real pleasure to meet you, Mr. Barile. You have a fine family." He extended his hand.

Nico hesitated, until Teresa said, "Donal is Mrs. Wunders' driver. Remember, I told you they brought me and Lauri home?"

Nico immediately thrust out his hand. "Yes, yes. That was good of you. Tell Mrs. Wunders I want to say thank you for bringing my family."

"I certainly will. I was just apologizing to Mrs. Barile for—"

"Oh, no, Donal," Teresa said. "I am not upset. It was kind of Mrs. Wunders to think of us. We are very pleased to have the tree and decorations. How do we thank her?"

"What about a tree?" Nico demanded.

Teresa felt a lump forming in her throat. "Nico, Mrs. Wunders said she couldn't use these, and offered them to us. We can have a decorated Christmas tree for the holidays."

The boys' eyes turned up to watch their father.

Nico frowned.

Donal stood quietly for a minute, and then said, "Only if it's all right with you, Mr. Barile. I was explaining to your wife that Mrs. Wunders told me to ask you first and, with the storm coming in fast, I forgot to do that. I'm very sorry." He paused briefly. "It's just an extra tree that she had cut. I can take it back if you have no use for it."

"No," Teresa said. "Please, Nico. It would be a sin to throw it away. Please, can't we keep it?" She held her breath through the silence that followed.

"Tell Mrs. Wunders thank you. We will keep the tree, but we will return the decorations after Christmas."

"Of course, I understand, sir," Donal said. "They were some leftovers that she wasn't using anyhow, but I'll be glad to take them back later." He squeezed the cap in his hands and then reached for the box. A Happy Christmas to all of you." His eyes swept in Teresa and the boys as he put his cap on.

"Donal, the snow is getting heavy," Teresa said. "Please come to the kitchen and have a cup of cocoa or tea before you go."

Nico stood still, saying nothing.

"Thank you very much, Mrs. Barile, but all the more reason for me to be gettin' on my way, before the weather turns worse."

As he opened the door, Teresa stepped up to him whispering, "Donal?"

He looked back. "Yes, ma'am?"

"Please tell her how very much ..." her voice cracked.

Donal nodded. "I'll be sure she knows how pleased you are." He walked to the carriage and took time to brush snow off the horses before he climbed up to his seat. The white air blurred his wave as he drove away.

***

"You let Wilfred and me watch the little ones and decorate that tree for you, Miss Teresa," Gregor said a couple days before Christmas. Gregor was their oldest boarder. "It's what we'd be doin' if we were home with our own families. You and Mr. Nico go on to church."

While Teresa dressed for Midnight Mass, she said a prayer of thanksgiving that Nico agreed to go, even if it was only because he wanted to be seen by his Knights of Columbus friends. Her fingers worked the buttons at the waist of the light gray jacket that matched her skirt. The neckline of the pale blue blouse fit high and tight around her throat. She felt elegant in this last outfit Mamma had made for her. She didn't like having to cover it, but she could remove the coat in church, and no one would notice her scuffed shoes in the dark.

Her light brown hair, long and wavy, was pulled back in a loose bun, the best she could do without help. Teresa's black velvet hat—old but presentable—had a gray bow in front and gray plume in the back.

"You look pretty, Mamma," Dante said, smiling at his mother when she tucked him into bed. The others were already asleep.

"Thank you, my precious son." She kissed his cheek. "You know, we already have this nice home to live in. LaBefana may not bring anything. She might not be able to find you here yet. Next year, she'll know where you live."

"I know, Mamma," he said, "but she has magic. She'll find us. If she doesn't have toys, I can say thank you for the house, can't I."

Teresa squeezed the burn out of her eyes. "Yes you can, my darling." She wrapped him in her arms, hugged him tight, and turned out the lamp.

She watched Nico put on his rarely worn derby and reach for the lantern to light their way to church. Hope stirred in her that this new life in Philadelphia would bring a peace to both of them. She took his arm as they walked through the light snow with the cold, crisp air stinging their noses. "Isn't it a beautiful night, Nico?"

His "humph" didn't dampen her enthusiasm. Carriages and pedestrians on their way to church services made the roads unusually busy for nighttime. The flickering lights from their lanterns and the windows of nearby houses created the loveliest Christmas Eve Teresa had experienced since coming from Italy. It wasn't first class yet, but for a while she could pretend.

Nostalgia filled Teresa's chest when she entered the church and saw evergreens lining the altar, with a life-sized, beautiful crèche on the left side. Candles glowed on the main and small side altars. Christmas incense and the scent of evergreens wafted through the air.

They squeezed into a pew in the already crowded church just as the organist finished playing Silent Night. Then came the beginning strains of the Mass music as altar servers and priests, dressed in the long, shiny vestments they wore only on special holy days, processed toward the altar. Teresa sighed. How she had missed these beautiful services.

After Mass, Nico introduced her to some of his Knights of Columbus' acquaintances. He seemed a different person interacting with this church group, chatting with the husbands and wives.

Teresa hooked her arm through his as they headed home. "Nico, thank you for coming to church with me tonight. I loved it, and I liked meeting your friends."

"They're not friends, Teresa. We're not inviting them to supper. They're men who have businesses. They can be helpful to me. That's why you go to church. I want you to get to know their wives, so they'll think of us when they know someone who's looking for a place to board."

"I am getting to know them, and I want to tell you that you made a good decision about moving to Philadelphia. I know I was upset at first, and the boarding house is very hard work, but life is much better here. I want you to know that, Nico."

"Of course I know it. Why do you think I came here? Your uncle wasn't doing us any good in New York. I told you, there's money to be made in Phila—watch out." He pushed her to the edge of the road as a carriage drove by, splashing slush on them. "Stupid driver." He reached for Teresa's hand to help her back onto the road.

Teresa brushed off her coat and held onto his arm again. "Nico, I still don't understand...never mind. You made a good decision." She would not chance spoiling the holiday by bringing up the money he took from her, but she had to find some way to make it up.

When they arrived home, the boarders waited for Teresa's reaction to the tree. Strings of multi-colored, bright shiny paper rings draped the limbs, and exquisite ceramic, hand-painted small figurines hung on the tree. A beautiful paper angel crowned the top, and a miniature Nativity Crib lay underneath. Her gasps of delight brought wide smiles to the men's faces.

For Teresa, it capped a perfect evening. Pulling out the small bags of marbles she brought from Italy, she put them into the boys' shoes by the fireplace. She added a few pieces of store-bought candy the Yosts left for the children. Thanking the men profusely, Teresa wished them *Buon Natale* before heading to bed. Nico stayed up.

Teresa looked at her beautiful sleeping children and, for the first time since coming to America, felt the hope that life might be better. She fell asleep minutes after crawling under the covers, dreaming of Leo and Christmas trees—and then a tree was falling on Leo. She screamed and tried to get to him, but she tripped and something held her down. She awoke to find Nico on top of her, grappling to get her gown off.

"Nico, the children!" she whispered.

"They're sleeping," he hissed.

"I'm so tired."

"And I'm tired of your excuses. You owe me thanks for tonight, *mi esposa,* and it's long overdue."

The smell of liquor on his breath nearly gagged her. Her protests would be useless.

His sexual advances were crude and assaultive, but it would be over soon, she told herself. She prayed her children wouldn't wake.

It took little time for Nico to satisfy himself and fall into a snoring slumber. Teresa finally drifted to sleep near dawn. Her startled eyes popped open a short time later to the grinning faces of Dante and Alberto as they shook her.

"Mamma, get up. It's Christmas!"

Teresa forgot all else as she watched the excitement on her boys' faces when they saw the decorated tree. Lauri, understanding none of it, babbled with delight. Dante and Alberto whooped and jumped and ran around the glistening tree examining it from all sides. And then Teresa told them to look in their shoes.

The boys ran to hug their mother when they found the rare candy treats. Then they opened the bag of marbles.

"Mamma, Papa…look." Dante's eyes widened with disbelief.

Alberto gaped as he clutched the small bag. He held it up for their inspection. "Little balls, Mamma."

Teresa smiled. "They're called marbles. Maybe Papa can show you how to play a marble game."

"Papa, can you?" Dante's eager eyes looked up at Nico.

"I don't have time. You can put them on the floor and make up your own game."

First Class to America

Then Alberto said, "Please Papa, show us."

Nico's tone softened. "Maybe after breakfast."

Teresa saw the hurt that flickered in Dante's eyes. "Come on, all of you. I have special Christmas bread for breakfast, like my mamma used to make." The boys ran after their mother, marble bags in hand.

***

Two days later, with the ironing board set up in the kitchen, Teresa reached for the last shirt to press when she heard voices in the front hallway. Nico had gone to shovel snow off the front steps. She looked out to see who he was talking to.

Donal stood inside the doorway.

"Why, Donal, how nice to see you again. I hope you had a good Christmas."

"It was a fine Christmas, Mrs. Barile. Thank you. I hope you did, too."

Nico handed an envelope to Teresa. "Donal brought this from Mrs. Wunders. She told him to bring back an answer."

"I'll just wait in the carriage," Donal said, turning to leave before Teresa insisted he sit in the parlor. Nico pulled her into the kitchen to read the note aloud.

> *Dear Mr. and Mrs. Barile,*
>
> *My brother is visiting for the holidays and we plan to drive to town on Wednesday to see the Mummers Parade. It is quite unique and entertaining. I would like to have you join us. I am sure you both, and the children, would enjoy it. The parade begins at noon, so we could pick you up about 10:00. Don't worry about lunch as we will have a picnic basket with plenty of food. Please consider it and give Donal your answer.*
>
> *Your friend,*

Letta Wunders

"Nico, we could do it. I can make extra bread the day before and have everything out for the men. They don't mind. It would be such a treat for the children." And for me, she thought.

Nico looked skeptical. "Why does that woman want to do all this for us?"

"I don't know. I think she's a good person and likes to be generous. She probably enjoys sharing with other people, and I don't mind us being the other people. We'd never be able to do something like this on our own, Nico, and the children should get out more."

Nico frowned and said nothing for a couple of minutes. "You take them and go with her. She could turn out to be good for us. But I have things to do. Just make sure everything is taken care of here."

"I will, Nico. I can do it."

"And you will pack your own picnic basket. We don't take handouts."

Nico returned to tell Donal that Mrs. Barile and the children would be ready at ten o'clock on Wednesday morning and would bring their own lunch.

8

By nine-thirty the morning of January 1, 1902, the aroma of spaghetti sauce, simmering on the stove for supper, filled the house. Teresa had everyone fed and the kitchen cleaned. She packed the picnic basket with sandwiches, pickles, cheese, and a metal container of steamy hot chocolate.

A large cloth bag held extra diapers for the baby, besides the two cotton diapers Teresa pinned on her, with a wool cover that buttoned over them. She made it herself, and then soaked it in water with lanolin—one of her treasures from Italy—that kept moisture from seeping through. With Lauri in her arms, she opened the front door as Donal turned the corner.

"Hurry, Mamma," Dante said, running down the front steps with Alberto on his heels.

"Don-Don," the younger boy called out.

Donal sat on the far side of the driver's bench. A man sitting next to him—apparently Letta Wunders' brother—climbed down and walked toward Teresa.

Reaching for the picnic basket with his left hand, he tipped his hat with the other as he flashed her a smile. "Well, my goodness, if it isn't Mrs. Barile. So this is where you got to."

Teresa's mouth dropped open. "Mr. Hahn?"

"What a coincidence," Jakob Hahn said. "I'll have to tell Lilly and Paul...and Gina. We've all been concerned about what happened to you. Letta mentioned the children's names, but not yours. Whatever are you doing in Philadelphia?"

"It is long story, Mr. Hahn." She forgot to move.

"I'm sure it's an interesting one, but we'll have time for that later. Right now, let's get your children out of this wind." He looked down at the boys. "You would be Dante, and you are Alberto. It's very nice to meet you, gentlemen." He shook their hands. The boys beamed.

"He called us gennelmen, Mamma," Dante said, as Jakob set down the basket to lift each boy into the carriage.

"You are Letta Wunders' brother?" Teresa was still stunned.

He took her arm and helped her step up while Letta leaned over to take Lauri.

"Guilty, ma'am. Your family has made quite an impression on my sister, you know. And this beautiful lady," he nodded toward Lauri, "well, I can see how she's grown."

"You two know each other?" Letta's eyes widened.

"Mrs. Barile will tell you about it." Jakob helped Donal put Teresa's bags in the cab before hopping up on the front seat again.

Letta looked toward the house.

"Nico can't come," Teresa said. "He said to thank you, but he has too much to do."

Letta waved Donal to go ahead. "Please tell me how you know my brother."

"Incredible," Letta said after Teresa told her the story of meeting Jakob at Ellis Island, and later at Lilly and Paul's apartment. "It has to be fate. If you had come into New York a day earlier or later, he wouldn't have been there. He doesn't like taking so much time away from his own business."

"Oh?" Teresa raised an eyebrow.

"Jake has a real estate office in Hartford like I do here in Philadelphia," Letta said. "He comes here periodically to run my board meetings. The board is, of course, made up of men who don't take kindly to a woman director."

"You run a business?" The idea fascinated Teresa.

"Quite a successful one. Actually, my husband and I ran it together until he died seven years ago." She stopped talking and looked away long enough to clear her throat. "By then, Jake had his own company in Hartford."

"I am sorry about your husband."

"I wish you could have met him. Claude was a fantastic man. I still miss him terribly, but I thank God for the wonderful years we had together." She sat back. "And Jakob is such a good uncle. He's been a blessing to me and my children since their father died."

"Do they still live with you?"

"When they're not at school. Abigail is a freshman this year at Bryn Mawr, and Lance is a junior at Pennsylvania State College. They're both home for the holidays, but they went to the parade with friends. And it looks like they'll be in the midst of quite a crowd." Letta motioned toward sight-seers filling the roadways to town. "There already seem to be more people than last year."

As she gazed at the bustling streets, Teresa's chest pounded with excitement. "This is difficult to believe. I mean that I am here because your brother rescued me in New York, and then you rescued me in Philadelphia. You must be my guardian angels."

Letta laughed. "I don't know that either of us has been called that before, and I have to agree with you that the coincidence is remarkable. But then, I believe in signs and I think this is a sign that we are to be friends."

Teresa didn't know whether to be flattered or suspicious. What did she really know about Letta Wunders? That she exhibited generosity and a need to help poor people? Teresa's family had apparently become one of her causes. Teresa didn't care. She'd be one of Letta Wunders' causes if it got them out like this and brightened her children's Christmas.

Thickening crowds indicated they were getting close to the parade route. Teresa recognized it as one of the main thoroughfares they had passed on their way from the train station. Then Donal turned the carriage into a lot behind a large gray stone building near the corner.

"Here we are," Letta said. Jakob jumped down and opened the door. He gave each of the boys a wide swing in the air before setting their feet carefully on the snowy ground.

"Welcome to Wunders' Real Estate." Letta unlocked a back door to the building.

Teresa followed her along a hallway into a huge room with a ceiling twice as high as the ones in the boarding house. A large framed map of Philadelphia hung on the longest wall, flanked on both sides with historical pictures of the city. Teresa stared at the pictures for a full minute. It was a lovely city.

Several groupings of upholstered chairs and small polished tables sat in clusters around the room. The walls were covered with dark wood finish about four feet high, and brown and yellow striped wallpaper from there to the ceiling. Golden yellow drapes framed the windows.

"This is all your business?" Teresa's gaze swept the room.

"Just two floors. The top four are rented. We have no problem keeping them full. There are a lot of businesses in Philadelphia," Letta said.

Jakob took Lauri. "You relax and visit with my sister. She's been looking forward to seeing you again."

"Yes, I have." Letta put a hand on Teresa's arm. They both turned when they heard Lauri's happy gurgle as Jakob bounced her on his knees.

"You are good with children, Mr. Hahn," Teresa noted. "You must have little ones."

"I'm sure I would if I was married." Teresa glimpsed a shadow of sorrow in his brown eyes for a few seconds, before another smile lit his face. "But I have a fantastic niece and nephew. Unfortunately, they are all grown up." His eyes weren't brown, they were green...no they were brown with green specks.

Still carrying Lauri, he motioned to the boys. "Come on, gentlemen, we're going upstairs for the best place in Philadelphia to watch a parade."

They all followed him to a second floor office, where two large windows overlooked Broad Street. "This is my office," Letta said. "The advantage of being the boss is that you can pick your colors and your view." She chuckled. "That's about the only advantage."

Teresa gaped at the furniture. She let her fingertips graze the edge of the huge, shiny cherry wood desk. Two stuffed chairs in front of it were nicer than any in her home. In the back corner, a small round wooden table sat beside a brown leather sofa. Flowered wallpaper matched two Oriental rugs. She pictured herself working in a room like this.

Thunderous cheering from the crowd signaled approaching marchers, while loud music and drum beats filtered through the glass.

"Look, look." Both boys yelled happily as they peered out the window at the brightly colored, feathered costumes of marchers.

"Mamma, look at the big balls." Dante pointed toward the sidewalk where large balls, dark orange in appearance, bounced around at the end of a string. Many children were walking with them. "Can we have one?"

"Another time, Dante." Teresa put an arm around his shoulder. "Today is for watching the beautiful colors and listening to this wonderful music."

There was no complaint from either boy. They had too much to see. Band members played instruments of all kinds—from bagpipes to wooden flutes and banjos—and dressed in the most pompous costumes had ever seen. Some looked like Indians decked out for special ceremonies; others appeared to be huge birds with elaborate, brightly colored feathers that bounced in rhythm to their marching. Hundreds of revelers crowded the street.

Letta recited a history of the parade. "They come from all over. Most started as street party groups celebrating the New Year and eventually evolved into city parades. Mummers actually date back a few hundred years. We love it. We hope it will become a tradition here."

"I can see why."

A few minutes later, Teresa heard her boys yell with delight. She turned to see Jakob handing a balloon to each of the boys.

***

"Papa, Papa! It was great big parade," Alberto cried. He and Dante ran toward the house, little fingers clutching the strings of their balloons. They raced inside to show off their prizes.

Embarrassed, Teresa looked at Jakob. "They are too excited, but they should thank you before running away."

Jakob reached up to help her out, not letting go of her hand. His eyes seemed to be poking fun at her. "Your boys have already thanked me several times. I haven't had so much fun in years. Watching a parade as an adult is not the same as seeing it through the eyes of children. So thank you, Teresa Barile, for making our day brighter." He raised her hand and kissed the back of it.

The flush that crept up Teresa's neck spread over her face as she gently wiggled her hand out of his. She lowered her eyes, forcing herself to breathe slowly, and then she lifted Lauri from Letta's arms. Donal handed her bag and basket down to Jakob.

"Teresa," Letta said, "please think about my invitation. I would like to have all of your family for Sunday dinner before Jakob leaves us again. May I send

Donal for an answer, after you've talked it over with your husband?"

"I will ask him," Teresa was sure Nico wouldn't go.

Jakob set the bags on the front stoop. "I hope we meet again." He tipped his hat and walked back to the carriage.

Teresa stood for a minute to still her heart before moving into the house.

9

Nico agreed to accept the dinner invitation after Teresa told him about Letta's and Jakob's businesses. He insisted they all dress in their "Sunday best" for the visit.

A week later, Donal drove them along the edge of downtown Philadelphia toward the wealthier residential section of the city, meandering through areas of palatial brownstones. Regal carriages sat in front of most, while a few nannies braved the winter air, pushing baby strollers along sidewalks and by beautiful parks. A light sprinkling of snow gave it all a winter wonderland effect. For a while—just a little while—Teresa could almost pretend they belonged in this carriage, on this street.

Soon they were on the outskirts of the city. Though not paved here, the streets were in much better condition than the ones in south Philadelphia. These homes weren't crowded together, like many in town. The magnificent homes sat on acres of beautiful fertile land.

How could single families use so much room? Teresa's mouth opened in awe as they passed one estate after another, each seeming to be more majestic than the last. "Oh, Nico, aren't they beautiful?"

"I'm going to live like this someday," he said.

"You mean we all are, don't you?"

"What?" He glanced at her. "What did you say?"

"You said you were going to live like this someday. You meant we all are, didn't you?" She waited for his answer.

"Of course. What else would you think I meant. Don't you want to live in a home like these?"

"I dream about it." She breathed a wishful sigh.

"Well, remember then, today could be our start. I told you there were a lot of people with money in Philadelphia. Your fainting might've found us some."

Teresa's chest tightened with an uneasy feeling. She believed Letta Wunders and her brother were good people. She said a silent prayer that Nico would not spoil their chance to be friends.

The carriage turned into a circular driveway in front of a house that wasn't grander than others they had seen, but took her breath away. A huge three-story brick home with enormous white columns, it had two long windows with white shutters on each side of an elaborately carved front door. Four columns held up the portico roof in front of the doorway, over the drive where Donal parked the carriage.

As they pulled in, Teresa glimpsed a smaller two story brick structure behind the big house. That must be the carriage house that Donal had talked about—a house for horses and carriages. Imagine!

What grabbed her attention the most, though, was an attached, single story room to the right of the main house. Windows, surrounded with white frames, made up most of the room. She pictured the light and view in such a room. What a wonderful place to read to the children, or sew, or play music. This was how the rich lived.

Jakob Hahn walked out as Donal opened the carriage door and helped Teresa down. Her heart pounded. She hadn't told Nico about meeting Jakob in New York. She hoped her anxiety didn't show.

The boys scrambled out of the carriage, waving and yelling.

"How do you do, gentlemen? It's very nice to see you again." He shook their outstretched hands.

The boys grinned.

Before Teresa could say hello, Nico brushed past her. His stoic expression changed to a forced smile.

"You must be Mr. Hahn." He thrust out his hand.

Jakob grasped Nico's hand. "A pleasure to meet you, Mr. Barile. You have a fine family."

"Thank you." Nico used his best business voice. "You know my wife," he looked back at Teresa.

Jakob nodded to her. "Good to see you again, Mrs. Barile. May I carry Lauretta for you?"

"I will carry her, Teresa," Nico said. He uncharacteristically reached out and took the baby from his wife.

Jakob turned to the boys. "There's a surprise for you two inside."

Dante and Alberto looked at each other with widened eyes. Jakob opened the door and held it as the family stepped into a large white and black tiled foyer. A wide staircase ascended from the middle of the room. Six balloons, tied together with string, bounced on each side of the stair posts.

Alberto shouted, "Byoons, byoons. Can we have them?"

"If your parents say it's all right."

The boys looked at their mother. "Please, Mamma," Alberto said.

Dante turned to Nico. "Papa, can we?"

Silence pounded in Teresa's ears as she watched her husband.

"It's hard to say no to such kindness," he finally said. "You each take just one."

Jakob cleared his throat. "I should have asked you first, Mr. Barile. I'm sorry."

"It is all right this time. You do not have children, but my sons must know about working for what they get."

"You are absolutely right. My father said the same thing when I was a boy. Now let me be a good host and take you to the parlor. Nora fixed us some refreshments."

First Class to America

A breath of relief escaped from Teresa's lungs, and then her eyes swept over the majestic foyer. White railings followed the stairs partway to a landing where they divided, and with a few more steps on either side, led to the second floor. The oak stairs shone like glass. A large crystal chandelier hung in the middle of the entrance way. Teresa envisioned the brilliance of the gas lamps radiating from it in the evenings.

Letta Wunders appeared from a nearby room and welcomed her with a hug. "I'm so glad to see you, dear. And Mr. Barile, it's a pleasure to finally meet you. Welcome to my home." She extended her hand. "I appreciate that you took time from your busy schedule."

Teresa knew Nico did not approve of women shaking hands. He said the custom belonged to men. But he would want to make a good impression on Letta and her brother. He handed the squirming Lauri to Teresa, took Letta's hand and bowed. "It is the day of the Lord, Mrs. Wunders. It is kind that you invite us."

He was, indeed, intent on making an impression.

***

For a while, they sat in the richly furnished family parlor, warmed by a bright fire that burned in the huge fireplace. Letta offered to show Teresa more of the house, suggesting that her brother take Nico and the boys to see the carriage house.

When the men left, Letta said, "Come, we'll start with my favorite room."

Teresa followed to a room at the other end of the hall as large as the parlor. Shelves of dark wood on each side of the doorway held volumes of books. The cozy fireplace and large windows allowed streams of light to read by. A pleasant scent of evergreen drifted through the room from fresh fir limbs that decorated the mantel. One end of the room was set up for conversation, while a table and cushioned chairs invited study or board games at the other end.

"This was my husband's refuge when he came home in the evenings. After the children were in bed, we'd sometimes sit in here and talk for hours. This is where I still feel closest to him." Letta's gaze around the room seemed filled with memories.

"Everything in your home is wonderful. You must be very happy here."

Letta looked pensive for a minute. "Things don't make people happy, Teresa. But when your life is good, having nice things is an added blessing." She reached out and took Teresa's hand. "I have a special room I think you'll enjoy."

Teresa remembered the beautiful kitchen at Dr. Janys' house. "Is it the kitchen?"

"No, but would you like to see the kitchen?"

"Oh yes, if that is all right?"

"Of course, I should have thought of it. You spend a lot of time in the kitchen, don't you?"

Teresa nodded. "Yes, a lot of time."

"So did I, as a girl. Not that I ever learned to cook well. Now, I leave the kitchen to my experts. Come on, I'll let Beebe show you around."

They crossed to the hallway on the other side of the staircase, heading towards a room at the far end.

"Nora, Beebe, I'm bringing guests," Letta called as she opened the door.

A woman stood at the work counter kneading dough. She turned to look at her mistress. "I got me hands in dough, Miss Letta. Will you excuse me for not stoppin'?"

The lady's build, and hair, and round smiling face were so like that of Gertan Yost, reminding Teresa of how much she missed the woman.

"You don't need to stop. I just want you to say hello to Mrs. Barile and her daughter, Lauri." Letta nodded toward the servant. "Nora is the best cook in Philadelphia—probably all of Pennsylvania."

Nora laughed. "Miss Letta does tend to exaggerate. But 'tis a pleasure to meet you, Mrs. Barile. My Donny goes on and on about your little ones."

"Nora is Donal's wife," Letta explained. "They live in the apartment over the carriage house."

"Your husband has been very kind and helpful to my family, Mrs. Malone," Teresa said.

"Call me Nora, please."

"Thank you." Teresa felt an immediate liking toward this affable lady.

"And this is Beebe." Letta nodded toward a woman about Teresa's age.

"Nice to meet you, ma'am." The tall thin woman continued cutting vegetables at a counter by the sink. She was plain looking, with a thin face and sharp nose, but her compelling smile radiated contentment. Her soft, melodic voice made Teresa picture her in a church choir. She would be a soprano.

"Beebe, will you show Mrs. Barile around this part of the house. And I'll take little Lauri with me to the parlor." Letta reached for the cooing baby.

"I'd be delighted." Beebe laid the knife down and wiped her hands on her apron.

Teresa's mouth was already agape at the bright, colorful modern kitchen. Gaily flowered wallpaper covered the space above shiny white wallboard that was almost her five foot height.

"This is one of our newest and finest features." Beebe pointed to a deep sink under one of the windows, with drains on both sides and a real water spigot. A turn of the small handle, instead of vigorous pumping, brought a flow of water.

"Ohhh!"

"Quite something, isn't it?" Beebe smiled.

"It is wonderful." Teresa walked around the kitchen, touched the sleek enamel counter tops and looked longingly at the fine cupboard space, and the large kerosene stove that could be lit at the burner. No need to chop and burn wood for cooking.

"Blessed Mother, that is nice," she whispered.

Beebe led Teresa to a door in a corner of the kitchen and opened it to show the large pantry.

"It is like your own grocery store," Teresa said in awe.

"Look at this." Beebe opened another door. "They call this a Butler's Pantry, but it isn't really for a butler. It's my favorite work room." White cupboards lined the wall of a room with its own sink and another enamel counter top.

"This is where we put the food together, mostly, and ready it to serve. The silverware and good china are in here. And this," she opened a sliding door, "lets us take it right into the dining room."

"Oh, my." Teresa could only imagine the luxury of such a place to prepare meals.

Nora walked in and saw Teresa's expression. "It's an easy job these days, fixin' meals in a kitchen like this." Pride showed in her sparkling eyes.

Off the back of the kitchen, the laundry room sported its own spigot, with a tub and wash machine. A small closet held the ironing board, with a one burner stove nearby, just to heat the iron. Unbelievable. Teresa might never have all this, but her children would. Someday, somehow, she would make sure they did.

"And here is our new bathroom." Beebe beamed and stepped aside to let Teresa into an adjoining room with two entrances.

Teresa saw a water closet—but what a water closet. Nothing like the plain, crude wooden structures she used previously. The seat looked like it belonged on a comfortable kitchen chair, with clear water in the white porcelain bowl underneath. Beebe pulled the chain on a box above the seat and all the water went into the floor. Teresa looked at her feet, sure there would be a puddle, but the floor stayed dry. Then water reappeared in the bowl.

"Where does it come from?" she asked, wide eyed.

"Up there." Beebe pointed to the tank. "But I don't rightly know how it gets in there or where it goes."

A real tub for bathing, long enough to sit in and extend one's legs, sat against the long wall, opposite yet another sink and spigot. "Amazing," Teresa said.

"It amazes us, too. Ms. Letta often says she wishes her husband could've lived to see such advancement."

Beebe opened a door off the back of the laundry room. "This is my room." She walked in and turned in a circle, sweeping her arms out as though showing off a grand castle.

The small, pretty room with light painted woodwork, bright wall paper and colorful curtains reminded Teresa of Gina's pleasant bedroom in New York. "What a nice room," she said. "Would you mind if I sat for a minute? I've had a long day."

"Not at all, ma'am. That's a comfortable rocker." Beebe motioned to a wooden rocking chair in the corner, padded with red and blue cushions. "I often sit there in the evenings to read or knit."

"Thank you, Beebe. It is comfortable." Teresa sighed with relief at the chance to rest. "Do you mind being back here alone?"

"Oh, no. I love the privacy. And I've got my own outside door when I want to take a walk, or work in the garden, or even have a cup of tea with Nora and Donal.

They're just above the carriage house." She pointed to the brick structure across the lawn that Teresa had noticed earlier.

Nora came to the door. "I'm to tell you dinner will be served shortly, Mrs. Barile."

"I'll be right there, Nora. Thank you." Teresa stood up but quickly grabbed the bed post to steady herself.

"Are you all right?" Nora asked. Her face flashed concern.

Beebe reached out to grab Teresa, who waved her hand away.

"I'm fine. I just got up too quickly. I was so excited about coming today that I didn't take time to eat breakfast. May I use your bathroom before I go to dinner?"

When the door shut, Teresa wrapped her right arm across her abdomen. "Please, God, let it just be hunger."

10

Mamma always set a proper table, especially on Sundays, so Teresa was not intimidated eating at a formal table. In New York though, when she had sometimes cleaned for wealthy families, she noticed finer dishes and more silver put out for guests' dinners. She supposed that Letta kept the settings simpler for the comfort of her immigrant family. Even so, it was finer than any table Teresa had eaten at before. The boys had elected to have their meal in the kitchen where Beebe and Nora took turns entertaining them and their sister.

Teresa looked around after Jakob finished saying grace. "It is lovely."

She saw Nico watching carefully to make sure he used the right utensils. It surprised her that, in spite of his limited English, he engaged so well in conversation with Jakob and Letta. She was not surprised that most of her husband's questions were about their businesses.

"You own many properties in Philadelphia?" Nico asked.

"My sister and I own a few," Jakob said, "but our job is to sell properties rather than own them." He looked at Teresa. "How are you liking Philadelphia, Mrs. Barile?"

Teresa cleared her throat. She was much more comfortable listening than talking. "It is a nice city, Mr. Hahn. Thank you."

Later, the men smoked in the parlor while Letta showed Teresa the room that had grabbed her attention when they drove in. With windows on three sides, it gave her the feeling of standing in a glassed gazebo set in the middle of a park. A stone fireplace offered cozy warmth. Sparkling white woodwork and wicker furniture made sprinkles of color in the room stand out like bright pictures. Plush cushions covered in large multi-colored floral designs invited rest and relaxation on the wicker couch and armchairs. Bright vases waited for the coming of spring to be filled with fresh flowers. Lemon-colored window shades with matching tassels were ready to be pulled if the sun blazed through on a hot afternoon.

"I would sit in here all day if I lived in a house like this. And what a lovely room to sew in."

"Do you sew?" Letta asked.

"Oh yes. My mother taught me as soon as I could climb up on her lap. She did the dressmaking for most of the wealthy families in our village, and I helped when I wasn't in school."

Teresa walked around the room. "In Italy, Mamma used the kitchen table to sew on, and in New York, I sewed at my uncle's house, with the machine set up in a dark corner. A room like this would be..." She heaved a deep, longing sigh, and shook her head.

"You are welcome to come here anytime you want, to just sit or read or sew. It would be easy enough to put up a table for the machine," Letta said. She was quiet for a minute. She seemed to be thinking.

Finally she said, "I mean it, Teresa. I can have Donal pick up you and the children from time to time and bring you here for a few hours. It would be good for you. There's plenty of room out back for the boys to run and play when the weather is nice enough. And Lauri will be walking soon. She'd love it."

Teresa realized the truth in what Letta said. Lauri had already taken a couple of steps. There was so little outside space for the children at the boarding house. The offer overwhelmed her.

She smiled. "Thank you, but I do not think—"

"Don't answer yet," Letta interrupted. "I've been thinking about what I could do for you. Your life needs to be more than work and caring for others. Jakob said the same thing."

"He did?"

"We'd both like to see you take some time to enjoy life in Philadelphia. You and your husband, of course."

They must seem like pathetic figures to these wealthy people. Her smile faded. "Thank you, but I think Nico would not agree."

A short time later, Jakob walked Teresa and the children to the carriage. Teresa wondered what kept Nico. Finally he and Letta walked out, chatting like old friends.

Letta reached in to give Teresa's hand another good-bye squeeze. "Your husband and I have been talking about your coming here every other Wednesday and doing some sewing for me, Teresa. I've been looking for a seamstress and he says you are very good. Donal will drive you and the children."

Nico and Letta Wunders had negotiated her time and activity without even asking what she thought. And nothing had been said about pay. Still, Teresa realized it would give her the chance to get out. If Letta saw that she was good—

"If my husband says so, I am willing to try."

If Letta did pay, even a little, maybe she could begin to build up her first-class savings again. But what if…what if Letta agreed to give the pay to Nico? He would expect it.

On the ride home, Nico swatted at one of the six balloons that thumped his face. "I don't see why we needed to bring all of them," he complained, "but I guess it would've been rude not to."

"Is that why you offered my sewing services—because it would have been rude not to?"

Nico scowled at his wife. "I didn't make the offer, she did. It's a good chance for us, Teresa. These people are important in the community. You'll get to know how

Letta Wunders does business. Her brother said there are openings for new employees sometimes. I want to know when that happens."

Teresa took a deep breath. "It sounds as though you want me to spy on them."

"What are you talking—spy? You're spoiled, Teresa. We'd be fine today if your father had saved his money and not spent it on all your mother's senseless whims. He would've had plenty to give you when we married. Instead, here we are, practically beggars."

Teresa sat open-mouthed, too stunned to reply. Her father had been so good to Nico. She shook with indignation, but it was not worth an argument. "My father always took care of us, but whatever you say, Nico. We do need more income. I'll try it."

He sat back with a satisfied sneer. Letta must have discussed payment with him. Teresa swallowed her disappointment, but then envisioned days of sewing in the sun room, and open spaces where her children could play safely. Even if it was out of pity, Letta Wunders would be good to them.

***

They fell into a comfortable routine. Every other Wednesday, Teresa hurried through her morning duties so she and the children would be ready for Donal by nine o'clock. They could smell the fresh bread and oatmeal, or bacon and eggs that Nora had piping hot and ready when they arrived, and there was always a basket of leftovers to take home.

Letta pulled her aside at the end of the first day. "I told your husband that I would pay you three dollars a day, Teresa. However, I want to pay you five. It is worth it to me." Letta paused a minute, her brow wrinkled in a thinking mode. "I hope you will keep some of the money for your own needs and save some for the future. It's so important for a woman, you know. And I will not tell anyone, not anyone, how much I pay you. That is just between you and me."

Teresa looked at the woman in amazement. Mamma's words—so like Letta's—echoed in her head. *Always keep enough aside to take care of yourself and your children.*

Nico didn't complain about Teresa's long hours. His hand went out for the three dollars she brought home. "She could afford to give you more," he grumbled.

"Nico, that's a good pay for the little time I'm actually there."

"I guess so," he mumbled. He then quizzed her at length about any business information she picked up from Letta.

"She's at work when we arrive, and I'm busy with sewing when she gets home. We don't have time to sit and talk."

That wasn't quite true. Teresa finished the day's projects—from altering favorite dresses to making new kitchen curtains—before Letta arrived home those first weeks. In the beautiful bright room, she flew through her sewing on a machine she couldn't have imagined. She only had to peddle with her feet to make it work, so both hands were free to hold and guide the material. The pay she received exceeded anything she'd expected.

Maybe she would have another chance to build a savings, but she had to find a place to keep her money safe this time. As she picked up Lauri's diaper bag the next day, when they were leaving for Letta's, she knew where she would keep it. She made a pouch in the bottom of the bag. Nico would never look there.

***

Letta soon raised her salary to six dollars. Teresa told Nico it was a fifty cent raise. She begged God's forgiveness for the lie, and vowed to add it to her list of sins when she next went to confession.

A rare smile crossed Nico's face as he took the coin she held out to him. "If she uses you more, I can hire someone to work here and I'll be able to get another job. We can be out of here by next year—maybe sooner if things go well."

What did he mean, "...if things go well?" She felt her stomach tighten. She grabbed her abdomen, rushed outside and threw up.

"What's wrong with you?" Nico demanded. "Are you trying to get out of working?"

"Of course not," Teresa said, swiping her hand across her mouth as she lifted her head. "Probably something I ate unsettled my stomach. I'm fine."

"Well, clean up that mess."

***

Letta arrived home the last Wednesday in April to find a pasty-looking Teresa on the cot in Beebe's room.

"Whatever happened?"

"She fainted," Nora and Beebe said in unison.

Beebe moved about nervously, wringing her hands. "Do you think we should get the doctor?" Her voice was higher-pitched than usual.

Nora calmly loosened the tight collar around Teresa's neck. "She just needs a bite to eat."

Embarrassed by the attention, a wobbly Teresa sat up. "I will be all right. I felt a little bit dizzy, but I am fine now."

A knowing look passed between Nora and Letta.

"What is it?" Teresa said.

"How far along are you?" Letta asked.

Teresa hung her head and answered in a muffled voice, "I think about three or four months."

Beebe looked from one to the other. "What are three or four months?"

Nora gave her a stern look.

"Oh, oh, you mean...oh, I see now why you fainted, Ms. Teresa." Her worried expression faded into a big smile.

Later, when they were alone, Letta said, "I'm going by Dr. Janys' office tomorrow and make an appointment for you to see him."

"Oh, Letta, we can't afford a doctor. I am all right. I never had a doctor before, only a—what do you call them here—helper lady?"

"Mid-wife?"

"Yes, only a mid-wife when the babies came. Don't worry. I will get all your work done."

"You aren't to worry about the work when you don't feel well, Teresa. And don't be concerned about paying. I'll take care of that."

Teresa opened her mouth to argue.

"Just for now," Letta said. "We'll arrange a way for you to pay back later, but for now, please let me do this for you." She leaned toward Teresa. "Do you think I haven't noticed how thin you've become? I know you don't eat enough. And you need better nourishment for the baby's health. You must stop nursing Lauri. I'll make sure you have enough fresh milk for her and the boys."

Teresa stared at Letta. "Why do you do all this for us?" She'd wondered about it for weeks.

Letta heaved a deep sigh as she sank into a nearby chair. For a brief moment, she looked like she was going to cry, but she blinked the tears away. Staring at the far wall, she took several breaths before her gaze returned to Teresa.

11

"You know I have two children. But I had an older daughter—Sara." Letta's voice lowered and cracked, spilling sadness throughout the bright room. "She would have been two years younger than you."

"Would have been?" Teresa repeated. She thought back to the first day they met, when she asked about Letta's children as they waited for Dr. Janys. Letta had hesitated before she referred to, "both my children." There had been a third child.

"Sara was not quite twenty and had lost her father three years earlier. I think she was looking for someone to fill his spot in her life when she met Barrett—a good man, but both of them were so young." Letta's eyes drifted to the tightly clasped hands in her lap. "I begged them to wait until he finished school, but they were determined to marry, and both too proud and independent to accept help. They lived in terrible conditions. Oh, Sara said they weren't as bad as I thought, but her weight plummeted and she looked so pale."

She shut her eyes briefly, and then opened them and looked at Teresa. "Like you do."

Teresa felt a heaviness in her chest. She understood about living in terrible conditions.

"Truth is, Claude and I raised all of our children to be independent and responsible for their choices. Sara was doing what she was taught." Letta shook her head.

Teresa stayed quiet.

"Before her confinement we were downtown one day shopping for baby clothes. I stopped to talk to a friend and Sara started to cross the street just as a runaway horse and buggy turned the corner. She didn't have time or strength to jump out of the way." Letta took several breaths. "It could have happened to you."

She looked down, with eyes that seemed to have no tears left. "It was such a waste, two lives."

"Oh, Letta. I can't…I'm so sorry." Teresa's voice cracked. "Where is she now?"

A brave smile did not hide the sadness in Letta's eyes. She pointed toward the meadow behind her house. "She's buried there, next to her father. I'll show you one day soon."

Teresa pictured Mamma's grave in Italy. Losing a parent was hard enough, but… A cough cleared her throat. "I can't think how hard it would be to lose a child."

Letta patted Teresa on the hand. "I don't usually share that story, and I hadn't thought about it for a long time." She paused and shook her head. "That's not true. I think about it every day, but I've only shared my feelings with Nora and Donal. They loved Sara like their own. And Jakob, of course. He was only ten years older than Sara."

Letta paused. "She had asked him to be the baby's godfather. He was devastated when she died."

***

The late afternoon sun sent foggy streams of light through the window in Beebe's room, making Teresa blink when she awakened from the nap they all insisted she take.

Letta sat in the rocker reading a book. She laid it down. "I don't want to take over your life, Teresa. I just want to help. Tomorrow, I will ask if Dr. Janys can see you on Monday."

Teresa sat up. "Nico will not like it. He lets me work here and bring food home because he believes I earn it. He will not like charity."

"Let me talk to Nico. I'll come by your house on Sunday, when he has some free time. We'll work it out."

Teresa pictured Letta at her house. Donal had been there—but Letta? "I don't have a nice home like you do." Worry lines furrowed her forehead.

"Do you think I grew up in a place like this?" Letta leaned toward Teresa, not waiting for an answer. "Jakob and I had wonderful parents, but we were very poor. Our father was in a mine accident and couldn't work for years before he died. Our only income was the little my mother made cleaning for the church. We lived in a neighborhood like the one you are in now, in the very poorest section. It wasn't until I went to work that I even glimpsed how other people lived." She paused, and her eyes seemed to shift to a happier image.

Her voice softened. "That's where I met Claude. He was our section supervisor in the sewing factory and for some reason he took a shine to me—which worked, because I fell in love the first time I saw him. I didn't know then that his father owned the business. Claude had to work his way up like any other employee. He came from a good family. I was lucky to have wound up there instead of in one of the awful sweat factories."

Teresa listened in awe, picturing Letta living in a neighborhood like hers, and working in a…had she heard right?

"You worked in a sewing factory?" Teresa's eyes widened.

Letta bit her lower lip. Her face showed a moment of discomfort. "Just pretend you never heard that. I had to sew then, I don't have to now. I prefer not to. Come on, I want you to eat before you go home. And leave Nico to me."

***

By the time Letta finished talking with Nico that Sunday over coffee and the sweet rolls Teresa had baked, it was all settled.

"Letta said being pregnant here isn't like it is in Europe, where there are plenty of good mid-wives," he told her later. "American women go to doctors when they are pregnant,"

"Nico, we can't afford a doctor."

"That's why I'm going with you. Letta said this doctor—Jan something or other—told her he needs someone to do errands. That will pay for his fee." He had a smug expression.

"But we don't have a horse or buggy."

"No, but the doctor does. Donal is going to teach me how to drive it. There are a lot of people in Philadelphia I could work for." He paced the room, rubbing his hands together. "And Donal will give me milk to bring for Lauri and the boys. They need more than they're getting. You know, Teresa, you shouldn't still be nursing Lauri."

Apparently, Letta had covered everything with Nico. What magic did the woman have, besides money? But money was the magic for Nico, Teresa realized.

"That's awfully generous of the doctor and Donal." Teresa said.

"Letta wants to hire me to do some of her business errands, too. This is my chance to meet more wealthy families, and their drivers talk. I'll be able to pick up a lot of information about other jobs."

***

Dr. Janys estimated her due date as late September. She and Nico sat in the spacious office, on the patient side of the rich looking desk that reminded Teresa of the one in Letta's office. The doctor spoke with them about the importance of rest and diet for the mother-to-be.

"Regular work isn't going to hurt, but she is very thin," he said to Nico. "No strenuous lifting or riding over rough roads."

He looked at Teresa. "I want you to have a hearty breakfast every morning. Oatmeal is good for you and your children, and eat plenty of vegetables. Come see me at least once a month."

She nodded understanding.

He held the door open for her. "Now, if you make yourself comfortable in the waiting room with Mrs. Wunders, I have some business to discuss with your husband."

"He's so like my father," she told Letta. "Gentle and understanding, but firm. And he has the same kind of mustache and beard as Papa." Without warning, Teresa's eyes filled with tears. Had Papa received the letter she sent, so he would know where she lived now? She prayed her father was all right.

***

"I'll be driving for him one or two days a week," Nico said on the way home. "That will pay for the doctor and hospital when the baby is born."

"Hospital? I've never been in a hospital. Our babies are born at home."

"That's what I told the doctor, but he said in America only poor women have their children at home."

"We *are* poor, Nico."

"You've been lucky, Teresa." His voice rose. "Do you know how many women die in childbirth? Too many things can go wrong. Dr. Janys said you should go to the hospital when the baby is due. They have some sort of medication, eth—something, that can make you go to sleep so you don't feel the pain."

Teresa had heard one of Clara's New York neighbors talking about a new "wonder drug" called ether that made it possible to have a baby without pain. Supposedly, it just put you to sleep and when you woke, the baby was there. She couldn't imagine giving birth asleep and without pain.

"Dr. Janys said there might be more work for me later, if I have time," Nico said. "I told him I would have all the time he needed."

Maybe the work really will make him happy, and he can make a new life for us, Teresa thought. Mamma always said miracles happened if you believed. *God, I believe You opened the door for Nico to come here to Philadelphia and for Letta to come into our lives. Let me have faith enough to walk through the doors You open now.*

12

With the onset of milder weather, the boys began sitting on the front bench of the carriage with Donal, while he showed them how to guide the horse. Teresa smiled at her sons' excitement when they talked about driving the carriage, "and bossing Nickers." Donal told them he had picked out the nine year old gentle mare—chestnut with white markings—five years earlier at a local auction.

"She reached her nose out over the stall door and nuzzled me when I walked by. I knew right away she had to come home with me."

Dante, especially, begged to hear the story over and over.

They were pulling into Letta's driveway in late May when Teresa heard the boys yell. She felt a catch in her chest as she saw Jakob striding toward the carriage. He opened the door.

"Hello Mr. Hahn. This is a surprise. I wouldn't have come today if I knew you were here. This should be your time with your sister."

"Well, then, I would have been terribly disappointed. These little tykes are one of the reasons I most look forward to my trips to Philadelphia." He lifted each boy down and then reached for Lauri. Holding her in one arm, he held his other hand out to help Teresa. "And please call me Jake or Jakob."

She reached for his hand, and then jerked back like she had touched a hot stove. "I can do it." She grabbed the handle on the front of the carriage as she lowered herself to the ground. Jakob looked at her and grinned.

"You get up and down there pretty well, but should you be climbing like that in your condition?"

Teresa felt the flush spread across her face. Her condition? She already had to wear looser clothes, but she didn't show that much yet. Women who were obviously "in the family way" did not go out in public. Letta insisted that coming to her house was not "going out in public." Pregnancy was politely ignored by anyone except close female relatives or friends. Men were supposed to pretend they didn't notice the condition. Apparently, Jakob Hahn hadn't learned that. Teresa didn't know how to respond.

"I'm just fine." She was angry that he made her feel so uncomfortable.

"If you're sure." He gave a soft chuckle, walking toward the front door with Lauri babbling contentedly in his arms and the boys clinging to his legs.

They never behaved like that with Nico, but he never gave them the attention that Jakob did. A voice in Teresa's head admonished her. Nico hadn't had the kind of loving parents like Jakob's. Her husband had told her about his father's years of abuse. It might explain why he had so little patience with the boys.

Her children would do anything to please the people in Letta's home, or what Teresa asked of them. They seemed to do what their unpredictable father demanded out of fear. She put a hand to her chest and didn't breathe for a minute, thinking. How were her responses to Nico different from her children's?

***

Letta stood still one afternoon, shortly after Jakob's visit, as Teresa pinned pleats on the dress she was wearing. "You really are very good at this, Teresa." It was her third new dress in less than two months.

"Until you came along, there just wasn't a dressmaker that I liked or trusted." Letta turned around, looking into the full length mirror, admiring her new outfit. "I've gotten several compliments on the dresses you made for me. Some of my friends have asked if you were available to do dressmaking for them. I promised I would talk to you about it. You could do the fittings in their homes and the sewing here."

Teresa stopped and looked up at Letta. What an appealing, and impossible idea. "I can't do more than I am. It pleases me more than I can say to sew for you. But I can't take more time from the boarding house."

"Well, I've been thinking about that, too. If you came here four or five days a week, and did dressmaking and alterations for just two or three more families, you could earn enough to pay a woman to do your work at the boarding house. You would still have more wages for yourself than you do now. These people pay well. They are not pleased with the shops in town for themselves or for their children." She paused briefly. "And you know how much we all love having your children here. Nora and Donal, and Beebe too. They miss having little ones around as much as I do."

Teresa envisioned herself as a real dressmaker. If she continued to work for Letta two more years, she had already calculated that she would be able to buy her own machine. The idea thrilled her. It lasted a few seconds.

She reached out a hand and touched Letta's arm. "Thank you for the wonderful offer. I have three children and another one coming. I have a boarding house to run. I dream of doing something like that some day. Maybe after this baby—"

"Look here and listen to me, Teresa."

She was eight years old, sitting with her mother in the kitchen of their small home in Gaeta, telling Mamma that she couldn't sew that stitch.

"Look at me, Teresina, and listen. You are not going to let a stitch be smarter than you are. You will be a strong woman someday. You never say can't. I will show you once more. Then you do the stitch. You can do it."

"Yes, Mamma, I can do it."
"Yes, Mamma, I'm listening."
"What did you call me?"
"I called you…oh, Letta. I'm sorry. Sometimes you remind me so of my mother."
"That is indeed a compliment."
"Yes, it is."
"Then think about what your mother would advise. You trust my staff with your children, don't you?"
"I trust them like my own parents, and the children love them. That is not the problem. My children are my responsibility, and so is the boarding house. We can't keep relying on you."
"And don't you feel responsible for making a better life for your children and yourself?"
What would Mamma advise? She'd say do it, and so would Leo. It had been a while since she had felt Leo's presence. She shivered now as she sensed the familiar brush against her arm. She felt the warmth of his breath on her ear. *You can do anything, mia cara. This is an opportunity you must take. Isn't this what we planned? Now you must do it for both of us and your children.*
If Leo was with her, it wouldn't be a question. They had often talked about setting up a small dressmaking shop for her after they married. But that was Italy.
"Teresa?" Letta said again. "Do you think your mother would want you to pass up this chance?"
Teresa didn't have to think about it. She shook her head. "Of course not. But Nico will never consider having someone else run the boarding house."
Letta would not be put off so easily. "What if he would? If he knew it meant you could make more money?"
"I don't know," Teresa mumbled slowly, already with an idea in her head.
"Let me talk to him," Letta said.

"No, this time I will talk to him."

***

She made Nico's favorite dessert for dinner that night—apple crumb pie, and fresh perked coffee to go with it.

"This must be a special occasion, Miss Teresa." Johnny, their youngest boarder, took a bite of the pie that Teresa had just placed onto his plate.

"Not really, Johnny. Letta gave me apples today, and I know Nico likes apple pie." Teresa smiled at the pleasant young man. He always offered assistance when he saw her lifting a heavy pot, moving furniture, or even clearing off the table, especially since her pregnancy became noticeable.

"It is good with a cup of coffee, isn't it?" she said.

"You're right about that, Miss Teresa. It's delicious. And my Annie would think so, too."

"Oh, Johnny, I forget that you are just married a few months. I wouldn't want to lose you, but I wish you and Annie could be together."

"Matter of fact, I wanted to talk to you and Mr. Nick about that. Do you have a few minutes to spare?" Johnny looked at Nico.

Nico had paid little mind to the conversation until he heard the last comment. He pulled his chair closer to Johnny's. "Now, what do you want to talk to us about? You're not leaving, are you?"

It was one of the few times Teresa saw him look concerned. She walked to the stove and picked up the large blue-grey enamel pot, steaming with fresh coffee, refilled their cups, and sat down on the other side of the boarder.

"Well, Annie and I was talking about her moving here with me and looking for a job, 'cause there really ain't any good work for me back home. With all the rich families in Philadelphia— she's a great housekeeper, you know, and I'm sure she'd find plenty of work here. I wondered about that attic room where the Yosts stayed after you came. I think it's only used for storage now, but if Annie and I moved into it you could put another boarder in my bed."

He took a deep breath. "And the other thing is that Annie could help you with the kiddies and some of the work here, Miss Teresa. She's good with little ones."

Teresa didn't move, but her mind was in a whirl. Trying to contain her excitement, she thought Nico just had to say yes to this. It was right for Johnny and seemed the perfect answer to her prayers. She looked at Nico and chose her words carefully.

"I was thinking we might use that room for the children, but we have space enough for them where we are now, at least for a couple more years. It could mean extra money for the boarding house, I suppose. What do you think, Nico?"

"I think the attic room will hold three. You stay where you are, John. Your wife will move in with you and Gregor will go to the attic room. Then we can get two more boarders in there. But we can't make a lower rate for your wife."

Johnny gave a quick, tentative smile. "Thank you, Mr. Nick," he said. "I was hoping that if Annie helped here, maybe you could make the fee a little less, but I understand."

Teresa spoke up quickly. "Johnny, let Nico and I talk about that. You know we both want to see you and Annie together, and we will do all we can to help. You have been a good boarder. We want to keep you, don't we, Nico?" She didn't allow herself to react to his harsh glance.

Later, she tucked the boys into bed, fed Lauri and was rocking her gently in her cradle when Nico walked in. His frown and tight lips screamed displeasure. She had to be the first to say something. She spoke softly, to not wake the children.

"Nico, I'm sorry I spoke out when we were talking to Johnny, but he has been one of our best boarders. He doesn't drink like some of the others, and always pays on time. I just wanted you to know that I will do whatever you want so we can keep him." She could hear Nico breathing hard, but he didn't interrupt her. "And Letta talked to me today about an idea she was sure you'd be interested in. I didn't see how it could work until Johnny told us about his wife."

"What are you babbling about, Teresa? What were you and Letta Wunders talking about?" His demanding tone matched the anger in his eyes.

She backed away and sat on the bed, taking a deep breath to calm herself. "Some of Letta's friends saw the dresses I made for her, and… "

"And what? Get to the point."

She told him about Letta's proposal, and the possibility of making more money. He listened intently.

"When Johnny told us about his wife, it seemed like maybe God was opening a door," Teresa said. "But you know more about what we need and you have made good decisions for us. And I don't know if I am a good enough seamstress to do all of that."

"What do you mean, good enough? Wasn't your mother the best seamstress in Gaeta, and didn't she train you?"

Her mother was absolutely the best seamstress in Gaeta, and trained Teresa well. She knew she could do it. "You are right, Nico. She was the best, and I suppose I could do it."

"I know you could. I guess we'd have to give Johnny and his wife free rent in that upstairs room instead of payment." He paced back and forth, pursing his lips in thought. "But if business is as good as Letta says, you should make enough to pay the boarding house bills, and when I get into business I can pay Johnny to be here full time. It could work. It could be our chance. I hope you didn't tell Letta that you wouldn't do it," he said.

"Of course not. I told her it must be your decision."

13

Annie arrived with Johnny the following Sunday evening. They came with two huge bags that contained "...all our worldly possessions."

From the start, Teresa loved Annie like the sister she always wished she had. Four years younger than Teresa, and taller by almost a head, the sturdy built young woman was a bundle of pleasantness. Teresa found her laugh contagious, and loved the style of Annie's long sandy blonde hair, pulled back and held loosely away from her face with a large bow at the back of her neck.

Nico, on the other hand, described her as annoying. Not used to gregarious women, he told Teresa Johnny was downright henpecked. The young man asked his wife's wishes about everything and never seemed to tire doing things for her.

"You are going to have to be strict with that girl," Nico told Teresa, "or she'll waste your time and never get the chores done. I'm not so sure this is going to work."

"Give her time, Nico. I can already see that she is a hard worker and a quick learner. I think she'll be perfect. And the men like her."

"That's because she's always laughing and jabbering with them instead of tending to her work. She's not here to entertain the boarders. I want you to make her pay attention to her duties. Maybe it isn't such a good idea to have a husband and wife together."

Teresa felt her heart beat faster. "Please give them a chance. I think they have more energy working together. They are getting everything done. You'll see. We couldn't have found anyone better."

"I'll give them a month."

***

By the second week, even Nico noted Annie's frugalness and special skill in turning leftovers into tasty feasts.

"They are a lovely couple, and both hard workers," Teresa told Letta, "so good with the house and boarders. My only fear is that Nico doesn't have much patience. He thinks Annie talks to the boarders too much. But she is never idle. They love the attention. And Johnny—my goodness, he is like a school boy with her around. He is doing so much more than we expected."

"It sounds perfect to me. Nico will see that too, I'm sure."

Teresa hesitated, opened her mouth to respond, and then closed it. Finally she said, "I think you know my husband, Letta. He isn't fond of strong women, except you. For some reason, he doesn't seem to mind listening to you. But I don't know any other woman that he would take advice from, certainly not me."

"I don't know that Nico appreciates taking advice from anyone, but I can see that he does have respect for people who are successful and wealthy. It isn't a bad trait, Teresa, if it will encourage him toward his own success. He has been raised in a society that doesn't give credit to women, and in that, he is not so different from most American men. That's why Jake comes here to run my board meetings. Thank God for him." Letta smiled. "He used to stay longer when the children were young. He should have been a father, and I hope someday yet he will be."

"It seems odd that a man like your brother isn't married."

Letta's expression turned solemn. "Jake was engaged a few years ago to a lovely woman. They had known each other a long time and had a wedding date set.

Margaret was on her way home one stormy evening and—well, no one knows exactly what happened, but they think the horse panicked and reared on the Connecticut River bridge. The carriage overturned and she was thrown into the river and drowned."

Teresa gasped. "How awful for your brother."

Letta nodded. "It was a very hard time for him. I didn't think he would ever come out of his grief. Then Sara died. Another horse accident. That could have done him in, except he was so concerned about me. I don't know how I would have gotten through that time without him." Letta stopped talking and closed her eyes for a few seconds.

"But now, since he met you and your children, he looks like he is reborn. I haven't seen him enjoy life so much since before Margaret died."

Teresa had no reply.

✢✢✢

The winter gave way to a summer that heated up fast. By July, it was especially uncomfortable at the boarding house, with tenements crowded in on both sides and no space for air to circulate. Occasional breezes coming through the front or back windows were limited by near-by buildings and streets filled with people, carts, and animals. Teresa and Annie made sure all the house windows were open to take advantage of any little bit of air, except when the odor of animal eliminations was too strong. Keeping the flies out always presented a challenge.

Letta's house, on the other hand, had acres of country land and trees surrounding it, making plenty of shade and cooler air. Her huge windows opened to let in unencumbered breezes from all directions. Teresa felt increasingly grateful for the long days she and the children spent there.

As Letta promised, the two new families that Teresa began working for paid well. Within a few weeks, her first customer, Regina Billingsley, asked her about taking on another family.

"They are in the neighborhood, Teresa, so it wouldn't be out of your way, and you'll like Edith Smithers. Please think about it."

Letta encouraged her to add the Smithers as customers, and Teresa agreed only if allowed to pay toward Donal's fee.

"I know I'm taking his time away from you, Letta. I will take the trolley unless you let me pay."

They settled on a nominal fee, and Teresa increased her workdays from five to six a week. Still, with the amount Nico insisted he needed for house expenses, she rarely had a dollar left each week—that he knew about. She continued to keep aside almost half of her fees plus bonuses, which she regularly received from pleased patrons.

Nico still complained about John and Annie's wages, but agreed that the two new beds had filled quickly.

Annie's dresses were heavy and hot, though. Teresa gave Letta five dollars to purchase a few yards of lightweight material so she could make a couple of summer dresses for the young woman. Letta came home with several bolts of colorful, light cotton fabric of various designs, and light-weight wool suitable for pants or skirts.

"The materials are beautiful, Letta. But it is much more than I needed."

Letta smiled. "You, expectant little mother, are going to make two dresses for Annie, then three for Teresa. You do for everyone but yourself. And your growing children need new outfits."

For the next month, Teresa sewed feverishly. She first made lightweight shirts, pants and a jacket for Nico.

Even Nora commented on how good he looked, when he came by with Donal one morning. "Mr. Nico, you're goin' to have all the ladies' heads turnin' to look your way in them new clothes."

Teresa had not seen Nico blush before, or look so pleased. It never worked when she tried to compliment him.

Annie's clothes were next. A dress, skirt and two blouses had a thrilled Annie twirling around the house, showing off her new clothes to the boarders. The men whistled and praised both women. Annie hugged Teresa until she winced.

"Annie, easy, please. I'm glad you like them, but you are going to squeeze this baby out of me if you aren't careful."

"Oh, oh, I am sorry. It's just that I've never had two new outfits at once before, and such pretty ones. I'll be able to work twice as fast now."

Making new clothes for her children felt like an early Christmas present to Teresa. She made all the clothes large enough, with hems that could be lengthened or elastic that could expand, to allow for growth.

"Look at you handsome boys in those pants and shirts. You look so grown up." Tears stung her eyes as she watched her children dressed in clothes that had no patches. "And look at my Lauri."

Teresa beamed with pride when Lauri toddled over, holding out her skirt. "I like, Mamma."

"I like too, precious." She hugged her beautiful daughter.

Finally, she made herself two lightweight skirts—one a dark blue and the other with black, white, and red stripes. The waistlines were expandable. She could tack them in to fit her after the baby. She did not attend church during her confinement, but when she did again, adding ribbons and decorative stitches would dress up her three new blouses.

***

Teresa's small body bulged with child by August, when her eighth month rolled around. She and the children looked more robust every day from the healthy diets and lifestyle imposed on them six days a week at Letta's.

Her formerly shy, quiet boys now talked incessantly and knew most of the words in the story books that Nora and Beebe read to them daily. Even Lauri, toddling around the house with her blonde curls bobbing, already mimicked some of the phrases.

Donal taught Dante and Alberto—Dan and Bert to most by then—how to brush the horses, measure oats and toss hay into their feeders.

"Both your lads can hold the reins on their own now," Donal told Teresa. "Dan'll be drivin' before you know it, and Bert won't be far behind."

Leo, I wish you were here to see him. Teresa looked around, sure she had felt a hand on her shoulder. There was no one.

14

On his visit to Philadelphia that month, Jakob sat Letta and Teresa down for a talk.

"It doesn't make sense for Donal to drive back and forth all the time, now that you are here every day, Tesa."

She bristled with his use of the nickname he called "an American version of Teresa." Her frown didn't stop his using it.

"I don't like Donal to make that trip every day, either. I told Letta I could take the trolley."

"No, you couldn't," the siblings said in unison.

"That wouldn't be an option even if you weren't with child," Jakob said decisively.

Teresa felt herself flush. She wished he would stop talking about her pregnancy.

"That's not what I meant," he said. "I do have a suggestion, though. If Nico had his own carriage he could drive you, and also be able to pick up extra deliveries from merchants out there in Little Italy."

Teresa sighed. "We cannot afford a carriage."

"Letta would make him a good deal." Jakob eyed his sister. "When is the last time you used that little carriage of yours, Letty? And how many times have you told me you were going to look for a new one?" He didn't wait for an answer.

"The extra work Nico could get with his own transportation should give him enough to pay the carriage and horse off in a year or less. Dan and Bert know how to take care of the horse. What do you think, sister?"

"Actually, I think it's a grand idea. I should have thought of it. You are useful at times, brother." Letta grinned as Jake swept his hand in the air and made an exaggerated bow.

Teresa's brow furrowed. "There's just one thing. Please don't tell Nico I know about this. It is just—well, it wouldn't be right for me to know before he has made a decision."

Jakob sat back down, eye level with Teresa. "I wouldn't have told him, and neither would Letta."

"I think Teresa has a good point, though," Letta said. "Why don't you talk to him about the carriage, Jakob? He may feel better about it coming from a man."

Jakob agreed.

"I've been wanting a new I can drive myself," Letta said. "You and Donal can start shopping for one."

"As a matter of fact, I've already talked to Donal about looking at carriages, but the kind that don't need a horse." Jakob held up his hand to fend off protests ready to pounce from his sister's mouth.

"I'm seeing them more and more in Hartford, and I know you've noticed them here. Many people say they won't last, but I don't agree. Think of it—streets full of carriages that don't need hay and oats. The original models are already improved. You'll be able to get good modern transportation with the new autos coming out in oh-three."

Teresa, eyes wide with fascination, bit her bottom lip to keep from laughing as she watched Letta's mouth gape. She had never before seen the woman speechless.

***

Nico never told Teresa how much he paid for the carriage and horse, but it couldn't have been what they were worth. Letta had given them Nickers, the boys' favorite, and they found an affordable horse stall two blocks from the boarding house. The small black carriage had an enclosed, single bench passenger seat covered with a thick, comfortable pillow. One of the boys sat in front with Nico, leaving plenty of room for Teresa and the other two children in back. Both boys vied to sit up front, though Nico chose Alberto most of the time. Teresa saw the hurt in Dante's eyes when Nico would swing his brother onto the driver's bench day after day.

"The oldest should sit in back to help you," he insisted.

Dante never complained.

***

The days continued to sizzle in mid-August. With the children asleep, Teresa and Nico walked to the back porch one evening and opened the door to allow some teasing breezes into the house. She heard Johnny humming as he snuffed out lanterns in the sitting room and followed Annie upstairs.

They hadn't discussed their jobs or wages since Johnny took over Nico's boarding house responsibilities. This freed Nico to begin working full time for Wunder's Real Estate, assisting with maintenance and business errands. With a regular salary and extra income from occasional side jobs, he seemed in a better mood lately. Teresa thought this might be a good time to talk to him about her concerns.

She had poured two glasses of iced tea and now handed him one, and then walked to the top of the porch steps hoping for a little more air. "Nico, I am trying to pay Letta back for all the loans she made us, but I'm not able to do any extra work 'til after the baby, so I don't have money to spare. I thought your new wages would cover most of the boarding house expenses. Are there some that I don't know about?"

She lifted her glass to take a sip of tea and never saw his hand coming. The blow smashed against the side of her head and, for a moment, everything was black. Her arms flailed. Grabbing at air, her fingers clawed desperately to find the edge of the door jam. Nico yelled her name, but his attempt to grab her was not quick enough to prevent her plummet down the steps.

The crash against every step sent pain screaming through her body. When she slammed into the hard ground, Teresa was sure her baby could not have survived, and wondered if she would. And then she feared Nico would fall over her as he stumbled down the steps to reach her. She cried out when he tried to pick her up.

"Don't move me," she whispered hoarsely. "Call Annie."

"Annie, ANNIE. Come quick."

Two pairs of feet pounded through the house. "Nico, Teresa," Annie called.

"Where are you?" shouted Johnny.

"Down here," Nico yelled.

"Oh, no." Annie rushed to Teresa's side, cradled her head and instructed Johnny to get a blanket. Annie's arm swept Nico out of the way while she tried to sooth Teresa. "We'll have you inside in a few minutes. You'll be all right, don't you worry."

"My baby, Annie. Something's wrong. It feels like the baby is coming but it's too soon."

Johnny was back with the blanket and knelt beside her. "Teresa, can you get up if we help you?"

"I don't know," she moaned. "I don't think so. I hurt bad all over." She squeezed her eyes, fear and pain pulsing through her.

"We have to move her." Alarm filled Nico's voice.

Annie ignored him.

"You don't have to move, Teresa," Annie said. "Johnny and I will carry you." She looked at Nico. "Get your carriage and bring Dr. Janys as quick as you can, Nico. Hurry."

Nico looked from Annie to Teresa.

"Go, Nico. NOW." Annie had taken over and Nico left in a run.

Teresa tried not to shriek as Annie and Johnny carefully eased the blanket under her, and then used it like a stretcher to move her in the house and onto her bed.

Dante came out from behind the curtain that separated the children's section of the bedroom from their parents'. "Is Mamma sick?"

Annie put her arm around him. "She's going to be all right, Dante. But she isn't feeling so good right now, and your papa has gone for the doctor. Can you be a really big boy and watch Alberto and Lauri if Johnny takes them up to our room?"

Dante nodded and followed Johnny when he carried the other two upstairs.

When he came back into the room, he told Teresa, "They're fast asleep on my bed and Dante insisted on sitting up to watch them. He's a fine boy."

She nodded as the image brought a brief smile to her lips. "Thank you."

Dr. Janys arrived an hour later and confirmed that Teresa's labor had indeed begun. "It's going to be a while, but I'm sure there will be a baby by morning."

Teresa felt worry cover her face.

The doctor took her hand. "Many babies come early and do just fine. Your job is to relax as much as you can. Let us do the work right now." He gave instructions to everyone: Johnny to the kitchen to light a fire and boil water; Nico to gather up towels, scissors and extra sheets; Annie to get the outer clothes off Teresa. He then had Johnny bring a wash basin with cool water.

Teresa writhed with pain, not sure what was labor and what might be broken, but her right arm throbbed.

"Annie, I want you to keep wiping her down and talk to her calmly. Johnny, as soon as you get some hot water in here, put more on and wait in the kitchen 'til I call for it. Nico, put the linens where we can reach them, then I want you to go into the kitchen with Johnny."

"But, but I should be—"

"Nico, I want you out of here. You need to rest. You'll have plenty to do later, but now do what I say." It was not a request.

"Come on, Nico. I'll make us some coffee. Let's keep out of the doc's way, so he can take care of Teresa," Johnny said. Nico looked back at his wife, and then followed Johnny out of the room.

Teresa let out the muffled scream she had been holding back, biting onto the cloth that Annie put between her teeth. Dr. Janys pulled a pill bottle from his bag and gave her two pills. Annie gently held her head up so Teresa could sip water.

"Annie, thank you for being here," she muttered. "What would I do without you?"

"Oh, shush, where else would I be?" She looked up at Dr. Janys. "What did you give her?"

"Just something to help her rest. This baby isn't due for another five or six weeks, but it's not going to wait. And I think she is having more than labor pains." He listened to Teresa's heart and abdomen with his stethoscope.

"You hit your head hard when you fell down those stairs. You could have a concussion, a broken arm or dislocated shoulder, Teresa. You should be in the hospital, but that will have to wait 'til the baby comes. We'll do our best to make you as comfortable as possible for now."

Teresa mumbled a thank you through her pain.

"Do you have towels under her for when her water breaks?" he asked Annie.

"I do. I helped with plenty of birthings in my home town."

Dr. Janys peered at her. "Annie, why haven't you gone to nurses' training? You are more competent than most of the nurses I work with in the hospital."

Annie smiled as she rinsed the washcloth again in the cool water. She continued to sponge Teresa. "It was a dream of mine as a girl. If it's to happen, I believe the Lord will open—oh, I think her water just broke, Dr. J."

Several hours later, Teresa drifted from dozing to crying out in pain. During the dozing periods, Dr. Janys let Nico in for a few minutes, but admonished him to sit quietly.

Teresa knew morning was drawing near when she heard Annie say, "It's getting near time to fix breakfast, but I can't leave Teresa."

"Nico and I can get enough food out for the men," Johnny said. "None of them will mind making do, under the circumstances."

Nico didn't argue.

"What happened here, Annie? How did she fall?" Dr. Janys asked when the door closed.

"I don't know, Doctor. Didn't Nico tell you?"

Teresa opened her eyes, wanting to say something, but couldn't make her voice work. She knew Nico didn't intend that she would fall down the steps, but...

"He said it was dark and Teresa didn't realize she was close to the edge of the porch, that she wanted to drink her tea and get some fresh air. He claims he heard her yell and when he ran out she was on the ground by the steps. Do you think that's how it happened?" The doctor's voice was skeptical.

Annie looked at Teresa's fluttering eyes. She said nothing for a moment, and then whispered, "I don't know, Dr. Janys. I heard them both talking on the back porch when I was on my way upstairs. It could have happened like that."

"But you don't think it did."

Annie shifted her gaze to the doctor's face. "I really don't know, Dr. J. It doesn't change this, though, does it?"

Her head nodded toward Teresa. "She's hurt and needs our help."

"She is lucky to have you, Annie."

Teresa's loud groan grabbed their attention. The doctor checked her and said, "I don't think it will be much longer. You're doing good, Teresa."

"Hail Mary, full of grace, the Lord is with Thee," Teresa whispered frantically. "Blessed art Thou among women and blessed…Ohhh!"

Annie reached for the cloth and wiped her gently, letting Teresa squeeze her hand until she again fell into a fitful, brief sleep.

"The sun's coming up," Annie said sometime later. She raised the window. The dark sky was fading to pink and already warm air promised another hot day.

They could hear the boarders move around the kitchen to help themselves to an assortment of foods that Johnny and Nico would have set on the table. Noises from the street announced the beginning of a new busy day for cart vendors.

Then the pain came again and Teresa knew her baby was coming with it. She thought her teeth would break off from biting so hard on the cloth when she gave a final push.

***

Annie opened the door to a pacing Nico. "Come in."

He walked into the room, uncertainty on his face as he looked at the others. He stood at the foot of the bed and watched Teresa hold the tiny baby close, tears in her eyes.

Dr. Janys continued to wash his hands at the bedside washstand, saying nothing.

Annie gathered up soiled towels and sheets. "You have a daughter, Nico." She left the room.

"Doctor, is something wrong? Tell me." Nico's tone was more a plea than a demand.

Dr. Janys sat down on a stool at the side of the bed. "Your daughter is premature. That would be concern enough. But the fall Teresa had, I'm afraid, might have damaged the baby as well as your wife."

"Damaged...damaged. What does that mean? How damaged?"

"I had a hard time getting the baby to breathe, and she is very frail. We need to get both of them to the hospital as soon as possible."

"What could a hospital do that we can't do here?" Nico argued. "Wouldn't that be expensive?"

Dr. Janys did not hold back his exasperation. "Nico, we talked about that. Your wife and baby were both injured tonight when Teresa *fell* down those stairs."

Nico's expression remained stoic.

"Teresa may have some serious injuries. And the baby will need around the clock special care or you could lose her. If you are so worried about the cost, I'll work out a payment plan with Teresa. But she needs to get there today, do you understand, as soon as possible."

"Yes, I will work to pay. I don't mean I won't." Nico's face reddened. "But how can I take her in that small carriage?"

"I'll take her in my carriage. I want Annie to come along. You get to the hospital and tell them to have a stretcher and room ready. Now!"

Nico turned and hurried out.

15

Four weeks into the hospital stay, Teresa—still in an arm splint—cradled Eva close to her breast, hoping the baby would nurse better today. Mamma's dead babies didn't have a chance to be baptized. At least the priest had come to baptize Eva. "Jesus, Mary and Joseph," Teresa whispered, kissing the rosary crucifix and crossing herself, "please make my baby well." She prayed her beads every day.

Dr. Janys insisted she stay in the hospital, where she could nurse her baby as often as possible, and have time to heal herself. He came by later in the day, when Nico was there. "It will take some time for your baby to catch up." The doctor looked at Nico. "Unless you can hire someone to care for the children, plus full time private nurses, Teresa and Eva should not go back to the boarding house."

Nico looked stunned.

"I know that Annie would help, but she can't take care of the boarders and all of you, too. Your baby needs twenty-four hour care, and so will Teresa for a while."

Teresa didn't know what to say and could only imagine what Nico was thinking.

"What do you want us to do?" Nico looked glum.

"Eva's care will be costly, Nico, but I have extra work for you if you're willing. I can arrange for the nurses and take the pay from your salary."

Nico swallowed and shifted his feet, looking uncomfortable. "Of course."

"About caring for Teresa and the other children, I have a suggestion, but it will be up to the two of you."

They waited for the doctor to continue.

"First, we have to talk with Mrs. Wunders."

***

Letta's rarely used downstairs room, next to the library, was converted to a comfortable bedroom/nursery for Teresa, her baby and Lauri, while the boys slept in Lance's upstairs room. Two pediatric nurses took turns caring for Eva around the clock. The children easily adjusted to living full time in the "big house." For Teresa, it felt strange to depend on others.

Nico came most evenings for dinner. Teresa tried her best to appear pleased when he arrived, though her smile and easy manner changed to a cautious, defensive attitude as soon as he walked in the door. She noticed Letta's concerned glances.

She couldn't remember her children being so happy, though. Beebe and Nora fussed over them and taught them something new every day. The boys' delight in spending time with Donal was not lost on Nico.

"It's time for Dante to come with me and start learning how to make a living," he said one evening. She had walked to the door with him as he prepared to leave.

"Nico, he's only six years old. I'm sure he'd like to spend time with you, but why would he need to know how to make a living now? He's just a little boy."

"He's going on seven, Teresa. I was picking up coal and wood by the railroad tracks when I was his age. It was the only fuel we had for cooking or heat. He needs to learn that life is not all play."

She could not talk him out of it, but she did argue for Dante's going just one day a week. "The boys have learned so much. They will be able to have better lives if they learn to read and write well. They can already print their names."

"You mean if they have better learning than me, don't you?" His tone was accusing.

"I mean they can have a much better education than either of us. Wouldn't you want that for your children? For *all* of your children?"

He looked at her saying nothing, but for a minute she saw loathing in his eyes. He walked out the doorway, and then turned abruptly. "I will take him every Monday. Have him ready."

***

A few days later, Teresa hurried toward the excited voices of her sons and saw Jakob play boxing with them in the front hallway. He stood when she walked out. "Hello, Tesa."

She was unnerved when he addressed her with such familiarity. He had no right to do so

"How are you feeling?" His blue-green eyes showed genuine concern.

I must look a sad sight, she thought, as she unconsciously smoothed her hair with her hand. "I'm quite fine, Mr. Hahn. Thank you."

"Letta wrote me about your fall and the premature birth of your baby. I'm truly sorry. How is she doing?"

Before she could answer, Dante said, "Jake, come see my baby sister."

Teresa was horrified. "Dante, you never call a grown up by their first name. You call him Mr. Hahn."

Dante looked confused.

"My fault. I told them they could call me Jake." He smiled. "I'd really prefer it, if you don't mind." His green speckled eyes pleaded.

"I suppose that is up to you, but it is not the way I raise my children. They do not call grownups by their first names. I suppose they could call you Mr. Jake."

"Don't they call Donal 'Don'?"

"Well, yes, but that's just a nickname he said they could use."

"And...?" His irritating cheeky smile was back.

"You win." She felt annoyed.

"I don't want to win. I just want it to be easy for them. May I see that new baby now?"

"Mamma, can I take Jake?" Dante asked.

"Me too, Dannie," Alberto piped in.

"All right, you can both take *Jake* to see the baby, but be very quiet."

Jakob grinned and put a finger to his lips as he followed the boys. The nurse had Eva up, trying to coax some milk between her lips with a new nipple bottle from the hospital.

Dante and Alberto both leaned in to give their sister a kiss on the forehead.

Jakob's smile disappeared when he looked at the tiny infant. He stared at her for a minute. "She really is small, isn't she? But she's perfect. That must be what you looked like when you were a newborn, Tesa."

"I wouldn't know."

Jakob asked if he could sit in the rocker and hold the baby. "I can feed her." He looked at Teresa's surprised expression. "I do know how to feed babies, you know."

"I'm sure you do. It's just that most men don't like holding such small ones."

"I'm different." His eyes twinkled. "So may I, Mamma?"

She sighed. "I guess it would be all right."

He nestled Eva gently in the crook of his arm and put the bottle to her lips. She didn't move them until he drew an index finger softly across her chin and cheeks. Her lips pursed around the nipple and she began to suck.

"Well, my goodness," Helen exclaimed.

Teresa watched in awe. Nico had never even held Eva. The baby took several sips, and then closed her eyes in sleep again. Teresa heard a movement. She looked up to see Letta watching from the doorway.

"You look very natural there, Jake."

"It's been a while, hasn't it? I haven't held one this young since Abbie was a baby."

"You're home early, Letta," Teresa said.

"I intended to be here before Jake arrived. There's a board meeting in a few days, and we have business to go over. He'll be here a week or two—or more if I can hang onto him." She eyed her brother with affection.

"Will we be in the way?" Teresa asked.

"Of course not." Jakob carefully handed Eva back to the nurse. "I get so enthused being around your children that I can do twice the work." He deepened his voice and lifted a boy on each side as they held onto his forearms. "I turn into a power man."

"Or an idiot," his sister teased. "Come on, power man. Say hello to Nora."

"That's right, and I haven't seen my beautiful Lauri yet. You told me she was walking." He lowered the boys and followed Letta, calling over his shoulder, "Don't go away, Tesa."

Why did she feel so disconcerted with him around? But he had a wonderful influence on her children, and they loved being with him. Teresa just didn't want them hurt when he disappeared from their lives.

***

The only one who didn't smile when he saw Jakob was Nico. "Living in the same house with my wife and children—it's not right." He had led Teresa outside after dinner.

"Nico, he and Letta are at work and meetings all day. It doesn't make any difference to us. I am in my room with the baby most of the day. I rarely see him."

"I don't like it."

"Do you want to stay over and sleep in the boys' room? It has a big bed." She hoped the suggestion would make him feel as ridiculous as he sounded.

"Maybe I will. How much longer do you expect to be vacationing here?"

"Oh, Nico. I've told you, the doctor said my arm can't be moved for another two or three weeks. I still get headaches, and did you even look at Eva? Have you held her? Do you see that she isn't gaining any weight? She could die." Saying the words brought a reality of fear Teresa hadn't allowed herself to face before.

Nico seemed speechless for a moment, and then his face twisted in anger. "I suppose you are blaming me for everything." He grabbed Teresa's left arm to pull her further from the house.

She stumbled. "Nico, you're hurting my arm."

The front door burst open, and Jakob rushed out. "Are you all right, Mrs. Barile?"

"She is all right. I am with her."

"No offense, Mr. Barile. I was just coming out to have a smoke." Jakob pulled a pipe from his jacket pocket. "I saw your wife slip and thought maybe you needed some help." His gaze shifted to Teresa. "But if you're both fine, my pipe and I will take a walk to the back. Enjoy your evening if I don't see you before you leave, Mr. Barile. And you, too, Mrs. Barile. I'm sure Letta and I will be long gone before you are up in the morning."

"Thank you, Mr. Hahn," Teresa said.

"Yes, thank you, Mr. Hahn." Nico's voice echoed an edge of sarcasm.

"Please, both of you, call me Jake." He disappeared around the side of the house.

"He was watching us," Nico hissed.

"Of course not. He wouldn't do that. It was just coincidence. Come back in with me, Nico. Come see Eva." Teresa reached for his hand, but he pulled it away.

"You know, Teresa, if you hadn't been on the edge of that back step, you wouldn't of fell. All of this didn't have to happen."

Her mouth opened. No words came out, but the guilt cut like a knife slicing into her stomach. She had been thinking the same thing. She should never have let her guard down with Nico. If she hadn't challenged him about their finances, he wouldn't have hit her. She had put her baby's life at risk.

16

Dr. Janys's expression was grim when he checked Eva in mid-November.

Teresa tried to steady her voice before speaking. "You told me she would catch up, but she isn't, is she?"

"I had hoped she would be better by now. Medically there's not much more we can do. However, I do have another suggestion. I want to hire a third nurse, so each can provide eight hours of greater activity for Eva."

"Didn't you say she needed rest?" Teresa asked.

"Rest isn't helping. I want her held, rocked and walked more. There's a new type of baby cart that will allow you to roll her outside for fresh air."

Letta had been listening from the doorway. "How do we get this baby cart, Sam?"

"There's one at the hospital. I can bring it tomorrow."

"Never mind," Letta said. "I'll have Donal pick it up today."

***

"Another nurse to pay for?" Nico said that evening. They were in Letta's sitting room with the door closed. "We can't afford this kind of care forever."

"Nico," Teresa cried, "whatever happens, I will take care of her if I have to work all my life to pay for it. I just want her to live. Don't you?"

He threw up his hands. "You always do this, Teresa."

"I always do what?"

"You always try to make me look bad." He slammed his fist on Letta's delicate serving table. It crumbled to the floor.

Footsteps plummeted down the stairs, and then Letta opened the door, motioning her brother away. "Excuse my intrusion, but it sounded like someone fell. Are you both all right?" Her eyes found the broken table. "Oh, it's just the table." She gave a relieved sigh.

Teresa felt color drain from her face. "It's your beautiful serving table, Letta. I am so sorry...so sorry."

"Tables are replaceable. The table isn't important, as long as you and Nico are all right."

"I broke it." The words burst from Nico. "I will pay. You take the money from my pay."

"We'll look at it tomorrow. Maybe it can be fixed. Now, I want you both to come to the kitchen and have some of Nora's delicious cake and tea."

Teresa glanced into the hallway and saw Jakob on his way back up the stairs.

A new table replaced the old one by the following evening. Letta didn't allow them to mention the incident again.

***

Jakob stopped to see the baby every morning. In the evenings, he retired to his room after dinner and then came down again when Nico went home, heading directly to the nursery. "How's my little Eva doing today?"

Teresa watched as he walked around the house with the baby in his arms. He described everything he saw as they visited each of the other children. "Here's your sister. Let's read to her."

Lauri laughed and kissed the baby's cheek, then threw her arms around "Yake's" neck. He held Eva with one arm and pulled Lauri onto his lap with the other, before reciting Jack and Jill. Lauri asked for the same rhyme every night and repeated each line after Jakob.

Next he took Eva upstairs. "Time to say goodnight to Dan and Bert. They're your big brothers, the ones who are going to protect you and fight off all the bad men who make eyes at you. You want to stay close to them."

The boys giggled at the ritual.

By the time Jakob left, two days after Thanksgiving, Eva was sucking voluntarily on the nipple. She swallowed better, opening her eyes more and moving arms and legs on her own.

Dante, Alberto and Lauri crowded the front doorway, waiting for one last hug from Jakob and his promise to return soon

"I'll be back when Santa comes. I might even pass him on the way. Remember, after Christmas we're going to another big Mummers' Parade. This time we're going to watch from the street and maybe you can touch some of the feathers."

Teresa wanted to tell him he couldn't go. With a third nurse, Eva was in someone's arms most of the time, but none of them seemed to have Jakob's magic.

***

With her baby showing improvements, Teresa became anxious to resume her dressmaking, even with limited arm movement. "I want to make a holiday dress for you," she told Letta. It was mid-December.

"Are you sure you feel up to it?"

"I'll feel better getting back to work."

"You have something in mind, don't you?"

Teresa nodded. "You wear nice outfits for work and church, but nothing bright. I think red would be a wonderful color on you, especially for Christmas."

Letta's expression turned melancholy. "I had a lovely red dress and used to wear bright colors quite a bit when Claude was living. We went to dinners and dances often. I gave several dresses away, but kept some favorites. They're in a trunk in the attic."

"You have favorite dresses packed in a trunk?" Incredible, Teresa thought.

"Maybe it is time to get them out. They probably need altering. It's been a few years and I've lost weight." Letta looked excited about the idea. "And if it hasn't disintegrated, I kept the red one."

It took Teresa three days to take apart and alter the beautiful red dress that Letta had once worn. She added new black trim and taffeta underskirts that gave more flair to the bottom. She changed the straight waist line to a V shape to match the V that lay at the tip of the long sleeves.

While she was fitting the nearly completed dress on Letta, Teresa cleared her throat. "I've been wondering about something, but I don't want—you don't have to answer."

"What is it? You should know I'd tell you anything."

"You are such a beautiful and bright woman. There must be men who want to keep company with you. Are you not having guests because we're here?"

Letta laughed. "Heavens no. And, yes, there have been men who have asked me to be their companion for social events. I've gone a few times, but it's not the same. I've never felt comfortable, or enjoyed myself with anyone else since Claude died. I finally decided that I would know if it was the right time, and the right person. So far, it hasn't been."

She looked down at the dress. "It's beautiful. It looks like a completely new dress. I have a red hat that will go nicely with it, but it needs black trim."

"Get me some black ribbon and lace. I'll have it done Friday, and then Saturday we will be leaving, Letta. I promised Nico we would be home for Christmas."

As she said the words, Teresa felt a knot tighten in her stomach.

"Are you all right?" Letta asked.

"Yes, yes I'm fine. Just a twitch."

***

Teresa and Annie hugged as though they hadn't seen each other for years. Annie had prepared a lunch of ham sandwiches on bread just out of the oven. She garnished them with canned pickles, homemade cottage cheese and apple butter. Everyone "ummed" when she brought out her special apple-walnut pie for dessert. When Gregor came in and saw Teresa, a broad grin covered his face.

"How do you like your new roommates?" she asked him.

"They're a good pair," Gregor said. "And we could have filled their beds three times over. Word's gettin' 'round about Annie's cookin' and good nature—almost as good as you, Ms. Teresa. All the new fellows are wantin' to board here."

It felt good to be home, and Nico seemed in a better mood than Teresa had seen since Eva's birth. He continued to complain about the expenses of her private nurses, though. It was the only concession Teresa made to coming home.

"Eva is doing better because she has constant care," she said. "If we have to give up the nurses, then I cannot work at all."

Nico grudgingly gave in and Dr. Janys found a nurse, Mary, who lived nearby. She guarded Eva like a bulldog and faithfully fed her every three hours through the night. Helen continued to care for the baby at Letta's, where Teresa resumed her dressmaking.

17

Letta talked more about her children as their Christmas homecoming drew closer. She bragged about what a good student Lance was and her hope that he would one day take over her real estate business. "And Abigail is working toward a nursing degree." Letta sighed. "She also spends a lot of time volunteering with the poor, then stays up all night studying."

"She's got a spirit like her mother," Teresa observed.

Letta smiled and nodded. "I guess you're right. I keep telling myself that as long as they both have a good education, they can choose whatever they want."

Teresa determined her children, too, would have a good education. She was slowly building her first class savings again. But she needed a different hiding place. She feared that Nico might notice the diaper bag getting bulkier.

***

Letta had asked Nico to bring the family to her house Christmas morning. "We have gifts for the children, and I'm anxious for Lance and Abigail to get to know all of you better."

To Teresa's surprise, he agreed.

The excited children chattered noisily as Nico turned the carriage into Letta's driveway. Two large evergreens, outside the front door, glistened with shiny decorations made of painted wood and bright metals. Candles shone in every window. Teresa breathed in the beauty of the scene, and then felt her heartbeat quicken when Jakob opened the door.

Nico's glowering expression melted into a forced smile as he walked toward the house. "Well, Jake, you are back so soon."

Jakob extended his hand. "I wanted to be here for the children's Christmas. They bring the holiday spirit back to us. You're a blessed man, Nico."

Nico shook the offered hand without comment.

Jakob bowed slightly to Teresa when she was inside. "How are you, Mrs. Barile, and how is Eva?" The baby had stayed home with Nurse Mary.

"Much better." Teresa smiled as Lauri pulled at Jakob's jacket.

He reached down and picked her up. "I haven't forgotten my little princess here."

"Up, Yake," she cried, pointing a finger to the ceiling. When he gave her a mild swing in the air, she giggled with glee. "I up, Mamma."

"I see you are." Teresa smiled broadly. She felt a hand on her back and turned to see Letta in her new red dress.

"Oh, Letta, you look beautiful in it."

"I had numerous compliments at church services last night. A couple of friends wanted the name of my seamstress. We'll talk about that later. Come see the decorations now."

Teresa looked around the hallway, decorated on both sides with green and red gaslight holders that flickered on evergreens wrapped around the stairway banisters. "It's lovely, Letta."

They moved into the sitting room where candle light shimmered from each branch of a huge tree covered with glimmering crystal and white-crocheted ornaments. A large papier-mâché angel adorned its top. Tall candles on the fireplace mantle stood in the middle of garlands of greenery, holly berries and pinecones. Spices placed through the greens filled the air with aromas of cinnamon, mint, rosemary and other scents that blended to make the room smell like church incense.

The children's excited exclamations echoed their mother's.

Letta pointed out a small hillside village that wound underneath the tree, with homemade replicas of houses, streets and trees she said Donal and Claude had made years earlier.

Teresa sank to the floor, beside her boys, to look at each piece. She pictured herself walking through such a village in Italy on Christmas Eve. She looked up. "How did you get it all done?"

Before Letta could reply, the front door banged open and two young adults burst into the room, laughing and slapping snow off their clothes. They looked at the stunned group in front of them.

Abigail reacted first. "Oh, my golly. We wanted to be here before you came. How do you like the Christmas tree?" She dropped to her knees, talking to the boys and Lauri. The children stared wordlessly at the woman in front of them.

Lance threw his head back, laughing. "They think you are a wild person, Abbie."

"Introduce yourselves, you two, so my friends won't think you are strange," Letta said.

"Ah, but they are strange. Fantastic, but strange. Here, let me." Jakob knelt beside his niece. "Abbie, this is Dan, and this is Bert, and this lovely little lady is Lauri. Now," he addressed the children, "you know how that lady is your mamma?" He pointed to Teresa.

They nodded.

"Well, Letta is their mamma. Her name is Abbie." Jakob put an arm around his niece. "And this is her brother, Lance." He pointed to the young man.

"How do you do, gentlemen?" Lance bent down to shake hands with the boys.

Their beams told Teresa her children had just found two new friends.

"Did you open your presents yet?" Abbie asked the children.

Three wide-eyed children shook their heads, looking at the gifts under the tree. Then Abbie and Lance were on hands and knees helping the children rummage through the pile to find ones with their names on.

Letta glanced at Teresa and laughed. "I think my children are more excited than yours."

Lauri's baby doll had its own blanket and baby clothes. The boys each opened a new bag of marbles and a drum.

"You can practice outside later," Jakob said, "and then you'll be ready to play with the marchers in the Mummers parade." He looked at Nico. "Maybe your papa can show you how to shoot marbles now."

Teresa waited, remembering the previous year.

"When I was a boy, I never had time to play like you did." Nico didn't move from his seat in the corner. "The only thing I played with was sticks and stones."

"Sure. We played with sticks and stones in the street, too," Jakob said. "My parents couldn't afford toys, but one of my friends had these little glass balls. We boys gathered nearly every afternoon to shoot marbles. I wasn't always the champ, but I got pretty good. You'd like it, Nico. I can teach you."

Nico stood and headed toward the door. "Maybe later. I'm going outside for a smoke first."

"All right, men." Jakob stood and looked at the boys. "We'll do marbles later. I hear Nora calling us for breakfast now. Is anyone as hungry as I am?"

The big and little children all gave a loud affirmation and headed eagerly toward the aromas of ham, eggs, potato pancakes and hot chocolate that drifted from the dining room.

When they finished eating, Letta said, "Before we do anything else, Donal is waiting for you youngsters in the barn. He said Santa left more presents there for you. We'd better go see."

The children scrambled to the door while Teresa looked at Letta with a puzzled frown.

"Nico knows about it," Letta said. "We had to make sure it was all right with him, even though we knew they couldn't be taken to the boarding house. I guess he wanted to keep this as a surprise for you, too."

What couldn't be taken to the boarding house, Teresa wondered.

***

"Careful, sweetheart. Don't squeeze her too tight." Abbie showed one and a half-year old Lauri how to hold the fluffy gray kitten in her lap as they sat on the barn floor a few minutes later. A ribbon around the cat's neck had Lauri's name on it. The little girl rubbed her cheek into the soft fur of her new pet.

Meanwhile, Alberto tried to hold onto a puppy that licked all over his face. He laughed until tears came. "I wanna' call him *Lick*, because he licks my face."

Teresa thought her young, going-on-six-year-old son was at a good age to appreciate a dog. And a kitten was perfect for Lauri.

"I call my kitty *Kitty*," Lauri held the kitten against her chest.

"They are both good names." Teresa looked back at Dante, who would soon be eight. His eyes showed the disappointment of being the only one without a pet. He and Alberto could share the care and enjoyment of *Lick*.

"Come help me feed the horses, Dan," Donal said.

Teresa watched them move toward the back of the barn. Then Jakob walked out of the last stall leading a pony.

"This one has your name on it, Dan." He handed the straps to Dante.

The stunned boy didn't move for several seconds, and then led the pony to the front and looked around at the adults until Letta said, "He's yours. Isn't he beautiful?"

Dante nodded. "He's…" He put his arm around the animal's neck and laid his head against it. His eyes glistened. "I love him."

18

January 1, 1903, dawned cold and bright as Teresa and the children dressed for the parade. With so much extra to bring for the day, she forgot the diaper bag when she walked out with Eva in her arms. She sent Dante back for it. In a few minutes, he came toward the carriage, lugging the bag with two hands.

"Hurry up, Dante," Nico called angrily. "Are you too weak to carry a diaper bag? You'd think it was full of bricks."

"It's feels heavy on the bottom, Papa. But I can carry it."

"Why would a diaper bag be heavy?" Nico started to get down from the carriage bench.

Teresa thought her heart would thump out of her chest. "It's just the baby's milk bottles." Hoping Nico didn't hear the nervousness in her voice, she grabbed the bag from her son and swung it into the carriage. Then she pulled Dante along. "Hurry, we'll be late."

Still breathing hard, she pulled the door shut as Nico reached it, watching her. She forced herself to be busy settling the children into their seats.

Nico frowned, and then turned and climbed back onto the driver's bench.

When they reached Letta's, Teresa made sure she had the diaper bag hooked over her arm as she carried the baby inside. She resolved to find another hiding place for her money as soon as possible.

***

Feeling better about Eva's progress, Teresa extended her dressmaking hours after the holidays.

Customers were pleased to have her back full time. She was treated well in their homes, but noticed a difference between their attitude toward servants and Letta's. She'd ask about it when she found an opportunity.

It came one afternoon the next week, when Letta arrived home earlier than usual carrying two large shopping bags. "Wannamakers had some new fabrics, Teresa. It's been a while since Beebe or Nora had new dresses. When you finish sewing for Regina Billingsley, I'd like you to make them each a couple of outfits if you have time."

"Of course. I would always make time for them. But could I ask you something?"

Letta set the bags on a nearby table. "Certainly. What is it? Is everything all right with your bank account?"

"Oh, yes. That is just fine. Such a relief, Letta. Thank you again for your help." When Teresa had confided about her diaper bag hiding place, Letta took her to the Girard Bank to open a saving's account. Finally, her money would be safe from Nico.

"I'm relieved, too, that your money is in the bank. Now, what is it you wanted to talk about?"

"Well, I am treated very well by your friends, but---"

"I hope so. You let me know if they ever say anything out of line to you."

"No, no. It is nothing like that. It is just that I see how different they seem to be toward their servants than you are. You treat Beebe, and especially Nora and Donal, almost like they are a part of your family. Other people don't do that. Their servants are...well, they are just servants."

Letta nodded. She folded her hands in her lap and leaned back in the chair. "I know. And if Nora and Donal didn't insist on keeping a distance, I'd make them a part of the family, but they say it wouldn't be proper. I've left it up to them."

She sat down. "Claude and Donal worked at the sewing factory together. They were best friends. Donal was the maintenance supervisor when I began working there." The memory brought a smile. "Neither wanted to remain at the factory when Claude's father decided to sell it. Claude was already interested in real estate and Donal planned to go into business with him, but he went back to Ireland first to marry Nora."

For a moment, she had a faraway look. She shook her head. "Too long a story for today. But the important part is that Donal and Nora did come to America and worked on a farm for a few years, while Claude learned the real estate business. Turned out they loved the farm work and were able to save enough that Donal insisted on giving Claude money toward purchasing our real estate company. He never became a partner, but he's still a shareholder in the business."

Teresa's eyebrows furrowed. "But he is your servant."

Letta nodded. "Only by choice. We were always friends. Several years after Claude and I married, we bought the land here and built our home. Claude asked Donal to help set up a barn and purchase a few horses. He and Nora couldn't have children, and they were ready to leave the farm. Somehow, we worked out this arrangement and it seems to still be satisfactory to them."

A look of nostalgia crept into her eyes again. "Claude and Donal sat out back nearly every evening in good weather, smoking their pipes, talking over the day and laughing at each other's outrageous jokes. They got even more outrageous when Jake was here. Donal was lost when my husband died."

Letta pulled out a hanky and blew her nose. "That's why he is so pleased when Jake comes." She shook her head and looked back at Teresa. "And how did I happen to tell you all of this?"

Teresa smiled. I asked you—never mind. I understand better now."

***

Nico began dropping off Dante at Letta's real estate office on Mondays, after she told him she could train his son to be an "office worker." It was soon clear to Teresa how quickly Dante was picking up reading, writing, and simple math from Letta. He played "teacher" at home, helping his brother and sister with letters and words. Teresa loved watching them.

"Where could I find a school for Dante?" she asked Letta one day. "I think he is ready for formal education."

"I've been thinking the same thing. He's a very bright boy, but you'll have to convince Nico."

Teresa nodded. "I know."

Later that week, Letta met with both of them. "I've been letting Dante do simple figures when he is with me. He is good with them, and he reads exceptionally well." She put her elbows on the desk, folded her hands together and leaned forward. "He should be in school. He will make a fine business man one day if he gets an adequate education."

Teresa held her breath, watching Nico.

"There is an excellent boys' school here in Philadelphia," Letta said. "I know the headmaster. Actually, I provide a scholarship there, in my husband's name, for worthy students. I would like to offer Dante the scholarship for the 1903 school year. Of course, it would continue through his graduation."

Nico scowled. "That is good of you, Letta, but I think Dante will be a good builder. Alberto will be the business man."

"Of course he will, but Alberto isn't as old as Dante. I didn't mean to exclude him," Letta said. "I think both your boys deserve a good education. Alberto will be able to go next year."

Nico thought for a minute. "Alberto first. Dante works with me."

"Nico, that's not fair," Teresa exclaimed, then put a hand over her mouth. "I'm sorry," she mumbled, taking her hand away. "But think about it, Nico. If Dante goes first, he will be able to help Alberto next year. They should both have the chance."

"Just a minute," Letta said. "By this coming school year, Alberto will be old enough to go, too. I should have thought of that." She threw up her hands in a helpless gesture. "They can start together, and you will still have all summer for Dante to work."

She looked at Nico, as though he had won the argument. "But they will have to be enrolled now, because this school fills up fast. Can I do that for them?"

Nico was quiet for a moment, and then said, "If they both go, it is all right."

Teresa blew out a breath of relief. "Letta, I don't know how to thank you."

"Your husband just did." She smiled.

"You don't really provide a scholarship to that school, do you?" Teresa asked her later.

"I surely do. Your sons will be the first, but not the last recipients. I want to do this, Teresa. I'll have the boys registered next week. And my Claude would say it's a wonderful idea."

19

Teresa struggled to adjust to life back at the boarding house. Although glad to be in her own home again, she noted even Annie and Johnny were careful of what they said with Nico around. And Teresa dreaded the times Nico wanted to have sexual relations. A curtain between the parent's and children's beds did not keep out sound. "They're getting too old," she whispered one night. "They'll wake up."

"They're young," he snarled. "They sleep like the dead."

"I'm so afraid of getting pregnant again, Nico."

"You're always afraid of something. Do you forget that you are my wife?" he said angrily. "You must think you don't have wifely duties anymore. I've been plenty patient. I don't know any other man who would put up with what I have."

"Nico, it's not that at all," she lied. "I'm sorry. I don't want to argue." She put her hands on his face and kissed him—anything to quiet him.

It didn't take long for him to finish, roll over and fall asleep. Teresa lay awake for a long time. She couldn't continue like this. She would have to talk with Dr. Janys, as uncomfortable as she felt bringing up the subject with a man.

At her next visit, the doctor told her about a method many doctors recommended for regulating pregnancies. "It's believed that there are certain times of the month when a woman is least likely to get pregnant. You should wait for those times to have intercourse." He coughed as Teresa's face turned red. "It might be better to sleep apart on other days."

She tried to relay the information to Nico.

"Isn't that nice for you. Now you have the doctor telling me when I can have relations with my wife."

"Please, just talk to Dr. Janys. He'll explain it better than I can. You know we can't afford another baby right now."

Nico finally agreed, though he still complained two days later on the way to their meeting with Dr. Janys. "You think the doctor is greater than God? What does our church say about wives obeying their husbands? Are you telling all this to the priest in confession, or don't you care about being a sinner?"

Teresa had never felt like a sinner, but maybe Nico was right. She remembered Sister Maria Giuseppe's long ago admonishment that faith mysteries were not to be questioned. Did God mean for them to never understand anything? Was she being punished because she questioned Leo's death and became pregnant before marriage? No, she did not believe it would be God's will for her to keep having children they could not care for. Surely a priest would understand.

Nico listened to what the doctor had to say, and then asked, "Is that what our church says?"

"I can't answer that, Nico. I can only tell you that, for the health of your wife and baby daughter, Teresa should not have another pregnancy for at least a couple of years. By then, both she and Eva will be stronger. You would have to talk with a priest about the church's teachings."

When Letta arrived home that evening, she looked at Teresa. "You're upset. What's the matter?"

Teresa didn't intend to involve Letta, but it was a relief to talk with another woman. She described the visit she and Nico had with the doctor.

"I think Dr. Janys made a good suggestion about talking to your pastor," Letta said. "Ask Nico to go with you. If he listens to anyone, it will be the priest."

Surprisingly, Nico said he would take her. "We will go tomorrow. I want to get this settled."

***

Faithful parishioners, mostly women, walked toward the open doors of St. Mary Magdalene church early the next morning, holding coats tight to their bodies against the cold air. Nico stopped the carriage in front of the gray stone structure and tied his horse to a hitching post. They arrived early enough to attend seven o'clock Mass. Father Rossi, mingling with his flock after services, agreed to see them in the rectory.

"God be with you." He blessed them with the sign of the cross when they were inside. The house, also a gray stone, sat beside the church. It was the largest home in the neighborhood.

The priest was a head taller than Nico, middle-aged with a crop of wavy dark hair and a build that showed he enjoyed good meals. He gestured for them to sit. "I understand you both work for Letta Wunders." They nodded.

Teresa stole a look around at rich dark woodwork that trimmed the spacious room. She noted the fine upholstery on their comfortable chairs, recognizing that this parish of poor and middle class Italian immigrants did well for its church.

"Mrs. Wunders is not Catholic, of course, but I know her through business connections," the priest continued. "She's a fine woman and quite influential in this community."

His words eased Teresa's discomfort.

"How can I help you?" Father Rossi asked. He had a kind voice.

Teresa looked at Nico. His eyes focused on the man in black.

"Father, my wife went to her doctor, without telling me, and told him she did not want to—to do the marriage duty—because she was afraid she would get pregnant. The doctor said we should talk to you about God's will in our marriage."

Teresa's mouth fell open. "That's not all, Nico."

"No, he also said not to do lovemaking on certain days of the month. It has nothing to do with a man's feelings," Nico said with indignation. "What does God think about that, Father?"

Teresa's face burned. It had been hard enough talking with Dr. Janys. She didn't know what to say.

The priest cleared his throat and looked directly at Teresa. "God's will is very clear, Mrs. Barile. The man is head of his family, and a wife's duty is to her husband. God shows His will through the man. It is a sin for a woman not to submit to her husband's wishes and needs."

"But…but Father, we already have four children, and the baby is very sick, and our doctor said we should wait at least two years before we have any more. Surely we are doing God's will."

The priest leaned forward. Mrs. Barile, please calm down. You must pray. God will not give you more than you can handle with His help. You must trust that He will be in control, whatever happens. Take time each day to pray. Then listen to your husband. You don't want your soul damned to hell because of mortal sin. Remember, man and wife are one flesh, and the husband is the head. God will work through him."

"But Father, what if a husband has a weakness, like gambling or drinking, like some men do. I don't mean Nico," she said quickly. "But doesn't a woman have to protect her children?"

She didn't need to look at Nico to feel his anger. She would have to deal with that later. Now, she had to plead her case.

"Many men have weaknesses, my daughter," Father Rossi said. "God shows us that in the Good Book. You remember the story of David and Bathsheba, and what an occasion of sin she was to one of the greatest heroes in the Bible. But God forgave David his weakness and worked His will through that great king's magnitude. So it is with your husband. He will take care of you. Trust in the Lord."

He looked at Nico. "Do you understand also, Mr. Barile?"

"I understand sin, Father. I've felt it from my wife in these last few weeks, and in New York when she hid money from me. I felt betrayed." Nico glared at Teresa.

Her money—her first class savings. How could he bring it up here? Surely Father Rossi would agree with Teresa's reasons.

Turning toward Teresa, the priest said, "Mrs. Barile, when you married, did you not understand the meaning of your marriage vows?"

Teresa was astonished. "Of course, Father. But I did not have children then. I put a little money aside to take care of my family. Any mother would do that."

"And you hid it from your husband?"

"I…I just didn't have a chance to tell him about it."

"Teresa." Nico's tone was harsh. "You are lying to a priest."

"Mrs. Barile," Father Rossi said calmly, "I will be glad to hear your confession before you leave. I'm sure you don't want anything to happen to you while you are in a state of sin."

Teresa followed the priest to the church confessional. She did not tell him about her new savings.

20

In June, about the same time she knew she was pregnant again, Teresa realized Eva hadn't shown any progress in the past few weeks.

"She has seemed a little peaked, but that happens sometimes when babies are teething. I'm sure she's fine," Nurse Mary said.

Teresa felt her panic building. She prayed the rosary daily. She would pray it twice a day—stay up all night to pray if that's what it took. God couldn't ignore so much pleading.

"How do you think Eva looks?" She and Nico were preparing to leave the house the next morning. Teresa tried to keep her voice from shaking.

"She looks fine to me," he said. He barely glanced toward Eva. "Don't all babies lose weight when they start teething?"

He and Mary were probably right. It must be the teething.

***

By July, even Nico made concerned comments about Eva's failing, in spite of extra nourishment and attention by the nurses, and three rosaries a day prayed by her mother. Teresa wished Jakob would come back. Eva needed the magic he seemed to bring.

Dr. Janys asked to see the parents together. "I know you don't like it, Nico, but staying at Letta's home is best for your daughter right now. We can manage her care better there.

After dinner that night, Teresa began to pack clothes for herself and the children, who were already asleep.

"What do you think you're doing?" Nico had just walked into the bedroom.

"I can't be away from her, Nico. You know that. The children and I have to stay at Letta's again until Eva is better."

"It's always about you, isn't it, Teresa." He grabbed a handful of her hair and jerked her toward him.

"Nico, you're hurting me."

"Mamma, what's wrong?" Dante stood in front of the curtain that separated the bedroom.

Nico dropped his hand from Teresa's arm and turned toward Dante with a furious expression. "Nothing's wrong." He thrust an arm out, pointing his finger at the boy. "This is grown-up talk. You go back to bed. Now!"

Dante's frightened expression did not stop him from standing still and looking at his mother.

"Everything is all right, Dante. Go back to bed dear, please."

Before Teresa realized that he had moved, Nico rushed across the room and slammed the back of his hand against the side of Dante's face, knocking him down. His head cracked against the floor.

"Nico, STOP." Teresa ran to her son.

They heard a knock at the door. "Is everything all right?" Johnny called.

"Everything's fine, John. A chair just fell over and scared Teresa." A shaking Nico stood over Dante, breathing hard.

"Thank goodness," Johnny said. "I'll be at the kitchen table awhile reading this good book. Call if you need anything."

"What the devil—he doesn't stay downstairs at night," Nico growled.

"Nico, Dante's hurt." Teresa was on her knees, cradling her son's head. "Dante, open your eyes." Her voice rose with alarm.

"He didn't obey me. It's your fault, Teresa. He didn't obey me."

"Nico," she yelled. "We have to get him to Dr. Janys. Get the carriage. Tell Johnny to help you. Hurry…ohhh!" She bent her body further and grabbed her stomach with one arm.

"What's wrong now?" Nico's voice cracked.

They heard Johnny again. "Teresa, Nico, do you need help?"

"Johnny," Teresa called, "Dante's hurt. Please help Nico get him to the doctor."

"Sure. Come on, Nico," he said, opening the door. "Looks like we should be taking you too, Teresa. I'll get Annie to watch the children."

***

"I'm sure he has a concussion." Dr. Janys had finished examining Dante. "He'll need to be watched closely and kept on bed rest for several days. He's not going to get the rest he needs in either your home or Letta's. Too much activity. It could be done in the hospital, but—" He held up a hand to stop Teresa's protest.

"As I was trying to say, I have a better plan. Bea would delight in caring for the lad right here. He'd have her undivided attention and the best care a patient could get. She was a nurse, you know. She'd be thrilled to have her own patient again."

"I didn't know that," Teresa said weakly.

"Sure, that's how we met. I was a new young doctor and she came to work for me. I found it was cheaper to marry her than pay her." He smiled.

Later, when Johnny and Nico were in the kitchen with Bea, Dr. Janys examined Teresa. "What happened tonight?" he asked, in a tone that demanded the truth.

"I don't think he meant to hurt Dante," she said in a faltering voice.

"Nico?"

Teresa nodded, feeling the guilt of not having protected her son. "We were arguing and Dante came out. I should have taken him back to bed right away."

Dr. Janys sat on a nearby chair. He removed his glasses and laid them on his lap. His head and shoulders slumped and he rubbed a forehead that Teresa knew must be weary with all that a doctor sees and hears over the years. Finally he stood up and called Nico in.

"I think it would be better if Teresa and the children remained at Letta's, where there is more room and help. I know neither of you want to put this pregnancy at risk and have something happen again, like it did with Eva." The doctor's eyes didn't stray from Nico, who offered no argument.

***

A few days later, Sam Janys brought a smiling Dante back to Letta's. "I had a hard time prying him away from Bea," the doctor said. "He's doing fine, though, and I know he missed his family. He still has to stay quiet for at least another week."

"We'll be sure he does." Teresa gave her son a welcoming hug before sending him on to see his brother and sister.

"You look better," the doctor said. Then his expression turned somber. "I wish I had more encouraging news about Eva, though. We're doing all we can."

Teresa nodded. "Nico wants me to go back to the boarding house, but I can't leave her." They walked into the sitting room where Letta was waiting for them.

"Do you think that Nico would want to stay here, too, if I offered? We could move Eva and the nurses into the sun room, and he could stay in your room," she suggested.

Teresa began to tremble.

"Sam, I'd like to talk to Teresa alone," Letta said.

"Of course, and I want to see Eva again." He walked out, closing the door.

Letta sat down on the sofa beside Teresa. "I have a thought—something that might work for both you and Nico."

"I can't think of anything that would work right now, Letta."

"There just might be a way," Letta said. "But I need a few days to check with my brother."

Her brother—what would he have to do with anything? Jakob had already been there twice since the doctor told them Eva was failing. Even though the visits were short, Teresa always thought her baby was just a little better while he was there. It could have been her imagination, or maybe Jakob Hahn was her daughter's savior. At times, it seemed that he was hers.

21

It happened a few days later, July 20th, a month from her first birthday. Eva's little body could no longer keep up the struggle that living required. Jakob, who had arrived that morning when life already started to ebb from the frail baby, could not save Eva this time; nor could Dr. Janys and all his good nurses, nor Letta, or Donal and Nora, or Beebe, with all their love and support. Nor could the desperate mother who prayed tirelessly and tried beyond her daughter's last breath to will life back into her.

***

Because of the pregnancy, Sam Janys gave Teresa a very mild sedative which allowed her worn-out body to fall into a deep slumber. Mamma was there, smiling and assuring Teresa that she would take care of Eva and the little girl would never be ill again. And then she saw Leo walking toward her. *"Ciao, Bella."* He reached out to touch her, but he was too far away, and then they were gone.

She opened her eyes later to find Nico sitting on a chair beside the bed upstairs, where they had taken her to rest. The tears in his eyes surprised her. Her eyes had no more tears to shed.

"I didn't think she would die." Nico seemed to be talking to himself. He stood and paced the room, and then walked back to the chair and sat. "What do we do now?" He swiped the back of his hands across his eyes. "I guess I have to contact the priest."

She nodded. "Probably. Ask Letta." Teresa put her feet on the floor, stood and followed him downstairs. It seemed the right thing to do.

Uncharacteristically, Nico listened as Dante told him their baby sister "went to sleep and now lives in heaven with God, and she isn't sick anymore." He went with the boys into the nursery, where Eva's little body lay on the bed—freshly washed and dressed—looking beautiful and peaceful. The boys kissed her. Teresa stood nearby, feeling numb and watching as though the scene was somewhere far away.

The children left pictures and a farewell note that Nora and Beebe had helped them write. Nico waited in the background, and then told them to go out and play. He asked Teresa to leave, too. He closed the door and stayed in the room another fifteen minutes.

He walked into the sitting room where Letta sat with Teresa. "Should I get the priest?"

"I wanted to talk to you both first," Letta said. "I've already asked a carpenter friend to make a burial box for Eva. I hope that is all right."

Nico nodded. "Thank you, Letta."

"Also, unless you have a site of your own, I would be very pleased if you would use one of the burial sites at the corner of our meadow. It's where my husband and Sara are buried, and where I will be."

He gave a deep sigh. "I don't have...I did not think about—yes, that is fine."

Letta reached out and put her hand on Nico's arm. "I am so sorry, Nico."

He stood abruptly. "I will go and see the priest. What should I tell him?"

"We should have the graveside service tomorrow." Letta looked from one to the other.

"I will go now and tell him to come tomorrow," Nico said.

Teresa nodded. "I'm staying with Eva tonight." No one tried to talk her out it.

***

She found comfort in seeing that her baby daughter would be protected somewhat from the heat of summer and snows of winter by willow trees that shaded the small burial plot.

Letta had lined the tiny pine box with white satin, a soft blanket and a comfortable pillow for Eva. Teresa insisted that everyone leave the room while she said good-bye to her baby. She remembered the glimpse she had of Mamma and Leo when Eva died. That wasn't just a vision; she was sure they had been there with her. Knowing they would be taking care of Eva finally allowed Teresa to move on to her baby's burial service. She picked up the coffin lid and placed it on top before she walked out of the room, dry-eyed. If she shed a tear now, they might never stop.

"You can take her," she said to the men she trusted—Jakob, Johnny, Donal, and Lance—who waited to carry the tiny coffin to its burial site.

In the suffocating grief that Teresa felt, Jakob's quiet strength seemed, at times, to be all that held her together—that and her children. If she didn't have them, she wouldn't care about living. But she had to, for them and her new baby. She touched her stomach protectively.

The priest arrived early enough to spend time with her before the service, but she refused to see him.

"Teresa, Father Rossi wants to pray with us before the burial. It's rude for you not to see him," Nico admonished.

She looked at Nico. "Father Rossi does not have a wife and has never been a real father, and certainly not a mother. What would he know about how to pray with me? No, I do not want to see him. You let him pray with you if you want. He can pray at Eva's service. That will be enough. Tell him I am ready and will meet him outside."

Nico walked out with the priest, and later stood beside Teresa at the prepared site. She felt the brush of Leo's presence and knew he was there to keep the promise he made to always be with her. She pictured Eva—a happy, healthy, laughing baby—in his arms.

***

Afterward, Donal and Lance saddled Brownie for the children to ride and take their minds off the confusion of seeing their sister closed in a box and put into a big dark hole. The rest of the adults mingled inside. Teresa, showing no outward emotion, acknowledged their condolences.

Jakob wandered to the back of the parlor where Teresa sat beside her husband. "Have I told you how sorry I am for your loss?" He looked at Nico.

"Thank you. I was surprised that you were here when my daughter died. How did you know?"

"I didn't. I came to see you, Nico. I wanted to talk to you and Teresa about some help I need in Hartford."

"Help? In Hartford?" Nico looked puzzled. "How could we help you?"

"Actually, it would be just you. But I don't think we want to talk business now. We can talk tomorrow."

"I work tomorrow. I do nothing now. We can talk."

"I don't think Teresa would wan…"

"It's all right," Teresa said in a monotone. "We can go to the sun room."

They followed Jakob into the bright, inviting room that she used for her sewing—except the brightness had vanished for Teresa. Jakob waited for them both to sit before he did.

"You know that I run a real estate business in Hartford, similar to the one my sister has here."

Nico nodded.

"I am looking to hire someone for a research project. I'd rather it be someone not known in the business community there. It would involve travel to other areas in Connecticut and Massachusetts, to assess growing populations and businesses. My sister suggested that you might be a good choice, Nico. Of course, that was before we knew about Eva." Jakob paused and cleared his voice. "It would mean leaving your family and relocating to Hartford for an undetermined amount of time. I doubt that you would want to consider that now."

Teresa said nothing. Nico pinched his lips together, shifting his eyes away for a moment. "How much do you pay for such a job?"

Jakob stated a figure comparable to what Nico made from the combination of jobs he was doing in Philadelphia. The generous amount astonished Teresa.

"Of course, the position would also include an apartment, the use of a horse and carriage, and living expenses," Jakob said.

Nico looked at the floor for a couple of minutes. Then he lifted his eye to meet Jakob's. "Tell me more about this job."

***

A few days later, Jakob sought out Teresa to say goodbye. "I know this is a terrible time for you, Tesa. I don't want to do anything to make it harder. Nico does not have to come now."

"It won't be harder. Nothing brings back my baby. It is better for Nico to go now. I believe this new job will make him happier. And, I think, me too. Thank you." For a few seconds, they stood and looked into each other's eyes.

"Tesa ..." his hand reached out to touch her cheek, but she pulled back.

Her hand sprang nervously to her throat. "I must get to my work while you say good-bye to the children." She turned and rushed toward the sun room.

Nico left for Hartford two days later, and Teresa told Letta she and the children would be moving home. "Everyone here has been wonderful, and you make life easy for us, but we need to be in our own home. We have the carriage now and Johnny can drive us here each day so I can keep up with my sewing."

They returned to the boarding house the following weekend.

Part III

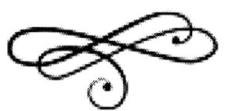

LIFE IN PHILADELPHIA
Teresa
1903-1913

22

Letta's accountant helped Teresa set up a bookkeeping system for the boarding house. It showed that income and expenditures should allow a reasonable profit. By fall, Teresa began to realize how much Nico had been making and, she was sure, gambling away.

"Annie, do you and Johnny have everything you need?" she asked as the two women sipped tea in the kitchen one evening. Annie grew her own peppermint leaves, and Teresa said she made the best cup of tea in the county.

"Oh, yes. I mean, at times we wish we were able to offer the men more fresh fruit and meat, but we all understand, with everything that's happened…" she reached out and touched Teresa's hand, "and Nico missing so much work to be with you. We just cut down. Don't worry about it."

Teresa's nails dug into the fists on her lap.

Annie hesitated. "It's been over two months, but Nico said he would send us some money when he got to Hartford. I'm sure he will soon."

Teresa stood, trying to contain the deep, angry knot building inside her stomach. She began pacing.

"Teresa, it's all right."

She looked into Annie's beautiful blue eyes. "No, it's not. I am making enough now to pay you and Johnny each week. It will take some time, but you will get everything you're owed, and I want good food for these men." She realized she would have to cut out her own savings for a while. At least she would not be giving most of her money to Nico now, or ever again if she could help it.

"What do drivers do when they have time to spare during the day?" she asked Donal the next day.

"Oh, different things. Some of us use the time to groom our horses and shine up the carriages. Sometimes the drivers stand around and talk. You know how men like to tell tall tales." He chuckled. "Do you need me to do something for you?"

"Oh no, Donal. I was just curious. Do many of them drink?"

Donal cleared his throat. "I suspect some of them do at the end of the day. Now and then you hear of one who drinks while driving the carriage. He doesn't last long."

"What about gambling?"

He made no reply for several seconds. "Many men gamble. Drivers are no different.

"Was Nico gambling, Donal?"

"I never saw him."

"But you talk to other drivers. You know. What do they say? Please tell me."

Donal hesitated. "They say Nico gambled a lot. He liked to play cards, mostly."

"He lost a lot, didn't he?"

He sighed again. "That's what they say." Donal coughed. "Miss Teresa..."

"It's all right, Donal. I already suspected. Thank you for being honest with me."

***

Dante and Alberto began school in mid-September, both of them admittedly excited and nervous. Everyone fussed over how handsome they were in their uniforms of brown knickers, long-sleeved tan shirts and dark blue blazers, topped with matching caps. Knee-high brown socks covered their lower legs, and Johnny had their brown shoes polished bright enough to see his reflection.

Donal had taken them to the barber. Both had their newly shorn hair smartly combed when they left for school.

They came home the first day telling stories about new friends and exciting experiences. They came home the second day with a note from the headmaster requesting a visit with the boys' parents.

Letta accompanied a nervous Teresa the next morning. They met with Br. Broadwater, the headmaster.

"You aren't to worry," he said. "It was a little altercation between Dante and one of our other students. I have already talked with both of them, as well as Alberto and children who saw the scuffle. Dante was defending his brother after the other boy had apparently been picking on Alberto all morning. Unfortunately, it often happens with new students. I am meeting with the other boy's parents, too. There will be no more discipline at this time, but I do hope, Mrs. Barile, that you will talk to your boys. Help them understand they are to come to my office if something like this happens again, instead of trying to settle it on their own."

"I will, Mr. Broadwater. I promise."

"They are good boys," Letta said. "Dante must have been very upset to have acted the way he did. I wouldn't want them bullied or hurt."

"Trust me, Letta, I'll see to it that this isn't repeated. I'm glad to have the youngsters in our school. I can tell they are well-mannered and bright young men. We'll take good care of them."

"I know you will, Frank." Letta reached out and shook hands with the man.

Teresa felt better after meeting with Mr. Broadwater, though she suspected it would have gone differently if Letta had not been with her. "You called each other by first names. Are you good friends?"

"Not that good, but we have done business with him over the years. He and Claude were on first name basis.

Then Frank began calling me Letta after Claude died. I will not address any man as 'Mr.' when he uses my first name."

Teresa looked at her friend. "I think you are my hero."

"Thank you." Letta smiled. "Now, back to your boys, I think they're going to do very well in life."

Teresa agreed, but did not voice her worry about the fighting. It seemed so unlike Dante. He had seen Nico erupt in anger many times, and Teresa prayed he would not follow Nico's example

***

Letta walked into the sun room, and sat down to share the news from her brother's latest letter. Teresa always wondered if the parts about Nico spoke the truth.

> *Tell Tesa that Nico has taken to the job very well. He has a two room apartment in our real estate office building in downtown Hartford, and the livery stable is just behind it. I have given him a small carriage to use and one of my best horses. The carriage is enclosed to keep out the weather, so she doesn't need to worry about his being exposed to the elements. I also have a tutor working with him, to help improve his English with businessmen. He is doing quite well with it, and seems to be enjoying the traveling and new business acquaintances. I'll tell you both more when I see you at Thanksgiving. I am sure that Nico wants to see his family, too. I am anxious to hear about Dan's and Bert's school experiences. Tell Lauri to say 'meow' to Kitty for me. I hope Tesa is taking care of herself.*

"If my brother saw how pale you are, he would be on the next train from Hartford. Other than me and my children, I haven't seen him so concerned about anyone since Margaret," Letta said.

"He is a kind person like you, Letta." Teresa told herself Jakob's concern for her was no more than kindness. "I'm all right. Some days are harder, but...it is always like yesterday to me since Eva died. I can't get used to it. I think I never will, but I have my other children. It just takes time."

Her thoughts drifted back to Eva's funeral service, and the bitter memory of the priest's comments after Eva's burial.

"Remember, Mrs. Barile, your daughter is in a better place. We can't question God's will. It is a cross He will help you bear. We must put these difficult situations in His hands and go on with life."

That's what he thought her Eva's death was—a difficult situation, a cross to bear, God's will? She had looked into the man's eyes, her mouth open to reply, until she decided that he and his small mind were not worth her time or breath.

"Please have some food before you leave," she had replied before walking away. She vowed to never seek advice or consolation from a priest again.

Now she looked at the sad expression Letta wore and realized that her friend had been so busy comforting everyone else that she hadn't dealt with her own grief. She walked over and put her arms around Letta.

"I know you miss her, too."

Weeks of pent up tears unleashed as Letta wrapped her arms around Teresa's waist and sobbed until little Lauri wandered into the room and toddled over to the weeping woman. Her small hand reached up and touched Letta's wet cheeks.

"Don' cwy, Etta," she said.

Letta's head came up. She reached out and swung the little girl onto her lap. She laughed and fumbled for a handkerchief to blow her nose. "I won't cry any more, pumpkin. How can I be sad with you here?

23

With Thanksgiving nearing, Teresa was busy with holiday sewing and didn't hear the sun room door open.

"Hello Tesa. Doesn't my sister ever give you time off?"

She jumped at the sound of Jakob's voice.

"Sorry, I didn't mean to startle you." He closed the door as he came in.

Why did his presence always cause her to blush and feel nervous? "I didn't know you were coming today." She made herself stay busy.

"I wasn't sure I could until a couple of days ago." He settled into the rocking chair beside her sewing table.

She hadn't told him to sit down. Didn't he see that she was busy?

"I'm not disturbing you, am I?" he said nonchalantly. He gave no evidence of moving.

"I…No, of course not. Well, I do have this dress to finish for Abbie, but please tell me about Hartford. Did Nico come with you?"

His expression turned serious. "I tried to talk him into coming—even offered to stay and work for him so he could be here with you. He insisted he has things to finish so he can come when you have the baby. I try to let him be as independent as possible, you know."

Teresa tried not to let her concern show, but Jakob must have sensed it.

"I'm sorry, Tesa. I know you and the children hoped he would be here for Thanksgiving."

"Oh no." Did she answer too quickly? "It's just that I, well, hope everything is all right with his job." She did not want to tell Jakob that she feared his absence would give Nico a perfect opportunity to gamble.

"He's doing all right. He hasn't had much schooling, has he?" Jakob said.

Teresa laid down the material and turned toward him. "My husband doesn't like to talk about his past, but I will tell you what I know."

"You don't have to," he said softly.

"You and your sister have been very good to us, Mr. Hahn. You did not have to take Nico to Hartford. You deserve to have information about him, more than I can give. I only know what he has told me." She paused, realizing how little she did know about her husband.

"His mother died when he was young, nine or ten, and that's when he quit school. His father drank quite a lot and mistreated Nico terribly, I gathered. He can write his name and a few simple words, and read a little Italian. He found jobs on ships mostly, and some farms, until he came to Gaeta and worked with my father in his carpenter shop. I don't know anything more, except that he sometimes gambles." She wanted Jakob to know. Maybe he already did.

Jakob leaned back, folded his arms, and looked at her for several seconds.

An uncomfortable Teresa wondered what he was thinking. Was he going to send Nico back to Philadelphia? She could hardly swallow.

When he spoke, it was slow and deliberate. "You don't have to answer this if you don't want to. It's none of my business and you can tell me that. But I'd like to know—is Nico Dante's father?"

She didn't have to say a word for him to have the answer. She knew it was plain in her face. Her voice wouldn't work. She lowered her eyes and shook her head. Then she looked at him with alarm. "Please, Dante doesn't know."

He leaned forward. "I will never tell anyone, and it makes no difference to me. It explains a lot, though, and I do have one more question. Again, you don't have to answer, but I'd like to know. Were you in love with Dante's father?"

Her eyes filled with tears as she nodded. "We were to marry, but he…died in an accident."

Jakob clenched his fists. "Look at me, Tesa."

She looked up, wiping the tears from her face.

"I will never bring this up again, but I will be here for you anytime you need help. Do you understand?"

She nodded, feeling self-conscious, but aware that the terrible knot wedged in the middle of her chest since Eva's death had begun to crumble.

Jakob stood and walked to the door. Turning the knob, he looked back at her. "Just one more thing."

She glanced up with apprehension. "What is it?"

"Do you think you could call me Jake now?"

***

Teresa walked into the parlor later as Jakob asked the boys about school.

"It's good, Jake," Dante said, sounding too grown up. "We're learning lots of new things and have a bunch of new friends."

"Yeah, since Dan put that Bobby Brown in his place," Alberto said. He told, in detail, about the early school incident. "Dan socked that boy good, Jake. He didn't push me again. My brother is tough."

Teresa sat quietly in a corner.

"There are times when a man has to be tough enough to stand up to a bully, but we don't ever want to be like them, do we, men?" Jakob seemed to read her thoughts. The boys shook their heads vigorously. Their attention quickly turned to the excitement of the holidays.

Jakob returned to Hartford after Thanksgiving, but promised, "I'll be back before Santa comes. I want to be here on Christmas morning to see whether you get candy or coal in your shoes."

***

Her first signs of labor came on December 21$^{st.}$ She was working on a customer's dress, listening to her children in the next room as they helped Beebe hang Christmas decorations. The boys were determined to be exceptionally good since Jakob's remark about the coal.

Teresa had planned to have Christmas morning at the boarding house, and spend the afternoon with Letta's family. Carlo, if a boy—or Carleen, if a girl—changed the plans. Nora sent Donal to fetch Dr. Janys.

"I don't want to be away from my children for two weeks, Sam," Teresa referred to the usual confinement period.

"If all goes well, I'll get you home sooner," he promised. "But I want you in the hospital now."

They pulled out of the driveway and met Jakob coming from Hartford. Donal stopped long enough to tell him where they were going. Jakob jumped down and ran to the carriage door, ignoring the snow that blew into his face.

"Tesa, I'll be there later and I'll get a message to Nico." In the excitement, no one else had thought of Nico.

***

Carlo Dominic Barile squalled his way into the world in the wee hours of December 22, 1903. Teresa chose Leo's middle name, telling Nico it was the name of an uncle. The Dominic, of course, was after Papa.

Papa. The hospital stay gave her time to think of him and wonder about his life. Was he well? Was he still living? Her heart ached to see him.

Letta visited every day. Jakob came twice a day. He and Donal brought the children each morning, holding them up one by one as she waved and blew kisses from a second story window.

On his afternoon visits, Jakob brought her plants or flowers—amaryllis, Christmas cactus, poinsettias—and gave animated reports about the children and their activities.

"Thank you for the flowers, Jakob," Teresa said. "They will brighten the boarding house. And thank you for keeping my children entertained."

"Me, entertain those youngsters? They're the ones that keep all of us entertained." He turned serious. "I've sent word to Nico. He should be here any day, unless the weather is too bad in Hartford."

She knew Jakob made excuses for her husband. She tried to ignore how much more his visits lifted her spirits than Nico's ever had.

Her husband arrived two days after Christmas, the day Dr. Janys said Teresa and Carlo could go home, "…only if you remain in bed another week."

She promised.

"I can't stay more than a couple of days," Nico said. They had just returned to the boarding house. "I have a lot of customers to see in Hartford."

"I'd like you to tell me what you do there." Before he could answer, Teresa's attention was captured by the cooing infant in her arms. "Don't you think he's a beautiful baby, Nico? He's healthy and he sleeps and eats well. He's going to be another wonderful son."

"I'm sure he will be. Maybe someday he'll be helping me in my own business."

Surprise covered her face. "I thought you were happy working for Jakob in Hartford, and Letta here. You don't have to worry about the expense of running a business of your own."

"I will be my own boss someday," he said firmly.

"What kind of a business do you want?"

"With all the experience I'm having, and the builders I'm getting to know, I'll have my own real estate company in a few years."

Teresa was aghast. "But that would be in competition with Letta. Surely you wouldn't do that after all she's done for us."

"I'm not talking about Philadelphia. I think this job in Hartford will last a long time, maybe several years. That will give me time to build a following there."

"Several years? You plan to stay in Hartford several years?" The news brought her both relief and concern.

"Hartford's a good business center. There's opportunity there," he said.

"Nico, Jakob is the one who gave you that opportunity. How could you even think about going into the same business?"

"You don't know anything. Hartford's growing fast. Jakob knows that other people are getting into real estate."

"Have you talked to him about it?"

"Of course not, and you'd better not, either. I'm not doing anything for a while. I'll talk to him then." He stormed out of the room.

Her mind reeled with unanswered questions.

The following day, Teresa tried in vain to talk to him again. He made it clear she could expect no financial help from him. "I have to build a savings for my business, and you should be making enough to cover expenses here."

Johnny took him to the train station the next morning.

He had not mentioned Eva and spent little time with his children, but they didn't seem to notice.

***

Letta, Jake and Donal took the youngsters to the 1904 Mummers' Parade. Even two and a half year old Lauri could anticipate the excitement by then and joined her brothers in bringing home balloons and stories.

"Next year, you bring baby Caro, Mamma," Lauri said.

Teresa laughed. "All right. Next year we'll all go."

She returned to work a few days later, as Jakob prepared to leave.

"You're looking healthier Tesa, but is everything all right?"

Teresa realized her worry showed. Without thinking, she placed a hand on his arm. "Jakob, I don't know much about Nico's job, but are you watching him? How is he doing?"

He covered her hand with his. A quiver shot through her arm. "I have good friends all over Connecticut. I know where Nico is and whom he sees. He gets more than enough to cover expenses, plus his regular pay. Don't worry." He leaned down and brushed his lips against her cheek. "Just take care of yourself." He picked up his bag and walked out.

The quiver rippled through her body.

24

"Teresa, do you think I should go back to the factory for a while?" Johnny asked a few evenings later. "I don't want you to work so hard, and Nico says he can't help because of extra expenses."

"No, I need you here, and the work isn't a problem for me, Johnny. But what extra expenses did Nico say he had?"

"Mostly travel expenses." Johnny cleared his throat and looked at the floor. "He wanted to borrow money from me, but I didn't have any to give him. You understand, don't you?" His head lifted as his eyes sought Teresa's. "He didn't want me to tell you."

She struggled to stay calm. Her voice stayed low, but firm. "I don't think Nico lies deliberately. He is embarrassed that he doesn't handle money well. Please promise me that you will never give him any."

Johnny and Annie exchanged glances, and then he looked back at Teresa. "We won't, but Annie and I want you to promise that you will tell us if he ever tries to hurt you again."

Her mouth opened, but no words came.

***

Donal began teaching Dan and Bert how to hold the reigns and drive the horses. "It's an important skill for young men," he told Teresa, "though I think driving an automobile is soon going to be just as important."

He and Jakob still had their minds on a "horseless carriage" for Letta, who continued to express her skepticism. "I can't imagine they will ever take the place of a horse," she said one day. She watched Teresa trace a dress pattern for her on new material.

"It is exciting, though, even to my boys, Letta. Some of their friends talked about the horseless carriages they saw at the World's Fair in St. Louis this summer." Teresa's expression turned solemn. "There is something else I have to talk to you about. You may not want us in your home anymore when you hear, and I will understand."

Her eyes filled with tears of regret and anger as she told of Nico's plan to have his own real estate business. "After all you and Jakob have done for us, I couldn't believe it. Nico didn't want me to tell you, but I had to. I will let you decide how to tell Jakob."

Letta reached out and took Teresa's hands. "Look at me."

Teresa raised her head.

"And listen carefully so I don't have to say this again." Letta pinched her lips together before she spoke. "You can't tell me anything about Nico that would be a surprise. Jakob and I both know he has mistreated you. We worry about you and the children when he is home."

Teresa's hand flew to her mouth. "I didn't think…I tried not to show it." Tears spilled onto her cheeks.

"I could see that you did."

"I know Nico won't take care of us; I have to do that. But I am still his wife by the law and the church, and he is still my children's father. I don't know what else I can do."

"Nico is paid a good enough salary," Letta said, "but he doesn't know it's only part of what Jakob budgeted for that job. My brother plans to talk to you about it on his next trip. He has the rest in a savings for you and the children. It's yours anytime you need it."

She squeezed Teresa's hands. "I'm not going to put you out. And we won't talk about this again."

A stunned Teresa watched Letta walk out. Jakob had money set aside for her? Money that Nico earned and didn't know about? That meant she had a savings again, even though Jakob controlled it.

***

Teresa soon had all the work she could handle, with more requests as word of her dressmaking skill spread. She sewed more hours daily, taking advantage of the lengthening summer days.

Letta came home early one warm day in late August. "I want you to come with me Sunday. I'm driving to my office to meet with one of our board members, and I don't want to go alone." When Teresa began to protest, she said, "Don't argue. The weather should be nice, and it will do you good."

On Sunday, the children stayed with Annie. Teresa had begun weaning Carlo, who drank well by then from one of the new baby bottles Dr. Janys had brought for them.

As Teresa climbed into the carriage, Letta said, "Sundays are so much more enjoyable in the city than busy weekdays."

Soft breezes hinted of an early fall, allowing for a pleasant drive. Letta guided the horse at a comfortable pace. Teresa had seen downtown only in the hustle and bustle of a business day or the Mummers Parade. Now she leaned back and breathed in the fresh air, enjoying time to take in the sights of the breathtaking homes they passed. Some day her children would live like that, she promised herself. They would live first class, even if she never did.

In the quietness of a Sunday, the city seemed quite grand. Teresa gazed at the blocks of huge buildings that represented different businesses and industries. Then she noticed smaller shops she had not previously paid attention to. A shoe cobbler's sign hung on a corner building, with nearby women's and men's hat shops, a jewelry store and others, including one with a sign that read *Tailoring for Men*.

"Letta, do you see that store?" Teresa pointed to the sign.

Letta nodded. "Mr. Hemmings has been there for years. He made most of Claude's suits, but he'll be retiring soon. It will be a loss to the men around here."

"Is there a dress shop for women in town?"

"Not that I know of. Most of the women have a seamstress, but none as good as you." She turned into the driveway of the real estate building.

Teresa followed her inside, to the end of the hall. Letta opened the door to a huge room that covered the width of the building, with windows on three sides.

"I don't think you've seen our boardroom yet. I'm meeting with Mr. Broadwater in a few minutes to discuss moving the furniture upstairs. Jake and I have long thought this was too nice a room for just quarterly board meetings. We'd rather rent it to a good business. Come on. We're meeting him in my office."

"You go ahead, Letta. I'll wait here."

"Well, if you'd rather." She pulled out a handsome, leather arm chair for Teresa to sit in. Several others surrounded the long shiny, cherry wood board table.

"How do you like this room?" Letta asked.

Teresa looked around. She liked everything about it. The floors were polished like glass. Cherry wood wainscot covered the walls about four feet high, with attractive aqua and light gray striped wall paper from there to the high ceiling. Two long windows on each end, and two sets of double windows along the length, let in an abundance of light. Aqua valances and ties offset the light gray drapes.

"It's a wonderful room—so big, and look at the light that comes in."

Letta nodded. "We think so, too. I'm sure we wouldn't have trouble attracting a suitable business. I won't be long. Then we can see some more of the city and stop for lunch at one of my favorite tea rooms."

When Letta left, Teresa stood up and walked around the room. This would be a perfect dressmaking room, she told herself, looking again at the space and the light shining in from three sides. It would perfect for her business.

"*My* dressmaking business? What am I thinking," she said. She had a dressmaking job, but a business? She would need too much. The equipment and materials—how could she do it? And she would be farther from the homes she had to visit for fittings. No, it wouldn't work. She was dreaming.

Even if otherwise possible, she couldn't begin to pay the rent Letta would need for this space. And she would have to put in an outside door for her own entry—it could go there by the front windows.

Stop it, Teresa, it's not possible, she told herself. But she did have the carriage, and she could learn to drive it. She wouldn't want to give up seeing her customers in their homes. They liked the personal touch.

She had a little savings that Nico didn't know about. She'd have to tell him that Letta loaned it to her. And there was the money from Jakob, which he had confirmed on his last visit. The account was in his Hartford bank. He offered to transfer it, but they both agreed it was probably safer in Jakob's account.

She couldn't buy much at first, but it would be a start. She could look for a rebuilt sewing machine and a large cutting table, and…she was sure she had the rest for now: scissors, tapes, and such. But could she pay the rent?

And she would need a fitting room, maybe a curtained-off space in that corner.

She walked around the room again, her heart beating fast as she envisioned it as a dressmaking shop—her dressmaking shop. What would Mamma think? It would be a big risk, but she had to do something. Nothing would bring Eva back. She had to start working and living for the children that were still with her. She couldn't depend on Nico. Should she take the risk? Maybe Letta wouldn't want a sewing shop here.

She jumped when the door opened and Letta walked in. "Whatever are you doing standing there in the corner?"

Teresa took a deep breath, trying to calm her pounding heart. "I'm dreaming about impossible things."

Letta laughed. "Dreams are never impossible, Teresa. They may present challenges, but that's what makes life interesting. What is your dream?"

"Sit down. I want to tell you about it. I'll need your help again. I hope you will say yes."

***

Letta said, "Maybe."

"I think it's a wonderful idea, Teresa, and I do believe a dressmaking shop would work very well here." She looked around. "It would be perfect for you. I have to discuss it with Jakob, of course. He'll have no objection, but our board will have the final say."

"Oh. I hadn't thought of that." Teresa's shoulders slumped.

"Well, the good thing is that Regina Billingsley's husband, Anthony, is on the board. Regina told me how pleased he is with your work. I think he might sway the others, but I can't promise. It will be almost three weeks until the next meeting. I'll make sure Jakob is here."

The next three weeks passed in a mass of flurry for Teresa, with so much to think about and prepare. She followed Letta's instructions in gathering information for Jakob to present to the board.

Jakob came a week before the meeting. "They'll want to hear it directly from you." He helped her with the figures and facts that would hopefully convince the board of her ability to run a successful business and make a profitable return for herself and their company.

Teresa learned more about what it would take to operate a business than she had ever thought possible. Could she really do it? Her nerves felt like lit fireworks when she thought about presenting to the board.

"They'll know you aren't a speaker, Tesa," Jakob said. "Just answer their questions. If you feel uneasy about anything, look at me. I'll be there to help you."

When she walked into the board room a few days later, filled with anxiety, Jakob immediately arose and strode over to take her arm and introduce her. Her panic vanished.

Letta was right about Anthony Billingsley. It helped that he wore the suit Teresa had made for him. "The smartest suit in my closet," he told the other members.

They agreed to allow her six months to prove she could build her business and make the payments.

"Thank you, gentlemen. I appreciate your confidence and I won't let you down." She hoped she sounded more self-assured than she felt.

25

Business people of Philadelphia, passing by on their way to and from work, quickly discovered *Tesa's Dressmaking and Tailoring*—Jakob's suggestion. Mostly men, they sent their wives to meet Tesa and discuss their dressmaking and tailoring needs. After that, word of mouth brought new patrons weekly.

Customers welcomed Teresa's suggestions of modifications, fabrics and some of the new styles she found in European magazines. Also, most women liked the popular fashions seen in *McCall's* magazine each season. Teresa soon added a sketch board that helped customers visualize her suggested alterations.

Beebe, working part time with Letta's approval, was a great help with hand stitching, but Teresa needed another seamstress. She put a sign in her window. A day later, Hanna walked in.

Hanna Groft appeared to be in her mid-40s. She wore her hair pushed into waves in the front, and pulled into a knot in the back. Her smiling eyes crinkled in the corner.

"You would be the owner, yes?" the woman said.

"Yes, I am. Can I help you?"

"My name is Hanna. I can do sewing good. I am hoping you give me job."

She could do sewing good, very good, and proved to be a hard worker. Each day she thanked Teresa for the job and wonderful working conditions. She had spent months in the grueling, demeaning environment of one of New York's infamous sewing factories.

By Thanksgiving of 1904, Teresa had hired another seamstress, Magan, a niece of Hanna's. The young woman proved as reliable, and almost as good a seamstress as her aunt.

Nico came home only for Christmas that year. He arrived December 23rd, dressed in a nicely made dark gray woolen business suit with a matching waistcoat. His shirt had the fashionable winged collar, complimented by a gray and red striped bow-tie. His gray homburg and new shoes completed the picture of a well-dressed, handsome business man.

Teresa had never seen this Nico. She recognized how much work and cost went into making such a suit. "You look very nice, Nico."

"I have to dress well in this business, you know."

The children hung back until he called them. He shook hands with Dante, pulled Alberto into an embrace, bent down to hug Lauri, and then went into the bedroom to see Carlo. He brought a gift for each one—small inexpensive trinkets that put big smiles on the children's faces.

Teresa was puzzled but relieved when Nico made no attempt at lovemaking.

"I don't want to take a chance of leaving you pregnant when I'm not here to help," he told her. She had not asked.

Her business impressed him, though. The business had indeed done well—better than she would let Nico know. She suspected he did not want a pregnancy to interfere with the money she was making. It should, after all, be accessible to him as her husband. She was determined it would not be.

Teresa closed early on Christmas Eve and, at his insistence, took Nico to see her dress shop. She told him about the expansions she'd had to do to keep up with increasing business.

"You must be making good money here." He walked through the rooms, opening doors and looking all around.

Teresa knew what was on her husband's mind, but this was for her children. "I might be some day, but it will be a while and then only if another shop doesn't open."

She grasped the edge of the long cutting table, leaned forward and looked directly at Nico. "I am still paying off Letta for the equipment. And since I've had to hire two more people, I have nothing left after our expenses and boarding house costs. Some day, I want to begin a savings. I hope you are doing the same." Her look feigned sincerity. She once again had a healthy percentage in her first class savings.

"How much are you paying these women? Probably too much." His sneer and tone blasted judgment.

"I give them fair wages. If I didn't have them, I wouldn't have the customers I do. They are very talented and loyal workers."

An unpleasant laugh burst from him. "You know nothing, Teresa. No one is loyal. You could pay less, and they would still be happy. It's your business, but you are anxious to give your money away."

"Nico, I am going to treat my employees the way I would want to be treated. I will pay them what they deserve and, as you say, it is my business. As long as I don't ask you for money, you don't have to worry about it."

He "humphed" and walked away from the longest conversation they had during his stay.

Teresa felt blessed relief wash over her the day after Christmas as she watched her husband leave.

***

She found herself looking forward to the 1905 Mummers Parade as much as her children. She tried, though, to avoid being alone with Jakob, who stayed until mid-January. He unnerved her. He came to the office every day to help Letta with end-of-the-year reports, and always stopped in the shop to say hello before closing time. The other women anticipated his visits like children anticipating Christmas morning.

"Hey there, Hannie and Mag and Beeb," he'd greet them, using his personal nicknames for each. "How are the prettiest women in Philadelphia today?" And then he'd wink at them and glance back at Teresa. "And how's *the boss* treating you?"

While the boss concentrated on ignoring him, the other women chuckled. "Mr. Jake, you know she's the best boss in Philadelphia," Magan always replied.

"He's such a bright spot in the afternoons. We'll be missin' him awful when he goes back to Hartford. Won't you, Teresa?" Hanna said one day.

Teresa shook her head and laughed. "He's a distraction to all of us. We'll get lots more work done when he's gone." She wouldn't admit to watching the door every afternoon for his visit, or how it quickened her heart. And she wouldn't let herself think about how much she'd miss him when he left.

***

Near the end of the school year in June, Teresa insisted that Nico come to Philadelphia for the class awards ceremony. Both Dan and Bert were receiving achievement awards. He came the day of and left the day after, but he was there.

After the ceremony, Alberto told Jakob, "Papa said he was proud of us."

Teresa later overheard Jakob talking to his sister. "He told them exactly what I said he should. I made it clear that he was to do nothing but praise his sons. I believe I would have put a fist to him if I heard him criticize them for anything."

Nico hadn't come for the boys. He'd come, apparently, only at Jakob's insistence.

***

His Christmas visit that year was, as usual, short, but his trinkets pleased the children. This time he had pencils and paper for the boys and ribbons for Lauri.

"Now you two can write to Papa about your school experiences." Teresa tried to sound excited about the gifts. "And won't these look beautiful with your new dress." She held the ribbons up to Lauri's hair.

She had purchased a nice pocket watch for Nico.

He expressed genuine surprise and pleasure. "I didn't have time to shop for you."

"There's nothing I need," she said. His thoughtlessness didn't even disappoint her.

"Yes, there is. There's something we both need."

Teresa looked puzzled.

"Did you forget about our citizenship?"

Her hand rose to her mouth to cover the "Oh" that jumped from her throat. "I guess I did. But what if we decide to go back to Italy some day? Don't we want to keep our Italian citizenship? We can't have both, can we?"

He looked at her incredulously. "Why would we want to go back to Italy? There's nothing for us there. If we ever go back, we'll go as American citizens. I want you to start studying for that examination next year. Jakob will get the material for you."

"But what…what about the time I was in Italy?" She hated reminding him.

"Jakob already talked to the authorities, and they said it'll be all right, *if* you pass the exam. But you'll only have one chance. You'd better not mess this up Teresa," he warned her.

***

That September of 1906, Jakob came to Philadelphia with Nico the day before the citizenship exam.

He and Letta reviewed questions with Teresa later in the evening. Nico said he had studied enough.

"Nico's tutor is concerned that he might not be ready," Jakob said, "but Nico doesn't seem worried. I hope he's prepared."

"I'm very nervous," Teresa said.

"You know more about this government than I ever did," Letta told her. "You're ready. You'll do fine."

As nonchalant as he tried to appear, Nico couldn't hide his rapid breathing and shaky hands when they were on their way to the exam the following day. Afterwards, he refused to discuss it, but looked no less worried. He left for Hartford the next morning.

It would take several months to know if they passed.

26

The following morning, Teresa rode to work with Letta, but Jakob showed up at her shop shortly before closing. "My sister had to leave early, Tesa. I told her I'd take you home. Besides, I want to talk to you."

"I guess I don't have a choice." Teresa wrinkled her face into a mock frown, hoping the quip would cover her uneasiness at driving home alone with him.

"Sure you do. You can walk."

In spite of the joking, Teresa had not missed the seriousness in his voice.

She sat beside Jakob, on the seat of the small two-person buggy he kept at Letta's. He told her of a conversation Nico had with him about plans to move his family to Hartford. Teresa remained quiet.

"I can't tell you more than that. I asked him if he had discussed a move with you. He said it would be his decision, and he was sure you could find work in Hartford. I let him know that I was going to tell you, but I'm sorry you're getting the news this way."

She shook her head. "I never know what he may be thinking." She noticed Jakob tense. His pursed lips indicated he had more to say, but he remained silent.

"I knew that we might have to move some day," Teresa said. "I hoped it wouldn't be until the children were through school." She looked at Jakob. "Thank you for telling me." Her hand moved toward his arm, but she yanked it back, clasping her hands together. She saw him glance in her direction.

"You know that no matter what happens, I'm here to help. I try to hold my tongue when Nico starts talking about things that don't make sense, especially when they concern you." He looked straight ahead and urged the horse on a little faster. His face was grim.

Teresa folded her arms around herself, afraid to comment. For a few minutes, both of them were silent.

Without looking at her, Jakob said, "Teresa, if he took you—all of you—away, it would be very hard on my sister and her family. And it wouldn't be fair to you. I can't imagine treating a wife of mine like that." He paused. "My only consolation would be having you in Hartford, where I could be near to help watch out for you."

Her body stiffened. "Jakob, you and Letta, and everyone here has done more than I could ever give back, but I can't be responsible for what you lost. I can't take Sara's place."

"Is that what you think?" His head shot up. He guided the horse and carriage to the side of the roadway and stopped. His eyes bored into hers. "Do you really think that I see you as a replacement of my niece?"

Teresa took a deep breath. "I know that's why your sister has done so much for us. She's doing what she wished she could have done for Sara."

"That may have been true at first, but that's far in the past. Whatever Letta does for you now is because you are her friend. And she has come to love your children. We all have. It has nothing to do with Sara anymore."

Teresa absently stroked her hair. "Maybe so, but we can't be your responsibility. I know you are trying to make up for your sister losing her daughter. You couldn't save Sara, so now you want to save me. You can't do that, Jakob. You deserve a life of your own, and I don't see you doing much about that. You would be a wonderful father. You should be out courting an attractive woman and making plans for your own future."

He looked at her intensely, saying nothing for a moment. "If it's to be, it will be, Mrs. Barile. In the meantime, I won't stand by and see you done an injustice by your husband or anyone else if there's anything I can do about it. And if you think my feelings about you are those of an uncle, well, you are sadly mistaken. If you want me out of your life, you will have to tell me so."

He started the horse with such a quick, loud, "Giddyup" that she fell against the back of the seat. They didn't exchange a word for the rest of the ride to Letta's.

Teresa gathered up Carlo and the other children.

"Teresa, it's late," Letta said. "Why don't you stay and eat with us, and then Donal will drive you home?"

"Thank you, but I need to go now. I have things to do." Teresa tried to avoid looking at her friend.

"Did Jakob have a chance to talk to you?"

"Oh, yes, he talked to me." Teresa sighed. "It was just about some of Nico's business. Jakob can tell you. I have a little headache, Letta. I want to get home."

Letta frowned. As she walked Teresa and the children to their carriage, the barn door slammed. Jakob, looking angry, strode toward the house.

"That's not like Jake," his sister said, with a questioning glance at Teresa.

***

After dinner that evening, while the children played table games with Annie and Johnny, Teresa strolled outside to sit on the front steps and watch the day close down. Street odors from animals' waste, and garbage mixed with the lingering scent of vendors' vegetables and smoked meats, drifted through the area. Creaking wheels of produce carts and merchandise wagons, to be freshly filled early the next morning, rolled toward home. Men stood in groups talking and smoking, while bored, boisterous teens roamed the neighborhood. Nevertheless, the spot gave her a relatively private place to think.

She replayed Jakob's words in her head, not wanting to give them any significance. He couldn't have meant anything more than a concern for her physical safety. But why did they sound so personal? She could tell that her children were special to him, but...no, she couldn't let herself think that way about Jakob.

She and Nico should never have left Italy. He would have eventually found a job and they would be where they belonged. If she hadn't left, maybe Mamma would have lived. And Papa would have his grandchildren to live for. But they were here now, and she could not let Nico come back and take them away from all they had achieved in Philadelphia. Still, the law would be on his side regarding any property or earnings of hers. She determined to talk with Letta about how to protect what she had.

A few afternoons later, Jakob met her at Letta's front door when she stopped to pick up the children. Teresa had avoided him since their last conversation, but she needed to talk with him now.

"I'll be gone before you come in the morning, Teresa. I wanted to say good-bye."

"And I wanted to talk to you before you leave. Can we sit in here?" She motioned toward the parlor.

"Of course." Jakob followed her into the room and waited for her to sit.

She tried to keep the quavering from her voice. "I don't like it that you are in the middle, Jakob, but I don't have any other way to send messages to my husband, or to know what he is doing. You said he knows you were going to talk to me?"

Jakob nodded.

"Please tell him that I want to see him. I have to know what he's planning for our lives; even if I have to make a trip to Hartford."

Jakob didn't respond for a few seconds. "I don't think Nico would want you in Hartford right now. If I tell him that, he'll probably be on the next train here and he won't be happy." He paused. "Please don't do anything impulsive. Let me talk to him. I'll write and let you know what he says."

Teresa looked puzzled. "Why would he not want me in Hartford, when he is talking about moving us there?"

"I don't think he has plans to move you for a while. You know how important it is for Nico to be in control of his life and his family. Your showing up in Hartford would not be in his plans."

She knew Nico well enough to understand what Jakob said was true.

***

His letter arrived two weeks later.

> *Dear Tesa,*
> *I gave Nico your message. He wants you to know that he has no plans for moving his family for at least another year. He will have plenty of time to talk to you about it, and will do that when he comes back at Christmas. He is trying to consider what would be best for his family when you are all together again.*
> *I can assure you that you have nothing to worry about regarding any changes in the near future. Nico remains busy and content with his life and work here.*
> *Please tell the children that their Papa and Jake will see them again before Santa comes. And please take care of yourself.*
> *Sincerely,*
> *Jakob*

She read the letter through once for the information. She read it again because it came from Jakob, though she told herself it was to make sure she understood the information. She tucked it into a pocket in her dress and pulled it out to read again after the children were in bed that night. She knew it by heart when she finally placed it in a drawer between her handkerchiefs.

A second letter came the next week. She read it several times, too, before placing it into her drawer next to the first one. By then, her tears had dampened the letter.

> *Dear Teresa,*
> *I am sorry to tell you that your papa died about two months ago. Mrs. Retalino took care of him at the last and he told her to write to me. He said to tell you he loved you always. Now he joins your mamma. He was a good man. I hope all is well with you.*
> *Uncle Sal*

***

"Do you want Donal to drive you to church so you can talk to your priest?" Letta asked.

"No!" Her reply was immediate and emphatic.

"I just thought—" Letta sighed deeply. "You look so sad. This time, I don't know what to do for you. My parents both died, and I loved them, but they weren't so far away. I thought maybe the priest could say something that would comfort you. I don't know what to say."

"The priest says what he has to say, and it's not comforting." Her eyes watered. "You are comforting, Letta, just being here. You don't have to say anything." Letta opened her arms and Teresa stepped into them.

***

She had a small tombstone engraved:

In Memory of
Domenico 1850-1906 and Maria 1852-1901
SANTORA
Beloved parents of Teresa
and grandparents of Dante, Alberto,
Lauretta, Eva and Carlo

The three older children, who had heard many stories about their grandparents, made pictures for them. Teresa wrote a note:

> *Dearest Mamma and Papa,*
> *You were the best parents in the world. Thank you for loving me so much. I will miss you and love you always. I know you are together in heaven. Someday, I will be with you.*
> *Your loving daughter, Teresa*

They placed the tombstone next to Eva's. Teresa and her children put their papers in a tin box and buried it by the memorial. Abbie and Lance came home for the weekend, and Teresa found herself surrounded by dear friends as Donal read the Twenty-third Psalm and led them in the Lord's Prayer. He then prayed a simple, spontaneous prayer—lovelier than any of the church prayers Teresa had ever heard.

"Donal, I didn't know you could do religion," she told him later. "Thank you. It was beautiful."

"Most Irish can do religion, you know," he smiled, "and it was my deep pleasure."

Another letter arrived from Jakob, offering condolences and letting her know that he was thinking about her. He added:

Nico sends his sympathy and love. He regrets that he can't be there.

She felt sure the words from Nico's mouth came from Jakob's pen. She didn't care. The people who mattered most had been with her.

27

Nico brought decent gifts for Christmas that year: a doll for Lauri, a baseball and gloves for the boys, and a set of baby blocks for Carlo. He even had a stunning new hat for Teresa like ones she had seen in the new fashion magazines. Yellow and peach-colored flowers adorned the top and back. Light tan in color, heavy pleats gave the hat a straw effect. The gift astonished her.

"Thank you, Nico." She placed a kiss on his cheek. "It's lovely."

She later asked Jakob if he had picked out the hat for Nico. He cleared his throat before answering. "I made some suggestions, but I didn't pick it out. I imagine Nico asked one of our secretaries to help." Teresa wondered why the question seemed uncomfortable to him. Maybe he still resented her confrontation on his last visit. She hoped not, yet each time she saw him, she felt tension between them.

***

The evening before Nico planned to leave, he still hadn't set aside time to talk with her. After the children were in bed and the boarders retired, Teresa asked him to come into the sitting room so they could talk privately. He followed her and closed the door.

"I have packing to do and things to discuss with John yet," he complained. "What's so important?"

Teresa turned to face him. "Nico, our lives are important. You promised you were going to tell me about the plans you have for our future. I have to know what to expect."

He paced the room without answering for several seconds. Finally he stood in front of her, grasped her shoulders and pushed her into a nearby chair. She grabbed at the sides to keep from falling.

"You don't have to know anything," he snarled in her face. "You think you are an important business woman and can tell me how to run my life. For your information, I have already been in touch with Mr. Woodhill at the bank and told him to inform the Yosts we are giving up the boarding house by the end of this year. In case you can't count, that is next week."

She couldn't have heard him right.

"John and Annie can stay and keep running the place if the Yosts want them to, but you are not to pay them another cent of wages. After next week, you will either owe rent here or look for another place to live. Your business," he spit out the words, "should earn you enough money for a rent. And I expect you to put aside your profits for me. Don't worry—I'll leave enough for you to live on, but the rest is to come to me."

He straightened for a moment, and then leaned toward her again. "And another thing, don't you ever threaten to come to Hartford unless I tell you to. Do...you... understand?" He waited.

She couldn't talk. She tried to comprehend what he had just told her.

"DO YOU?"

Her heart beat so fast and loud she was sure he could hear. Would he hit her? With Johnny nearby in the kitchen, she didn't think so, but—

She forced herself not to flinch as she saw Nico's fist raised. With barely room to squeeze out of the chair, she stood up and backed toward the door, squaring her shoulders and swallowing hard.

Nico's face got redder. "Answer me, goddamn it." He came toward her again.

Teresa put out a hand. "Nico, stop. I heard what you said." She tried to keep her shaky voice low and calm. "I just don't understand why you couldn't talk to me about your plans." Keep it reasonable, she told herself. Keep him calm. "If we were still in Italy—"

"Hah! If we were still in Italy, you think I would talk to you about decisions? The man is the head of the household in Italy. Even your dead father would tell you that!"

She gasped.

"Do you think old Domenico told his wife everything? Never. Do you think women have more power in this country? Hah! They'd like to, but it's not going to happen. So you, *donnaccia*, bitch, learn to stay in your place and I might let you keep your business. Or I might sell it. But you never come to Hartford until I tell you to. And when I say come, you'd better be ready."

He stormed out of the room. She stood, shaking, unable to move, trying to understand what was happening to her life.

The next day, a letter arrived congratulating her for passing her United States Citizenship examination, with information about the upcoming Oath of Allegiance ceremony to receive her Certificate of Naturalization. She tossed it on her desk.

***

Jakob and Letta brought the children to see their mother become an American citizen that February of 1907. Johnny and Annie were there, too. All beamed with happiness for her. Teresa felt conflicted. America was finally opening more opportunities for her than she ever expected, yet she mourned the loss of her Italian citizenship. Giving it up seemed a betrayal to Mamma and Papa—and Leo. But she had to pretend for the others, especially her children.

The only one who seemed to notice was Jakob. "It's overwhelming, I know, but you don't look as happy about becoming an American as the rest of these people." He looked around the crowded room.

"I am. I just have so much on my mind and, as you said, it's overwhelming." Her eyes misted.

He reached in his pocket, pulled out a handkerchief and handed it to her. "I'm sorry, Tesa. I hoped this would be a good day for you."

She blew her nose and smiled at him. "It is, Jakob. It really is. This is the right thing to do for my family, and that's what counts."

Nico didn't come. He had not passed the exam. He blamed the tutor.

***

Johnny and Annie begged her to stay, but it was time to find more room for her family. They understood. "Besides that," she said, "you two can move into this space, and it will give you another room to rent to two more boarders."

She looked all over Philadelphia for a reasonable apartment in a location that could accommodate getting Dan and Bert to school and herself to work, and with a place for the horse and buggy. She couldn't continue to depend on Donal for the boys' transportation. Finding an affordable place that fit her needs seemed impossible, until Sam Janys heard about her need for a rent.

She took Carlo in for a checkup. "I hear you're looking for a rental, Teresa, and I have just the place," the doctor said. "

By the way, this young man is in fine health. He'll be riding his own pony shortly."

He closed his office for lunch, insisting Teresa come with him. Everyone knew that Bea Janys fed whoever appeared in her kitchen. She sat at the table holding Carlo, spooning him bites of her applesauce, while Teresa ate the tasty sandwich made with Bea's homemade bread.

Sam, on the other side of his wife, leaned over and whispered something to Bea. She smiled and nodded vigorously. They both looked at Teresa.

"I'm planning to retire next month," Sam said. His wife continued to smile.

"Oh, no," Teresa said in alarm. She depended on him for the care of herself and her children. "What will we do without you?"

He swatted his hand in the air. "There are plenty of good docs in Philadelphia. But that's not the point. Listen to me."

She put down her sandwich.

"Bea and I want to make a trip to the continent—something I've promised her since we were married—and it's time to get on with it. We need someone to take care of this place while we're gone, and you would be perfect."

He put a hand up to stop the comment coming from her mouth. "Hear me out. Since I won't be practicing anymore, I don't need my office and patient rooms. We've already contracted to have them converted to an apartment. If you think this would be a good location for you, there's no one we would rather have as a tenant. You can move into our house when we leave, and your rooms should be finished before we get back."

Teresa's mouth hung open.

"You don't have to answer today, but I can't think of any reason why this wouldn't work well for you, Teresa. It's close to your work and is walking distance to the boys' school. The space should convert to a comfortable home for you and your children. And I have an extra stall for Nickers."

Bea watched her. "It would be perfect for you, Teresa."

Teresa shook her head. "I wouldn't have to think about it. What a wonderful offer. But I can't pay what it's worth."

"Sam, talk to her," Bea said to her husband.

"Listen to me, young woman. We've made up our minds that we want you. We need to cover expenses, of course, but we don't care about making a big profit. We'd like you to say yes so we can relax and get on with planning this trip."

***

She moved into the house in April. Sam had told the workers to apply whatever colors and room modifications Teresa wanted in her rental unit.

She and the children overcame the strangeness of living on their own by the time they moved into their apartment in June. Still, she awoke each morning feeling the wonderment of having her own place

Like most wealthy families, the Janyses had electricity and running water installed in their home and the apartment during renovations. Teresa finally realized what it felt like to live first class.

28

Letta insisted Teresa should have a telephone for her shop. "It's 1907, Teresa. Many families, and all real businesses have them now."

As soon as Nico learned about her move and the telephone, he called to let her to know that he expected to see her books the next time he came, and would be making a plan for "investing our money."

Jakob and Letta helped Teresa set up an alternate book system that he could examine when he did come.

"He won't understand it," Jakob said, "but let him see it and explain the figures just the way we showed you."

He wasn't there yet by July, when Teresa baked a cake for Lauri's sixth birthday—in her own oven, in her own kitchen.

"Imagine, Mamma, a real home for me and my children." Teresa hummed as she layered frosting on the cake, until an unexpected lump rose in her throat. Memories took her back to the kitchen in Gaeta, watching Mamma bake cakes for her when she was a child.

Abbie and Lance came for the party, with their mother and Lance's fiancé, Melody. By then, Lance was a partner in his mother's real estate business. Abbie had completed her nursing degree and worked in the children's ward at the Jewish Hospital of Philadelphia.

Lauri became Abbie's shadow. "I'm gonna be a nurse, too, when I'm big like you, Abbie."

Teresa could see Lauri as a nurse. Whatever her daughter wanted to do, Teresa determined to make possible for her.

"I've something to ask you before I leave," Letta said. They were lighting candles on Lauri's cake. "It's nothing that can't wait. Birthday party comes first."

They carried the decorated cake into the parlor, where everyone sang *Happy Birthday* to a beaming Lauri. All her special people were there. All but Jakob, and he promised he would come in a couple of weeks, "just to see you, princess."

"What did you want to ask me?" Teresa asked Letta before she left.

"I'd like you to come to a meeting with me and Abbie next Tuesday after work. I think you'll find it worthwhile."

Teresa's brow wrinkled in puzzlement. "Of course. What is it about?"

"You'll see. We're called Suffragettes."

***

From the first meeting, in a room filled with bright, energetic, enthused women, Teresa was awed. A passionate addiction to their causes—her causes—grabbed her by the end of her second meeting.

Many of the women had supportive husbands who wanted the world to be a more just place for their daughters. Voting was the primary, but not only issue of the Suffragettes.

As one of the few female business leaders in the community, Letta had a leading role.

"Why didn't you tell me about them earlier?" Teresa asked.

"You had too much to work out before, but I knew this was your time."

***

Nico didn't come that Christmas. He showed up at the apartment, unannounced, on a Saturday afternoon in

February, almost a year after Teresa moved from the boarding house. The children were at Letta's with their pets.

"Nico. I didn't know you were coming." Jakob always let her know when to expect him. This must have been a last minute decision.

"I thought it was time I checked on my family." He walked past her into the parlor, taking off his coat and dropping it on the sofa. "I would've been here for the holidays if it wasn't for that banking crisis in New York. One of us needed to stay and calm down our customers, you know."

She'd heard about people pulling their money out of the banks in November. Letta told her not to worry. "Jake and I are watching the situation, but we're confident the funds are fine for now."

Jakob had come for Christmas, satisfied that the country's finances were stable. Teresa suspected Nico had another reason for staying in Hartford.

"I heard you received your citizenship." She picked up his coat and hung it on the coat tree. "Congratulations."

"I would've got it the first time if I'd had a better teacher," Nico grumbled.

"Well, I was lucky to have Letta. Come on, I'll show you the apartment."

Dr. Janys had extra windows put in, making the parlor bright, cheery, and airy when the weather allowed them to be open. Teresa had picked out light green and pale blue striped wall paper. Splashes of the same colors were seen in chair, sofa and drape fabrics.

With new friends from the Suffragettes, as well as the Lutheran church she now attended with Letta, Teresa had occasional visitors. She prayed none would show up while Nico was there. He didn't know about her involvement with either group.

"You didn't discuss this move with me." His voice and expression were accusing.

"You are the one who told me I needed to find a rent, Nico."

He followed her to the kitchen. She poured two cups of coffee, placed them on the table and sat down.

"You're lucky to have so many people taking care of you, and getting all of this free." He pulled out a chair, sat, and took a sip of coffee before pushing the cup away.

"What do you mean, free? I'm paying the Janyses a fair rent."

"Hah" he retorted. "If you're paying anything, it's got to be a pittance. I know these kind. They've been taking care of you since we got to Philadelphia—the poor little immigrant. You think you're special to them? You're just their charity project."

"And do you think I don't know that?" She would not be defensive. "I haven't asked for anything, and yes, they have been generous, but not just to me. Think about it, Nico. You would never have gotten to Hartford without Jakob giving you the opportunity. We should both be grateful."

"I'm not so sure about that. I don't trust these people. They're using both of us. Jake's business is better than ever, thanks to me. He bought himself one of those new automobiles last year, a brand new '07 Ford Model T. I'm the one traveling, but I still have to use a horse and buggy."

She shook her head at Nico's sense of entitlement, wondering why Jakob tolerated it. Even Letta still drove a horse and buggy, though more and more horseless carriages traveled the streets of Philadelphia. Jakob reminded his sister of that each time he came.

"He's traveling in style now, and I'm getting tired of making money for him. I deserve more than he's giving me." Nico stood, walked to the window and back. "And you think Letta doesn't have her own motive? You just wait. She'll find a way to grab profit from that business of yours and you won't even know what's happening."

Teresa's mouth opened. She stood and glared at Nico. "After all they have done for us, I can't believe you mean the words that are coming from your mouth." She turned to walk away when he grabbed her arm and yanked her back into the chair.

"You are forgetting your place, Mrs. Barile. Having all this doesn't change that you are still my wife and you owe me. I want to see your books. If you are such a wonderful business woman, you should have a good profit. I'm here to get some of it before you throw it all away."

She tried to pull free, but he squeezed harder. "Nico, quit!" No one was nearby to help this time.

"You're going to stop being such a high and mighty. You should've had the good doctor deal with me about this rent before you moved."

She winced, and he finally let go. "Tomorrow morning, Teresa…first thing. You take me to see your books."

"I can show them to you right now." She felt mild satisfaction at the surprised look on his face. "I bring all my receipts and bills home and do the books here."

Rubbing her aching arm, she walked into her bedroom and took a set of record books from a small corner cupboard. At the kitchen table, she opened them for Nico's inspection.

"You can see that there is really no profit yet. I'm getting more sewing requests than I can handle, though. If I expand, I'll need more help, more equipment, and more space. But I can't make that commitment until I know what our future is."

He looked at the figures for a minute, and then took his finger and underlined them, trying to understand what he was seeing. Simple daily income and expense columns showed how little she had left for her own living expenses, plus debts that she still owed.

She did not tell him about the other set of books—the ones that showed her true income. Even after operating and living expenses, she already had a sizeable enough profit to purchase new equipment for expansion.

"You can see that I will have a fair profit after the equipment is paid off, but I could have much more if I expanded."

Nico studied the books another minute. "How long will it take for you to have these big profits?" The scoffing tone couldn't hide his curiosity.

"Letta thinks my business could be doubled and everything paid off in two or three years." She let him think about it briefly. "There are already other tailor shops here, but none give the personal attention I do. My customers like that. And remember that Philadelphia is growing. Business will be growing too."

He squinted his eyes and pulled on the corner of his moustache, saying nothing for a couple of minutes. Then he stood up and paced the kitchen before turning to Teresa.

"I can wait another year to start my business in Hartford. That will give me time to make more contacts and for you to make more profits. In the meantime, you send me at least $15 a month for my business. You can afford that."

She swallowed hard, hoping Jakob was keeping an eye on Nico's spending. He left early the next morning, after seeing the children briefly.

A month later, Letta received a letter from Jakob describing Nico's new automobile. She told Teresa about it. "It's called a—oh, goodness, what was that name?"

"Cameron," said Donal. "It's called a Cameron Runabout—1905 model, I believe. It only holds two people, but it's a nice little automobile, as they go. I expect it will be good for Nico's travels about the countryside."

"Yes, I imagine it will." Teresa was sure Jakob had made it happen.

29

After a year of persuasion, Jakob convinced his sister to buy an automobile, though not before she had Donal do some research.

"Donal says they're not without trouble, but he's convinced they're here to stay and it's time for me to have one. Claude always said if Donal suggests something, it's the right thing to do," she told Teresa.

Jakob said Henry Ford was the most progressive automobile maker in America. After looking at several models, he and Donal settled on a 1908, six cylinder, four passenger, forty-horse powered Ford Model K.

"What about my horses?" Letta asked. She and Donal were in the driveway, showing the shiny gray new automobile to Teresa, Beebe and Nora. The women walked around the vehicle, touching it, climbing in and out, and talking about how "simply beautiful" it was.

"The horses, Donal," Letta said again. "They can't just stand in the barn all day."

"'Course not," Donal said. "They're important backup if this new contraption breaks down. And we need more than one transportation vehicle. The horses are getting old, though. It's time to give them a break, but they still need exercising. I've an idea about that."

"I'm afraid to ask," Letta said.

"You'll like it," he assured her. "I hope Teresa will, too."

Teresa looked at him in surprise. "What ..."

"I think we should hire Dan and Bert to drive them a couple times a week. They know how to hitch and handle the horses well enough by now."

Donal looked at her. "What do you think?"

She studied him for a few moments. "You know better than I do, Donal. My boys would be thrilled, if you think they are ready for the responsibility. They seem awfully young to me, but I'll leave it up to you and Letta."

"If Donal says they can do it, that's all I have to know. Eleven and twelve are not too young," Letta said.

"No pay, though," Teresa said. "Letting them handle the horses is pay enough."

"No, no," Letta said. "I want them to take this seriously. Donal is right. We'll offer them the job and make a contract for them to sign. They'll have to earn their pay."

The Dan and Bert Team launched that summer. At first, Donal oversaw their preparation and hitching of the horses, and went with them on neighborhood rides. He watched them unhook, cool and brush down the horses before putting them in their stalls, and then properly clean and store the reins and halters. When convinced they no longer needed supervision, he began letting them take the team out alone. Teresa cautioned them to be careful.

"Mamma," Dan said, "Donal's been letting me and Bert drive since we were kids. We know what we're doing."

"He taught us all about horses and driving," Bert chimed in. "We're experts!"

Teresa laughed, gazing at her young sons. How did they get so grown up without her noticing? She felt as though she had missed too much of her children's lives, still thinking of them as her babies. But Lauri was almost seven, and Carlo would be five in December. Teresa had been so busy building a business…. For a moment, she felt cheated. Nothing in life could be more important than her children.

She thought about the Suffragette movement. More and more of her time involved meetings and attending public stands on women's rights. Did it take too much from her children? She looked over at Lauri, who folded material for her.

The world was evolving, but women still fought for their independence and the right to vote. Teresa wanted life to be better for her daughter. And she wanted her sons to appreciate and respect the women who would become a part of their lives. They never learned it from their father. She had to stand up for all of their rights. She also had to find a balance that would allow her to have more time with the children before they were grown and gone. She resolved to hire more help before, not after her expansion.

***

She promoted Hanna to a supervisory role and let her assist with home consultations. There were more than enough applications from well qualified seamstresses to fill Hanna's sewing spot, and most were eager to work at *Tesa's*.

Mr. Hemmings, just a block away, let her know that he planned to retire and sell his tailor shop. She'd already talked to him about buying it, and then got a stomach ache thinking about taking on such a large mortgage.

"I've had this business for many years," Mr. Hemmings said. "I feel responsible to my faithful customers to make sure it goes to someone who will continue to serve them well."

"I understand," Teresa said.

"I've been watching you and listening to people talk about you, young lady."

Teresa stood tall. She had to look up just a bit to make eye contact with the elderly tailor.

"I hear fine things about you. I would be comfortable selling my shop to you." They shook hands.

She'd have to find a way to get Nico's approval, but she didn't worry about that. Jakob would work it out.

***

In 1911, Teresa modified the original *Tailoring for Men* sign to *Tesa's Tailoring for Men,* deciding to keep Mr. Hemmings' store strictly for male patrons. It pleased him that she retained his long time employees.

Tesa's Dressmaking and Tailoring Shop became *Tesa's Tailored Clothes for Women and Children.* Both businesses had grown considerably in the two years since Nico convinced his wife to "go ahead with the shop expansion." Teresa never knew exactly what Jakob had said to Nico, but her husband seemed to become excited about the expansion of her shops, even though he returned to Philadelphia only twice in those two years.

"I'm busier than ever," he told her. "I have to travel every week to keep building up my business contacts here. It won't be long 'til I'll be on my own." He gave no evidence of making the change, though. That suited Teresa.

With each visit, he stayed long enough to spend a little time with the children and let his eyes verify the success of his wife's enterprises, criticize her wastefulness, and make an updated plan for his share of her profit.

Much as Teresa tried to protect her earnings, she understood that money was Nico's only incentive for allowing her to continue her business. She showed him the ledgers she kept for his eyes only. The profit line indicated a third of her real profits, but the amount satisfied Nico, and he insisted she could well afford to send more to him for "investing."

"Nico, those profits are for the business and my living expenses. And don't forget how much your children are growing. The boys eat like men now."

"As a matter of fact, I've noticed that Dan and Bert are old enough for jobs, especially Dan. I think Bert should have more education, but it's time for Dan to start earning money. I might take him back to Hartford with me on my next trip. I could use an assistant."

Teresa's hand flew to her mouth. "Oh no, Nico. He is doing so well in school. They both are. They will have a chance at much better paying jobs if they finish their education and go on to college. They could be business leaders in the community, like Letta's son." Lance was now vice-president of his mother's real estate business.

"I'm not so sure you're right." He said no more then. He did leave with a sizeable check from Teresa, and a promise that she would send him a third of her profits each month.

***

Teresa's business had indeed grown. It filled the bottom floor of Letta's building now, with a consultation room, three fitting rooms and a children's suite. That had been Beebe's suggestion.

"There are mothers who come with several children. Wouldn't it be helpful to have a playroom for the little ones while they or their mums wait for fittings?"

"What a splendid idea, Beebe." They began planning.

She asked Nora and Donal to describe Sara's childhood playroom, and then followed the same theme for the shop's playroom. Half a rainbow covered the top part of the door around the room's name, *Sara's Place*.

A huge rainbow rose above clouds painted on the back wall, with a variety of animals and *Mother Goose* characters traipsing around the other walls. Musical notes hung in the air from threads attached to the ceiling. When they began decorating the room, Teresa learned about the piano that had been in Letta's house.

"She had it taken out after Sara's death," Nora explained. "The girl took an interest in music when she was just a child and heard it in church."

Teresa wondered what happened to the pianoforte that had been in her home in Italy. She hadn't touched it since Leo's death when, like Letta, the music disappeared from her life. Now she realized how much she missed it.

"Do you think Letta would mind if we put a piano in the playroom for children or their parents who like to play?" she asked Donal.

A smile began in his eyes and traveled to his lips as he remembered. "I am sure she will think that is a fine tribute to her daughter."

Teresa picked out a piano that day and had it delivered the next morning. She also picked out sheets of music. Most were children's songs: *Twinkle Twinkle Little Star*, *Mary Had a Little Lamb*, *Rock-a-Bye Baby* and others. She included a few popular songs of the day that adults might enjoy—*Sidewalks of New York*, *The Band Played On*, and *O Sole Mio*. That one for Leo.

Bright braided rugs were placed on the wooden floor, and white cabinets held an assortment of toys and books. Drapes on the long, double windows were splashed with rainbow colors.

When everything was ready, she brought Letta.

"What's all this mystery abou...?" Letta began as Teresa led her toward the playroom door. Letta stopped in mid-step, with a hand to her mouth. Her eyes filled with tears. Teresa feared she had made a terrible mistake, until she heard a soft whisper, "What a beautiful thing to do."

They opened the door and Letta gasped as tears ran down her cheeks. Then she spied the piano. "Oh, Teresa, how did you know?" She walked over and touched the keys.

"Is it all right?"

"It's perfect, just perfect."

***

Mothers raved about the playroom for their children when they came for dress fittings. As the demand for more children's clothing grew, Teresa realized the need for more workers and someone to supervise the playroom full time. Beebe was so good with little ones. Teresa spoke to Letta first.

"Of course I wouldn't mind," Letta said. "She's been there part time since you opened, and she loves it. I have enough help in the house."

Beebe became the official Nanny of *Sara's Place*.

30

"It's time for you to have an automobile," Letta told Teresa one day.

Nico wouldn't like her spending the money, but it made sense, especially with the growth of her business and the need to be out more in the community.

Even Dr. Janys had succumbed to the horseless carriage rage. "It's the way to travel in these modern times," he said.

She asked Donal to help her scout for a vehicle. They both liked the red 1909 Buick Model F that had been owned by friends of Letta's. The price was right for the five passenger touring model. Donal gave her driving lessons until she became comfortable behind the wheel. Dan and Bert learned much faster.

The brothers were making a fair amount of money with their expanding little business. More neighbors found it convenient to use them for running errands and transporting servants. Teresa made sure Nico didn't know. She took each boy to the bank to open his own savings.

***

The Boys Academy of Philadelphia graduated fifty-nine young men in 1913. Dante Barile, class president and valedictorian, stood at the podium, looking out at the family and friends who came to cheer and support him.

"I could never have achieved this success without their tireless support and constant encouragement," he said to the crowd.

Dan then turned his attention toward classmates and talked about the importance of believing in themselves and making the future better than the past. He concluded,

"As men, we must strive especially to make a better future for our sisters and wives and daughters. Women have the same ability as men to lead this great country, and it is time that they stand beside us at the voting polls."

Teresa heard a scattering of applause at first. She found it hard to restrain herself from cheering out loud with pride. Dan had been aware of her activities with the Suffragettes, and she told him about Letta's trip to New York the previous May, for the big Suffragette march with women from all over the country. He questioned why women weren't allowed to vote, and wondered what other rights they were denied. But she never realized, until now, that he had given any thought to what she said.

Then she saw Jakob stand to clap and cheer. Others joined him until the whole audience was on its feet. However, Teresa noted several men, like Nico, who made a pretense of clapping while looking less than enthusiastic. She didn't care. She watched her handsome son, who looked so like his father—his hair, those eyes that sparkled like Leo's did when he laughed at her, the dimple on his left cheek.

She wondered what effect Dan's message would have on Nico. He had arrived the previous day, expecting to drive "their automobile" to the ceremony. Teresa didn't care. It wasn't worth arguing about.

Afterwards, they went to Letta's, where a large tent was set up for the graduation reception. Teresa watched her two oldest sons together, chatting easily with guests in Letta's backyard. She thanked God her boys remained best friends through the years, and that neither had questioned the differences that were more noticeable as they grew older.

Bert's straight light brown hair, with red highlights, contrasted with Dan's black, longer curly locks. Dan, slim and muscular, stood almost a head taller. He had Leo's dark brown eyes and darker complexion. The other children, with fairer complexion, had light brown eyes, like hers and Nico's.

She worried at times about the quick temper Bert seemed to have inherited from his father; but unlike Nico, it was short-lived and he was easy to reason with. Dan seemed to always be in a good mood and able to see the bright side of any situation. He could talk or joke his siblings out of their occasional grumpiness...like Leo used to do with her, and like Jakob did with her children.

Later, she saw the boys talking with Jakob. She walked toward them, but stopped when she overheard their conversation. Jakob saw her, but the boys had their back to her.

"What are you two going to do about your business if you go off to college, Dan?" Jakob asked.

"We've talked about that," Bert spoke up. "We both have a good savings, and Dan has enough to pay most of his first year at Penn State."

"That's where you've decided to go?"

"Yes. They have a campus right here in Philadelphia you know, and it's a good school. They've offered me a scholarship. That leaves me enough money to buy a small auto, and we're thinking we could keep the business going."

"But not with the horses," Bert interjected.

Jakob raised an eyebrow. "Oh?"

"They're getting old and they've earned a rest."

"Besides, it's getting too dangerous for them with so many autos on the roads anymore," Dan said. "Carl is big enough to exercise them in the pastures, and it will give him a chance to start earning. We make enough to pay him." Dan used his younger brother's now familiar shortened name. "We thought we'd use my car for the business—that is, the one I'm going to get."

"That's until I get one," Bert said. "We figured this year for Dan and next year for me."

"Sounds like you two have been doing a lot of figuring. It's pretty ambitious. What do you plan to study?" Jakob asked Dan.

"I'm hoping to get into the School of Veterinary Medicine."

"That's a fine profession and a good choice for you, Dan. Does your mother know?"

"I mentioned it to her a couple of times, but I think she just thought it was a kid's dream."

Jakob's eyes met Teresa's as she flinched. "Tell her again. I could see how proud she was with your speech today about supporting women. That was a fine thing to say."

Later, as Teresa sat with Beebe, she saw Nico pull Dan aside. Whatever Nico said to him caused her son's face to bland. Then they were arguing. Teresa stood and moved toward them. Jakob walked up to her and put his hand on her arm.

"He's grown up, Tesa. I don't know what it's about, but give them a little time. You know Nico is not going to hear anything you say in the heat of an argument. Try to let Dan handle this. He'll let you know if he needs you."

She hated it, but knew he was right.

***

"Nico, you can't take him away." Teresa pleaded with her husband that evening.

"Don't tell me what I can and can't do, Teresa. You're the one who begged me to let him stay until he finished his schooling. Well, he's finished. I kept my part of the bargain."

"He wants to be a veterinarian and he's been offered a scholarship. Think about it. You can have a college educated son, and it won't cost you a thing. Please, Nico, you can't make him lose this chance." With fingernails biting into her hands to keep from shaking, she held back bitter tears.

"Nothing is free, Teresa. A scholarship might cover some costs, but he won't earn anything for four more years, and there will still be expenses."

"But he has his own money for the expen..." She slapped a hand over her mouth. "I mean he—he has been doing some errands and...and has saved enough to start school."

Nico didn't miss the blunder. "No, he has more than enough to start, doesn't he?" He eyed her coolly. "Just how much, and how long were you going to keep it a secret from me?"

"Nico, listen to me. It's Dan's money. It's not that much; just enough to pay his own way, so he wouldn't have to ask you or me for help. He's worked so hard. He wanted you to be proud of him."

"Isn't that touching. How much, Teresa? When were you and your precious son going to tell me about this? And what else haven't you told me? How much more money is hidden away by you and Dan?"

"None. You see my books. I don't know how much Dan has, but it's what he earned and it belongs to him. It can't be much. Please don't take it from him, Nico."

"Shut up, Teresa. Just shut your mouth. You always talk too much. Have you been filling his head about this women's rights' trash? A woman's right is to do what her husband says. If I ever see you in one of those groups, I'll put a quick stop to it, don't think I won't. I might even put a quick stop to your business." He stalked out, slamming the door.

She could never guess if Nico's threats were real or meant for intimidation, and she never wanted to test him. But she couldn't let him ruin Dan's future. Would it be possible for Nico to close her business? She reasoned that it would cost him the tidy little income that had been flowing his way for several years, and he surely wouldn't want to give that up. On the other hand, Nico could be unpredictable if he felt pushed.

The next day, she asked Hanna to cover for her. "Nico is leaving this afternoon. I need to see him before he goes."

Dan was packing his clothes when she returned home. Nico's bags were already waiting by the door. "What are you doing?" Her voice shook with alarm.

He stopped and put his arms around her. "I love you, Mamma." He hugged her tight, and then stepped back and looked down at his mother, with a hand on each of her shoulders. "I'm going to miss you terribly, but I've decided to go to Hartford with Papa. You don't need me here anymore. Bert can take care of anything you need. Papa can teach me his business and that will be better than any college education for me. And he said next year, when Bert is graduated, he's moving all of you to Hartford so we can be together again."

"But what about your plans for Vet school? What about your scholarship?" she said frantically. "That was your dream."

"That's all it was, Mamma, a dream. And who knows—I might have another chance to go in a few years, but not now. The scholarship? This will give someone else a chance. Maybe I wouldn't have made such a good veterinarian anyhow."

"You'd make a wonderful veterinarian." Fighting tears, she wrapped her arms around her son. "Please don't go, Dante."

He unlocked her arms and held her hands. "I have to."

She shook her head. "No, you don't. I'll talk to your father."

"It's settled, Mamma. I want to go. It'll be good experience for me. And I'll be working with Jake."

That Jakob would take care of Dan was her only consolation. But it didn't make this fair. She walked outside, where Nico waited. "I will not forgive you for taking this chance away from him, Nico."

"That's going to keep me awake at night," he jeered. "You can drive us to the train station—but stop by the bank on the way. Dan wants to get his money."

31

"He didn't even tell me. How could he leave without telling me?" Bert paced back and forth in the parlor, disbelief on his face. "All the plans we had. How could he just go off like that?"

"Don't blame Dan, sweetheart," Teresa said, perching on the edge of the sofa. "Whatever Papa said to him made him think he didn't have a choice." She told him everything Dan gave as his reasons for leaving. "I tried to talk him out of it. Now we just have to trust him."

"Then why didn't Papa talk to all of us about it? He didn't even say good-bye to us. He just left—like he always does. He doesn't care about us."

"Of course he does." Teresa tried to make it sound true. "That's why he has been working so hard in Hartford all these years."

"Mamma." Bert stood still finally and looked at his mother. "We're not children anymore. You can stop pretending. Don't you think Dan and I noticed a long time ago how little Papa comes to see us? And when he does, he's just looking for money. He never brings us any. It's your money. That's what's been taking care of this family and, we're pretty sure, of Papa, too. For gosh sake, Jake has been a better father to us since we were kids—and Donal, too."

She didn't know what to say. She stood and put arms around her son, leaning her head against his chest. "I'm so sorry, Bert. You all deserve better. I'm sure your father loves you. He just never learned how to show it."

"Don't make excuses for him. He's not worth it. But Dan is, and it's not right that Papa took him away. He should be going to school, not to Hartford." Bert paced some more. "I can do the business myself, and Carl can help me. He's old enough now. I'll make a good business man out of him."

The thought brought a slight smile to Teresa's face. She gave her son a squeeze. "I know you will."

She needed to tell Jakob about Dan before he left. Teresa found him in the carriage house with Donal the next morning. They had the hood up on Jakob's automobile, comparing his engine to the one in Letta's car.

"Could I talk with you?" She looked first at Jakob, and then said to Donal. "Just for a few minutes."

"Take all the time you need," Donal said. "I'm done here. I've got chores to do for me lovely wife."

"Do you want to go inside?" Jakob asked.

"I'd rather stay out here."

He pulled out two wooden stools, grabbed a cloth hanging on the wall, and dusted them off. "Sit down. You look upset, Tesa."

Fighting tears, she told him about Nico taking Dan, and about her conversation with Bert.

"Damn," he said. "He talked about bringing Dan to Hartford, but I didn't think he'd really do it. Teresa, I'm sorry. I'm so sorry. I don't know if I can change his mind, but I'll try with everything in my power."

"It's not just about today, Jakob. I want to know what's going on," she said emphatically. "When Nico first went to Hartford, it was supposed to be temporary. Then he began threatening to move us there with him. It hasn't happened, but I'm tired of living with his threats. It's no secret that Nico and I do not have a loving relationship. I was willing to be a good wife—if I was treated like one." She clenched her teeth and looked somewhere beyond Jakob.

"I don't mind that Nico isn't here. Our life is more peaceful when he isn't, but I can't stand that he just walks in and out with anything he wants, including my children." Her gaze came back to Jakob. "I want to know what's going on with him in Hartford. You can't shock me about Nico, Jakob. Please tell me everything."

"All right." He sighed, leaned back in his chair and returned her gaze. "But first I want some truths from you. What are your feelings toward me?"

"What...what...my feelings toward you?" she muttered. "What has that got to do with anything?"

"It pretty much has to do with everything," he said, matter-of-factly.

Teresa's breathing quickened. What was he talking about? She wasn't sure she wanted to know. "I don't see how—"

"Why do you think I suggested Nico come to Hartford in the first place?"

"Well...because you needed someone for your business, and—"

"And it didn't occur to you that I could have found dozens of better applicants than your bumbling husband?"

Teresa's lips opened, but no words came. Her mouth went dry and her heart pounded. She should get up and leave, but she couldn't move.

Jakob leaned forward, took her hand in his and looked directly into her eyes. His voice softened. "Tesa..." She tried to pull her hand away, but he held it firmly. "It definitely wasn't love at first sight, but you pinged my heart a little that day on Ellis Island. I admired your determination. And then when I saw you at Lilly and Paul's in New York, I just thought it was a pleasant coincidence. But when you turned up at my sister's here in Philadelphia, I realized that fate had to have put us together. Didn't you ever think about that?"

"No...I mean, I did think it was odd, but coincidences happen." Her heart thumped so hard she knew he could hear. She tried to swallow. Her mouth was spit dry. This was not what she wanted to talk about. She couldn't allow herself to hear this.

"Yes, they do. But it's been more than coincidences with us, hasn't it?"

"Jakob, I came here—"

"You came here to get information that you've put off too long. And that's what I'm giving you. I've put it off too long, too. I should have told you all about Nico, and about my feelings, long ago."

"Jakob, you are doing just what Nico does, except you aren't as ugly about it as he is." She yanked her hand away and stood abruptly.

At that, Jakob jumped up. "What are you talking about? I would never, ever treat you—or any woman—like Nico does."

"You think you wouldn't, but I came to get some truths from you, and you are talking about what you want, not what I want. That's just what Nico does."

Hands on his hips, Jakob looked down at her and took a couple of frustrated breaths, blowing air out of his nostrils like an angry bull.

"I don't like the comparison." He scowled. "And I don't think you're right, but I promise you I will give it some thought. Now though, Mrs. Barile, it seems to me that you are the one trying to avoid the truth."

"How can I be avoiding it? I want answers about my husband, and you don't want to tell me." Now she was scowling.

He sat again, took her hands and gently guided her back to the stool, then pulled his around to face her. "One of the things I love about you is your persistence and determination, even though it makes me crazy at times. I don't know when I began to really love you, but I have for a long time. You must know that."

"Don't say that, Jakob. Please, this is hard enough."

"Tell me you don't feel the same way. Look at me, Tesa. Tell me."

She looked to the floor and then shook her head. He put two fingers under her chin and lifted until her eyes found his. "Tell me," he whispered.

Tears sprang to her eyes. "It doesn't matter. It doesn't change anything."

"It matters to me," he said. "It's the reason for everything. I took Nico to Hartford to get him away. I knew he was mistreating you, and I knew that it would only get worse if he stayed. I've done everything I could to help him do better in life. I thought if he could learn better English and make a good living, maybe he would turn into a decent husband for you and father for your children. It hasn't happened. The more he gets, the more he gambles. He hasn't done anything for his family's benefit. Sometimes he has unexplained bundles of money, but he loses it on one thing or another."

"Where does the money come from?" Teresa wasn't surprised by what she heard.

"I've been told by a couple of people I trust that he is doing more than gambling. He's booking, too. To Nico, I'm sure it seems like a way to get rich quick. The truth is that it can be perilous. I don't know any private bookie who hasn't gone under sooner or later. When they do, there is more at risk than money. These are dangerous people. I've tried to tell him, but he keeps denying any involvement."

"Do you think he'll get Dan involved?" Alarm filled her chest.

"I don't think so. I think he'll try to get Dan to cover his work so he has more free time to expand his gambling. But that's not all, Tesa." He took a deep breath. "I've not wanted to tell you this, but it's time you knew. He's got a mistress. He'll deny it if you ask, but he's been supporting one or another for several years." He waited for her reaction.

She said nothing.

"I'm sorry. You don't deserve this."

"Oh, it's not the mistress. I don't mind that at all. I never loved Nico. It's actually a relief to know that he has someone else. It makes me feel less guilty for not being a loving wife, and it explains…" She stopped talking, feeling her face grow hot. She looked away.

"The only thing I resent is his spending all that money on his own pleasures and giving nothing to his family. And I have to give him what I should be saving for my children's future." Her hands clenched into fists. "If that's the cost of keeping him away, it might be worth it, except now he has Dan. Now it's become too high a price. What can I do?" She looked at Jakob again.

"Divorce him and marry me."

Her eyes widened. Her mouth opened, and then closed. Clutching her arms, she sighed and shook her head.

"I mean it, Tesa. I've been in love with you for years. I've had the company of other women, but all I do is think of you. I've tried making Nico into a suitable husband for you, and that didn't work. We were meant for each other, I know it. I can make it happen—your divorce—but I've got to know you love me too, and I'm pretty darn sure you do."

She felt as though she was standing precariously on the edge of a deep hole. If she started to fall, she wouldn't be able to stop. She couldn't let herself get off balance. She hoped her voice still worked.

"Jakob, I can't have this conversation with you. Not now. I have to think about what to do to protect my family."

"Just tell me, do you love me?"

She hung her head. "I can't," she whispered.

"You can't what? Love me or tell me?"

Tears dropped onto her lap. It was a full minute before she whispered, "I don't love you."

"I don't believe you." Jakob stood up and walked toward the doorway.

"Jakob?" Her tearstained eyes followed him.

"What?" He paused, without looking back.

"Please take care of Dan."

"Like he was my own son," he promised and continued walking.

32

"I'm sorry, Mrs. Barile. He had identification showing he was your husband. The law says that's all we need," Anton Dahlberg, president of Girard Bank, explained to Teresa a few days later. "He told us he was withdrawing it for you, and we had no reason not to believe him."

Barely able to breathe, Teresa stood and spread her hands on the man's desk. She leaned forward, her eyes boring into his. "If the account had been in my husband's name and I came in to ask for a withdrawal, would you have given it to me?"

"Why certainly," he said, "as long as you had a signed statement from Mr. Barile giving us permission."

"But you didn't have permission from me," she pointed out.

"But, Mrs. Barile, he is your husband. We don't need permission from a wife."

Squinting at the little bald man—who seemed to try and make up for the lack of hair on his head by the abundance of it on his face—her words were slow and deliberate. "Doesn't that seem terribly wrong to you, Mr. Dahlberg?"

She didn't wait for an answer before turning abruptly toward the door. With her hand on the knob, Teresa looked back. "I'll be withdrawing the balance of my money right now. Please clear it with your teller."

He followed on her heels trying to explain, placate, and promise that they could find a way to keep the rest of her money safe and secure.

She turned to him. "Mr. Dahlberg, when I opened my account here, you promised me all of that in front of

Mrs. Wunders. Our customers will know that this bank is no friend to women." She left the man sputtering.

***

"What can I do?" She directed the question more to herself than Letta. Feeling sick to her stomach and enraged at her husband, she couldn't keep from worrying about her business.

Letta looked at the clock on her office wall. She was angrier than Teresa had ever seen.

"That weasel!" Letta said through clenched teeth. Teresa didn't know if she was referring to Nico or Anton Dahlberg.

"You don't have to worry about the rent," she said. "And whatever you need to get through this, I can lend you. Your business is good, Teresa. You'll have it paid within a year. I know Jake and Lance will agree. Right now—"

"No, Letta, this is my problem. I underestimated Nico." She stood and paced the floor. "Not that I thought he wouldn't take my money. I just thought I had it safe enough. But I have to get the business out of my name before Nico takes that, too. I want to transfer it to you. I'd rather give it away than have him get it."

"I don't want your business, Teresa, but transferring may be a good idea—at least on paper. We've seen that we can't trust the law to protect a married woman. Come on. We have to get back to the bank today."

Letta faced Anton Dahlberg a half hour later. "I want my accounts closed now."

With a tormented sigh, and concern pulling the man's face into a sea of wrinkles, the bank president had no choice. In a few minutes, he handed a check to Letta while continuing to mutter apologies to both women and moaning about having to follow the letter of the law.

Teresa asked about Dan's account.

First Class to America

"I'm sorry, Mrs. Barile, but I'm not allowed to give you that information," Mr. Dahlberg said apologetically.

"Dan is her son. Tell her, Anton," snapped Letta.

Worry covering his face, the man "ahemed" a few times before checking his records. "Mr. Dante Barile withdrew his funds."

"All of them?" Teresa felt sick again.

"Yes, ma'am."

"And what about Alberto Barile?"

The man turned toward Letta with pleading eyes.

"Tell her," she demanded.

He examined the ledger book. "His monies are still intact."

Teresa sighed with relief. She would make sure Bert had his funds transferred by the next day.

When they returned to the real estate office, Letta lifted the receiver of her candlestick phone. "I need to let Jake know about this."

"Letta, I'd rather you didn't."

She hung up the receiver and leaned her elbows on the desk, looking at Teresa. "Listen, my friend, I don't know what's going on between you and my brother. He certainly won't tell me and it's none of my business."

Teresa didn't utter a sound.

"Well," Letta clasped her hands and rested her chin on them, "maybe it is. However, right now I'm more concerned with your business. If the law can't do something about it, maybe Jakob can." She picked the receiver up again and asked the operator for a Hartford connection.

Teresa listened as Letta told Jake what happened. They exchanged a few more words before hanging up.

"Nico is out of town for a few days, but Jake thinks he can get him back. In the meantime, he expects to see Dan this evening and find out what he knows. He'll call me at home."

"I'll be waiting for you in the morning." Teresa didn't expect to sleep much that night.

The next day, Letta's attorney drew up an agreement transferring *Tesa's Seamstress and Tailoring* businesses to a partnership that would require both her and Letta's signatures for any financial or business decisions.

Jakob called Teresa two days later to tell her that he had demanded to know what Nico did with the money he stole from his wife. "He insisted that was money you had promised him for your home in Hartford. He says it is already spent on a house he bought here, and this time I think he does intend for you to move."

***

Three tormented weeks later, Teresa heard from Nico. "Start packing, and give the good doctor your notice. I bought a home for us. You're moving to Hartford."

"I don't think so. I've got a business to run here, or have you forgotten?" She shook with anger. "How could you do such a rotten thing, Nico—steal the money I worked so hard for? I've given you enough. Did you have to take what I was saving for our children, and what I needed for my businesses?" She had promised herself she would stay calm and rational when she talked to him, but her emotions gave way. She could not let go of her fury this time.

"I left enough," he said. "You lied to me, Teresa. You told me you were just keeping what you needed for living expenses. I only took what you owed me. You'll have to sell the businesses there anyhow. That will give us money to start your business here. Don't worry, I already have a space for you. You're gonna love it."

"First of all, Nico, I am not leaving here. But if I did, I wouldn't have any money to bring, because I don't have the businesses anymore. You didn't leave me enough to keep them running. I turned them over to Letta. I work for her now."

"You what?" he shouted.

"That's right, Nico. You succeeded in making me lose everything I worked for. I have nothing left to bring to Hartford. But I don't intend to come. The children and I at least have a home here."

She could hear his angry breathing...and then silence...and then his eerily calm voice. "All right. Stay if you want, but the children are coming with me. There's a good school over here for Bert, unless he has to stay home to take care of his brother and sister."

"I won't let you take them, and they wouldn't go." She spoke with determination, though fear filled her chest. "You can't do that, Nico."

"My judge friends say I can, Teresa."

Part IV

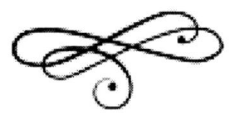

HARTFORD
1913 - 1917

Joyce Senatro

33

Leaving Philadelphia felt almost as hard as leaving Italy. I should never have left Italy, or married Nico, Teresa thought. Then she pictured life without her children, or without the friends in Philadelphia who had become surrogate family—or without Jakob. She wouldn't give up any of it.

What could she do about Jakob, though, now that she would be living in Hartford? She felt guilty at times, wondering what life might be like married to Jakob. At other times she wanted to blame him. If he hadn't manipulated her husband away from Philadelphia, she wouldn't be facing this move. But the last few years without Nico had allowed her to grow in ways she never could have otherwise. She had to find a way to get back on her feet and take care of her children. She would bide her time.

Leaving the people they had grown to love disheartened the children. They were inconsolable about parting with their pets. Dan had turned his pony over to Carl, but their father said they could not bring a pony to Hartford. Nico finally consented to Kitty and Lick coming. Both were growing old.

"You know Donal will take good care of Brownie." Teresa put her arms about the sobbing Carl. "We'll come back to visit. You can ride him then." She prayed it would happen.

There hadn't been a choice about the move. Nico made it clear he had powerful allies—including lawyers and judges. She knew he would follow up on his threat of trying to take the children away from her, and the law would always side with a husband.

"I have a fine shop ready for your dressmaking business in downtown Hartford," Nico had told her. She didn't trust him. Whatever he had set up, he would find a way to control.

Bert and Carl had the car packed full when they left early in the morning for the drive to their new home.

Letta drove Teresa and Lauri to the train station a short time later. "I'll come to see you," she promised.

Nico met them in Hartford. Teresa felt sure she would remember the hot July day as one of the dates that tore her life apart. Expecting the worse, she was relieved to see a decent neighborhood between downtown Hartford and the Connecticut River. They passed an attractive park a few blocks before turning onto Capen Street. Nico stopped the car in front of a house that typified ones Teresa had seen in Philadelphia's nicer middle class areas. The home designs were known as American Foursquare.

"The house is completely furnished," Nico said. "I knew the previous owner and was able to make a good deal." Teresa didn't ask any questions. She had long ago learned that Nico's words had no meaning.

The white frame house, with blue-grey shutters on the windows, had a large front porch that ran the full width of the house. Though not fashionable like the Janys' home, it was not unattractive. She found the inside rooms and furniture to be in good condition, but old and not to her taste. Four bedrooms and a partially finished attic made it roomy enough.

"That's Dan's room," Nico said when they reached the attic.

"Dan sleeps up here?" It was Teresa's first comment since entering the house.

"It was his idea. Gives him plenty of room."

Showing her the bedrooms, he said, "Lauri will have one of the small rooms and I—you'll be pleased to know—will take the other. I'll be gone a good deal, so I won't need much space. You, my dear wife, can have one of the large rooms. Bert and Carl will share the other, since Bert will be away at school most of the time anyhow."

He had everything mapped out. This would be her life now. His plan for separate bedrooms gave her a breath of relief. At least she wouldn't have to pretend they were a happily married couple inside their home. But what did he mean—Bert would be away at school?

"I thought you said there was a good school right here in Hartford."

"There is, but Jake said there was a better boys' prep school in Salisbury, and he's willing to pay the tuition. It'll give Bert a good start on college."

"What about Dan? He should be going to college now," she insisted. "And why is Jakob paying Bert's tuition? We should be doing that."

"Because he wants to, and can afford it, so why should we deny him the pleasure." Nico sneered. "Dan doesn't care about college anymore. He likes the work and he's getting a good business education."

Teresa didn't believe it. She would talk to Dan when they were alone.

***

Nico said nothing on the ride into town the following morning. As they turned onto Capitol Avenue, the amount of industry and factories in Hartford surprised Teresa. It hardly compared to New York and Philadelphia, but the town appeared larger and more industrialized than she expected. They passed an enormous building called the Pope Bicycle Manufacturing Company. Although she had seen people on the two wheeled machines in Philadelphia, the streets were full of men and boys on bicycles here. They easily maneuvered around the carriages and automobiles, which now outnumbered horse-drawn coaches.

Nico turned the corner onto Main Street and stopped the auto in front of a large building—not unlike the one Letta had in Philadelphia—with a huge *Hahn's Real Estate* sign over the door. Then Teresa's attention was riveted to a sign in the far front corner window.

Opening Soon
Tesa's Dressmaking and Tailoring
Shop.
The best in Connecticut.
Adult and children's clothing.
Experienced dressmakers may
apply after August 1.

Teresa wanted to run—but where to and how? She had no funds left.

"Why is my shop here, Nico? I don't want to depend on Jakob."

"I've noticed how much he likes to do things for you, my dear." Nico opened the door for her. "Since I needed all our money to buy the house, it was a perfect solution. Jake said you could set up the shop here and he would give you a loan for equipment and material to start it. After all, we need to build our account again."

She looked at him with disbelief.

"Don't worry. You won't be here long. He's going to keep ownership of the business and give you a salary—the greedy SOB. As soon as you've made enough, we'll get a place where we can be our own boss."

She stood still, too stunned to respond. Jakob set up a shop for her, but she would be working for him. And she had turned her shop in Philadelphia over to Letta. Could Nico have been right all along? After all the work she had done these past few years to build independence and a future for her children, it all belonged to others.

"Come on, Teresa. Don't just stand there," Nico barked. "Jake'll be waiting."

I'll get it back, she resolved. She may have to start over, but she did it once. She could do it again. She braced herself for the meeting with Jakob. She would make sure it was all business.

***

The next day Nico accompanied Teresa to register Lauri and Carl in school. He insisted any issues were to be addressed to him. "My wife will be busy with her new business," he told the principal. "I wouldn't want any more burdens on her. We're sure you'll see that our children are model students."

On the way out, they overheard the principal remark to his secretary, "What a nice couple. It's refreshing to see a father who is so concerned about his family."

Teresa cringed. Nico was determined to control everything.

***

She had little time to talk to Dan alone. Some days, the business kept him away almost as much as Nico, who now had a newer automobile. At least, Dan had his old one.

"The horse and buggy was getting too slow for all the places I needed to go, so Papa let me buy his car," Dan said. He was finishing breakfast before leaving for work.

"He made you pay for it?" Teresa tried to keep her voice even.

"It was the easiest way, Mamma. It's all right." Dan gave his mother a kiss on the cheek before he went out the door.

None of this is all right, she thought. But any complaint by her would only make it harder on her children. She watched Dan drive off. Being with him again was the only bright spot about their move.

※※※

Teresa forced herself into the work. From dozens of applicants, she hired two well qualified women.

Letta called her with updates about the businesses in Philadelphia. "The customers miss you, but your staff is running everything well." Letta paused. "Do we have a bad connection, Teresa, or is something wrong. You sound upset."

"No…yes. No, Letta. I shouldn't be here."

"I know. You should still be here. I miss you so. We all do."

"I miss you, too, but I meant that I shouldn't be here in Jakob's building. We shouldn't still be depending on him. I'll never be on my own again."

"Oh dear," Letta sighed. "Jake said he would explain it to you."

"Explain what?"

"Jakob put the business in his name, like I did, so Nico couldn't get your money. He knew you wouldn't like the arrangement, but it seemed safest for now. Talk to him about it. He plans to help you open an account that only you can access. You can trust his banker."

Teresa felt better, but still didn't like being indebted. Jakob probably hadn't explained anything to her because she didn't give him a chance. She had to build a successful business, though, and that meant she needed his help. With luck, she might be able to open by the first of September.

The following day she was out in the community, purchasing equipment and visiting warehouses where she could buy fabric and establish credit. That proved no problem. She only had to mention Jakob's name, and any merchant was pleased to do business and refer customers to her.

***

She made the September opening and had a sizable clientele within weeks. When word got around that Teresa made home visits for consultations, her business boomed. She soon interviewed more applicants, but couldn't find any like Hanna or Beebe.

As Christmas approached, she longed to be in Philadelphia. Jakob offered to take the children, but Teresa said no until Bert talked her into it.

"With all the changes Lauri and Carl had this year, it'll be good for them to have Christmas at Letta's. And to see the parade."

"You're right, Bert. It would be good for them. All right. Tell everyone I'll try to come in the spring." She wanted Dan to go, but Nico insisted he was needed in Hartford.

"I'd rather stay here with you, Mamma," Dan said. She knew he lied to make her feel better.

34

The day before they left, Jakob made a rare visit to Teresa's shop to tell her about the account he set up for her at the Hartford National Bank.

"Speak to the bank president. No one, including me, is to be given information about the account except you. Mr. Harrison wants you to sign the paperwork this week if you can."

"Of course. Thank you, Jakob. You know that I don't like asking you for help."

"So I've noticed," he said. "I want you to understand, Tesa. This will be your money, and only yours."

She had already repaid Jakob's initial investment and resigned that the building was a good fit for her shop and a good location. But they had not discussed rent.

"Jakob, I want your figure on a fair rent here. And where could I find estimates on what it would cost to refurbish our house? It's something I want to do as soon as I can afford to. Nico won't like it, but I'll find a way." It had been on her mind since their move.

He tapped his chin a few times while he looked at her. "For what my opinion is worth, if you want to refurbish I don't think you should put it off. Why don't you buy whatever you want, hire the workers, and have them send the bills to me. I'll work out a payment plan with you."

Her mouth opened to protest, before he added, "I'll even add interest if it will make you feel better." He suggested places to shop and gave her names of the best workers in town.

"Also, you might like to take a look at the renovations I had done to my home."

When her brow furrowed, he quickly added, "Now's the perfect time, while I'm away. My housekeeper will be there." He rolled his eyes and shook his head as he turned to leave.

"I might do that," Teresa said to his back. Her first impulse had been to reject any further loans from Jakob. However, getting her house redone before Nico thwarted her plans took preference. If her business continued to grow, she should have Jake repaid, with interest, in less than a year.

***

Dan drove her to West Hartford two days later. The still-developing community boasted fine homes with large, well-cared for lots. Teresa knew that many needy immigrants found employment as caretakers of such estates.

"This is Jakob's home?" Her eyes widened when they stopped in front of a large brick two-story, colonial style home. She didn't know why she felt surprised that he lived in such a house. She had never thought about Jakob having a real home. She noted the one story, white framed room attached to the far side of the house. Shaped like a half circle, it was made of mostly windows. Jakob had a sun room, too. The idea pleased her.

Mrs. Talon, the housekeeper, greeted them warmly, obviously glad to see Dan again. The woman appeared to be in her late forties. Matronly in appearance, her manner made Teresa feel welcome and special.

"Mr. Jakob told me you might be stopping by. I've been looking forward to meeting you."

She insisted they have tea and biscuits, and then said to Dan, "You know your way. Why don't you show your mother around?"

The home was as large as Letta's. Even with a different layout, Teresa could see the influence of Jakob's sister in the colors and furnishings he had chosen. His home, though, had more of a colonial influence inside as well as out. The rooms, rather than using high wainscoting, had fully painted or papered walls, with baseboards around the bottom. Teresa liked the effect of white woodwork throughout.

Finally, Dan took her to the large back porch, furnished with a table and comfortable outdoor chairs. It overlooked two acres of well- manicured lawn, trees and shrubs, with a large pond at the edge of a wooded area.

"Is that pond on Jakob's land?" she asked Dan.

"Of course. That's where he and I fish sometimes on weekends."

Teresa's hand covered her mouth as she blinked at tears, remembering how much Leo wanted to teach their son to fish. "I had no idea," she whispered.

Dan turned toward her. "Do you feel all right, Mamma?"

She put an arm around his waist. "I feel fine, Dante. I'm just a little overwhelmed with all this beauty. I'm glad Jakob shares it with you."

"So am I, Mamma. I don't know what I'd do without him."

On the way back to Hartford, she tried to erase from her thoughts what it would be like to live in a house like Jakob's. More specifically, she wondered what it would be like to live in Jakob's house.

***

Nico left for one of his "business trips" in early January, 1914, planning to be away at least a month. Teresa shopped for paint and wallpaper for the rooms, and material to recover the furniture. The house bustled with workmen papering, painting, and refinishing.

She hadn't asked Nico's permission. If she had no choice about the community, house or marriage she had to live in, she would, by God, choose the colors she wanted to surround herself with.

She chose an apple green theme to brighten the darkness of both downstairs and upstairs halls. Green and white striped wallpaper topped apple green wainscoting. A white settee, with green cushions, sat beside a small white table in the downstairs hall. A green vase on the table—ready for spring flowers when they bloomed—contributed to a cheerful entrance. Red stain covered the entrance hall, stairway, and upstairs floors. Large throw rugs, complimenting the colors of each newly painted room, gave smart final touches.

The children each picked their favorite bedroom colors. Lauri's room, the brightest, had hues of yellow, decorated with white and pink ruffles on everything. Bert and Carl chose crimson colors, which Teresa softened with light grey accessories. Dan had no preference. She had his attic room painted a dark blue. Pale blue and light tan fabrics, set off with tasseled shades on bedside lamps, spruced up the formerly dull attic.

Teresa selected violet and a very pale gray for her bed coverings, drapes and floor rugs. She finally had a space that felt like her own. The only room that remained untouched was Nico's.

Downstairs, the dining room and parlor shone with fresh white paint on the wainscoting and fireplaces. Flowered wallpaper with a light rose background covered the dining room walls. Chair cushions with the same pattern surrounded a new table. A pale blue and gray theme worked nicely in the parlor. Colonial blue stain on the floors blended well in both rooms.

Lastly, cream colored wainscoting in the kitchen matched the flowered wallpaper's background. Blue and brick-red colors were seen in the wallpaper and floor linoleum of the kitchen, pantry and enclosed back porch.

The only other significant change was a kerosene range Teresa ordered to replace the wood-burning kitchen stove. She decided that the ice box and copper sink were adequate for the time being, as was the upstairs bathroom, which had been added shortly before Nico bought the house.

The children delighted at the changes. Teresa asked Dan to give Jakob a tour when it was finished, but to do so while she wasn't there.

"Jake said you ought to go into home decorating, Mamma," Dan told her later. "He said no one in Hartford could have done a better job."

Teresa turned away, to not let Dan see the pleased smile that brightened her face.

"I told him it was hard to talk to you about anything these days," Dan said. "And he said, 'Don't I know it.'"

Dan watched his mother closely. She looked at him from the corner of her eye. "I'm glad you and Jakob had something to talk about."

***

Teresa saw him coming out the back door when she pulled into the driveway after work the next day. His angry expression didn't surprise her. She was determined he would not have the first word.

"Hello, Nico." She forced a smile as he yanked open her door. "Did you see how nice the house looks?"

"Where the hell did you get money to do all this?" he demanded.

"From my business, of course. You don't think I would use any of yours? But then, I don't have any of yours." When he raised his hand, she braced herself and looked directly into his eyes. She did not allow her body to flinch.

He lowered his hand, drew it into a fist by his side, and clenched his teeth. "Where did you get the money?"

"I told you, from my business. Where would you think? Have you even looked through the house to see how much better it looks, which means it will have more value when you're ready to sell?" She had gotten his attention, if only for a moment. She decided to press her advantage. "I just knew, especially in the real estate work you do, that you look toward resale value when you buy anything. And this house needed a lot of work to have resale value. Come on, let me show you." She walked past him toward the house.

He let her go a few steps before grabbing her wrist and wrenching her around. She cried out as pain shot through her arm. Then she was angry. "Don't do that, Nico. Let go of my wrist."

"You're lying to me. You didn't make enough money to pay for all this. Jake gave it to you, didn't he?" It wasn't a question.

She stopped pulling. "Let go of my arm, Nico."

"Tell me the truth." He yanked her harder.

"Papa, stop!" They both turned when Carl came running from the back of the house. Nico dropped her arm immediately. "Don't hurt Mamma," the boy cried out.

Nico forced a laugh. "Look at the little hero. You're a scrapper, just like me. I'm proud of you, son."

Carl didn't know what to say.

"Go inside, sweetheart," Teresa said quietly. "I'll be there in a minute."

"Go ahead," she said again when he hesitated. Finally he turned and walked inside.

She looked at Nico. Her words were slow and deliberate. "Nico, don't…ever…do that to me again." She turned and walked toward the back door. He climbed into his car, slammed the door and drove away.

Teresa shook as she came into the house and found Carl waiting for her.

"Are you all right, Mamma?"

"I'm fine, sweetheart." She kept her voice as calm as she could. "I'm sorry you were scared for me. Papa and I were just talking. You know how excited he gets at times. Come on, let's have some supper."

She had Lauri and Carl tucked into bed before Dan got home. It was almost nine o'clock.

"You put in long days." She gave him a hug.

"I like to talk to Jake when I get a chance, and evenings are usually his only free time. We had supper, Mamma. Don't bother fixing anything for me."

"You didn't see your father, did you?"

"No. I didn't know he was home."

"Yes." She tried to choose her words carefully. "He wasn't too pleased with the changes we made here, but I think he'll see that they make the house a better investment when he thinks about it."

"Did he hurt you, Mamma?"

"No…no. You know Papa. He'd rather things be his idea. I thought it would be a nice surprise, but …oh, well, it'll be all right," she said. "You, my darling son, go to bed now. You look tired."

He started up the stairs, and then turned to look at her. "Mamma?"

"What?" She gazed up at Dan. If he couldn't have Leo in his life, thank God he had Jakob. The thought made her aware of how important the two had become to each other.

"You'd tell me if he ever hurt you, wouldn't you?"

"Of course, but it won't happen. Now go. I'll see you in the morning."

Teresa set out dishes for the next morning's breakfast—a habit carried over from her boarding house routine—before she shut off the lights and climbed the stairs. She snuggled into bed and shut her eyes, hoping tiredness would bring sleep. Then she thought about the empty milk bottles. Had she put them out for the milkman?

"Better check." She reluctantly slipped into a robe and walked downstairs again. Turning on the hall light, she opened the front door. The bottles were there. She sighed, annoyed at herself for not remembering. She had just reached the stairs when she heard rustling and a clang in the back yard.

What now, she thought warily, the encounter with Nico still on her mind. She walked through the kitchen and looked out. It was only Lick chewing something and walking around in the fenced area they had made for him. Carl had forgotten to put him in. Teresa went out and unlocked the gate to Lick's yard. "Come on," she said, as the old dog ambled into the porch room. Back in bed a few minutes later, Teresa quickly drifted off to sleep.

An hour later, the shrill ring of the phone woke her with a start.

35

Jakob's voice was on the other end of the phone. Teresa listened, and then said, "I'll be right there." Hurrying back to her room to dress, she saw Dan standing in the hallway.

"I heard the phone, Mamma. Is anything wrong?"

"There was a fire at Jakob's building. The fire department is there now. He said most of the damage seems to be to my shop."

"I'll drive you."

"No, I need you to stay here with Lauri and Carl."

Twenty minutes later, she stared at her still smoldering dressmaking shop. The outside of the building remained intact and the upper floors were not damaged, thanks to a night guard's quick action and fast response from the efficient crew of Hartford's new, nearby fire station.

Inside, though, only two of her sewing machines had been salvaged. Water damage to them could be resolved with a good cleaning and oiling, the fire chief told her. That wasn't enough to keep business alive. She would lose it and have to let her employees go.

"He always wins." She fought back tears of anger and despair.

"What did you say?" Jakob walked back from talking with the fire chief. "Tesa, I know this is upsetting, but we'll find another place until this is repaired. You'll be back in business in a few days. Your customers will understand."

She shook her head, swiping tears from her eyes with the back of her hand. "Have you seen Nico?" Her voice shook.

"No. Is he back?"

She nodded.

"Why? You don't think Nico…This is where he works."

"It's also where you and I work."

Jakob took her arm and guided her away from the site that still teemed with firefighters and on-lookers. "What are you saying?"

She told him about Nico's reaction to the house. "I was a fool to think I could outsmart him! He was furious. I know Nico. He would have to get even. This can't be a coincidence, Jakob." She shook with fury.

"Try to calm down." Jakob held her by the shoulders. "Where do you think he is?"

"You tell me. You have a better idea than I do of who would give him an alibi."

"We have no proof."

"We'll probably never have proof, but I know. I just don't know what to do anymore." Her voice broke, the tears came, and Jakob wrapped his arms around her.

"My offer is still on the table."

She pulled away.

"I always pick the wrong time to say what you don't want to hear." He took her arm. "Let's go find the chief and see what they've discovered."

They found Chief Brennerman on the outskirts of the sewing shop, talking to his men. "We're pretty sure it was arson. There's a strong smell of kerosene in this area." He indicated the main room of the sewing shop and then turned to Teresa.

"Mrs. Barile, do you use kerosene for anything in your work?"

"No, nothing."

"Do you have any disgruntled employees?"

Teresa went through a mental image of the four women seamstresses and one male driver who now worked for her. She would trust any of them alone in her shop. She tilted her head up to look at the tall, muscular, mustached man in front of her. His manner, though strictly business, was caring and his eyes were kind.

"I pay them well, and any of them would tell you that my hours and working conditions are the best around. None of them would do this."

"What about anyone else in your life? Can you think of anyone who might want to cause harm to you or your business? This could be aimed at Mr. Hahn, of course, but it seems that your shop was the target."

Her head dropped and she said nothing for several seconds. Finally Jakob spoke.

"I have an employee, Brad. He would not be beyond harming Mrs. Barile's business to get to me."

"Oh?" The man's eyebrows shot up.

"It's Mrs. Barile's husband, Nico."

The chief looked at Teresa. "Do you have reason to suspect your husband, ma'am?"

"Tell him what happened this evening, Tesa," Jakob urged.

When she finished, the chief noted, "That hardly seems like a reason to burn you out."

"Not to you or me, but Nico has an intense need to be in control of everything, especially his wife," Jakob said. "We can't let him get away with this."

"You're right, Mr. Hahn. But we aren't accusing anyone at this point. We'll be questioning everyone, though, so let your employees know. Do you have any idea where your husband is now, ma'am?"

Teresa shook her head. "He left the house about six o'clock when I came home, and I haven't seen him since."

"We have to work with the police when arson is suspected. I'll make a report and they will question him. In the meantime, please try to consider anyone else who could be suspect for harming either of you. And be careful."

"First he takes all of my money, and now this." Teresa choked back sobs as she turned away and walked toward her car.

"Leave your car parked here. You're in no shape to drive. I'll take you home and Dan can bring you back in the morning," Jake suggested.

"Back to what...ashes!" She turned and looked up at him. A laugh, coupled with a sob, sprang from her throat. "That's what my life has felt like since I came to this country. I don't mean to be ungrateful, Jakob. You and Letta have given us the possibilities of a fine life—a great life here—but Nico will never let it happen. We should have stayed in Italy."

"Come on, Tesa. You are going to survive this. We'll get to the bottom of what happened, and I'm determined that someone is going to pay. We'll find another space for you, and my business won't suffer that much. Yours will have to be rebuilt, but we aren't going to let him win."

"He has won." She walked on toward her car.

He went after her, put his hands on her shoulders and turned her toward him. "Don't you ever say that again. Don't even allow it to be a part of your thinking. You are the stronger one, and don't ever forget it."

She looked up at him with no expression, then pulled away and walked on.

***

Teresa didn't leave the house for over a week, in spite of the collective efforts of her children and Jakob to get her out. He brought dinner every evening. She refused to move from her room while he was there, so he sat in the kitchen and ate with Laurie, Carl, and Dan, who had taken over all of his father's responsibilities for Jakob.

A week after the fire, Teresa sat quietly one evening at the top of the stairwell, listening to her children in the kitchen.

"Mamma wants to go back to Italy," Laurie said. "She said America doesn't like her, Jake. We don't want her to be sad, but we don't want to move away from you. It was bad enough leaving Philadelphia."

"Have you told that to your mother?"

Laurie nodded. "She just hugged me and said she knew. She said I shouldn't pay any attention to her, but I know that's what she wants."

"No it isn't, honey," Jakob said. "What all adults want now and then is to be able to go back to a happy time when they were children. Even grown-ups miss their parents at times, and your mother, I think, is missing her mamma right now. That's why she's thinking of Italy."

"I was born there, you know," Laurie said. "Mamma said my grandmamma thought I was the most beautiful baby she ever saw."

"That's because she never saw me," quipped Carl.

"Okay you two, it's your bedtime. Tell your mother I'll bring supper again tomorrow if she doesn't feel like cooking for you."

"Jake, Mamma isn't going to die, is she?" Carl's voice cracked.

"'Course not, champ. She's not sick. She's just sad about losing her business, but she'll get over it. You keep talking to her."

The next morning, Teresa stood by the kitchen range cooking breakfast for her children when they got up. She kissed them good-bye before Dan drove them to school, assuring her oldest son she would have a plan in place by the end of the day. She had no idea what it would be.

By late morning, she still sat at the kitchen table with a pencil and tablet, intent on making a list of what she could do to support her family. The first—and thus far only item on the list was *apply for job in sewing factory*. She would start over today. She jumped at the knock on her door.

"Letta! Oh, Letta, I am so glad to see you." Teresa threw both arms around her friend's neck.

"Have they arrested Nico?" Letta asked, after they talked awhile.

"I'm pretty sure they haven't found him yet."

"Where could he go?"

Teresa sighed and shook her head slowly. "I don't know. It isn't like him to get into obvious trouble, with so many powerful friends here. But he was so angry that he may have acted without thinking of the consequences."

"They'll find him." Letta's eyes glanced to the paper in front of Teresa. "This is your plan?"

"It's what I can do."

"Getting your business back together is what you can do."

"But... "

"No buts. Jake said your shop would be ready for business in three to four weeks. Your customers will wait that long."

Teresa sighed. "I won't put Jakob in danger again because of me."

"Stop it, Teresa. You don't think he's going to let Nico hurt his business, do you? Jakob told me to give you this and ask you to please go see the lady. She's a business friend of his and apparently she needs some help."

Letta handed her a piece of paper with a woman's name and an address just a few blocks from Jakob's business.

A woman business friend of Jakob's? What kind of help, she wondered. She had nothing to lose—might as well go meet the woman. Letta stayed to wait for the children.

Teresa drove downtown to a side street near the real estate building, stopping in front of a small two story frame house painted sky blue with yellow trim. A sign on the large front window read *Marta's Creations*. Colorful flowers bloomed in window boxes around the front and sides. The building stood out as a bright spot amid all the brown and gray business structures that dwarfed it.

How unusual, Teresa thought, wondering what kind of business it could be. She opened the front door to the tinkling of a bell. It took a few minutes for her to realize she stood in a dressmaking shop. She looked around at equipment much like hers—what she had before the fire. The rooms were smaller, but everything was there—sewing machines, dress forms, cutting tables. She hadn't known another dressmaking shop existed in this section of Hartford. Confused, she wondered why Jakob would have her set up a competitive business so near a friend's.

An older woman—probably the age her mother would be if she were still living—walked out through a curtained doorway. "Hello. May I help you?"

"I'm looking for a Marta Torrenti."

"You just found her," the woman said pleasantly. "What can I do for you?"

"I—I'm not sure," Teresa stuttered. "My name is Teresa Barile and—"

"You're Jake's friend." Teresa found herself wrapped in the older woman's tight embrace. "I'm so glad to finally meet you. I've been telling Jake to bring you by for weeks." She held Teresa by the upper arms and looked her straight in the eye. "He said you would think he was trying to force me on you; that you preferred to do things yourself. Now that may be true, but we women have to support each other, don't we?"

Teresa didn't know what to do but nod.

36

"No mystery," Marta told her later. They drank tea at a table in a small kitchen. "Jake opened his real estate about the same time my husband and I opened this sewing shop. We became business allies and friends. It's been my home and business since then, but I'm ready to make a change."

Teresa waited.

"Before my Robert died in '04, he asked Jake to keep an eye on me. The boy took him seriously," she chuckled.

Teresa smiled at "the boy" reference. "I would never have agreed to open my business in that location if I had known about yours, Mrs. Torrenti."

"Oh, that's no worry, and please call me Marta. Everyone in Hartford does." Marta waved her hand in the air. "I actually suggested it. I'm just sorry we have to meet at a time like this, though. How much did you lose?"

She suggested it? Did Teresa hear her right? "Uh, they were able to save two sewing machines and a few pieces of equipment, but most of it is gone…and all the material." Marta *suggested* it?

"That's all replaceable, dear. Your talent isn't. I hear you are quite good at what you do, which is why I've been sending most of my customers to you."

"You've been sending…why would you do that?"

"Look at me, Teresa. I'm no youngster. I've loved this business, but I'm tired. If someone like you doesn't buy the shop, one of these gray businesses," she swept her hand in the direction of the neighboring buildings, "will get it and tear it down. That would be a pity. Let me show you around, dear."

The shop was much smaller than the one at Jakob's building, but Teresa loved the bright, homey setting and efficient layout. Marta's residence was on the second floor.

"Downtown is not a good place to live these days," Marta said. "I'm planning to move to a nice tenement on Blue Hills in a couple of months. Then the business could be expanded to the second floor." She said nothing for a minute, allowing time for Teresa to think of the possibility.

"I'd like you to consider coming to work for me while your shop is being renovated. See how you like it. If you can get some of your help back, we should be able to catch up on most of your orders. My assistant and I just do alterations these days. I realize that this setting may not appeal to you for a business."

"Oh, Marta, it's a lovely setting, but I don't have the money to buy it."

"Of course you don't now. But if you do as well here as you apparently have in Philadelphia, you will be able to have me paid off in a few years. I can afford to hold the mortgage. As a woman, I avoid banks as much as possible."

Only then did Teresa notice a large picture on the wall that she recognized. It showed women marching in New York City...the Suffragette march that Letta had participated in a few years ago. She nodded toward the picture. "Were you there?"

"Oh yes, indeed," Marta said.

***

Before she made a commitment, Teresa had to make sure any earnings would be protected from Nico. She promised Marta an answer by that week-end. She could already envision Marta's shop—with the use of both up and downstairs—as the better choice for women and children. The location in Jakob's building would make a fine men's tailor shop. She took a deep breath. Like it or not, she would need his help.

The next day she and Letta drove to Jakob's real estate building. When they opened the door of his office, two police men were talking to him. Both turned to look at Teresa. She recognized the taller man as Lt. Amberson, who had already questioned her about the fire.

"Lt. O'Malley and I just came from your home, Mrs. Barile," he said, introducing the other man.

"Oh? Do you have any information about my husband, Lieutenant?"

"As a matter of fact, I was just telling Mr. Hahn here that Mr. Barile himself came into the station this morning—said he heard we were looking for him. He apparently has been out of town on business. He seemed to think you should have known that."

Teresa felt pain grab her stomach. She glanced at Jakob. His expression showed concern.

"Mrs. Barile already told you what happened with her husband the night of the fire, Lieutenant," Jakob said. "How could she have known that he was away on business? If anyone knew, it should have been me, since I'm his employer."

"He told us that, too, Mr. Hahn. But he said you give him the freedom to make his own schedule, and he reports results to you when he returns. Therefore, you wouldn't necessarily know when or where he might be all the time. Is that right?"

"That's right sometimes," Jakob said, "but Mr. Barile had just gotten back from a road trip. He hadn't given me any report yet, and would hardly have been planning to leave again the following day. He always spends a few days here to plan and schedule his next trip."

"Yes, he told us that was common. Except this time, he said he already had some contacts scheduled with business owners who would be gone if he delayed."

"Have you contacted these business men?" Jakob asked.

"He gave us the names of two. The others are already away, he said. We've been in touch with one, and he confirmed the story. I've no doubt the other will, too," Lt. Amberson said.

"You've no doubt?" Jakob's brow wrinkled.

"The other thing, Mr. Hahn," the lieutenant said, "is that he has a good alibi for the night of the fire."

"How could he?" Teresa asked incredulously.

"Oh, he can and he does, ma'am," Lt. O'Malley said. "Seems he was playing cards with one of our judges, and a couple other leading Hartford citizens."

"All night?" Jakob asked.

"No, but a good part of it. You said he left you at six o'clock?" The lieutenant addressed Teresa.

"Yes."

"Well, he was with the judge from nine-thirty 'til about one-thirty a.m. Chief Brennerman said the fire started between nine-thirty and ten o'clock."

"And he didn't leave there at all?" Jakob asked.

"Never left the room more than five minutes a couple of times to relieve himself, according to the witnesses. And they are all reliable witnesses."

Jakob shook his head. "It doesn't add up. Did he say where he was the rest of the night?"

The men glanced at each other and, for the first time, both looked uncomfortable. Finally, Lt. O'Malley said, "He was with a friend."

"A friend? Does this friend have a name?" Jakob asked.

"I'm sorry, sir," O'Malley said, "but we can't give you that information. However, we have checked the story, and the friend confirmed he was there."

"And this *friend* would also, of course, be a reliable witness."

"Mr. Hahn," Lt. Amberson said, "we know you're a reputable citizen, and we don't like this either. But someone set fire to your building and our information tells us that it couldn't be Mr. Barile."

"And you don't have any other suspects?"

"Oh, I didn't say that, sir," Lt. Amberson said.

"You have a suspect? Who?" Teresa asked.

"As a matter of fact, Mrs. Barile, we have reason to wonder about your whereabouts on the night of the fire."

Teresa grabbed for a nearby chair to steady herself. She couldn't have heard right. Then she felt Letta's arms around her, helping her sit.

"Lieutenant, I can't believe what you're implying. Mrs. Barile lost everything in that fire," Jakob snapped.

Letta spoke up. "I am Mr. Hahn's sister, gentlemen. I've known and worked with Teresa Barile for years. She is professional beyond reproach, and what you are suggesting is preposterous. Whatever would make you believe she could be considered a suspect?"

"Well, ma'am, with all due respect to your friendship and allegiance to Mrs. Barile, her husband made some pretty serious charges. He said she never wanted to move to Hartford, and that she definitely was displeased that her business was located in this building. He admitted being unhappy about the overspending she had done on the house, but he planned to work that out with his employer, who had loaned her the money. As we understand, Mr. Hahn, you had done so without consulting Mr. Barile."

Jakob looked surprised, but unshaken by the criticism. "The business was Mrs. Barile's and the 'loan' was money from her profits. It didn't involve her husband."

"As we understand from Mr. Barile's attorney, Mr. Lawrence Critterton—I'm sure you know of him, Mr. Hahn—the business may have been run by Mrs. Barile, but it was in your name, and the profits were to be administered by her husband," Lt. O'Malley said.

"Well, then, lieutenant, you understand wrong. Yes, I know of Mr. Critterton. He is a fine attorney. So is my attorney, Raymond Billings. I'm sure you've heard of him. And we are through here, Lieutenants, until I speak to him."

"I'm afraid not, Mr. Hahn. Mrs. Barile," Lt. Amberson turned toward Teresa, "unless you have reliable alibis for the night of the fire, we are going to have to take you to the police station now."

Teresa couldn't move. This couldn't be happening.

Jakob snatched up his phone receiver and dialed Ray Billings number. He gave his name to the secretary, and talked to his attorney within a minute. "Ray, I need you here now." Jakob listened a few seconds, and then hung up. "He'll be here in ten minutes. You will not ask Mrs. Barile any more questions until her attorney arrives."

"Oh, he's her attorney now?" Lt. O'Malley said. "And is Mrs. Barile paying him?"

Letta spoke up. "Yes, as a matter of fact, she is. Mrs. Barile still has a business in Philadelphia, which I administer since her move to Hartford. I am here to review the books with her. She makes quite a profit there, gentlemen, so retaining an attorney is no problem for her. She may not have been happy about the move, but she loves her business and was devastated by this loss. For you to suggest otherwise is shameful and only shows how much you have been duped by her husband."

For the first time, the officers looked uncertain.

True to his word, Ray Billings arrived a few minutes later. Jakob quickly briefed him.

"Do you want me to represent you, Mrs. Barile?" Ray asked.

"Please," Teresa said.

"All right. I want a few minutes with my client, gentlemen."

Teresa told him everything, including her suspicion that Nico's mistress had supplied an alibi for where he spent the night.

"Is there anyone who can confirm that you were home the whole time?"

"Yes, my children."

"How old are they?"

"Lauri is thirteen and Carl is almost eleven. And Dan was home about eight o'clock. He's eighteen."

"They can testify that you were home all evening?"

"Of course. I was with them until they went to bed. Dan went to his room before I did—probably eight-thirty, but he heard me get up to answer the phone later."

"Did any of them see you between nine and ten o'clock?"

"Well, no, but..." Suddenly her mouth was uncomfortably dry. "Oh, God, he's made them think I did it. What am I going to do, Mr. Billings?"

"First, let's go see what they've got. It doesn't look good right now, but I believe you. I don't want you to talk with anyone unless I am with you, understand?"

She nodded.

"Keep thinking of anything or anyone. No matter how insignificant it seems...and be prepared. They'll have plenty more questions."

37

They interrogated her again at the police station. This time Jakob and Ray were with her. Suffrage friends had told of women being abused by the police. She wasn't. It helped that Jakob was a personal friend of the chief, well respected by the officers who patrolled the downtown area, and one of the city's biggest contributors to the police department's annual fundraisers. Jakob waited outside the interrogation room while Ray went in with Teresa.

"Mrs. Barile, I'd like you to tell me everything again about the night of the fire," Chief Arnet said, talking to them in his office.

Teresa took a deep breath and began with finding Nico in the driveway.

"He had already been through the house, is that right?"

"Yes," she said. "My children—Lauri and Carl—told me that he had been there about an hour before I got home. They were excited about showing him the house, and said he walked all through it with them. He asked them questions about who had done the work, and if Jakob—Mr. Hahn—had been there. They said he didn't talk much, but that wasn't unusual for Nico. They had no idea how upset he was."

"I realize this is personal, but I have to ask. What has your marital relationship been like in recent months?"

Teresa felt herself flush. She cleared her throat. "You probably know that my husband has been living in Hartford for the past few years, and I have been living in Philadelphia, running my business there. It's true that I didn't want to move, but I also wanted to do what was best for my children. I came here willingly so they could be with their father."

"Did Mr. Hahn have anything to do with your willingness to move to Hartford?"

Her reaction to the implication was immediate. "Absolutely not. Mr. Hahn has been a good friend to both me and my husband. He was the reason my husband moved to Hartford. He offered Nico a wonderful job here."

"And you don't think he may have done that hoping you would follow?"

"I know he didn't."

"So there is no romantic link between you and Mr. Hahn?"

Teresa felt the heat of her face give her away.

Ray spoke up. "Chief, what has this line of questioning got to do with the fire?"

"Maybe nothing, Mr. Billings, but we have to explore anything that might be a motive, and extramarital affairs are often motives."

Teresa gasped. "You aren't accusing me…you can't possibly think…"

Before her attorney could object, the chief broke in. "As a matter of fact no, Mrs. Barile. I am not accusing you of anything…yet. I would like you to tell me what you know about your husband's affair, though."

"Chief Arnet, I think that's out of line," Ray said.

Teresa looked at him and shook her head. "It's all right, Mr. Billings. I do know that my husband has had more than one mistress here for several years. You already know that there is no love lost between us. If Nico is happy with someone else, that is fine with me."

"You probably know that we've questioned her," the chief said.

"I assumed you had."

"I think you should also know that the young lady had no idea Mr. Barile was married."

Teresa was sure skepticism showed through her eyes.

"We think she was telling the truth about his being with her, but it was after the fire. It just gives more credence to his story."

"But it doesn't implicate Mrs. Barile," Ray said.

"No, it doesn't," the chief admitted. "Frankly, Mrs. Barile, you are a suspect strictly because of your husband's accusations. You need a strong alibi. There is something else, though. We're sure kerosene was used to fuel the fire. Did your husband do anything that would require the use of kerosene?"

"Not that I know of."

"I understand that you recently bought a new range."

"Yes." Teresa, puzzled, answered slowly. Then she understood. She had a kerosene range, and Nico knew it. She looked directly at the chief. "My husband told you that, didn't he? Chief Arnet, I had nothing to do with that fire."

"I believe you, Mrs. Barile," the chief said.

"Then why—"

"Because your husband made serious allegations about your motives and opportunities, and there are others who do believe him. Unfortunately, you are not in a good position. All the more reason for me to question you carefully. Now, I want you to go over that night once again."

Wearily, she repeated the story, and then stopped abruptly when describing her time in the kitchen. "There is something that I forgot. I don't think it means anything, but I heard noises in the backyard. I opened the back door and saw our dog in the yard eating something…that's odd. I didn't think about it at the time, but Carl had already fed him, and he was fenced in, so what could he have been eating?"

She stopped for a minute as she pictured Lick in the fence. "Anyhow, I let him in and locked the door."

Before she could continue, the chief said, "Tell me more about that. I want you to try and remember exactly what the sounds were like and describe them to me. Take your time."

She closed her eyes for a minute. "I heard some...sort of shuffling, then a clang. It wasn't loud, just sounded like something banging together, then...that's about it."

"Could another animal have gotten in the fenced area with your dog?"

"Oh, no. The gate was locked. And Lick would have barked if there was anything moving in the yard."

"But he didn't?" said the chief.

"No. That's very strange. Maybe he did and I just didn't hear it."

"Or, maybe it was someone he was familiar with who knew what he liked to eat."

Teresa shuddered. Had someone been in her yard?

"Where do you keep your kerosene, Mrs. Barile?"

She didn't say anything for a minute, and then her words came slowly. "In two cans in an enclosed compartment under the back porch. Cans that would make a banging noise if one was moved and hit the other."

"Have you checked to see if any are missing?"

Teresa shook her head.

***

Jakob, Ray Billings, and Chief Arnet accompanied Teresa home, none surprised that she could only find one can of kerosene.

"I had two filled last week. There's only one here."

"You're sure you didn't move it?" the chief asked.

"I know I didn't."

"That gives us another concern," he said. "I'll be in touch if I find anything new, Mrs. Barile, or if I have more questions. You're not planning to go anywhere, are you?" It was not a question.

"Of course not."

Ray Billings bid them good-night. "Call me for anything, Mrs. Barile," he said.

Jakob and Teresa walked into the kitchen. Letta, who had stayed with Lauri and Carl, was still upstairs with them.

Dan burst through the door a few minutes later. "Are you all right, Mamma?" His voice overflowed with anxiety.

"I'm fine. Have the police talked to you?"

"I just came from the station. Apparently they wanted to question me away from you and I couldn't believe it when they said you were a suspect." He stomped back and forth across the kitchen floor.

"The bastard," he spit out. "Do you know what he's been doing, Jake? I spent most of the day contacting your Connecticut and Massachusetts customers. Nico hasn't been out there doing all that work for your business. He's been trying to talk these men into investing in his make-believe company—telling them you're going out of business soon; and he's booking with them. He's just been pretending to work for you while he's been taking your money!"

Teresa had never seen Dan so livid. She didn't miss the reference to "Nico" instead of "my father."

"I knew," Jakob said calmly.

Dan stopped and looked at him, astonishment covering his face. "You knew—you knew! How could you let him do it?"

"Sit down, Dan." They were in the kitchen. Jakob sat at the table, then took Teresa's hand and pulled her into a chair beside him. He waited until Dan sat.

"Your mother has known about your father's gambling for some time, but she wanted to keep it from you kids—except you aren't kids anymore."

"Mamma," Dan said, looking over at her, "is that true?"

She nodded, tears of frustration springing to her eyes.

"But that means you knew he was using your money—and mine. The money he stole from us. All of it was a scam. How could you let him do that?" Dan bounded out of the chair, throwing up his arms.

Before Teresa could answer, Jakob stood up. "Dan, sit down and calm down. Your mother doesn't need another ranting man in her life. She needs your support. Whatever she didn't tell you was to protect all of you. Now she needs you to be grown up."

Dan slumped into the chair, took a deep breath and looked at them. "What else?"

"I think you know that I have built up a good business reputation here over the years." Dan nodded.

"Most of my long term customers have become close friends. They weren't fooled by your father. When I brought him here, I thought—I really did, Tesa," he looked at Teresa, "that I could make a decent business man out of him…a respectful husband and father. I got the word back early on about what he was doing. Why did I put up with it?"

He paused, seeming to let Dan think about the question. "If he wasn't going to change, I wanted to keep him away from all of you."

Dan's brow wrinkled. "You put your business in jeopardy for us?"

"I'm not that dumb. My business was never in jeopardy. After I realized what Nico was doing, I had a talk with him first—told him he hadn't understood the assignment. I wanted to give him another chance. Next time, I put him off on clients that I knew had already made commitments elsewhere. It never affected my business."

"But…you did all that for us?" Dan frowned.

"Not just for you. I did it for me, too."

"I don't understand."

"That's because you haven't been in love yet."

"Jakob, don't…" Teresa began. He cut her off.

"Don't what, Tesa. Do you still want to pretend that your children have happy parents and all is well? Do you still want to pretend that I don't love you?"

"Oops." Letta stood in the hall doorway. "Should I go back upstairs?"

"No. Come on in, Letta. I've put this off too long."

Teresa sprang to her feet, pacing the kitchen, trying to still her heart—angry at Jakob's insensitivity. How could he bring this up now? Dan sat at the table looking bewildered. Letta sat still and quiet, but didn't look surprised.

"Dante…" Teresa began, not sure what she would say next.

Jakob spoke up. "What your mother wants you to know, I'm sure, is that she certainly has never reciprocated my feelings."

Dan looked at Jakob. "So you're saying that you put up with my father all these years because you love my mother?"

"Heck no, Dan." Jakob sat down facing Dan. "I don't just love your mother. I love all of you. Truth is, I loved you and Bert—and Lauri and Carl—way before I knew I loved your mother…ever since you came with us to that first Mummers' Parade. You were the family I always wanted."

Teresa took a deep breath. She had to get back in control. "I guess we should all be grateful to you, Jakob, but I'm in the middle of a crisis, and I will not let you sidetrack me with this…this…"

"She's right, Jake," Letta said. "Much as I know how good your heart is, we don't know where Nico is or what he might do next."

Dan stood up, frowning. He looked at his mother first, and then at Jakob. "And my mother is still a suspect."

38

Teresa stopped by Jakob's building a few mornings later to check on her shop renovations. Angry voices caught her attention as she neared his office and her heart beat faster when she recognized one as Nico's. She gasped when she heard the other voice. It was Dan's. She didn't want them together, not in her son's frame of mind.

Her hand froze on the doorknob. "Your mother won't do anything," she heard Nico say.

"She won't have to. I will," Dan threatened.

"I don't think so. You wouldn't let her name be run through the mud."

"The only mud my mother's had to run through has been you."

"You'd better watch your mouth, boy. What if I told you that your mother and your buddy Jake, here, was having an affair?"

She had to go in, but her body wouldn't move.

"I'd say good for them if it was true," Dan shot back, "but I happen to know that it's not. You, my dear father, are a lying bastard."

Teresa gasped. Her hand went to her throat at Nico's next words.

"Well it's a good thing then that I'm not your dear father. That's something your mother never told you, did she?"

Teresa burst through the door. "Nico!" she screamed. "How could you?"

"How could I what?" he spat back at her. "Tell your son that you were another man's whore? That I married you to protect your reputation?" He laughed.

The fist that shot out and connected cruelly with Nico's head belonged to Jakob.

"That was way overdue," he said to the stunned man who struggled to pick himself off the floor. No one gave him a hand. Jakob rubbed his sore fist.

"You'll be sorry about that," Nico said between clenched teeth, his narrowed eyes focused on Jakob. His hand held the side of his head.

"Don't ever come near this building again, Nico. And by the way, you're fired."

Spitting at Jakob's feet, Nico's eyes filled with revulsion. "You owe me two weeks' wages. My attorney will be in contact with you about that."

"You know what, Nico, I'm going to give you a month's wages—right now." Jakob opened a desk drawer, pulled out his checkbook, wrote a check and handed it to the fuming man in front of him. "That will give you a start in finding another job and place to live. Just don't use me for a reference."

"Oh, I have a place to live," Nico sneered. He reached out and yanked the check from Jakob. "The house on Capen Street is in my name. I'll be home for supper, my dear." He turned and stomped through the door.

Her heart still pounded from Nico's words to her son. "Dante, please let me explain…"

"You don't have to, Mamma. Bert and I sort of figured it out a long time ago."

"You figured out what?" She had a hard time breathing.

"Well, it always seemed funny to us that I looked so different from the others. One day Bert said I must have a different father. I think he was kidding then, but we talked about it later. That's why you married Nico, isn't it?"

She couldn't move. Tears spilled down her cheeks.

"You know what Bert said?"

She shook her head.

"He said if it was true, he wished that he did, too—have a different father." Dan looked down at his mother. "Where is my real father?"

"He died before you were born." Teresa choked back sobs.

"So if it wasn't for me, you wouldn't have—"

"If it wasn't for you, I wouldn't have Bert or Lauri or Carlo," Teresa said. "I wouldn't trade you or them for anything in the world."

Dan put his arms around his mother and looked at Jakob. "What can we do?"

"I'm going to explore the ownership of your house," Jakob said. "If you need to vacate for now, you'll all move in with me. I have plenty of room and a live-in housekeeper, so we'll be well chaperoned." His raised eyebrows and side glance toward Teresa indicated that should appease her.

She wiped her eyes and returned his look with a piercing stare. "I will not get out of that house—not after all the work we did to fix it up. It is our home. I may not have wanted it, but by God I will not give it up to that…that leach!"

***

"I want to meet her," Teresa said. She insisted Jakob take her to Nico's mistress. She has to know something more about Nico than she told the police."

Teresa refused to give in to Jakob's arguments to not go. He finally drove her to a fairly new section of Asylum Street, filled with apartment buildings that housed businesses on the ground floors. They stopped in front of a nice looking, five story brick building.

"How did you learn about this place?" Teresa watched him push the elevator button for the fourth floor.

"I told you, I have good friends all over this part of the country. And this woman is just one of several that

Nico has housed here over the years. I don't know how long she has been with him."

Teresa shook her head, not even surprised at this revelation.

He pushed the bell for apartment 4C. "Who is it?" a timid voice answered.

"Jake Hahn," he said. "I'm Nico's employer, Nellie." Teresa didn't miss that he knew her name.

"Just a minute." It was a long minute before the door opened.

She's just a kid, Teresa thought, staring at the thin, pale girl who peered at them from a narrow opening. She couldn't be much older than Dan…mid-twenties at the most. She was pretty—not beautiful—with long, straight blonde hair. She looked frightened, then defensive when she spied Teresa.

"Who are you?"

"I'm Nico's wife." The anger Teresa previously felt succumbed to pity.

"I didn't know he was married 'til a couple a days ago. I'd a never…I'm not that kinda girl. It wan't my fault—he never told me."

"I know," Teresa said. "I know, Nellie. Is it all right if I call you Nellie? I don't know your last name."

"Engles," the girl muttered. "Why're you here?"

"I know that my husband lied to you," Teresa said. "He's lied to all of us."

"Is that why you came—to tell me that?"

"We have four children, Nellie. Did you know that?"

She shook her head without saying anything, but she had the look of a cornered animal.

"I have to take care of them myself, because he doesn't help. Now he has accused me of something awful, and I need your help. The police talked to you about the night of the fire. I'm hoping you can think about that night again, and maybe you'll remember something more. Please," Teresa said.

"I told the police all I know," the girl said defensively. "Nico came in late. I was asleep, so I'm not sure what time, but when I looked at his watch it said 2:30, and he'd been here about a half hour by then."

Jakob and Teresa looked at one another. The alibi sounded rehearsed.

"Did he tell you where he was earlier in the evening?" Jakob asked.

"He was playing poker with some friends," she said. "The police already checked that." They were still standing by her open door.

"Nellie, may we come in and sit for just a few minutes," Jakob asked.

"I have things to do." She glanced nervously up and down the hallway.

"We'll only be a few minutes." He edged himself and Teresa in while they talked, and then closed the door.

They sat down on a worn sofa. Nellie looked uncomfortable as she chose a chair on the other side of the small, sparsely furnished room. The wall paper looked old. Two windows on the front of the building let in adequate light; but dark woodwork around the windows and floors took away any brightness to the place.

"Nellie, I'm not your enemy," Teresa said. "I'd just like you to think about my position. Please tell us about all the contact you had with my husband that day."

"I don't know any more. I have things to do now. You'll have to go, please."

"Are you scared of him?" Teresa asked.

"You have to go. I told you everything." She stood up and the shawl dropped off her shoulder. She grabbed at it, but not quick enough. Teresa saw the ugly bruise on her arm and, as the girl turned her head, a fresh red bruise was visible by her ear.

"You're hurt. Nico did that, didn't he?"

She shook her head. "No, I tripped and fell against the window sill."

"I've had bruises like that, Nellie. I know how they happen. When did he do that to you?"

She began to cry. "Please, you have to go before he comes. He'll be really mad if he knows that I let you in. Please go."

"Why are you staying here if you're afraid?" Jakob asked.

"I don't have…anywhere else," she sobbed.

"Get your clothes. You're coming with us," Teresa said.

She shook her head violently. "No, I can't. He'd kill me." She shook all over.

"You can't stay here until he beats you to a pulp, girl," Jakob said. "Do what the lady says. We're taking you out of here."

"Come on. I'll help you." Teresa reached out her hand.

Nellie stood still, looking bewildered.

"Come on, Nellie," Teresa said again. "We need to hurry before Nico comes."

The girl took Teresa's hand and followed her to the bedroom.

***

Nellie spent the night at Jakob's house with Letta and the housekeeper. Jakob insisted on staying at Teresa's home, sitting up with Dan to keep watch. Unable to sleep, Teresa saw the automobile stop out front about midnight, and then move on. They were sure it was Nico's.

"He probably saw my auto here and decided to keep going," Jakob said. "But we can't do this every night. Please come to my place."

"No. Take the children, but I will not move into your home, Jakob. Besides, if I leave, Nico will tell his lawyer that we abandoned the house and he'll get it for certain."

They were on the way to pick up Letta and take her to the train. Then they would work on a plan for Nellie.

"Listen to me, Tesa. I didn't tell you everything about Nico's gambling. He's not just making bets, he's booking them."

"You told me that before. Why is it different now?"

"Your husband is dancing with some pretty dangerous men. When we were in Nellie's apartment last night, there wasn't much furniture left."

"What do you mean—left?"

"I was there once before, with Nico. I didn't know it was his then. He told me it was a client's. Anyhow, the place was filled with expensive furniture and antiques. Nearly all of them are gone. I'm sure he's been selling them. That means he's getting desperate for money again." Jakob glanced at Teresa, and then back at the road as he turned onto his street. "He can't get it from you, but that won't stop him from trying."

"Do you think he'll sell the house?"

"Or wager it. That's how he got it—won it in a bet. He didn't buy it. He used your money for pay offs."

She looked at Jakob in astonishment. "When were you going to tell me?"

"I only found out yesterday. I had Ray check the sale. I thought you had enough bad news for the time being." He steered the automobile into his drive.

"Jakob." Her tone implied he would not like what followed. "You've tried to control my life—or protect me from bad news—ever since I came to Hartford. I know you've meant well, but controlling is what Nico has been doing all our married life. I'm pretty sick of it."

"Tesa—"

"Don't say anything." She looked away, trying to focus on a workable plan for Nellie. She nearly laughed out loud at the irony of it. Wasn't that just what she needed—another child to worry about? But she couldn't let Nico hurt the girl again. She walked to the house with Jakob trailing.

Letta's and Nellie's bags were both packed, sitting by the doorway. "We're ready," Letta said.

"We?" Teresa looked puzzled.

"That's right. We can't leave her here for Nico to find," Letta said with determination. She asked Nellie to carry her bags to the car, and then turned to Teresa.

"Nora needs more help, and they'll be good for one another. I don't think she's a bad girl, Teresa. I think she became an easy victim for Nico, and didn't know how to get away. She said her parents are both dead. Will you be all right with this?"

Teresa looked at her friend, shook her head and began laughing. "Letta, you are amazing. How could I possibly not be all right with it after all you have done for us? Yes, take the poor girl if that will work for you. It's a worry off me, but I don't want you to do it just for that."

"Of course I wouldn't."

"Remember, we don't really know anything about her, and I'm sure there is more that she hasn't told us about the night of the fire."

"When we get away from here, she'll feel safer. I'll talk to her then."

When they reached the train station, Nellie reached out timidly to touch Teresa's arm and thank her "for saving me."

Now she had to find a way to save herself.

39

Two days later, Jakob came to Marta's shop to tell Teresa about the phone call from his sister.

"Nellie wouldn't say anything until she was away from Hartford. She told Letta that Nico came to the apartment about six-thirty that night. She saw him talking to the caretaker's teenage son—called him a 'thug'—said he's often in trouble. Then they left together in Nico's car. The kid came back around midnight, apparently walking. Nico came in about two o'clock, after the game I guess, and left again with the boy. They were back an hour or so later. Nico pounded on Nellie when she asked where he'd been, said it was none of her business and she'd better not tell anyone if she knew what was good for her. He told her exactly what to say if anyone asked."

Jakob huffed out an angry breath. "I'm going to see Chief Arnet right now and I think you should come with me."

"Of course I should," Teresa said. "I just have to let Marta know."

"How did everything go last night?" Jakob asked when they were on the way. He had hired two police friends—after getting her permission—to take turns keeping watch at Teresa's home overnight.

"I slept much better with someone there," she admitted.

***

"I thought there was more to it than she told us." Chief Arnet had finished listening to Jakob tell about Nellie's story. He also had news for them.

"A neighbor said Nico had been by the apartment last night, but left a little while later. I'm guessing that he's a worried man since he found the mistress gone. He could be on the run. Do either of you have any idea where he might go?"

Teresa shook her head.

"He wouldn't go to anyone locally. He might try contacting gambling friends if he has money," Jakob said, "but I'm pretty sure Nico is broke. He probably owes them money. I suspect he's on the run."

"We'd better get to that kid before he takes off, too," the chief said.

***

They found him hiding in the basement of the apartment building. The boy crouched behind a box of wood. He told them he had been successful in evading their first search of the area. This time, he could tolerate the mustiness and dampness only so long before a sneeze gave him away. A small, defiant looking seventeen year old, Jeremiah could have passed for fourteen.

"Jer's been a problem to us since he was twelve." The father's voice was filled with irritation.

Chief Arnet confirmed that the boy was known to the Hartford police as a member of a youth gang that pillaged downtown neighborhoods. He'd been lucky enough to slip away in the past when they made arrests of other gang members. His luck had finally run out.

When the chief questioned him about the night of the fire, an anguished Jer said, "He'll kill me if I tell you."

"I'll kill you if you don't," growled his father. "It's time you owned up to the things you been doin' around here, like a man."

"It—it was his idea. I woulda never done nothin' like that, but he said no one'd get hurt, and he'd give me a lotta money. He said he just wanted to send a message to 'the bitch'—them's his words, not mine. I'd never call a lady a bitch."

"Course you wouldn't," the chief said. "Okay son, you'd better tell us everything that happened that night if you want to save any part of your hide. Now start with when Nico first talked to you."

It tumbled out then. He told them that Nico had found him hanging out on the corner of their street about 6:30 that evening.

***

After stopping at his apartment, Nico drove the boy to Capen Street, parking a few doors from the house. They waited until the downstairs light went out. He told Jeremy exactly where to find the kerosene. Nico also gave him Lick's name and had a piece of meat to keep the dog quiet.

"He won't care about nothin' else after you give him that to chew on," Nico told him.

It was dark under the house, and the kid banged the can against a post getting it out.

"That would have been the noise you heard," the chief told Teresa.

Then Nico drove Jeremy downtown to Jakob's building and showed him where to start the fire. "Just break one of those windows." He pointed to the front of Teresa's sewing shop. "Wait 'til you make sure no one's around. It'll only take a few minutes to get in and out. I'll be long gone, but you can walk home. Just make sure it's burnin' good 'fore you leave." It was about nine-fifteen when Nico dropped him off.

Jeremy waited until he saw the night watchman circle to the back of the building. He broke the window and didn't even need to climb in to get the kerosene thrown around the floor inside. After lighting, and throwing in one of the matches Nico had given him, the front drapes ignited within a few seconds. The blaze spread quickly from there. By then, the boy was a safe distance away. He hid the can in some bushes and began his trek home.

As he had promised, Nico returned by two o'clock in the morning, stopping at his apartment first. Then he picked up Jer and took him back to find the can. They drove by the still smoldering building.

"Good job," Nico told the boy. They discarded the can in a woodsy area outside of town, and then Nico stopped by a stream where he had Jeremy help him wipe down the backseat and floor, trying to get rid of the kerosene smell. He handed over the "lotta' money" that he had promised...all two dollars of it.

"You told me I was getting' a lotta money. You call this a lot?"

"Listen, kid," Nico said, "that's a million bucks to a punk like you. When did you ever make that kinda' cash for an hour's work?"

"Well, I expected more," Jer said.

"You'll get more, kid, if you ever say a word about this night to anyone, you hear? Wherever you are, I'll find you. Remember this—in the future, I could have more work for you if you keep your nose straight. If you don't, you won't have a nose left to worry about. Do you understand me?"

"That's fine, Nico. Sure, that's fine. I'll help you anytime," Jer told him, feeling the threat.

When he finished, the chief said, "It was pretty exciting, huh?"

"Well, I guess—but I wouldn' do nothin' like that again, chief, honest."

"I'm sure you wouldn't. I do appreciate your cooperation today, son, and I'll make sure the judge knows about it."

He clicked handcuffs on Jer before another officer took the boy away.

***

A month later they still hadn't found Nico. Teresa now worked full time managing Marta's shop. She consulted Ray Billings about getting the house in her name.

"Legally, the house is in Nico's name. However, under the circumstances I think a judge might turn ownership over to you."

It should have been that easy, but the record showed that Nico had remortgaged the house recently, in order to take out a large loan.

"How many times? How many times do I have to pay off his debts?" She slapped her hand on Ray's desk.

"I'm sorry, Teresa. The bank doesn't care who pays it off, as long as it's paid. Otherwise, they get the house. Are you sure you want it?"

"Oh, I want it. Would I love to go back to Philadelphia? Yes!" She blew out a breath. "But Philadelphia has changed. There's too much control by crime bosses now. I'd worry about my children there. Here, they're in good schools, I have a decent job, and I've put so much effort into that house. I just want to make certain that it will be in my name only. Can we do that, Ray?"

"We'll talk to Mr. Harrison tomorrow."

Reluctantly, she asked Jakob to come with them, "…because, well, I need your influence." She forced out the words.

He made her wait while he chewed on his lip. His brow wrinkled as he contemplated the request. He finally said, "Let me see if I understand. I'm not supposed to interfere, unless you need me, and you'll let me know when that is. Do I have it right?"

Teresa sighed in exasperation. "Darn, Jakob. Now you are twisting everything. You know women aren't taken seriously when they go to businesses by themselves. Yes, I need your help. Are you satisfied, and will you come with me?"

His brow smoothed and his voice softened. "I know it's not fair, Tesa. Of course I'll help you. And thank you for asking."

***

Teresa sighed in frustration the next day when they talked to the bank president. "We have been unsuccessful in making contact with your husband, Mrs. Barile," he told her. "We will be happy if you make the payments, but unless you pay off the mortgage, we can't transfer ownership to you. The house is actually due to become the property of the bank by the close of business today. Mr. Barile was told that when he remortgaged. I'm sorry you didn't know, ma'am."

They were going to lose the house. Shock registered on Teresa's face and the taste of panic filled her throat.

"But anyone who could pay off the mortgage would own the house, is that right?" Jakob asked.

Mr. Taylor nodded. "After today, that's right."

The next day, Jakob owned the Capen Street house. Teresa refused to allow him to put it in her name until she paid him in full, with interest. She had Ray Billings draw up a contract.

Finally, her home was out of Nico's name. Someday it would be in hers.

40

By 1915, they read of munitions factories springing up around the country, with one of the biggest—the Colt Manufacturing Company—in Hartford. The war in Europe became a mixed blessing to America. Even though President Wilson assured the country that "America is too proud to fight," he agreed to send ammunitions to the allies.

"Do you think the food lines will end, now that there is more work?" Teresa asked Jakob one morning when she stopped by his real estate office to pay her rent. She had watched the soup lines grow in the past year. Memories of New York, and the fear of homelessness through those years, crept into her mind.

"It's already made a difference," Jakob said. "In fact, with so few immigrants coming into the country now, factories are even hiring women to keep up with the demand for ammunition and war supplies."

"It's a sad thing when it takes a war to make our economy better, and to finally give women a chance to do men's work." Teresa shook her head. "Jakob, you do think it will be over soon, don't you…the war, I mean?"

"Are you worried about your boys?"

"Dan is old enough to go, you know, and Bert soon will be. I can see both of them thinking it would be their duty, if our country did enter the fighting." Her voice cracked, giving away concern that had been growing as war reports headlined the daily news.

"Don't worry. Your boys have plenty to keep them busy right here. I've not heard them say anything about the glamour of war, and the president has promised that America will stay out of it." Jakob sounded confident, but another concern pulled his brow into a frown.

"I hope you're right." Teresa turned toward the door, and then looked back. "What else is worrying you?"

"It's these labor unions. I know they can be a good thing for the employees, but some of the leaders are encouraging strikes, and the uprisings have gotten downright dangerous in places." Jakob served on a committee to prevent the kind of bloodshed in Hartford that other cities had experienced when they refused to deal with unions.

"Is there anything Marta and I need to know?"

He shook his head. "You already pay your employees better wages than the unions demand, and give them better benefits." He tightened his lips. "The Underwood Typing Factory downtown doesn't seem to have the employee problems they did before the Suffragist involvement last year, but the sewing factory is another story. Their wages and work conditions are pretty pitiful, and the use of children is especially troubling. Some of the ladies have tried picketing, but they're being harassed and assaulted. Ray and I are going to talk with the owners tomorrow."

"Does it only happen in women's work places?"

"No, but you know the law doesn't protect women like it does men. Tesa, please don't get involved in this."

She sighed. "I can tell that you don't approve of the Suffrage organizations, but it's the only way women can stand up for their rights."

He raised his eyebrows. "That's perceptive, but not quite true, you know. I support all the reasons for the Suffrage movement. I just don't want to see you, or my sister and niece in Philadelphia, get hurt."

"Do you know that Isabella Beecher Hooker started the Connecticut Suffrage movement right here in Hartford? It's big here, and now Lauri wants to come to the meetings with me. I love her spirit, but I do have concern for her."

He sighed. "I should have known. She's just like Abbie. She told me she's decided to be a teacher now instead of a nurse."

"I think it might be her calling," Teresa said. "I know she's young, but she loves school, and she's heard that teachers are badly needed, '...and their pay is disgraceful, Mamma.'" Teresa imitated her daughter. "She wants to make a difference and she sees Suffrage and teaching as the way to do it."

Jakob shook his head and sighed. "It's as pointless talking to you two as it is to Letta and Abbie. Just promise you'll be careful...both of you, please."

***

Marta's Creations became *Marta's and Tesa's Creations*. Women were choosing shorter dresses that rose above the ankles and allowed more freedom in movement. Most had given up the stiff corset for the lighter support of a girdle. And a new garment for the breasts, called a brassier, was growing in popularity.

The renovated shop in Jakob's building became a tailor shop for men's fashions. Teresa found a husband and wife team—both skilled tailors—to manage it. She began to despair, though, of finding the right person to run her children's program in Hartford. And then Betts showed up.

The young woman looked to be in her late teens. She walked with a noticeable limp, and her long dress did not cover the thick soled shoe on her right foot. But Teresa's attention quickly focused on the most striking eyes she had ever seen. Almost emerald colored, they were offset by long thick black lashes. The girl's flawless skin reminded Teresa of the cream at the top of milk bottles, and a contagious smile lit up the young woman's face.

Her clothes were obviously not new, but were clean, pressed, and tastefully put together. She wore her brown hair shorter than most girls. It fell just to her collar line in springy curls that hung beneath a soft green hat.

"May I help you?" Teresa asked.

"I'd like to talk to the person in charge." She had a soft, but confident voice.

"That would be me." Teresa introduced herself and invited the girl into her office, admiring the ease with which she moved in spite of the limp.

The young woman sat down and thrust a hand toward Teresa. "My name is Elizabeth Cummins. I'm called Betts."

Teresa reached out, surprised and impressed with the outgoing manner and strong handshake. "It's very nice to meet you, Elizabeth Cummins...Betts. How can I help you today?"

"I would like to work for you," the girl said. Most applicants simply said they wanted a job.

"Is there a reason you especially want to work here? Do you sew?"

"Yes, and yes," she answered. "I just moved to Hartford with my parents. We came from New York. A lady at church told me about your shop—said it was the best in the city. When she told me it was run by a woman, I knew this is where I should be."

"How old are you, Betts?"

"I'm almost eighteen. Please don't think my limp impairs my ability. I'm a very hard worker."

"I believe you," said Teresa.

"I am also a good seamstress. My mother taught me how to sew before I started school."

"Well, I might be able to use some part time help, but I don't have a full time opening right now. Let me show you through the shop while you tell me more about your experience, and we'll talk about whether this is the right place for you."

Teresa walked slowly to not hurry the young woman, but found that Betts had no trouble keeping up. First, they climbed the stairs to the sewing room.

Betts eyes widened. "I've never seen such a room."

Seamstresses' feet vigorously pumped treadles at sewing machines spaced around a large, sunny room. White woodwork framed pale yellow walls. Cutters, at each of two long tables, snipped around patterns laid on new materials that would soon be ready for the sewers. Three women sat by windows, taking advantage of the best light for hemming and hand stitching.

"You can see that we are small, but productive. Everything we do here is individual, unlike the factories," Teresa told her. "This room takes up most of the second floor space. There is a small kitchen and a water closet, too, so the women can take breaks and have their lunch."

"It's wonderful," the girl exclaimed. "Mrs. Barile, I'd be willing to work without pay for a few weeks, to show you how good I can be."

"That's a generous offer, Betts, but if you work, I will pay you."

Downstairs again, Teresa showed her the fitting rooms. Then they passed a closed door.

"What's that room?" Betts asked.

Teresa turned back to open the door. "We're saving this for our children's room, when we find the right person." She described Sara's Place in Philadelphia.

Betts eyes lit up. "I love children. I'm good with them. I could do that. I'd love to do that!"

***

At first Teresa took the girl with her to the homes of customers with children. It didn't take long to see that she wasn't just good with children, she was magical. All youngsters were curious about her limp, and Betts used it as a conversation opener.

"I was just born different," she told them unabashedly. "This leg didn't grow as long as this one." She pointed to her ankles, and showed them her shoes, with a thicker sole on one than the other. The children found they could talk with her about anything, and they did.

"I've found my Beebe!" Teresa told Letta that night on the telephone.

She and Betts shopped for furniture and had the room ready to open for their young customers within two weeks. Teresa set it up much like the one in Philadelphia, including a piano. But she used sky blue and sunset red for the background colors, with floating clouds, instead of rainbows. Teresa asked the talented Betts to paint the bright, cheerful sign for "Eva's Place."

41

Teresa assumed it was another request for a child's fitting when the phone rang in June, until she heard Jakob's sad tone.

"I have some bad news. Can you take a few minutes away?"

"Yes, but..." her heart thumped with anxiety.

"I'll be right there."

She waited for him outside, sure the news had something to do with Nico. He opened the door of his automobile for her.

"It's Nora, Tesa. She died early this morning. Letta didn't want to tell you over the phone."

Teresa couldn't get her head to accept the words she heard. She had known that Mamma was dying when she went to Italy, so she had been prepared. Letta talked about Nora not feeling well...but dying? The children saw her last Christmas, and Teresa planned to return this year. Nora had to be there.

"No. You didn't hear it right. I'm going to spend Christmas with her. She's making my favorite pie. She promised. She couldn't have died."

"Tesa, I'm sorry...I'm so sorry." He reached for her.

She pushed him away, opened the car door and bounded out, walking briskly for almost a block. He didn't go after her. She turned and walked back slowly, her face covered with tears.

Jakob stepped out of the car and waited. This time he didn't open his arms, but she walked into them anyhow. She let him hold her, while she sobbed out her grief. Finally, she pulled back.

"How am I going to tell the children?"

"Do you want me to tell them?"

"No...maybe. I don't know if I can. No, I have to. Jakob, I think it might be better if you tell Dan and Bert, though. I'll tell Lauri and Carl. I have to go home to them now. I can't work anymore today, but—"

"I'll let Betts know, and I'm driving you home." He didn't ask and she didn't argue.

This was the first loss her children had to face since their sister's death, and they were youngsters then. The news stunned Dan and Bert. Teresa had never seen them look so sad, nor had she seen them cry since they were small. Lauri burst into tears, while Teresa held her. Carl refused to believe that his Nora could be gone. He would have to go to Philadelphia and see for himself.

***

Early the next morning, they all squeezed into Jakob's new 1915 Ford Model T Town car, to make the trip in one long day. More roads were paved in the past few years, including the recently opened Lincoln Highway. By evening, as the tired group drove through downtown Philadelphia, Teresa realized how much it had changed in two years.

"Maybe I just don't remember how crowded it was," she said. "Hartford is a prettier town, isn't it?"

Jakob's eyes shifted toward her in a smug glance.

"Don't say a word," she said.

He didn't.

Then they were on the outskirts of the city, with the beautiful mansions and estates as breathtaking as she remembered. Letta's house came into view. Teresa felt a tightening in her heart as they neared. Her first homecoming should not have been for this. What could she say to Donal?

***

After tearful hugs, Letta walked them toward the parlor, where Nora was laid out. Teresa waited by the door for the children to say their goodbyes, and then couldn't make her feet move into the parlor. Thoughts of walking into this same room when Eva died made Teresa immobile. She caught the image of a dark wood, shiny casket in a room filled with flowers. Nora couldn't be there. She had to be in the kitchen, cooking something special for them.

Years of memories flooded her mind. Nora was the loving grandmother her children never had, who made them feel special no matter what they had done, and gently reminded them of better ways. Nora encouraged them to do more than they ever thought they could. She made their favorite foods. It felt like losing Mamma again.

"I can't go in now," Teresa said. "I'll come back later." She ran up to her room, fell onto the bed exhausted and slept through the night.

The sights and sounds that greeted them at Nora's service the next day were incredulous. An Irish ballad floated through the air from the Victrola in the parlor, which buzzed with conversations. Aromas of baked goods, tea and hot chocolate drifted to their nostrils. Huge bouquets of flowers, and balloons making dancing shadows on the walls, brightened the rooms.

Overwhelmed at seeing her old friends again, Teresa couldn't tell if she was laughing or crying. They were all there—Sam and Bea, Annie and Johnny, Hanna and Magan...so many others. And then she saw Donal, standing toward the back, waiting for her. That's when she knew she was crying. He held her and rocked back and forth with her, stroking her hair and telling her it was all right.

"My Nora's been hatin' the way she's been feelin' this last year, and all the things she couldn't do anymore.

She knew, before the rest of us, that this time was coming. She talked to me many times about it. I didn't want to listen, but she talked anyhow. You know, I could never shut that woman up when she had something to say."

Teresa laughed through her tears, while he wiped her eyes with his handkerchief. "Now blow your nose and come with me to see her."

Teresa froze. "I can't. Donal, I can't see her like that."

"Yes, you can, girl. You have to say goodbye. She will come back to haunt you if you don't. She said she wanted no tears—but that's too much to promise—and no morbid talk. She wanted good music, good food, and good friends to gather and remember the happy times."

Teresa looked around. It seemed that Nora had her wish. Then Letta was on the other side of her and the three walked to the casket together.

"Listen to our girl weep, Nora," Donal said. "The rest of us have been talkin' to you for a couple o' days now, but it's new to Teresa. You'll have to help her, darlin'. She doesn't know how much fun you're havin' up there. Let 'er know how nice it is to eat all the cake ye want without harmin' yer pretty figger or havin' to do the clean up after."

He stopped and blew his nose, and then put a hand on Teresa's arm. "It's party time all day long for my sweetheart now. Don't feel bad for her. She's not tired anymore."

Reverend Hoyt, from Letta's church, conducted the graveside service. It was a warm, sunny day in August, 1915. They laid Nora to rest beside Eva.

42

With *Marta's and Tesa's Creations* fully staffed and turning a good profit, Teresa felt comfortable going to Philadelphia for the 1916 Christmas holidays. It would be the first Yuletide season back with her "family."

Jakob planned to go, of course, and it didn't make sense to drive two cars, he pointed out. Frugality always won out with Teresa. She, Lauri and Carl drove down with Jakob. Dan and Bert were coming later by train.

"I've been good about not encroaching on your independence, haven't I?" Jakob asked as they speeded along at more than forty miles an hour on the better paved roads.

"You have," she agreed, "and it only makes me feel guiltier."

"Good God, girl," he said. "What can I possibly do to not make you feel angry, sad, guilty, or heaven knows what. Is there anything in this world that I could do that would just make you happy?"

"Jakob, we've had these discussions before. It would make me happy to see you have a life of your own, not feeling as though you have to always take care of me."

"Get it through your head—"

She put a finger to her lips. Lauri and Carl sat in the back of the automobile. Road and motor noises made it hard enough to carry on a conversation when side by side, but Teresa did not want to chance them overhearing this discussion.

Jake began again, this time in a harsh whisper. "Get it through your stubborn head that you are my life. I would change it if I could, but I can't control my feelings. I will be a happy man when we are married, and that is my life's goal. If we both have to hobble to the altar on canes, I am here until death do us part, legal or not. Until you look me in the eye and convince me that you don't love me, get used to it."

"I can't do that," she whimpered.

"You can't do what?"

"I can't look at you and say those words."

"What words, Tesa?"

"You know."

"Damn it, Teresa," he hissed, "what words?"

"I can't say that I don't love you. There, are you satisfied?" she snapped back.

He looked straight ahead, not saying a word. Her eyes shifted just enough to see his smile. She folded her arms and heaved a sigh.

Finally, he stole a glance. "Well, how many years have I waited for that little bit? But it's gigantic to me, sweetheart. And here we are, driving down the middle of the road, with your kids in the back. I can't even take you in my arms and kiss you, and I want to do that more than anything in the world right now."

"Jakob, don't you dare. I will move to the back right now if you stop this car."

"Oh, don't worry. I'm not going to embarrass you here and now, but I don't know who you think you're fooling. Your children all know how I feel about you. Wouldn't you like to be in my arms? Tell me the truth this time."

She pursed her lips, and then nodded ever so slightly. He reached over and took her hand, until he had to grab the wheel again at the next curve. The Model T was a great car, but safety demanded two hands for steering.

That night, when most of the others were in bed, he took Teresa by the hand. "Let's go see how Brownie's doing."

She put on her heavy coat to ward off the chill of the snowy winter weather.

"Now." Jakob pulled her into the barn. "I want to hold you and kiss you and... and just that. What I don't want is for you to go crazy on me again and run. Please, Teresa, may I kiss you?"

His hand cradled her chin, with her head tilted toward his. "Jakob, I can't marry you when I'm still married to Nico," she said sadly. There had been no word from or about him since his disappearance almost three years earlier.

"That's a leap, isn't it? I'm not asking you to marry me this instant. I just want to kiss you. All you have to do is nod."

She nodded. It was a soft, gentle kiss, but it rippled through her body like the pluck of a violin string.

"I love you, Teresa Barile. I love you and, when we can get you free, I want to change that name to Hahn. I am a patient man. You should know that by now. However long it takes, I plan to marry you. And I'll never be your dictator."

Her whole body sighed. Leaning against Jakob, she could hear the beating of his heart. "I love you, too. I have for so many years. It's a relief to finally say it, but—"

He put a finger on her lips. "No buts. Don't spoil the moment with anything else."

This time the kiss was long and hungry. She felt stirrings in her body that she hadn't felt since she was with Leo. She made herself pull away and he didn't try to stop her.

"I told you I only wanted to kiss you tonight. That's not true, but the rest will wait until we're married. I won't rush you."

"I know. It's just...never mind. I know you won't." This time she stood on tiptoe and kissed him on the cheek.

They sat down on the straw, her head resting on his shoulder, and talked about what needed to be done to set her free. Then he asked her to tell him about Leo, and she asked him to tell her about Margaret.

***

A bigger, brighter than ever Mummers Parade was planned for downtown Philadelphia in January, 1917. Daily news focused on the worsening war in Europe, and Americans worried about a possible involvement, in spite of the president's assurance. Philadelphians were ready for the parade's diversion.

"Mamma, we're old enough to go by ourselves," Lauri said, referring to herself and Carl.

"Even in Hartford, I don't think I'd want my thirteen and fifteen year old children walking the downtown streets by themselves. Philadelphia isn't safe like it used to be. You can go on without us, but only if you stay with Dan and Bert."

"We'll watch them," the older boys promised.

Letta's real estate building hummed with staff who brought their families to watch the parade from the warmth and safety of her front windows. She and Donal were in her upstairs office, mingling with friends. Jakob and Teresa watched from the street level windows of Tesa's shop.

"It isn't the same, having to look through bars," Teresa said. Letta had bars installed on the front doors and downstairs windows a couple of years earlier, when nearby businesses suffered a series of break-ins.

"The world isn't the same," Jakob said. "Some of it isn't as good. Some of it is much better. It's life. We change what we can, but there are times when things can't be made the way we want."

"These crime waves—why can't our police do more to protect us?"

"I guess because our laws aren't as powerful as the mob's laws. I don't know if they ever will be."

"The world would be a better place if women had more control. Jakob, if we ever marry, you have to understand that I want to continue my involvement with the women's groups."

"I'll come with you if they allow men. I have no problem with women having the same rights as men."

She took a step away, folded her arms and looked him over.

"I'm quite a guy, Mrs. Barile. You couldn't do better," he said.

"I think just maybe you are, Mr. Hahn." She stepped into his open arms, vowing she would see Ray Billings about filing for a divorce as soon as they returned to Hartford.

***

That night, after she finished packing for their trip home the next day, Teresa walked toward the stairs, intending to get a shawl she left downstairs. She trod softly to not disturb anyone, sure all were in bed by then. Voices in the downstairs hall stopped her. She didn't plan to eavesdrop, but couldn't make herself move away. The voices belonged to Letta and Donal.

"Whatever you want to do, love," Donal said, "is all right with me."

"I think we should tell them soon, Donal, but not just now. We have awhile 'til the wedding," Letta said.

"Whatever you think. You're not scared, are you, or embarrassed?"

"Embarrassed about us? Never. It's just that it's been less than two years since Nora…"

"My Nora would be our biggest supporter, darlin'. Don't you ever be concerned about that."

Teresa tiptoed back to her room.

43

"I don't like you being here alone," Betts said. She set the *Closed* sign in the shop window and walked back to Teresa's office. It was the middle of January, when the dark curtain of winter evenings fell early. "Do you want me to lock the door?"

Teresa looked up from her papers. "No, I'll be leaving in a couple of minutes. I just have to sign this letter and post it. You go ahead. I'll see you in the morning."

When the front door opened a few minutes later, she was sure it was Betts again. "Did you forget something?" she called.

"Matter a fact, I did. I think it was my wife."

Panic slammed through her body. After all this time, was her fear irrational? She didn't know. She stood, but had no way of escaping. He would already be in the front room. She could try to call for help. Her heart beat wildly as she grabbed the phone receiver and waited for the operator.

"Put the phone down, Teresa." Nico stood in the doorway of her office.

How much could she pretend? She had to keep her voice steady. She thought of the small handgun Jakob bought and insisted she carry after Nico had disappeared. He forced her to practice every day for weeks. She had changed handbags and, in her rush, forgot the gun. It was at home. Dumb, Teresa, dumb!

"I'm talking to a customer, Nico. I'll just be a minute. Have a seat. You should have let me know you were coming. My assistant will be back shortly." Keep him calm.

She heard the ring and operator's voice. Before she could answer, he stepped to the desk, grabbed the phone from her hand and slammed it onto the receiver. "I don't think so, Teresa. I just saw her leaving."

Feelings of fear, and then anger that she hadn't dealt with for almost three years, rushed back. "You have no right to walk in here like you belong, Nico. Where have you been all this time? What have you been doing?" She stopped.

This was Nico. She didn't want to make him defensive. She took a deep breath and noticed that he didn't look well. He was disheveled, extremely thin and pale. She may be quivering inside, but Nico shook visibly.

"Listen to Mrs. High and Mighty. You owe me, you know."

Her resolve to keep calm gave way to fury at his incredulous righteousness. "I can't believe you would say something like that. How do I owe you? You burned my business, and stole my money. You left me and your children broke, Nico. I owe you nothing." She slammed her right hand onto the desk.

He crashed his on top of hers. She cried out in pain.

"What did you do with Nell?" he demanded. "And I wasn't near your business when it burned. If that bitch told you I had anything to do with it, she's a liar. Who would believe a whore, anyhow? You sent the police after me with your damn lies." He ground his fist into the back of her hand.

She heard the bones crack as pain radiated through her entire arm. She screamed. "Nico, stop!"

"You always have someone to take care of you, don't you? Look at you here. Life's been easy for you, Teresa. But you haven't made it easy for me. You got more than your share. Now you share with me. I know you have money here. Give it to me."

He grabbed her hair and pulled her face into his. "Do you hear me, bitch. You tried to hide all your money from me. If you hadn't done that, I wouldn't 'v had to take it from you. You owe me, you hear?" He shoved her back against the chair.

She fell into it, holding the hand that now throbbed with excruciating pain.

"Do I tear this place apart or are you gonna tell me where you keep the money?"

"We don't keep it here, Nico. I'll give you all I have." She used her good hand and tossed her pocketbook to him.

He snatched the bag and tore into it. "You think I'm a fool? I know you got more. If you know what's good for you, you'd better tell me where it is."

"I'm telling you the truth. There isn't any here. The girl who works for me takes our money to the bank every night on her way home."

"Liar," he screamed, and slammed the back of his hand across her face. "You are a damn liar."

Her head spun. She thought she would throw up.

He pulled out the drawers of her desk, tossing everything onto the floor.

He's going to kill me, she thought. She couldn't get by him to run for the door. Even if she could break a window and scream, at this time of day no one would be around to hear. What could she do? He would kill her and no one would ever know who did it.

Her head throbbed and she couldn't lift the useless, painful hand. She had to think, or she would die. She almost laughed. How would thinking save her? Nico was beyond reasoning. Nothing could save her. He'd kill her and take the pitiful few dollars from her purse, and it was all so worthless.

A wetness ran out of the side of her mouth. Blood dripped onto her dress. She looked around desperately. A letter opener lay on the corner of her desk. She inched her left hand toward it. Her fingers wrapped around the handle and she slid it into her dress pocket just as Nico turned and screamed at her again.

"Where is it?" He grabbed her by the shoulders and shook until she thought she would pass out. Then he pulled a gun out of his jacket pocket and pointed it at her. "If you want to live, tell me where the damn money is."

"There isn't any here...I'm telling you the truth." Her voice slurred.

He heaved her chair onto the floor. She fell on her injured hand and cried out as pain jolted through her body.

Nico stormed down the hall into Eva's Room. Teresa heard drawers pulled out and stands knocked over as he searched the room. She had to get up and try to call someone.

"Mamma, you still here?" Bert's voice came from the front door.

She should have been relieved. But Nico's behavior was insane and he had a gun. She could face her own death, but not her son's. She couldn't let him come in.

Teresa tried to steady her voice as she called out, "I'm leaving in a minute, Bert. Go on home."

He was already at her office door. "Mamma, what happened?" He rushed to help her up and ease her into the chair. "What happened?" he asked again, his eyes flashing alarm. They heard the footsteps.

"Call the police," Teresa whispered, and then looked up.

Nico stood in the room with his gun pointed at them.

"Alberto," he said. He lowered the shaking gun, though his finger remained on the trigger. "Stay where you are, son."

"Papa," Bert said, looking at Nico, and then back at his mother. His face contorted with rage. "You did this?" He didn't need an answer. He moved toward his father.

Nico raised the gun. "Don't come closer, Bert. You don' unnerstan. I just came here t' ask your mother to help me. I'm sick, son. I need help. She don't care. She never cared. I know tha's not what she told you, but she's a liar. She took everything from me. I bet you know where she keeps the money. You'll help me." His legs wobbled.

"Yeah, I'll help you, Papa." Bert took a step toward the pathetic looking man. He threw himself at his father and the gun went off. He fell on top of Nico.

"Bert!" Teresa screamed, pushing herself out of the chair and rushing toward him. Bert groaned, and then sat up slowly, holding his arm.

"I'm all right, Mamma." He studied the upper part of his arm. "But it hurts like heck." He looked over at his father, moaning on the floor. Bert grabbed the gun with his good hand, stood up and pointed it at Nico.

"Bert, don't," Teresa yelled. "Put the gun down."

"Mamma, look what he did to you." His distressed voice cracked.

"I know, but look what he did to himself. Just get help here for us. Let the police take care of your father."

Bert didn't move. He kept the gun pointed at Nico.

"Don't, Bert," Teresa pleaded. "He's not worth it."

He gave a cry of despair as he threw the gun against a far wall. Nico screamed in agony at Bert's vicious kick to his ribs.

Teresa saw the bullet wound in the fleshy part of Bert's arm. It could have been to his head, or heart. Swallowing more pain, she looked at the man who had almost killed her, and would have killed their son. She raised the letter opener above his chest.

"Mamma, NO." Bert grabbed it from her hand. "Like you said, he's not worth it."

***

"I can't think what would have happened to you if Bert hadn't come when he did," Jakob said later. Teresa had never before heard his voice unsteady. He had taken both of them to the hospital. Nico was there somewhere, under police custody. Bert's bandaged arm hurt, but the bullet had gone through with no lasting damage.

"I would've killed him, you know, if I showed up and found you like this." Jakob's fingers gently stroked her battered cheek. "Thank God Bert got there. How did that happen?"

"It was coin…cadence—I can't talk. He jus' happen…" She moved a little, and cried out. "Sorry. I'n all right. It jus' hurts."

Teresa rejected the doctor's suggestion that she spend a night in the hospital. "I have plenny caretaker," she insisted.

Her splinted hand would need to remain bandaged for several weeks.

"You'll have to become left-handed for a while if you want to continue working," the doctor said. The discoloring around her left eye could be expected to move across to the right one by the next day, he told her. "You're pretty bruised all over. I'd advise you to take at least a week or two off."

On the way home, she muttered to Jakob, "He is a good doctor, but a week or two off? I can't do."

She woke the next morning and felt as though a freight train had slammed into her. She didn't try to go to work.

***

A week later, Teresa received a call from Chief Arnet, telling her that Nico had been discharged from the hospital, but would remain in police custody.

"How is he?" she asked.

"He'll be all right, I think. He'd been drinking heavily for some time, and taking strong medication, apparently stolen. I guess he's been living on the streets for a while. He may be glad enough to have shelter and food." The chief laughed, and then said seriously, "I'm sure he'll be charged with arson, at least, Mrs. Barile. But you and Bert should be there with your lawyer."

"Why would we need a lawyer?"

The chief coughed. "I'm sorry to say, ma'am, that we don't have strong laws for taking care of women. A lawyer will help protect your interests."

Teresa said nothing for a minute. She looked at her hand, and still felt pain in every movement of her body. Finally she said, "We'll be there…with my lawyer."

***

Jakob sat with them as they listened to Nico argue that he had been too sick to realize what he was doing. He insisted he "wouldn't 'v really hurt my wife, Judge. I just wanted to scare 'er. She owed me money."

The judge glanced down at Teresa's bruises and broken hand without comment. He listened to Ray Billings' description of the damage Nico did to Teresa's shop, "…the finest seamstress business in downtown Hartford, Your Honor. Practically all Hartford business men send their wives and children there. This man would have destroyed the business just to get revenge on a wife who had been supporting him since the day they married."

Then he brought up the arson charge and got the judge's attention when he identified it as happening to Mr. Hahn's building. Jakob added that he had substantial evidence from respected businessmen around the state about Mr. Barile's illegal gambling.

Chief Arnet described the arson evidence they had against Nico, his lies to the police and his evasion for the past three years.

Nico had no attorney and refused one when the Judge offered him the chance. "I've seen the kind of attorneys prisoners get, Your Honor. They're crooks themselves. No thanks. I can talk for myself."

"All right, Mr. Barile. That's your choice. A foolish one, but yours to make. The next offer is your right to a jury trial."

"Will that take longer?"

"It will take somewhat longer, as we'll need to select a jury."

Nico took a long look around the room, seeming to weigh the pros and cons of having his future determined by a group of local men versus one judge. Finally he reached a decision.

"I'll pass on a jury, Your Honor. I trust you to do what's right for a man who's been lied to and treated unfairly for years by an unfaithful wife."

Ray advised that they not bring up the abuse again, but present those issues that would be considered a convictable crime. They brought in a few men who testified about Nico's illegal gambling, though he proved clever enough to make their testimony questionable.

Then the Police and Fire Chiefs described the arson and how it was carried out under Nico's direction. When they brought a nervous Jeremiah in to tell his story, Nico could not outwit them all. In the end, he was sentenced to fifteen years in Connecticut's State Prison at Wethersfield.

Teresa looked at the pitiful figure of the man who had been so harsh and abusive, and taken so much from her life. She also remembered the Nico who had saved her from the unwed mothers' home in Italy, where she would have lost her first born son, and the Nico who fathered the other three children whom she loved more than life itself. She watched, with a mixture of relief and sadness, as he was led out of the courtroom in handcuffs. He never looked back.

Teresa waited for Ray Billings outside the courthouse. "Ray, what would have happened if I had been in that courtroom alone, without you men to speak for me and without the arson charges against Nico?"

Ray looked at the ground and shuffled his feet.

"Go ahead, tell her," Jakob said.

"I can't say that it's right," he muttered, "but probably Nico would have gone free."

"Because a wife is a man's property?" she said softly.

"Well, there's just no law that says otherwise, Teresa. I'm sorry. I know it's not right."

"No, it's not. We'll have to get that changed some day, won't we?"

***

"Don't you think it's time to get on with this divorce thing?" Jakob asked her a few days after the sentencing. Ray had begun the process for her almost a year earlier, but for a woman, it moved painfully slow.

She called the lawyer. "I don't know if it will be better or worse, now that he's here," Ray said. "It will depend on how he responds, and on the judge. But with Nico's history and incarceration, I think now would be the time to move forward."

They scheduled her hearing at the courthouse in Wethersfield. A guard brought in a shackled Nico, wearing prison clothes. He was placed in a chair at the end of the same table as Ray and Teresa, in front of the Judge. Jakob sat in a back corner.

Nico didn't look any better than the last time Teresa had seen him. A persistent cough plagued him throughout the hearing. That didn't stop him from being self-righteous and demanding.

"My wife never knew her place from the day I married her," he told the Judge between coughs. "Even when the priest talked to her 'bout respecting her husband, she lied about everything I tried to do for us. She knows how to get 'round people, Judge. She got money behind my back and tried to hide it from me. I wouldn't be here if I wasn't tryin' to get what shoulda been mine. Now she wants a divorce so she can keep all of it. Not right, your Honor."

"Mr. Barile," Ray said, "it doesn't sound as though your marriage has been a happy one for either of you. If I were in your spot, I'd be glad to get out of it." He reached into his satchel and withdrew some papers. "As for who took care of the expenses of raising your family, I have statements from several people who can attest that your wife was the one who bore that responsibility."

"Hah…that's 'cause—"

"And I have figures showing what you earned while you worked for Mrs. Wunders in Philadelphia, and for Mr. Hahn in Hartford. Suffice to say that both salaries were generous, and yet none—that's zero amount—went toward the care of your family. Would you like to see those figures, your honor?" Ray started to reach into his case when Nico threw out an arm to stop him.

"Never mind. The Judge don't need to see that." He looked nervous.

"I think I'd like to, Mr. Barile." The Judge reached out a hand.

Nico looked at the Judge. "It don't matter, Your Honor. I'm not arguin' against this divorce. I'd a had it a long time ago if I could afforded it. I'll give 'er the divorce, but the law still says that a husband has the right to at least half his wife's property. That's all I want, Judge, and that's more 'n fair."

"That's not exactly what the law says, Mr. Barile, but with extenuating circumstances, you may have a right to some of your wife's earnings. Mr. Billings, what is your client's position?"

Teresa hadn't moved since she entered the room. She sat in a straight backed chair, hands folded in her lap. Now she looked over at Ray and nodded.

"I have a statement here showing Mrs. Barile's worth, Your Honor," Ray said. "I've confirmed every amount as accurate. She is agreeable to turning over half to Mr. Barile."

Nico's surprised expression quickly turned to a satisfied one, until he watched the judge's face as he studied the statement.

"You may want to change your mind, Mr. Barile, but I'll leave it up to you."

Satisfaction turned to a frown of suspicion.

"This shows that your wife lost all of her investment in Philadelphia, and her former business there is now owned by a Letta Wunders. The home in Hartford, which apparently had been debt free, was re-mortgaged—apparently by you—and is now owned by Mr. Hahn. The Hartford business where your wife works is still owned by Mrs. Torrenti. Your wife is just an employee. She is getting a good salary, but with the expenses for your children's education, and trying to buy back the home for your family, the only thing left for you to inherit is half of her debt."

"That's a bunch of—" Nico jumped out of his chair.

"Sit down, Mr. Barile," the judge demanded. A bailiff was already moving across the room. Nico sat with a scowl.

Finally, he deliberately scratched his signature—illegible but legal—on the divorce papers and shoved them across the table to Ray. The judge told Teresa to leave the room first.

As she stood to leave, Nico vehemently whispered, "Bitch." Holding back tears of hurt, she saw Jakob waiting. She took a deep breath, feeling a freedom that she hadn't experienced since being in Italy with Mamma and Papa. She swallowed hard and walked straight ahead. Now it was her turn to run her life. She never looked back.

44

"Go with me to the Valentine's Day dinner and dance next week?" Jakob asked her on Friday. "Please," he added when she didn't respond. "It's at the Holiday Mansion downtown. You'll like it."

"That sounds wonderful Jakob, but how can I with my arm and hand in a splint, and my face is still bruised. Besides, I haven't danced since before I left Italy." A deep sigh carried her thoughts to the village dances she and Leo had enjoyed so much. "I'm sure the dancing here is different."

"First, you'll be dancing with your feet, not your arm. I'll help you. Your face looks fine, and I'll teach you the new dance everyone's doing."

He not only showed Teresa how to do the popular new foxtrot, but also insisted on teaching Bert and Dan.

"You two should be taking girls dancing. You can practice on your mother."

Teresa laughed as she watched Jakob dance the woman's part with Bert, then Dan.

"Remember—slow, slow, then fast, fast." His voice changed to falsetto. "Keep the rhythm and you'll have no problems, you handsome devils."

The boys rolled their eyes.

For the next few evenings, they cranked up the Victrola and fox trotted their mother around the parlor until they all looked like accomplished dancers. Still, Teresa felt nervous about the event.

"I'm not legally divorced yet, Jakob. I'm afraid people will talk."

"These are people we see and work with every day. If they're going to talk, they're already doing it. We can't let that stop us."

She pursed her lips, and then sighed. "It's easier for a man, you know, but you're right. I am ready to do something fun. I'll love going with you."

Marta and Betts worked all weekend on a new dress for her.

***

A nervous Teresa was on her way downstairs Wednesday evening when she heard Bert open the front door.

"Nice shine on that automobile, Mr. Hahn," he said. "And you brought flowers—for me?"

"You get your own girl and your own flowers, young man," Jakob said.

"Mamma, I believe your escort is here," Bert called over his shoulder. "You, sir, are dressed in very good taste, I must say. You will have our mother home before midnight, I trust."

Lauri and Carl giggled in the background.

"And I trust that you all will be in bed long before midnight." Jakob stood in the front hall. Then he saw Teresa, and his eyes sparkled.

Her simple dress, with a scooped neckline slightly off the shoulder, had one long sleeve gathered at Teresa's left wrist. A short cape-like sleeve covered the splint on her right arm. The waist of the amber colored dress was offset by a thick, black ribbon. Attached to a thin black ribbon around her neck was her grandmother's beautiful cameo pin. Finally, a black bow was clipped to wispy curls that hugged the back of her neck.

"I'll be the most envied man in the room," Jakob handed the bouquet to Teresa.

She beamed. "Amaryllis. They're beautiful. Thank you, Jakob." She took time to arrange the flowers in a vase on the front hall table. Then she put on the warm cape he held for her and slipped a hand through his arm.

"Have a good time," her children called.

"I'm actually nervous, Jakob. Do you know that this is our first formal outing?"

He held the car door open for her. "I'm nervous, too. I'd call this the beginning of our official courtship. I've been waiting a long time for this evening."

It was a memorable evening. They enjoyed delicious food—from the roasted lamb to the breaded, baked squash. Dessert was a tasty serving of bread pudding topped with a sweet sauce, and served with tea. Beautiful floral arrangements, and cutouts of hearts and cupids, decorated the hall.

They danced to tunes of the day, while Jakob hummed along to *Down Among the Sheltering Palms* and *The Trail of the Lonesome Pine*. Teresa loved dancing with Jakob. They both ignored winks between some of the men, and whispers among the women, when Jakob proudly introduced Teresa as "my good friend."

"It was a wonderful evening, Jakob," Teresa said on the way home. She snuggled close to him for warmth and comfort.

"If it wasn't so cold, we'd take a ride in the country," he said.

"It's late for a ride, but I'm too excited to sleep. I'll make us a cup of chocolate if you like. The children will be in bed...even Bert, I'm sure."

They opened the door to a quiet house. Jakob helped Teresa off with her cape before removing his top coat. He hung both on the clothes tree and followed Teresa into the kitchen.

She turned toward the cupboard, and then felt Jakob's hand on her arm.

"Wait, before you do that, sit down for a minute."

His serious expression filled her with apprehension. Teresa sat on a chair by the table. "What's wrong?"

"Ah, well, I had hoped for a more romantic setting, but the kitchen will have to do." He reached in his pocket before dropping to one knee in front of her. "Teresa Barile, I have loved you and waited years for this time to come. I know your divorce isn't official yet, but it soon will be. When it is, will you please do me the honor of becoming my wife?" He opened the small box, took out a simple, sparkling diamond ring, and held her hand...waiting.

Certainly they had talked about it often enough. This was Jakob. She loved him. She had dreamed about being his wife for years. His proposal shouldn't be a surprise. Why did she hesitate?

Teresa felt confused and speechless. She swallowed hard. Before she could say anything, she heard Bert's and Carl's voices from the hall doorway. "Mamma, say yes."

She burst into tears. "I can't."

"But he loves you, Mamma, and you love him." Lauri walked into the kitchen behind her brothers. "I know you do."

It was hard enough dealing with Jakob. How could she make her children understand?

Teresa nodded. Through sniffles, she said, "I do love him." She looked at Jakob. "I do love you. I just...I can't do this now."

He was on his feet. He took a deep breath and blew hard enough to extinguish a small fire.

"Mamma—" Bert said.

Jakob cut in. "No, Bert. Don't say anything more. I actually think I understand. Your mother has struggled with life so long that she doesn't know how to let it go. You go on to bed now, will you," he said to the siblings. He gave each of them a hug, adding, "I love you all, you know."

When they had reluctantly left the room, he sat down, leaned forward and looked at Teresa until she made eye contact with him.

"What's this about, Tesa? I never hid my intentions from you, so you can't be surprised. Have I been wrong all this time about you loving me?"

She shook her head. "I've loved you for years. You know that."

"Then what am I not understanding? I've certainly waited long enough for you, and isn't this why you pursued a divorce?"

Teresa put her head in her hands and sighed audibly. "I don't know if I can put it in words, Jakob. I'm not sure I understand myself."

She looked up at him, her eyes brimming with tears. He pulled out a handkerchief and wiped them, then handed it to her to blow her nose. She sighed again.

"I think you owe me an explanation," Jakob said quietly.

She nodded. "I do. I just don't know how to explain."

He waited.

"I've spent so many years in a bad marriage. Even when Nico wasn't around, he was always in control. I never felt that I had charge of my own life. I need time for that." She paused and he remained quiet.

"I'm not out of this marriage yet, Jakob, and thinking of another one right now terrifies me. You know I trust you more than anyone in the world." Her eyes, pooled with tears, begged his understanding. "Can you give me a little more time?" she pleaded.

He stood and paced the floor a few minutes.

Teresa waited, feeling torn. She knew she had hurt him, and she didn't know what to do about it. She couldn't pretend with him though...not with Jakob.

Finally, he sat down again, not touching her. "I'm willing to give you some time, Tesa, but I think you need more than time. You need distance from me. Our next contact, if there is one, will be up to you. I told you that I'd wait as long as it took, but I'm not sure I can do that anymore. If you're not ready to say yes to me now, I don't know that you'll ever be."

He stood and walked to the front hall for his coat. Teresa followed him, not knowing what else she could say—still trying to sort her feelings.

Jakob turned toward her. "You've told me often enough that I should get on with my life, and you're probably right. It's my misfortune that I'm stuck loving you, but with or without you, I've got to move on. Goodbye, Mrs. Barile." He leaned down and touched his lips to her cheek, then put on his coat and left, shutting the door gently, but firmly.

Teresa stood in stunned silence. He hadn't said good-night. He'd said good-bye.

***

When her phone rang the following evening, Teresa rushed to answer it. Maybe it was Jakob.

"I just talked to my brother and he sounded strange. Is everything all right there?" Letta asked.

"Did he say it wasn't?" Teresa tried hard to keep her voice steady.

"He said everything was fine. Maybe it's just me. I have news for you, Teresa, but I had to tell Jake first." She sounded excited.

"What is it?"

"Donal and I were married last evening. I know it may come as a surprise but, goodness, I've loved him forever. I just never thought of being in love with him until this last year, when I was afraid that he was going to leave. I couldn't imagine my life without him. He said he couldn't stay here any longer because he was having feelings for me that weren't appropriate for someone in his position. And…well, it just evolved. I am so happy. I know people will talk, but we don't care. Our families and close friends don't care, and that's all that matters. Please say you're happy for us."

Unexpected tears filled Teresa's eyes. "Letta, I am so very, very happy for both of you."

"You're crying."

"Don't pay any mind to me. They're tears of joy. I can't think of two people whom I love more, and who deserve happiness more than the two of you. I wish I could have been there—why didn't you tell us?"

"I knew it would be hard for you and Jakob to get away, and we didn't want to wait or have any fuss. We walked out back and talked to Claude and Nora first." Her voice caught a bit.

"And they both said it was a fine thing, didn't they?"

Letta laughed. "Yes, they did, as a matter of fact. We had the ceremony in our parlor. Abbie and Lance stood up with us. With both of them married now, I expect Dan will be next…unless…" she waited.

"I expect he will be, though I'm sure it won't be soon. He doesn't even have a girl yet," Teresa said quickly.

***

Woodrow Wilson was sworn in for his second presidential term in March, 1917. He declared war on Germany a month later. Fear gripped Teresa when she saw the headline.

In May, Dan asked if he could invite a special friend to dinner—someone he wanted his mother to meet. Just home from work, he grabbed one of the muffins Teresa pulled from the oven. Chewing on it while he talked to her, his "Umm" told her it was good.

"Of course," she said. "I'd love to meet a friend of yours. What's his name?"

He laughed. "Her name is Maryann."

Teresa saw her son's eyes light up when he mentioned the name.

"You'll love her. She's beautiful, Mamma. She's as pretty as you are."

The flattery brought a beam to her face, though there was a slight catch in her chest. "Are you in love?"

"I think I might be."

He told her about Maryann Perkins, the daughter of one of their business associates in Springfield. "She's almost nineteen and teaches piano. She's smart, Mamma, and you should see her with kids. She's just like Betts."

Now she understood why he made so many trips to Springfield. Maryann's father was a friend of Jakob's—and no, Jakob had not been keeping secrets from her, Dan said.

"You are the first one I told about our seeing each other, except her parents. I've been to their home for dinner a few times. You'll like them, Mamma. They're good people."

"I can't wait to meet her," Teresa said, swallowing a feeling she couldn't quite describe. Her son was a man, and in love. He should have a father to talk to. But he had Jakob, she reminded herself. Jakob would always be there for Dan.

He would be there for her, too, if she hadn't driven him away. "Dear God, I miss him," she whispered. But nothing had changed for her.

45

June 5th brought the beginning of the first draft registration. All men twenty-one to thirty-one were required to register within a month. Dan had turned twenty-one three months earlier.

Even while the President continued to say America would not join the fighting, citizens everywhere—including Hartford—saw the Army building its troop reserves. With so many young men anxious to get into uniform and participate in the glamorous life promised by recruiters, the draft was not widely used at first. That changed quickly after America began sending thousands of troops overseas daily. Most went to France. Teresa woke each morning in fear it would be the day Dan received his notice.

Her son showed no fear, only concern for increasing numbers of friends and neighbors being shipped out. By the middle of July, he told Teresa he and Maryann had been discussing their future.

"We want to marry before I have to go overseas."

"Maybe you won't have to go, Dan. Maybe the war will end soon."

"Whether it does or not, Mamma, we don't want to wait."

"What does her family say?"

"I asked her father a few days ago. We have her parents' blessing and we both want yours. Mamma, I love her."

He didn't need her permission, but it pleased Teresa that he asked. She would have preferred more time, but with the country in a hubbub over the war, she understood their urgency. The couple set their date with Maryann's pastor for Saturday, July 28, at the Old First Church on Court Square in Springfield.

When Dan and Maryann asked if they could stay with her after the wedding, until they found an apartment, Teresa made a different suggestion.

"I don't need so much living space anymore. We could easily convert this into a two-family home like many of our neighbors are doing. If it's all right with you both, I'd like that to be my wedding gift. You and Maryann can have the downstairs, and decorate it any way you'd like. I'll renovate the upstairs into a nice apartment for the rest of us. Then Bert can have your attic room." She laughed. "He always wanted it, you know."

Mary Ann hugged her mother-in-law to be and thanked her repeatedly, asking for her help with refurbishing. Soon, the house bustled with workmen once again. This time, though, Teresa didn't have to worry about Nico showing up.

***

The night before his wedding, a jubilant Dan told his mother about Jakob's surprise. "He called me into his office today. I thought it was about a new customer. Mamma, he had a contract ready for me to sign. Can you believe that? 'If that's all right with you, Dan'." Dan did his best imitation of Jake's voice, adding, "as though there was any doubt."

"You, madam," he bowed and kissed her hand, "are looking at the new partner of Hahn's Real Estate. Jake said my name would be on the door with his by the time we get back from our honeymoon."

Teresa was speechless. She blinked back tears. "Jakob is a good person, Dan. I am so happy for you." She hugged her son. "He made a good choice."

"Mamma." Dan paused a few seconds. "No, I promised Jake I wouldn't say anything, but I don't understand, you know."

"I know, sweetheart. But tomorrow is your wedding day. We'll talk later, if you want."

Teresa asked if Jakob was coming to the wedding.

"Of course. He's going to be my best man."

***

"People will have a hard time looking at my bride when they see you." Dan kissed his mother when she walked into the back of the church the next day, in her new royal blue silk dress.

She smiled at the compliment. "Your beautiful bride will have all eyes on her, Dan. She doesn't have to worry about any competition." She gave him a hug. "I am so happy for you, and I'll try not to cry, but I can't promise."

Lauri had styled her mother's hair the way it was for the Valentine's dance. The memory brought a wave of sadness that Teresa didn't want to deal with on this joyous occasion. She'd had no contact with Jakob since that night, and felt a mixture of excitement and dread about seeing him again. She wondered if he would come alone.

"Do you like it, Mamma?"

Teresa turned to see Lauri. "Oh my, yes."

The pale yellow taffeta dress, with cream colored satin stripes, glimmered as Lauri moved. The same satin trimmed her scooped neckline and the narrow train in back, which hung from the top of the dress to a hemline shortly above her ankles.

"You are beautiful," Teresa told her, with a lump in her throat. She felt sure she would not have Lauri with her much longer.

***

Letta and Donal had come from Philadelphia and spent the previous night with Jakob. Letta pulled Teresa aside before they went into the church.

"Jakob talked to us last night. He didn't say much, except that you and he decided this was not the right time in your lives to make a commitment." She sighed. "Whenever I've seen you together, it just seems right. But he made me promise not to interfere. I love you both. You know that, don't you?"

Teresa nodded, not trusting words. She hugged her friend. Today was about Dan, not her.

Carl, a few inches taller than his mother and looking all grown-up in his first three piece suit, came over to offer her his arm. As they walked up the aisle, Teresa noticed admiring glances toward her son from many young girls. One day, too soon, she would be attending his wedding, too.

Seating his mother in the front pew, Carl kissed her cheek before leaving to bring in the next female guest. Maryann's young brother, Ben, guided Letta to the seat beside Teresa. Donal followed them.

Mrs. Perkins smiled and nodded to Teresa from across the aisle. She had arranged for the church to be decorated with beautiful summer flowers. Small bouquets of peonies, attached to the pews, made a bright, colorful entrance as family and friends walked to their seats. Large baskets of hydrangeas were placed on each side of the sanctuary, with bouquets of pink and white roses on the altar beside lit candles.

Teresa's thoughts were on the beauty of the flowers, and the nervous excitement her son must be feeling at that moment, when the sacristy door opened. The pastor walked out, followed by Dan, Jakob and

Bert. Teresa could feel her chest tighten as she fought to control her breathing.

Dan wore a dark, solid jacket with tails. Matching pants and vest had subdued stripes. Teresa was amazed at how calm and in control he appeared.

Bert looked extraordinarily handsome in his new formal suit, and Jakob—. For a minute she forgot all else. She could see how proud Jakob felt, looking at Dan, the young man who had become like a son to him. She wanted to tell Jakob she had made a terrible mistake. She wanted him back in her life, but she was afraid. He might never want to come back.

Her eyes turned when she heard the beginning strains of music from the organ. Everyone watched the wedding attendants begin their slow march down the aisle. The bride's attractive cousin led the way, followed by Lauri, the maid of honor. Teresa heard murmurs of admiration as her daughter walked toward the altar.

The first strains of the *Wedding March* brought all guests to their feet, with eyes focused on the bride. Maryann walked through the vestibule doors on the arm of her proud looking father. Teresa took a deep breath and drank in the loveliness of her soon to be daughter-in-law, and then glanced at Dan. He obviously saw nothing but Maryann.

Letta squeezed Teresa's hand later as they listened to the exchange of wedding vows—the promise to love, honor and obey "until death do us part." Those were the words she had hoped to one day say to Jakob.

She understood now how much the word "obey" frightened her. Nico used the vow as a threat to control her life, and the church gave him the authority to do so. Jakob was not Nico. He would never use words to inflict pain on her. Jakob—her eyes found him again.

She couldn't let herself dwell in the regret that threatened to engulf her.

Looking at her son, she felt grateful for the man he had become. Dan deserved this good life. He would be a wonderful husband, and Teresa knew he would be the best of fathers. She could see him playing lovingly with his children.

In the middle of her thoughts, Teresa felt a presence that had been absent from her life for a long time. It seemed right, though, that Leo would be here today. She touched the back of her neck where she felt his warm breath. "Thank you for coming, Leo," she whispered.

After the wedding, the couple ran through the line of well- wishers and brushed rice out of their hair and clothing before climbing into the new Pope-Hartford automobile that Maryann's parents had given them. Carl and Ben already had their packed bags behind the seat, so they would be ready to go without paying attention to the trail of streamers, cans and other noise makers tied to the auto's bumper.

Teresa watched, with a mixture of happiness and concern, as her oldest son and his bride drove away. Glancing at Jakob, she found his gaze on her. She mouthed "Thank you," and he nodded, with a slight smile. Their only other contact that day was a brief, "How are you, Tesa?" at the reception. Whatever happened between her and Jakob, she knew he loved Dan—he loved all of her children, and she was filled with gratitude for that.

***

The following month, Teresa called Ray to ask about the status of her divorce.

"It's going to happen, Teresa. It moves slowly for women. The pity is that without an attorney, it wouldn't move at all. I'm sorry about that."

"But Nico signed the papers."

"I know. Connecticut is better with women's rights than it used to be, but not good yet. They want us to wait another year, even with the signature. I'm quite sure it's not going to take that long. A few more months, though."

"It's not fair, Ray. I'm tired of being treated like a second class citizen just because I'm a woman."

"I'm not arguing that, Teresa. It isn't fair, but that's the way it is. I'm pushing as hard as I can."

She resolved to increase her Suffragette's activity. Six women had been jailed in Washington a few days earlier simply for holding a peaceful demonstration outside the White House. They wanted President Wilson's backing on a bill that would allow women the right to vote. It was disappointing, and unforgiveable, that he not only refused to consider the measure, but that their leaders had actually been jailed. At the last meeting Teresa attended in Hartford, Marta suggested that it was time again for a local demonstration. All the women, including Teresa, agreed.

49

When she received a call from the Police Chief that Nico wanted to see her, her head screamed to ignore it.

"I'm just passing on the request that I got from the warden," Chief Arnet said. "That doesn't mean you should go."

She took a deep breath. "I'll go," she said, "but let him know I won't stay more than ten minutes, and maybe not that." Teresa told only Betts about the trip, insisting on driving the few miles by herself.

The ninety year old brick prison looked decent from a distance. Teresa rang a bell on the weather-beaten door of the main building. After she gave her name to the guard, he allowed her inside and led her down a dim hall to a small, dimmer room. Scarred walls and musty smells on the inside of the prison gave away its age.

A few minutes later, a buxom woman came into the room. She didn't bother with a greeting, just an order for Teresa to begin removing pieces of clothing. Teresa thought she would never again feel the humiliation of Ellis Island, but the woman's probing made her wonder if Nico's ten minutes were worth reliving that nightmare.

After she, and her pocketbook, and her hat and shoes had been thoroughly examined, another guard led her to a different room, further into the prison behind huge, locked barred doors. Their loud clanging startled her each time they were opened and closed. The din of noise from the prisoners' shouts and chatter increased and Teresa grew more uneasy. Then the guard opened a door and motioned her to sit on one of the two straight backed, dirty looking chairs inside the dimly lit room. He left her alone and locked the door behind him.

She looked around, but the low light made it hard to see. The four walls seemed to close in on her. Faint odors drifting in reminded her of the urine and garbage-strewn hallways of their tenement in New York. This was Nico's life now.

The door banged open again and there he was—shackled like he had been at the courthouse. A guard led him to the other chair. "I'll be waiting outside," he said to Teresa. "You have ten minutes. Just knock on the window if you want to leave sooner." He pointed to the room's only window on the corridor's wall, almost too high for Teresa to reach. She heard the door being locked when he left. The poor light made it hard to see, but Nico looked even thinner than when she had last seen him.

"Hello, Teresa." His voice was barely audible.

"Hello, Nico. How are you?"

"Been better. Thanks for coming." He coughed hard.

She couldn't remember, in all the years they had been together, that he had ever thanked her for anything before.

"You're welcome. I can only stay a few minutes. The Chief said you wanted to see me."

"I did. And they told me you wouldn't stay more than ten minutes. I don't blame you…it's not exactly the Ritz, is it?" He started to laugh, but a hacking cough stopped him.

She didn't reply. This was Nico's time. She had nothing to say.

"I…well, it's sorta funny. I don't even think I know why I wanted to see you. I just did." He looked at his feet and fidgeted a minute or two.

She remained silent.

He coughed. "I've been thinking about Dante and Alberto…and Carlo and Lauri…and Eva." He paused.

"Mostly Alberto," he said, coughing again. "I didn't get to know any of them very well, did I?"

She didn't answer, but it really wasn't a question. Nico seemed to be talking to himself. She wondered why he wanted her there. She waited.

"I guess they don't think much of me, but then I never thought much of my old man." He bent over with a deep hacking cough.

"Alberto—that day in your office—I think he really would've shot me if you hadn't stopped him." The coughing made it hard for him to get the words out.

"I don't know, Nico."

"I do. My father was a son of a bitch. I woulda killed him if I'd a had the chance. Alberto had that look." More coughing.

"He's a good boy, Nico."

"Tell him…tell him I'm sorry."

"Tell him—what?" Even now, she couldn't believe she heard right. Not this. Not from Nico.

"Just tell him." He wouldn't repeat it. He bent over again, coughing until he almost choked.

"All right, Nico, I'll tell him. I have to go now." She walked to the door and had to stretch to reach the window.

She could hear his coughing as she followed the guard down the hall.

***

"He seems awfully sick. Does he get any medical care in there?" she asked Chief Arnet later.

"They tell me he hasn't been eating and he coughs most of the time. The doctor has seen him. They'll call the doc again if he gets worse. There's not much they can do, though."

"That's an awful place." She shuddered.

"That it is, Mrs. Barile."

Bert was at the desk in his room when she told him about the visit.

"You can't trust him, Mamma. You should know that by now. What if he had done something to you? What if he has something contagious and you get sick too because you were there?"

"I hope I won't, Bert. But I had to go. You seemed to be his only reason for wanting to see me. I think he meant it when he said he was sorry."

"Sorry for what, Mamma? For being a terrible father? For not taking care of us? For beating you? For stealing from all of us?"

She walked to the chair, put her arms around her son and laid her cheek on the top of his head. "That's all true, Bert, and each of you deserved so much more. I think Nico wanted to be better than his father, whom he hated, and he realizes he wasn't. It seemed important to him for you to know that."

"It's a little late, isn't it? But I got the message, so you don't ever have to go there again."

***

Chief Arnet stopped by her business two days later. "Just wanted to let you know, Mrs. Barile. Nico was found dead in his cell this morning."

Elbows on the desk, Teresa clasped her hands together and leaned her chin on them, staring at a spot on the wall without seeing it. She felt...what did she feel? A relief that she would never have to deal with him again? A sadness for the man who had never seemed to find any joy in life? A deep regret that her children had a father who left them with no happy memories?

She raised her head. "Thank you, Chief. I appreciate all you have done for me."

"If there's anything more, or you have any questions, please call me, Mrs. Barile."

"I do have a question. What's going to happen to him now—I mean about a burial?"

"He'll be buried in the graveyard in back of the prison. No marker, just a plot. It's where they bury all the indigent prisoners who die there."

"Will we know when?"

"No. They'll get his body out as quick as possible, but with no family or anyone to pay, no one is notified."

"I'll pay, Chief." She said it without thinking. "I'll pay for his burial in a regular cemetery."

He looked at her curiously. "Why would you do that, ma'am? I mean, it's fine if you do, but why would you want to?"

"He was the father of my children. Even if they don't care now, maybe someday they will, and I want them to know where he is buried."

"I'll contact the prison and tell them your wishes. You'll need to get in touch with a funeral home to make arrangements." He gave her the names of a few.

***

They buried him in the Cedar Hill Cemetery in Hartford. Teresa gave a generous donation to St. Patrick's Church and asked the priest to say some prayers for Nico's soul. The children, and Maryann, came with her to the brief graveside service. Jakob offered to come, but Teresa sent word through Dan asking him not to.

"Tell him thank you," she told Dan, "but this is something I need to take care of." She wouldn't have asked her children, either, but they wouldn't let her go alone.

The early fall day had a chill in the air, felt more keenly because of the cold drizzle that accompanied it. The weather seemed to match their somber moods as the family followed the man in black, with a clergy collar, to a newly dug gravesite toward the back of the cemetery.

Beside a large pile of dirt, a deep hole held the plain pine coffin.

Dan stood between his mother and Maryann, holding their hands. Bert, on the other side of Teresa, squeezed her hand hard. He seemed to need something to hold onto as the priest began to read words of the burial service from the black book in his hands.

Teresa just wanted to get through the service and have it done with. Lauri and Carl looked on, standing near Bert. Their memories of a father they barely knew would be different from that of their brothers'.

The minister spoke his rote words, sprinkled the coffin with holy water, blessed it and the family with the sign of the cross—all in less than ten minutes. He asked if anyone wanted to add a comment or another prayer. There were no extra words and no tears for Nico. The priest picked up a handful of dirt and gave it to Teresa. She threw it on top of the casket. Two caretakers, waiting in the background, moved forward and began shoveling more dirt into the hole.

Teresa thanked the priest, and then she and her family went home.

The only comment about the service came from Bert. "Well, that's over."

She ordered a gravestone, carved simply with Nico's name, date and place of birth, and date of death. She knew she would never return to the site.

Part V

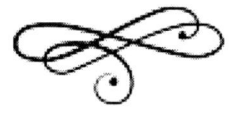

TERESA and JAKOB
1917 - 1919

47

The notice came in mid-August. Maryann saw it first and brought it upstairs. From the dazed look on her daughter-in-law's face, Teresa knew immediately what it was. They waited for Dan to come home.

"We knew it would be coming." He read his Selective Service Notice to appear for military duty.

"Yes, but I hoped the war would be over before it did," Teresa said. "Four days, Dan. You should have more time than that."

"But I don't, Mamma. I'll have to finish up all that I can with Jake tomorrow. It's a good thing I've had time to train Bert."

A few months earlier, Bert accepted Jakob's request to come work with them. He gave notice at his old job the same day and had been traveling with Dan to get acquainted with their outlying offices and personnel. He told his mother he couldn't take Dan's place, but he was ready to fill in until his brother returned.

Teresa didn't sleep at all that night. The next day, she explained to her staff why she would be taking a few days off. There was no use pretending she could keep her mind on work. She realized Dan would want to spend most of his time with Maryann, but she could cook his favorite meals and have his clothes washed and pressed. That would give the couple more time to be together.

Dan and Maryann took long rides, talking afterwards about the beauty of the Connecticut countryside. They went for walks in the evenings, arms around one another. They spent hours reminiscing about their meeting and courtship and the things they loved about each other.

Teresa caught wisps of the conversations and thanked God she had not tried to talk Dan out of marrying. She heard them discuss their plans for the future, when Dan would be home, and they would begin their family. She prayed God would keep her son safe and bring him back unhurt. But if he was hurt, she and Maryann would take care of him and make him well, no matter what. "Please, God. Please keep him safe."

Even when she felt deserted by her church, prayer had always been a part of Teresa's life. The only times she remembered her prayers having such intensity, though, were when the sea swallowed Leo and when God took Eva. Now the pain of those losses rushed at her again, like a flooding river she couldn't outrun.

How could she bear to have her son go to a place on the other side of the world where he had to shoot at someone else's son to stay alive? But she couldn't bear to have him go and be the one shot at. War was so wrong. Why should countries expect their young men to point guns and kill each other because governments didn't get along? It was crazy.

"They'll take us to camp, issue our weapons and show us how to use them." Dan explained what would happen before they were sent overseas.

That didn't sound like enough training to Teresa. Her son couldn't be ready to fight with so little preparation. Dan wasn't a fighter. She couldn't eat for two days before he left, and thought she would be sick that last morning when he came out in his uniform. She forced herself to tell him how handsome he looked.

After teases and hugs and rare "I love you" moments, his siblings stayed home, but waved until they could no longer see the automobile carrying their brother away. Teresa drove Dan and Maryann to the station, saying her farewell by the car so the couple could have their time at the train. She wrapped her arms around her son and felt his bigger, longer body envelop her and hold on tight. She remembered him as Dante, the young son who always tried to protect and please her. Now he was going to war to protect them all. She yearned to turn back time.

He gave her a last squeeze. "I love you, Mamma." And then he was gone. She clutched the side of the car to keep her shaking legs from giving way. When her son was out of sight, Teresa's body shook with sobs.

Fifteen minutes later, the train pulled out of the station. Maryann stumbled back, blinded with tears. "I'm so afraid, Teresa," she said. "I know he has to go, but I don't know how I can stand it."

Teresa wiped her own eyes and held her daughter-in-law, letting the girl's tears flow.

After a few minutes, Maryann blew her nose and said, "If Dan can go to war, I can be brave. I will be fine. I'll help make things to send to the soldiers. I have to. I have to do something or I'll go mad."

Teresa understood.

***

The Suffragette's march in downtown Hartford, planned for the following week, helped put their minds on something besides the war. The women were told that they could not have a "formal demonstration."

"You can gather a group of friends and walk together downtown," the mayor said, "as long as you don't advertise it as a demonstration."

"Public marches are allowed for every other purpose," Marta told the group later. "We will not allow them to deny us the same right because we are women. We just won't use the word demonstration."

That Saturday Teresa, Lauri, Maryann and Betts joined Marta and most of their shop workers downtown. Several hundred other Suffragettes gathered with them on

Main Street. They planned to march a mile through town, carrying banners and chanting for women's right to vote. Lauri and Maryann carried a large banner that read: *Equal Rights for Women—It's Time.*

The ladies were dressed in their Sunday best and, as they had been instructed, did not engage in any disagreements with hecklers. The day was cool, but pleasant, and it seemed that most of Hartford turned out to watch. In spite of a large number of protestors, there were throngs of women, and even men, cheering them on. And then, about two blocks into the march, a group of mostly young men began pelting the marchers with eggs and rotten tomatoes.

Lauri, marching on the outside, got hit first. Teresa felt enraged, and then scared. She could ignore the crude remarks, but when she saw eggs and squashed tomatoes dripping off her daughter's face and clothing, she wanted to get Lauri, Maryann and Betts out of there. She had promised Dan she would take care of his wife. She pulled at them. "I want you both to go home."

"And leave you?" Maryann said. "No. I'm staying. My husband was not afraid of going to war. I'm not afraid of these thugs." She wiped the gunk off her dress, lifted her head high and kept marching.

"Me too," Lauri said. "We're marching for all women, Mamma. We can't quit."

Betts agreed and ran to catch up with the others.

Most of the Suffragettes stayed, but the harassment worsened. Soon the youth came closer and tossed bags full of dirt and stones at the marchers. They had been prepared. Some flung horse dung at them.

Where were the police? Even if it wasn't considered an official demonstration, surely they would not ignore this harassment. Teresa looked around. She saw them with the onlookers, on the sidewalks, watching but doing nothing to interfere. And then several of the boys became physically assaultive and pushed a woman to the ground. When they began hitting her, police finally edged their way through the crowd. By then, chaos had erupted. The tormentors were in the midst of the women, hitting and shoving, cursing and slugging them. Teresa tried to push the girls out of the way as women screamed around them. She felt an excruciating crash to the back of her head before her body slammed onto the hard street.

***

Why did everything looked blurry? Where was she? Pain shot through Teresa's body when she tried to move. Bandages covered her aching head. She must be in the hospital. Groaning, she saw movement from the corner of her eye.

"Welcome back, sleeping beauty," Jakob said. He lifted his head and yawned. He sat in a chair by the side of her bed.

She groaned again, holding both hands to her head. "Jake, wha' happen?" The words were hard to get out of her dry mouth. "Why're you here?"

"Don't you remember the march?"

"Marsh? What mar...oh, no." She tried to sit up, whimpered and slumped back onto the bed.

He stood and walked to her bedside. "You'd better not move. You were hit pretty hard. The more you move, the more your head will hurt."

Her eyes widened with concern. "Lauri...Mayann—"

"They're fine. They were here all night. I sent them home a while ago, but they'll be back."

She closed her eyes and sighed with relief. "Thank gooness. How long...here?"

"You've been here since yesterday afternoon. I left my office early to go by the newspaper office—just happened to see the march and stopped to watch. That was about the time all the hoopla started. It would've probably been confined to hecklings except for a couple of gangs who thought they'd join forces for some good sport. Unfortunately, they got a little too sporty." He sounded angry.

"Police—should've stopped 'em before—"

"I know," Jakob said. "I've talked to Chief Arnet about that. He was mighty upset. He's already given some of the officers unpaid vacation. Seems he didn't tell them that his wife and sister were part of the marchers."

Teresa nodded. "I know. But what…happen…to me?" Her mouth felt as dry as a withered mud hole and pain came with every word.

"One of the guys started swinging a board. I was heading your way when I saw it slam into the back of your head. You went down hard. I'm sorry, Tesa. I tried to reach you before you got hurt."

She peered at him through eyes that didn't seem to work well. "Are my eyes swollen?"

"Darlin', your whole face is swollen. You're a mess, I'm afraid. But the doctor said he's pretty sure none of it is permanent. You have a concussion, too, but so does the guy who hit you."

"How—?"

"My fist connected with his head when I was trying to move him out of your way."

"Jakob, I'n sorry. I jus wan'ed to do right, but it…. I shouldn' make you involve." The words slurred from her mouth like cold molasses.

"Listen to me, Tesa. I was there out of curiosity. I didn't know whether you were part of it or not, so you didn't make me involved."

"Oh," she said. "Thank you anyway." She moved slightly in the bed, and bit her lip to keep from yelling with pain. Her body hurt everywhere.

"Most of all, Jake—thank you for," she stopped to swallow, "take care of girls. I shouldn've brought 'em."

"In case you haven't noticed, they're not girls. They are young women and they chose to be there."

She didn't know what else to say and besides, talking was too painful. "You can go, Jake. I'll be all right."

"I know you will. I'm tired and sore, too. And your family will be here soon." He stood up to leave. That's when she saw the other side of his face.

"Oh…Jake. Did 'e do tha'?" She pointed to an ugly bruise on his left cheek, and then noticed the bandage on his right wrist. "An tha'?"

"Actually, one of his pals did the face. The wrist happened when I was trying to catch myself on the way to the pavement." He laughed. "I haven't had so much fun since I was in school."

In spite of her annoyance and pain Teresa smiled, then grabbed her side and moaned. "It hurts." She looked at Jakob again. "Will you come back?"

His expression became serious. "I don't know. Do you want me to?"

"Maybe—when I look better."

"I don't know if I can wait that long," he chuckled.

***

Teresa drifted in and out of sleep for the next few days, helped by medication to keep the pain more tolerable. Anxious to get home, she insisted that she could heal as well there as in the hospital. Jakob did not come again until the day before she left. She wondered if he was seeing someone else.

"They tell me you're going home tomorrow."

"I am. Will you come to see me?"

"I don't know, Tesa. Are you inviting me?"

"Jakob, you know my marriage isn't a concern anymore."

"What does that mean?" He frowned.

She swallowed, her heart pounding. "I know I don't look very good, but..." she took a deep breath. "Would you ask me again?"

"Ask you?" He frowned. "Ask you what?"

"Jakob...you know." What was she thinking? She should not have said anything. He had obviously moved on. She could not move her eyes from him, though.

He looked at her without saying anything for what seemed too long. "You do look pretty beat up still, but that's not even an issue." He strode to a window and stared out for several long, painfully silent minutes.

Finally, he turned and walked back. "It's your turn."

"What do you mean, it's my turn?"

"Just what I said. I had my turn asking; now it's your turn. That is, if you have the courage to do it."

He couldn't actually mean what he was saying. "But it's a man's thing," she said.

The laughter that burst from his throat was immediate and mocking. "Look at you. All banged up because you had to go marching for women to have the same rights as men, and now you bring up the issue of a man's responsibility. I'm afraid it doesn't work like that. I'm giving you the right to make a significant choice, Teresa. The next move is up to you."

He did mean it. Her chest tightened. "Never mind." She turned her back to him.

"All right, Mrs. Barile. I'll never mind." He picked up his hat and walked toward the door.

"Jakob?" Her voice was barely audible.

He stopped. Without turning, he looked at her over his shoulder.

"What?"

"I'm scared."

"You? Scared of what?"

"You might say no."

"You won't know unless you ask, will you?" he said softly and walked out.

48

Home for almost two weeks, Teresa healed more every day...physically. Emotionally, she began and ended each day thinking of Jakob. She wouldn't talk to anyone about it, and her children didn't press her—at least not directly.

A few times, Teresa overheard them talking to each other about Jakob's stopping by the shop to bring a new customer, ask if they needed any supplies, or just to say hello and inquire about Teresa's health. They didn't direct the conversation to her, but they didn't lower their voices to keep her from hearing.

Her daughter-in-law had volunteered to fill in at *Marta and Tesa's Creations.* She turned out to be a good seamstress and excellent with the children.

Betts told Teresa that the youngsters loved Maryann's music and singing. "She's a perfect fit for us, Teresa. Can't we keep her?" So Maryann became part of the staff. Lauri helped, too, when she wasn't in school.

Teresa finally felt well enough to resume some of her former activities. With the swelling in her face almost gone and the bruising faded, she moved about with minimal pain. She decided it was time to call Jakob. When he answered, she knew her heart must be beating loud enough for him to hear through the phone.

"Hello, Jakob. I wondered if you would like to come to dinner tonight. I'm baking a chicken, with fresh corn on the cob and roasted potatoes and bread pudding for dessert." She had practiced reciting the menu all afternoon. She quickly added, "That is, if you don't have other plans."

"Whose idea was it to invite me?" he asked.

She sighed in exasperation. "It was my idea, Jakob."

"In that case, it sounds delicious and I can probably rearrange my schedule. Will the whole family be there?"

"Actually," she stopped to clear her throat, "they all made plans to spend the evening at Betts'. They're packing some things to send Dan."

"So it will just be the two of us?"

"Well, I had this dinner planned…and then there was no one to share it with, and it seemed too much to eat by myself. Do you mind?" He wasn't making it easy, and she was already off her script.

"I'll miss them, but sure, I'll keep you company."

***

Teresa's best tablecloth covered the dining room table, which she had set with her good china. She debated whether it would seem too pretentious to put candles on the table, but she liked the touch.

She fixed her hair in the upsweep that Jakob had admired the night of the Valentine's dance and chose a soft yellow and white dress that had a loose blousy top and a skirt that fell in soft gathers. She wanted to appear casual, but look as attractive as she could. Most of all, she wanted to cover her nervousness, and knew clothes wouldn't do that.

She had the dinner timed well. It was almost ready to serve when she heard his car pull into the drive. Her heart raced. By the time he knocked, it hammered in her ears.

He wore dark brown pants and a white, long sleeved shirt under a tan sweater. It was nice to see him not dressed in the full suit he usually wore for work. He looked relaxed and…darn, he was handsome. He handed her a bouquet of daisies and a bottle of wine and she remembered to breathe.

"You look good, Tesa. Your face is almost healed." Jakob turned his attention to the formal table. "Nice. Can I help with anything?"

"No, it's almost ready. Just have a seat. Thank you for the daises, Jakob. They're lovely." Teresa busied herself arranging them in a vase, and then poured a glass of wine for him and herself.

Her tenseness lessened as they began to eat. They talked easily about her recovery, his business, how well Bert was doing with the firm, how well Maryann and Lauri were doing at her shop, and the latest news from Dan.

Teresa served bread pudding after the dinner.

"That was an excellent meal," Jakob said. "Can I help you clean up?"

"No, no. This won't take me long."

"Well then, if there's nothing I can do for you, I'll say good-night." He stood and reached for her hand. "It's been a very nice evening, Tesa. Thank you for inviting me." He bowed and kissed her hand and held it while she stood. "Walk me out?"

"Uh, Jakob, if you're not in a hurry, would you like a cup of tea before you leave?"

He took a moment to answer. Her heart raced. "Matter of fact, that sounds good. Here or in the parlor?"

"Why don't you go to the parlor? I'll bring the tea in." She hoped her shaking hands wouldn't spill it.

Jakob sat in one of the covered chairs, waiting for her. "You did a fine job with the renovations on your home. You have a talent for it, you know," he said as she walked in with the tea.

"Thank you." She carefully placed the tray on the coffee table. "It's something I enjoy. Two sugars?" She looked at him questioningly while she poured—sure he could see her nervousness.

Jakob watched her for a minute, and then reached over and picked up the cup. "I'll do it. Let me fix yours, too." He stirred in one spoonful of sugar, remembering that's how she liked her tea.

Teresa took the cup he handed her, but set it down before taking a drink. She couldn't put it off any longer. She let him take a sip, and then lifted the cup from his hand and placed it back on the tray. She dropped to her knees, looked up at him and took his hands in both of hers.

"Jakob Hahn, I do realize that you may no longer want to marry me, but I can't let you go without trying again. I have loved you for years. I can't think of my life without you. I want to grow old with you. You have been more of a father to my children than their own father ever was, and I'd love for you to be a grandfather to their children. I want to be your wife, Jakob. Will you please do me the honor of being my husband?"

She held her breath while he said nothing. Was he going to turn her down? How would she survive if he did? She let go of his hand and dropped her head.

She felt his fingers under her chin as he lifted her head. His gaze locked onto her eyes and he bent down. His lips touched hers in a warm, gentle kiss that sent a shiver racing to the tips of her toes. Her eyes closed until he placed a kiss on one eyelid and then the other, and she heard his soft voice.

"It's been my dream since our first Mummers' Parade. I'd be delighted to be the grandfather of your children's babies, and being your husband would be the biggest honor of my life."

"Jakob—oh Jakob!" She jumped up, threw her arms around his neck and fell onto his lap. She laughed and cried at the same time. "I love you so. I thought I had lost you."

"Unfortunately, my love, you spoiled me for any other woman. I'll never know why, because you are anything but easy." He laughed.

***

They agreed to have the wedding as soon as possible.

"Here or Philadelphia?" Jakob asked.

"Hartford is our home now. This is where we should be married—and just with family and special friends."

Her decision pleased him. They would have the wedding in his back yard, weather permitting, and live in Jakob's home.

His pastor from the Lutheran church agreed to marry them.

***

The early November day dawned bright and unusually balmy. Pleasant breezes fanned a harmony of late autumn leaves that rained from overhead tree branches. They planned the ceremony for early afternoon, before the chill of evening. Two large tents were set up—one for the wedding and the other for dinner and dancing afterwards. Jakob hired the same band that had played for the Valentine's dance, with a request to begin with *Let Me Call You Sweetheart*.

He asked Bert to be his best man. Teresa smiled as her son's eyes lit up.

"It would make me proud, Jake." They hugged and back patted each other.

Lauri was her mother's maid of honor. Teresa asked her to wear the same dress she had for Dan's wedding. "You looked so beautiful in it, and the color is just right."

Betts, Marta and Maryann outdid themselves with Teresa's dress—floor length with layers of ecru silk chiffon over off white taffeta. Lovely wax lilacs decorated the shoulders and hem. A short chiffon train fell from the back of the waistline. Maryann styled Teresa's hair in a soft upsweep with lilacs woven through it, and let wisps of curls fall onto the nape of her neck.

Jakob selected a black tuxedo without tails, and a black bow tie. His housekeeper, Mrs. Tallon, made sure the suit was nicely pressed, his shoes shined to a gloss, and the tie perfectly straight. But Jakob always dressed well. Teresa said anything would look good on him.

Dan's absence marred the otherwise perfect day.

"He'll be home soon, I just know he will," Lauri said. "And he must have your letter by now, so he'll know about the wedding."

Maryann had been listening. "He should have the letter with my news, too, Teresa. I was going to wait to tell you, but maybe this would be the best time."

Teresa's eyes opened wide with curiosity.

"Your grandbaby is coming in the spring." Maryann's face broadened into a pleased smile.

Tears of joy stung Tessa's eyes. She gently put her arms around Maryann. "You're pregnant."

"Yes, yes—but be careful, you'll muss your dress."

"I don't care," Teresa said. "You have given me the best wedding present that I could ever have ...my grandbaby...Dan's baby. Wait 'til I tell Jakob."

"Mamma, it's time," Carl called through the door. He was giving her away. A head taller than his mother by then, he had grown into a handsome, confident young man.

Lauri led the way as Teresa walked across the lawn on the arm of her youngest son. Ahead she saw the man who had waited patiently for her for such a long time. How did she deserve him? When Leo died, she thought she would never find another love. She didn't know then the world had a Jakob.

49

Jakob reminded her that his house was now "our home," and had proven it on their wedding day by having her name added to the deed.

"This will always be your home." They were at breakfast the morning after their wedding. "You won't be needing the Capen Street house anymore, unless you want to keep it for your security. Otherwise, I'd like to deed it to Dan and Bert. But it's up to you."

Dan could come home to a job, a son or daughter, and his own home. Bert would be pleased to know he had a place of his own. He had already hinted at a future with Betts.

"I think it would be perfect."

It had been decided that Lauri and Carl would move to Jakob's house with their mother. However, they insisted on staying at their old home a few days with Bert, "so you newlyweds can have some privacy." The newlyweds appreciated the decision.

"Where would you like to go for a honeymoon?" Jakob asked. With the uncertainty of the war, they had put off making travel plans until after the wedding.

"I don't need to go anywhere." Teresa reached for his hand. "I'm content staying right here with you. But if you would like to take a short trip, many of my customers talk about what an exciting city Chicago is."

"That's a good choice for now," he said. "Bert's capable of handling my agency, and between Betts and Maryann, your business is in good hands. We could see the whole country if you like."

"I wouldn't want to be gone that long—not until Dan gets home."

"As soon as the war's over, I'm taking you on a proper honeymoon to Italy," Jakob said.

"That would be my dream, Jakob, to show you my home. But before we plan an overseas trip, there's something that's very important to me."

"If it's important to you, it is to me, too." He leaned over and kissed her cheek. "What is it?"

"From the time I was a young girl, my mother told me to always keep some money aside of my very own. She said someday I could use it to travel first class. I thought it would never happen after Nico—" She blew out a deep sigh. "But now that I have my businesses back, I can afford it."

She looked at him intently. "Jakob, I want to pay for our tickets—First Class—when we go to Europe. Will you mind? I want it to be my wedding gift to you."

"Mrs. Hahn, I wouldn't mind at all. I can't think of a better wedding gift."

***

When they returned from Chicago, Teresa rose early every morning to scan the Hartford Courant for any news of the war. The scarcity of information frustrated everyone. Maryann had received a letter from Dan in mid-December, telling her that his division was in France.

> *I've always wanted to come to Europe, but not like this. I wanted it to be with you. I don't think I'll be sent to Italy, but if I am, I hope I can go to Gaeta and see where my father lived. When this war is over, you and I and our baby will make the trip someday. I can't wait to get back to see you. Tell Mamma that I miss her and love her. I love you, Maryann, with all my heart. Now that our country is in the war, I think it will be over*

quicker and I might even be back before the baby comes. Give my love to all my family. Tell them Merry Christmas for me. We'll celebrate when I come home.
    Your Dan

***

"Jakob, I can't do it. I just can't put up decorations and celebrate Christmas when our country is at war, and Dan is fighting—God knows where—on the other side of the ocean." Teresa thought of the holiday nearing. They had always made it a special celebration in the past. "Maryann said the same thing. She and Lauri and I are going to spend Christmas at the Red Cross, helping put packages together for the troops. Maybe one of them will get to Dan. You won't be upset with us, will you?"

"Actually, I'm relieved. I couldn't enjoy the holiday celebration either this year. If you and your Suffragette friends don't mind, Carl and I will come along to help."

"What did you plan to do with me?" Bert asked.

"I thought you were spending the day with Betts." Teresa said.

"I'll see her this evening. We talked about driving to Philadelphia for the Mummers Parade next week, but neither of us feels up to that, either, this year."

"Next year we'll all go. The baby will be almost as old as Lauri was at her first parade." Teresa had a feeling of nostalgia remembering. She looked toward Maryann. "I'll be glad when we can call him or her by name, and not just 'the baby'. Have you thought of names yet?"

"Actually, we have. I wrote to Dan about my choices, and he agreed with me. If it's a boy, it will be Leo. If it's a girl, we'll name her Eva."

Teresa's voice didn't work. Jakob put his arm around her and looked at Maryann. "Good choices, honey."

First Class to America

***

January, 1918, blew cold wind and snow through Hartford. Jakob didn't insist on many things with Teresa, but he did insist on driving her to work when the streets were icy. January 31 was one of those days.

"Maybe February will be better this year." He pulled in front of Tesa's shop. She was still in the car when Betts ran out to meet her.

"There's a call from Maryann. Something's wrong, but I can't understand her. I think she might need the doctor."

"Oh, dear God." Teresa jumped from the car. "Jakob, wait for me. We might have to go to the house." She hurried to her office.

"Maryann, what's wrong? Do you want me to call the doctor? Or do you need to go to the hospital?" Teresa prayed it was not labor pains…not this soon.

"No, no, no" MaryAnn's sobbing choked off the words she tried to get out.

"What is it, sweetheart? Tell me."

"The tel-am," she muttered, barely able to talk.

"The what? Never mind. I'm on my way."

Then she heard the words. "The telegram—Dan."

"The tele—" Her body stiffened as understanding gripped her. Telegrams were rare, but they were a common means of notifying families of a soldier's death. The phone slipped from Teresa's hand as she crumbled to the floor.

50

Italy, October, 1919

    Teresa stood beside Jakob at the ship's railing, looking out over Naples. It had been twenty-one years since she and Nico had stood here with their sons; twenty-one years since she had held Dante's little hand as they boarded the ship that would take them to their new lives in America. And now—

    Jakob slipped his arm around her waist as they followed other passengers off the ship. "Are you all right?"

    She nodded, not trusting her voice. She had anticipated returning to Italy for so many years, but never could she have imagined it like this. She stepped off the ship onto Italian soil and experienced a rush of sadness. Her heart felt crushed for her personal losses, but her homeland had also suffered terrible losses. Port authorities warned passengers about heavy crime, especially in southern Italy. Lawlessness had worsened after a war that drained the country's finances. Then famine spread across the land when men came home to no jobs.

    Teresa felt a stab of guilt as she passed hordes of desperate-looking countrymen waiting for passage. She was sure most had hopes of going to a prosperous America, not realizing the end of the war also brought a termination to scores of jobs there.

    Automobiles were rare on the streets of Naples after the war, but a few drivers with horses and buggies waited near the dock. Jakob paid one generously to take them to the train station.

As they were getting out of the buggy, Teresa talked to the driver in Italian and then looked at Jakob. "It's too late in the day for us to go to Gaeta, and I'm sure we couldn't find a room there, anyhow. The driver said there is an inn next to the station here. They have meals, and we can get a train in the morning."

The next morning, the kind woman who ran the inn wrapped some bread and cheese in a towel for them to take. "I will have good soup for you when you get back tonight," the woman said.

Sorrow enveloped Teresa as she looked out the train window and saw mile after mile of desolate farmland and deserted buildings. "Oh, Jakob, it wasn't so good when I left, but it is so sad now. I wish you could have seen it—" Her voice broke.

He put an arm around her. "I will. We'll come back in a few years, when things are rebuilt. They will be." He sounded confident.

The train stopped at Formia, a few miles from Gaeta. A half hour later, they found someone who had a horse and cart to drive them to Gaeta. It seemed that transportation had changed little since Teresa left. She could not have imagined she and Jakob would ever be bouncing along a cart in Italy. The people could not afford automobiles.

"Jakob, I don't know what to expect when we get there."

"I know you don't, sweetheart, and I wish I could make all of this easier for you. I can't, though. But I can understand better now, all the things you told me about growing up here. As poor as it is right now, Tesa, look around at the hills, and the richness of the land. It will build back up. I can see it, can't you?"

She closed her eyes and nodded. A tear ran down each side of her face. And then she opened her eyes and called out to the driver. He stopped the cart.

"There…there it is. Jakob, that's my home." They were in the midst of a small community on the outskirts of town, looking at a small house with stucco-type finish. "And see," she pointed to a smaller building behind it, "that was Papa's shop."

She looked around. "They don't look so bad, do they? They look better than many of the other homes."

"Yes they do, in fact. What happened to them after your father died?" Jakob asked.

"They weren't worth much then. And Papa owed money to a few people, and needed to have a burial. Uncle Sol sold them just to pay the debts."

"It appears that someone has taken good care of them. Do you want to stop and ask if you can see the house?"

She was quiet for several seconds. "No. I'd rather remember the way they were, and I want to get on to—" her voice choked.

Jakob nodded to the driver and he drove toward the church.

***

Tears blurred the images in front of Teresa. "How did you find him?" she asked when they arrived at the cemetery.

"It took a little hunting," Jakob said. "I learned that most of the soldiers in France were buried at Meuse. That's where he was. Most stayed there, but I found a company that transferred some of the soldiers' bodies to other places in Europe. It seemed right that Dan should be with his father."

They stopped at Mamma's and Papa's gravesites first. She brought fresh plants for the four graves and arranged to pay the caretaker a small sum annually to keep them watered and trimmed.

"You'd be proud, Mamma. I finally have my fund and I am traveling real first class. And I have a first class life, because I found this wonderful man who loves me and my children. Papa, you would like Jakob. You and he could share marvelous stories." She carefully placed the plants in front of each parent's grave and let her fingers wander over the names on the stones for a few minutes.

They moved on, then, to the ones she dreaded seeing, but had come across the ocean to visit. She spotted the sites first by the huge bouquets of balloons tied to colorful boxes that were set by the gravestones. Tears spilled from her eyes when she saw the fishing pole. She knew Jakob had arranged these special touches.

Leo never had a marker before, since his body hadn't been recovered. Jakob told her that wouldn't do. Now she read the words on the beautifully carved memorial:

In Memory of Leonardo Carlos Legettia
Born in Gaeta, 1873 Died at sea, 1895
Beloved of Teresa Maria Sentora Barile Hahn
Father of Dante

She stood for several minutes…remembering. She still pictured the young, dashing Leo, but the memory was fading. It belonged to the young Teresa, the one who grew up in Italy. That seemed another lifetime ago.

She pressed her fingertips to her lips and then touched them to Leo's name before her feet moved to the second stone. Teresa swallowed several times. Her breathing quickened, though she was afraid it might stop altogether. She blinked hard to read the words:

Dante Francis Barile
Born in Gaeta, 1896

Joyce Senatro

Died in France, 1918, serving his adopted country,
the United States of America
Dearly loved son of Teresa and Leonardo
Beloved husband of Maryann and father of Eva
Danielle

Teresa didn't move—couldn't move—for several minutes. She swallowed the lump in her throat and wiped at the tears that washed her cheeks. She squeezed Jakob's hand before he stepped away to allow her privacy. He would need his own time with Dan.

"My darling Dante," Teresa said softly, in a shaky voice, "this is your father, Leonardo. I know he will take care of you now. And someday soon, Maryann will come to visit with your beautiful daughter. You would have loved her so. She looks a lot like you, and she will be a beauty like her mother." She knelt on the grave and leaned against the tombstone with her arms around it. Her mind couldn't grasp that she would never again be able to embrace her son.

Jakob stood nearby as he always had, keeping watch over her without intruding.

Finally, Teresa opened her pocketbook and took out the worn, faded picture of Leo that she had carried for so many years. She lifted the photo to her lips, then dug away some of the dirt at the base of Dan's stone and buried it, patting the dirt tight on top. "I don't need it anymore, Leo," she said. "It should be with our son now." She felt his presence brush her arm. Was it Leo or Dan? It didn't matter. They had each other now. She placed a kiss on the top of Dan's stone and turned back to her husband.

"Thank you."

***

"It's the first time I've seen her from this viewpoint." Teresa had just sighted "the Lady" as their ship sailed into the New York harbor on a frosty September morning. "Now I understand why I always heard such a cheer from the passengers up here. She's quite a sight, isn't she?"

"She is that," Jakob said. "And you have finally been able to travel first class. Big difference, isn't it?"

She sighed a loud, contemplative sigh. "Yes, it is. It almost doesn't seem fair, Jakob. If I had never traveled steerage—but I did. This was a hard trip for me, even first class. The next time we go, it will be better. Maybe then there won't be a third class. But to enjoy luxury when I know there are so many below…"

"How do you feel about coming back?" Jakob asked. There was hesitancy in his voice.

She gave a deep, thoughtful, mournful sigh. "Other than having to leave Dan, it's good to be coming home."

He exhaled a breath of relief.

As was customary, their clearance had been completed on deck, and they were moving with the other first class passengers toward the boat that would take them to shore. Teresa turned around to pick up her handbag and saw a young Italian woman, holding a crying baby. The woman stood with others, behind a roped off area waiting for the third class passengers to disembark. She struggled to hold onto her luggage and pacify her baby. There was no one with her.

"Jakob," Teresa said, "she needs help."

His eyebrows shot up. "And that would be you, I suppose."

"You don't mind, do you?"

"I'd be disappointed if you didn't do something."

Teresa walked back to the girl and Jakob explained to the Captain that they were going to remain on board for the third class transport.

"Do you have anyone to meet you?" Teresa asked in Italian, reaching out for the baby. The girl's name was

Patrizia. She had an uncle who might come, but he had no room for her and expected her to have a job within two days, he had written.

"What kind of work can you do?" Teresa asked as Jakob joined them.

"I am good with housework," Patrizia said, "and I am very good with sewing."

A smile spread across Teresa's face. She looked at Jakob and translated the girl's response.

He shook his head, laughing. "Good thing we have a big house, Mrs. Hahn."

Teresa reached for the young mother's hand. "*Benvenuta in America, Patrizia.* Welcome to America."

Acknowledgements

Deepest thanks to my daughters, Edie and Faun, for reading the original version—including 20,000 plus words that were eventually, (and thankfully for future readers) edited out—and to Patty, who taught us that you should never give up on your dreams. Their love and support gave me the courage to tackle this novel. Wishing the world to be a better, kinder place for girls and women everywhere gave me the persistence to keep at it.

Thanks to my neighbors, Bea and Evelyn, for being my first 'outside family' readers, and for their encouraging feedback.

And then there are my Florida Writers' Association critique groupies who picked it apart, questioned everything, and kept pushing me on. I am grateful to all of you. A special thanks to Veronica "Ronnie" Hart, our Daytona Writers' leader, for insisting that I keep Teresa strong and independent through all her adversaries; to Peggy Lambert, our Port Orange Scribes' leader, who critiqued every word and gave some of my most constructive criticism; and thank you, Jim Thompson, for your group leadership and for encouraging me to put the story into competition.

Christine Holmes, early fan whose suggestions always made my writing a little better, designed the book cover and helped me find my Teresa, Nico and Jakob. I am deeply grateful to her and to Mary Custureri, my publisher, whose dedication and tireless energy constantly amazes me.

The heroines of the story have to be the early Suffragettes who fought for the rights we women take for granted today, and for those still fighting for true equality.

Finally, this story would not have happened without the bits of history I learned of my husband's grandparents. Much appreciation to his sisters, brother, nieces and nephews who shared their memories. And thank you, Jim and Loretta, for taking me on the tour of historic Hartford, to visit today's Capen, Main and Asylum Streets, closed factories, St. Patrick's Church and Cedar Hill Cemetery.

First Class to America

Joyce Senatro

CPSIA information can be obtained
at www.ICGtesting.com
Printed in the USA
FFOW01n1551010217
31878FF